The Players Act 1

All The World's A Stage

Amy Sparkes

Sword and Fiddle Publishing,
a division of Sword and Fiddle Productions Ltd,
Unit 4 Cedar Court, Tiverton Business Park, Tiverton. EX16 6GT

ISBN-13: 978-1-0683279-1-9

Cover design: Sarah Christie

1st Edition 2025

Dedication

This book is dedicated to those struggling performers of all kinds,
today and throughout history,
who have found their lives made harder
by the prejudices and mores of a broken and unequal society.

***

All the world's a stage,

And all the men and women merely players;

They have their exits and their entrances,

And one man in his life plays many parts...

William Shakespeare

As You Like It, Act two, Scene seven

***

CHAPTER 1: Thomas

Thomas yanked open the front door of the Red Lion, scooped up his skirts and ran outside. He just about dodged the soggy cabbage which hurtled past him into the street. For Heaven's sake! It was hard enough running dressed as Titania.

The laughter of the drunken audience behind him rattled in his ears as an egg came flying through the door. It landed with a discouraging noise, and an even worse smell, at his feet. Dropping his skirts and catching his breath, he looked back at the inn with its uneven, timber-framed walls.

Where the Hell were the others?

There was a rumble of wheels. Thomas snapped his head around and gave a sigh of relief. Thank Heaven! The tattered old wagon, covered in canvas and decorated with colourful strips of rag, exited the stable-yard behind the building and headed right for him. It was pulled by Old Bess, a huge, sturdy horse, and driven by the man he so desperately wanted to impress. The red cloak of Oberon hung around his shoulders, and a hastily crumpled green curtain sat in his lap.

Robert pulled on the reins and the wagon rattled to a halt beside Thomas. "In!" Dark waves of hair framed a face marred by disappointment. He jabbed his thumb at the wagon. "Thomas, in!"

"You cannot be suggesting we leave the stage behind! All that wood!"

"*I'm* the manager: do as you're bloody told! Where are the girls?"

Before Thomas could answer, a couple of older men from the erstwhile audience staggered into the doorway, pissed as pigs in a cider orchard while smelling twice as bad, and more eggs flew in his direction. He jumped back as the shells smashed at his feet, releasing their vile odour. The men burst into drunken laughter and took aim again—

—but they lurched forwards, landing face-first on the ground as Caroline pushed past them, dressed in a scrappy green tunic with her wild, black hair still tamed for the performance. One of her hands gripped a bottle of – was that rum? – and the other pulled Annie, who was clutching her fiddle and apparently hadn't considered that removing the donkey head she wore might have hastened the exit.

"Catch!" called Caroline, throwing Thomas the bottle.

Thomas' sweating fingers just about caught it – definitely rum – as Caroline pulled the donkey head from Annie, hastily untangling it from long, red hair. Caroline threw the head in the back of the wagon, then bundled Annie in.

"We must go back for the stage!" Thomas looked desperately at the inn.

There was a roar of noise as the rest of the drunken men and women swarmed out of the door.

"Shit," muttered Thomas. Why was it an audience only seemed large when it was pissed off?

The red-cheeked innkeeper pushed to the fore, pointing at Caroline. "Bloody Puck stole me rum!" A fresh barrage of rotten food flew towards them.

"On reflection, let's leave the stage." Thomas turned to the wagon behind him.

There was a flick of reins; a rolling of wheels.

"Shit-shit-shit-shit-shit-shit!"

He swept up his skirts with his free hand, sprinted after the wagon and leapt, landing a little painfully upon the donkey head.

"Mind Horatio!" protested Annie.

He jumped straight back up. The wagon rolled away from the crowd, whose disappointed faces reflected his own heart. Why did this have to happen? He always tried so hard. So bloody hard. But he threw on the winning smile of a showman and raised the bottle of rum to the crowd.

"You've been a marvellous audience!" he called, and gratefully took a swig.

CHAPTER 2: Piero

Piero always walked upon the ground as if he were treading the boards. So even now, when the indigo evening was speckled with the keenest stars and the street was clearly empty, he tossed his dark tousled hair, held his head high, and strutted with purpose. He wore a smart, black jacket over his white shirt and knee-length breeches, with his spotless cravat neatly tied. Presentation was important. He kept himself clean-shaven to display his fine cheekbones, the favourite of his many remarkable features, and often the subject of others' admiration. His eyelids were smeared with purple powder, and he encouraged the pale green eyes beneath them to gleam with delicious and well-earned hatred.

A vain peacock, Caroline had called him. He had laughed in her face and told her it was a compliment. For a peacock understands his audience, and he commands them. When he takes to the stage in all his glory, everyone is compelled to watch until the peacock declares the show is over. He couldn't help but smile as he remembered Caroline calling him a few other names after that.

The breeze blew strongly around him now, swaying the lantern which hung by the front door of the inn. The painted sign of the Red Lion creaked as it swung, but it was not the inn itself which had Piero's attention, despite the merry laughter coming from within. No. There was something more specific he was after.

His eyes lit up as a piece of paper fluttered along the dirty ground, attempting to escape. He picked up the pace – with measured composure and dramatic style, naturally – towards his prey. He began to sing to himself.

"And if ever I should meet you, by the land or by sea,

I will always remember your kindness to me..."

The heel of his boot stamped down upon the paper, pinning it to the ground. He bent down to pick it up with his white-gloved hand.

THE TICEHURST PLAYERS PRESENT

A MIDSUMMER NIGHT'S DREAM

BY SHAKESPEARE

FOLLOWED BY A SONG AND A DANCE

THE RED LION

His heart missed a beat and a smile escaped him. Oh, he had waited for this for such a long time. Waited, and wanted. And he was so very close now. Holding the bill nearer to his face, he inhaled, trying to detect a certain scent, purely for the hunt. But he could not find it. Still, he did not need that scent. Not any more. He needed information. He folded the bill and tucked it inside his jacket. He strutted towards the inn door and held the iron ring in his gloved fingers, gripping it ever tighter as he prepared for his second-favourite thing.

He twisted the ring, threw open the door and left it wide open behind him as he strode inside, ready to devour the response to his entrance.

A wall of comfort hit him, but he had no time for the heady smell of ale. No interest in the hugging heat of the fire, or the plump lips and breasts of the hopeful harlots perched on men's laps. They eyed him up, and duly noting their attention, he accentuated the sway in his walk oh-so-slightly in appreciation. Lord, he loved taverns. An audience already sitting and waiting, with naught better to do than drink themselves out of their bored skulls – desperate for entertainment, desperate for something out of the ordinary to come and stir up the wretched monotony of their tedious lives. Well, here he was.

At the far end of the room, beyond the bobbing heads of the audience, stood a small stage raised upon trestles. It was unremarkable, save for the decaying vegetable matter bedecking the boards. On he walked towards it – every step perfectly paced and perfectly placed, revelling in the increasing murmurings which rose in his wake. A snoring man, face down on a tankard-strewn table, was shamefully oblivious of matters, and Piero delivered a sharp kick from his boot as he passed. The man sat suddenly bolt upright and stared at Piero. Better. Piero let the moment build and build, preparing for the glorious climax. It was all in the timing.

He passed the bar on the right-hand side of the room, behind which stood a red-faced man with greying hair and a handsome younger man with a square jaw. His shirt sleeves were rolled up high and he leaned his broad, muscly arms onto the bar, watching with interest.

Arriving at the stage, Piero took a moment to feed on the tense and curious mood which filled the large room behind him. Then he sprang up elegantly onto the knee-high boards, still facing the wall behind it. He waited for just a moment, then he spun around on a heel to address the room and extended his arms in a warm, open gesture.

"Ladies and gentlemen, I plead for just one moment of your attention." He paused long enough for the entire room to silence. "I find myself in need of your assistance. I seek the Ticehurst Players – a small, insignificant troupe, easily forgettable, but I beg you to search your memories as I believe they may have passed this way."

"Oh, they been here a'right," said the red-faced man behind the bar. "Bloody Puck stole me rum!"

"Most regrettable. Was it perchance a rather disagreeable, sour-faced woman with dark hair and brown skin?"

"Aye!"

“Disappointingly predictable,” said Piero, with a loud, forlorn sigh.

“Go on, show ’im what you got, Harry!” called a bald man from a nearby table, slapping the back of an older man with a matted beard and an ale-stained shirt.

Piero resisted the urge to glare at the interruption as the man stood up from a table near the stage, knocking over his stool with a noisy and entirely unnecessary clatter onto the bricked floor. Piero gave an inaudible sigh. Then the man picked up something from the table in front of him, and the audience laughed as he clamped a fake padded bosom to his chest.

“Ooh, I’m Titania, Queen of the Fairies!” the old man roared drunkenly.

There was a larger wave of laughter and cheers as tankards were raised. It took every ounce of Piero’s strength not to tut, and he took a couple of steps forwards on the stage to make it clear that the drunken fool would likely meet a swift and untimely end if he dared to step up beside him.

But the old man seemed oblivious and dropped the bosom in what was presumably an attempt at a dramatic reaction, his hands flying in feigned shock to his bearded face. “Ooh, I’ve lost me bloody paps!”

As the tavern erupted into more laughter, Piero was unable to repress a roll of his eyes.

“Too bad they didn’ leave the dress behind, an’ all,” called out the handsome, broad-armed man behind the bar.

Piero’s ears pricked up. “Dress?” He spoke more curtly than he’d meant to.

“Could ha’ put that lovely blue bow in your beard, Harry!” cackled someone else.

The dress with the blue bow...! How dare the bastard allow anyone to *touch* that dress, let alone perform in it? Piero took a deep breath and tried to soothe the fire twisting inside him. This was not the time... this was not the place. He pushed the beautiful dress from his mind and reined in the fury which made him want to shout and swear and hurl stools across the room. Instead, he presented a perfectly calculated smile.

"My good people!" he said with fervour. He raised a hand in a flourish as he began to pace upon the stage, emphatically stepping over the cabbage. Once more the witless merriment died down to a murmur, and everyone's attention began to return to where it bloody well should be. "I thank you for your valuable wisdom and insight. Now, can any kind soul here answer me this: when these inadequate players departed this *fine* establishment..." He paused for the predictable rumbling cheers and raising of tankards... "In which direction were they bound?"

"Andover way, wager," slurred Harry, trying the fake bosom on again and looking ridiculously pleased with himself.

"Aye, and in such a hurry, they forgot their bloody stage!" laughed the bald man beside him. He snatched the bosom from Harry, who hollered in protest as the bald man tossed it to someone else. Harry stumbled into tables as he attempted to chase after his prize.

Piero slowly cast down his eyes to the boards beneath his feet. Oh, *their* stage... Now, that was an unexpected and wonderful pleasure. His eyes danced with dark delight, and he looked up again, throwing his arms wide. "Good people, I thank you for your kind assistance and wish you all the merriest of nights!"

He held his hand aloft then dropped into a sweeping bow as several of the audience cheered and clapped. Of course they did. It was a shame not to linger, but his two travel companions were waiting, and the hunt was calling. He jumped down and swayed towards the handsome, broad-armed man behind the bar. He gestured with his white glove towards the main fireplace.

"Your fire runs dangerously low. I shall assist you in stoking it." His voice dropped to the most delicious, threatening whisper. "And savour the smell as it burns."

No one – *no one* – touched his dress.

CHAPTER 3: Thomas

Kneeling in the small wagon, Thomas unfolded the costume he'd worn for Titania. Evening was overpowering the day, but there was light enough to see the ribbons on the shoulders and embroidered detail on the top. He traced his fingers sadly over the blue bow which tied at the waist. Such a beautiful and valuable asset – why in Heaven's name was everyone so reluctant to use it? He brushed away a tiny piece of cabbage leaf caught in the fabric, folded up the gown and placed it back into the costume sack. The dress had such potential. *They* had such potential.

He looked around the rickety wagon. Beneath the patched canvas the hooped arches stretched from one side to the other like a giant ribcage – as if Thomas himself was its beating heart. Besides a sack each of personal possessions and Annie's crate of dubious handmade tonics, there were the costumes, the two swords, the drum, the donkey head, blankets and the small chest of props, half-buried by the green curtain draping over it and topped with Annie's fiddle... But damn, it looked painfully empty without the wood for the stage.

"Thomas!" called Annie. "Food!"

Was that... rotten cabbage drifting on the breeze? Oh Lord. Not for the first time, he sorely missed his ma's cooking at the inn. He looked out of the wagon across the tree-ringed common to where Annie and Caroline stood by the crackling campfire. Annie was barefoot, and her tangled red hair spread across her shoulders. She stirred the small iron pot which hung by a short chain from a tripod, then wiped her hands on the apron over her light brown dress.

Beside her, Caroline wore the brown breeches and white shirt she often donned when they kept their own company. She had cast aside her cap, as she and Annie often did, and her black hair was no longer restrained but wild and free. She stood with tension, watching Robert, who sat broodingly on the far side of the campfire. Her hands were on her hips, and her feet were definitely further apart than necessary. Oh Lord.

"Here's a health to the company and one to my lass..." sang Annie in her soft voice as she stirred.

There was certainly an uneasy feel in the camp tonight, and he was grateful for the forks of orange flame which danced determinedly against the gloom.

"Let us drink and be merry..."

"Merry? When we've just lost our stage?" Caroline said, peering at the pot suspiciously.

Thomas clambered out of the wagon, his wary eyes so fixed on Caroline that his foot clipped the donkey head, sending it toppling onto the grass below with a thud. Annie turned around, raising her dripping ladle in alarm.

"Oh, no! Mind poor Horatio!" she gasped as Thomas tossed the donkey head back into the wagon.

"Hard to tell which is the greater ass," Caroline said, looking pointedly at Thomas.

Thomas huffed. "Listen," he called across the common, "we were right to bring out that costume. It is woefully underused! Months it took to convince you all—"

"And we should never have agreed!" said Caroline.

Why was she always so difficult? Thomas walked over to Caroline, who faced him with tempestuous eyes. He raised his hands in surrender. "We ought not to be discouraged. Just because it wasn't quite an outstanding success today, it does not mean it will always be so."

"Wasn't quite an outstanding success?" Caroline folded her arms. "Where is our bloody stage?"

He waved his hand. "That is beside the point. We ought to give my Titania another chance! We were just unlucky!"

"THREE TIMES YOUR PAPS FELL OUT."

"*Very* unlucky," he said curtly.

"And on the third time you slipped on them and fell on your arse."

"Unreasonably unlucky!"

Caroline threw her hands up in the air. "And you wonder why they pelted us?"

Thomas pinched the bridge of his nose. The fire spat a shower of sparks up into the air. Frustration reared inside him as it did so often in any prolonged conversation with Caroline. Why did she always harbour such unreasonable frostiness towards him? Why could she not appreciate the vision, talent and encouragement he brought the company? And why did she always aggravate his doubts when he fought so hard to believe in himself?

He flung his arm out, causing his tatty, unbuttoned waistcoat to flap as he pointed in the vague direction of Winchester. "But you witnessed my performance! I poured my very heart and soul into that role! They *arrived* armed with vegetables! We clearly didn't stand a chance!" He whirled around to Annie, who was raising the ladle to her lips. He gripped her shoulders urgently, sending broth from the ladle flying over her shoulder. "Did we, Annie?"

"Oh... well..." Annie cast a nervous sidelong glance at Caroline. "They *were* unkind—"

"And wasn't the dress wonderful?" he said, stooping to search for reassurance in her big hazel eyes. "And didn't my Titania clearly display the breadth and depth of my talent?"

"If the breadth and depth of your talent is slipping on your paps and falling on your arse!" said Caroline.

"Oh, that's enough, you two," came Robert's voice from the other side of the fire.

Thomas scowled at Caroline. There was no point arguing with her when she stood with her feet that far apart. He released Annie and turned his attention to their manager, who sat with his knees drawn up and his arms slung loosely over them, staring at the flames. Robert shivered and pulled his brown jacket more tightly around him. He was only eight years Thomas' senior, yet he seemed significantly older of late. There was an increasing and concerning loss of enthusiasm for their performances now, even for such a bold and commanding portrayal of Titania. Thomas sighed and ran his fingers through his short, dark hair. Then he paused thoughtfully, mid-run. Perhaps next time... a rather elaborate wig?

Annie hastily poured brown liquid into bowls and handed one to Thomas and one to the woman who seemed to thrive on making his life difficult. Thomas curled his lip as slimy green vegetation floated on the surface of the broth.

Caroline stared. "Tell me that's not what I think it is."

"Well, it cost us naught," Annie said brightly. "That one landed in the wagon."

"Right. Robert," called Caroline, "we must lodge at an inn soon, for a decent bed and a decent meal. Surely we can manage one night!"

"And pay with what?" said Robert. "A song and a dance? We have nothing left."

"That's true enough," said Annie. "Even that lovely highwayman a fortnight ago refused to take anything and wished us better fortune."

Thomas dipped his head with the weight of shame. His pa's words drifted into his mind: *You're naught but a failure.* He pushed them away and edged closer to Caroline. "Fine, listen," he said in a low voice. "Times may be a little challenging..." He risked a glance at

Robert, then dropped his voice to a whisper. "We should sell your ma's ring."

"And why do that when we could sell your pocket watch?" hissed back Caroline.

Thomas dropped his mouth open in protest, grateful she didn't know he had already considered selling the watch his brother had gifted him. But if there was any other way... "You know I would sell my soul before that pocket watch."

"You'd fetch more for the watch."

"I have told you before," drifted over Robert's voice. "My players will not part with their most treasured possessions to pay for this company's failings."

"Damn his hearing," Thomas whispered to Caroline.

"And his principles?" said Robert.

Thomas grimaced a little, leaned back from Caroline and met Robert's brooding stare with an awkward smile before their manager turned back to the flames. Annie eyed Thomas and Caroline nervously, then tiptoed on her bare feet between them, holding a bowl of steaming broth. She placed the wooden bowl in Robert's hands, then squeezed his arm.

"We'll find more wood for a stage, sure enough, won't we? Eat up. You'll feel better."

Robert glanced at the broth doubtfully. "You are good people, good actors. You all deserve better than this company." He placed the bowl beside him.

Annie's face fell and she grabbed fistfuls of her apron. "I'll fetch the nettle tonic."

Thomas shook his head sadly. Poor Robert. The nettle tonic was a particularly vicious one. "How we are still alive is forever a mystery," muttered Thomas, earning a flick of the hand from Caroline.

He wagered he knew what the man would do next. Sure enough, Robert dipped his fingers below the neckline of his shirt and pulled out the rabbit's foot necklace, its fur matted and flat from Robert's repeated handling. They must have the most superstitious manager in the entire land. He wore it always around his neck and whenever he fiddled with it, a long, dark and solitary mood was never far away.

Thomas took a deep breath and encouraged his warm brown eyes to sparkle with the defiant passion of his heart. "Listen, this is just a minor setback. We'll find another stage! There are brighter days ahead and one day we'll play at the Theatre Royal in Drury–"

"Without a patronage?" said Caroline. "I doubt they'd even let us swill out the piss-pots at Drury Lane."

Yet again, the sneering voice of his pa floated into Thomas' mind.

"To be fair, it weren't Thomas' fault that Lord Blagdon didn't approve of him," said Annie, heading for Robert with a bottle of ominously dark green liquid and a wooden cup. "If you ask me, he only had eyes for–"

Caroline threw her a warning look. Annie gasped and they all looked at Robert anxiously. Thomas knew little about his predecessor, the one he struggled to live up to. The day Thomas had joined the company, Caroline had marched him behind a tree at sword-point and made it quite clear that no one mentioned the actor he was replacing. But it had been nigh on a year. Surely this man could no longer be of significance.

Annie knelt beside Robert, poured some of the vicious tonic into the cup and handed it to him. "This'll raise your spirits."

"Or kill you completely," Thomas muttered. "Could go either way." He earned another flick from Caroline.

"Go on," Annie said, with an encouraging nod.

Robert looked understandably doubtful, but he put his hand on her shoulder and gave an appreciative little smile. Screwing his face up in anticipation, he gulped it down, then coughed as if his lungs were on fire, which was quite possibly the case. Annie smiled back at Robert, but as she headed back to the wagon with the bottle, there was sorrow in her eyes. Thomas sighed. He took Caroline's arm and led her a little further out of Robert's good hearing.

"Less than a week since the last nettle tonic was administered," he whispered.

"You are not the only one counting." Caroline pulled her arm free.

Thomas drummed his fingers against his thighs as Caroline went over to Robert and offered the rum she had acquired at the unfair curtailment of their performance. She sat down beside him, so close their shoulders touched.

"You should visit a molly house," she said to Robert. "Now *that* will raise your spirits, and something else besides."

But Robert just drank from the bottle and seemed lost once more in his thoughts.

Thomas frowned. The mood was so painfully low! Surely he could do *something* to help them – but what? He paced around, patting his palms rapidly against his legs as he turned over options in his mind. They had knocked on the door of every potential patron in the area. They had exhausted the inns at Winchester. Perhaps the tavern at Eastleigh? Although they may no longer be welcome after Annie accidentally pissed in that barrel.

"Oh Thomas, stop marching around as if your arse is on fire," Caroline called as Annie went over and sat down beside her.

Possibly Romsey? Or—

"Andover!" He twisted around on his heels and extended his arms in a warm, open gesture. "We go on to Andover! We're in the right direction and I have not yet been there. You said you met with great success there before."

"When we were Lord Blagdon's Players, yes," said Caroline.

"And they will love us yet! We have a plan!" The brightness in his words was quelled by the silence which followed. He gave a little shrug. Well, no matter – they would surely warm to his excellent idea. In the meantime...

"Come on, a dance! A dance will bring us cheer tonight!" He bounded over to the wagon as fast as he could before anyone – especially Caroline – had chance to protest. He grabbed the scruffy old fiddle Annie held so dear, dislodging the donkey head once more as he did so.

"*Please* mind poor Horatio!"

Thomas tossed the donkey head back inside and headed for Annie. She might be the most dispensable member of the troupe, but at least she could play the fiddle well, and that served them in good stead. He handed her the instrument and gestured wildly with his hands to encourage her to get the Hell on with it before the gloominess became too much for even him to bear. Soon she was on her feet and a merry reel fought against the brooding silence, as the flames fought the ever-growing darkness.

A warm smile came to Annie's face as she played. It was working. Thomas clapped his hands in time to the music, then waved at the others to join in, but Caroline downed a generous amount of rum and belched at him defiantly. Robert returned to the flames, cradling the rabbit's foot.

Well, damn it all. He would dance by himself then! This company was his dream and his chance of success, and he would fight for it, whatever it cost. He stamped and leapt, frustration bursting through his feet every time they pounded the ground. And once Caroline's bottle lay drained beside her, even she gave a shadow of a smile and allowed him to pull her to her unsteady feet. He whirled her around the campfire, averting his eyes from the sight of Robert sinking his head deeper into his hands. The fiddle's determined, relentless rhythm flowed through Thomas' body like blood in his veins. He held his head high and chose hope.

Tomorrow, everything would be absolutely fine.

CHAPTER 4: Caroline

Why was it so cold for May? Caroline glanced up at the unbroken grey cloud and shivered. A chilly breeze danced around the road to Andover. Despite the shawl draped over her shoulders, the cap over her pinned-up hair and the kerchief around her neck, Caroline shivered once more.

"Right, that's it!" sighed Robert. "Please – just take the bloody thing." He slipped off his jacket and dropped it in Caroline's lap.

She shrugged and puffed out her cheeks. "Fine, if it makes you feel better."

He gave a tiny sigh. Good – he understood both her thanks, and the reminder that she could manage perfectly well by herself. But now she had his jacket, would he speak at all? Over the last two hours, his increasingly frustrated offers were the only words he had spoken. He always retreated when he was weighed with sadness. Although she would normally walk with the others to spare Old Bess, Caroline insisted on sitting beside him today, wary of the mood which devoured him. She wrapped his jacket over her shawl and pulled it around her shoulders. Warm, smelling of him. But although he sat beside her, he seemed a hundred miles hence. Fine, he didn't want conversation, but the sad silence which sat like an unwelcome fellow traveller between them was unbearable.

She glanced at Robert – one hand on the reins, the other still fiddling with the rabbit's foot around his neck. Her hatred for Piero rose once more – it didn't take long; it was never far away. The rabbit's foot should have been burned long ago. And that bloody dress. It must be nigh on a year since the bastard had betrayed them, since Robert had just cradled that wretched necklace and lain silent in the wagon, refusing to speak or eat. How many broken bottles had she wrestled from him? How many times had she bound his bleeding arms a little too roughly? She closed her eyes briefly at the memory, then cast Robert a quick glance. His frown was still there, unshakeable. Fear prickled her, as it often did. There were still broken bottles in his mind.

Muttering voices came from nearby. Caroline peered past Robert's brooding face and saw two grey-bearded men leaning against the gate of a walled field, pointing at her. Caroline sighed. Fine. Tension was already crackling inside her and it needed to fight its way out. It wasn't often people commented on the colour of her skin, but let their unkind words come. She was bloody ready for them. She drummed her fingers impatiently on the driver's seat, ignoring the sidelong glance from Robert.

"Too cold for you here, girl?" one of the men heckled. "Where you from?"

She opened her mouth.

"Shoreditch," Robert replied as they drove past. "Now, piss off."

Caroline whirled around to face him. "Why did you do that? I can speak for myself, and as it happens, I'm in the mood for an argument."

"I know. That's why I took pity on the bloody fools."

She glared at him, willing her annoyance to outweigh her gratitude. But it couldn't. He, of all people, understood unfair judgement. The world was not kind to men like him. Yet his own kindness had changed the course of her life when she had been alone, wandering, shunned by so many in her village. He had found her and welcomed her into the troupe.

She huffed louder than necessary. "Well, next time, let *me* do it." She flopped back against the seat as the wagon rolled on. She shuffled, her itch for a fight unsatisfied... unless... She shot upright, making Robert jump. "I reckon me and Thomas should show the swords."

"Swords?" came Thomas' nervous voice from somewhere behind.

Caroline sighed. Did Thomas have to complicate *everything*?

"No swords. She'll get carried away. Robert!"

"I promise I won't get carried away."

"You always get carried away! Last time I nearly lost an arm."

"Oh, you're lucky I went for your arm." Thomas and his bloody melodrama! Fair enough, sometimes it made her laugh, but sometimes it just made her want to punch him. She caught sight of the arched stone bridge as they approached Andover – there wasn't much time to persuade Robert. "Come on, it draws the crowds."

"Death scenes usually do! I said we should have blunted them."

"Just perform a fight, Thomas," said Robert.

"Well. Do. Not. Kill. Me. It's harder to perform at Drury Lane when you're a corpse!"

Frustration crawled under her skin again. His constant, all-consuming ambition! Just like someone else she knew. An image of Piero with his purple-powdered eyes sauntered uncomfortably into her mind. "And stop speaking of Drury Lane all the time," she called back. "I swear, if you mention it once more today, you'll be testing your theory about performing as a—"

The breeze swirled, bringing the smell of tumbling freshwater. She leaned forwards. That smell...

Time and place fell away. She was locked.

Her pale, lovely face.

Her heart drummed.

Tangled weed in her auburn hair.

She was breathing too fast.

No breath... no breath... screaming—

A firm hand rested on her shoulder. The world reappeared and time ran once more. She was back. She inhaled deeply to fight the dizziness. That smell. Lord, she hated that bloody smell. Caroline uncurled her tight, shaking fingers and rested back in her seat, Robert's hand still refusing to leave her shoulder. She turned her face away from him but pulled his jacket up further towards her cheekbones, grateful that it was now *his* scent filling her mind. She pushed her secret back to a place where, for now, it could be neither found nor felt. Tension burned in her shoulders, and as she forced them to relax, Robert's hand slid back to the reins. He demanded no explanation from her. He never did.

She needed to fill her thoughts with her surroundings when this happened, to keep those memories where they belonged. She studied the brown-bricked mill as they passed beside the stream that fed it and listened to the gentle rumblings of wheel and stone coming from within. They turned into the bustling main street with the octagonal market building in the middle. The ground floor was open, with thick wooden columns resting on a low stone wall, supporting the gabled floor above.

Either side of the building the wide road was lined with timber-framed houses and taller, brick ones, no two the same, their mismatched rooftops of thatch and tile at different heights. On the right, they passed the Black Horse Inn, a two-floored coach house with whitewashed walls and bay windows either side of the front door. She eyed it coldly, recalling their last visit over a year ago – staggering to bed in the early hours, full of food, ale and applause. The way Piero had captivated the audience that night was, admittedly, outstanding. Robert's eyes had shone with pride as he had applauded him.

BASTARD.

Horses pulled carts, folk stood in the street passing the time of day and scraggly dogs trotted around, searching for scraps. Caroline put a hand on her belly. What she would give for a decent meal.

Robert drove the wagon further up on the left, stopping between the market building and the White Swan. She had eaten the most delicious meat pies in that coaching inn, when they were Lord

Blagdon's Players. Those were the days they would arrive with a banging of the drum and waving of flags. Not slinking in unwelcome, without a licence to perform. She cast a wary eye towards the town clerk's house further up on the other side of the street, then looked ahead. A clear path for a swift exit. Yes, Robert had positioned the wagon well. This was their best chance.

Caroline reluctantly slipped off Robert's jacket and removed her cap and shawl, leaving them on the driver's seat. The chilly air gnawed as she jumped down to join Robert. He looked over his shoulder as Thomas came over, followed by Annie, whose tangled hair flowed loose around her.

Caroline reached into the wagon and threw Annie's cap to her.

"Watch for my sign," said Robert in a low voice. "Just long enough to get a few coins."

"Just long enough to win the fight," said Caroline, flashing Thomas a smile and at least gaining some small pleasure from his look of nervous disapproval.

Robert handed Annie her fiddle and Thomas the swords. Taking the drum for himself, he threw the strap around his neck. Caroline stared at the old drum, which had seen many a show. Was it not just like the company? Its once vivid red paint on its wooden rims was peeling and faint; the goatskin over the frame now fragile and worn; the zigzagged string around its side so tired, frayed, as if at any moment it might–

"Eyes sharp," said Robert.

Caroline gave a curt nod and smoothed her skirts. The wretched things were always in the way. "I ought to be allowed to do this in breeches."

"You know that, and I know that. But the town constables do not share that opinion."

"And you know, and I know, where the town constables may stick their opinion."

Robert laid a hand on her shoulder. "We're not performing a play: you know they would complain. A swishing skirt adds to the spectacle. Come on." He nodded at Thomas.

"You promised," said Thomas, reluctantly passing her a sword. "Follow the moves. It's not a battle, it's a show."

"I propose a tragedy," she said provocatively.

Thomas sighed, smoothed down his pale shirt and took his position. The fragile drum began to beat. Heads turned in their direction, and Annie's quick fingers delivered a lively reel. Thomas stepped into the road and stuck out his chest as if he were the most important person in the town.

"*Gather round, dear gentle folk and watch this wondrous fight—*"

"Lord Blagdon's Players are here!" called an old woman nearby.

Oh... The woman hadn't noticed the lack of livery, then? Caroline glanced at Robert. He shook his head urgently as Thomas flourished his sword.

"Yes! Lord Blagdon's Players!"

What the Hell? Caroline glared at Thomas as he swaggered around. A stream of wrong notes tumbled out of the fiddle. Did he not realise the trouble this could cause?

"Lord Blagdon's Players!" spread the word around the gathering crowd. Thomas flourished his sword again.

"*Gather round, dear gentle folk and watch this wondrous fight*

'Twixt Madeleine a villain and Sir John the gallant knight!"

"Why ain't you got Lord Blagdon's flags?" called a young woman.

Caroline opened her mouth to explain exactly why they didn't have the flags and where exactly Lord Blagdon could shove them, but Thomas quickly signalled to Annie to play the tune for the fight. Good! Caroline gripped the sword. She was bloody ready for him.

"What are you playing at?" she hissed. Why was Annie's introduction taking so long? Her muscles twitched. Oh, to Hell with it. She tutted and flew for him early, weapon outstretched, too furious to enjoy the surprise on Thomas' face.

"They know us as Lord Blagdon's," he hissed back as their swords clashed. "And you started too soon!"

The blades crossed.

"They should know us as Robert's!" She kicked his shin, making him yelp. "And I start when I bloody well like." She shoved Thomas backwards. He stumbled and laughter ran through the crowd. Served him right.

Annie played the reel faster...

Caroline went for Thomas with her sword, left and right, her skirts swishing in defiant rhythm.

"Now is hardly the time for an argument!" he pleaded.

Annie played faster...

"Oh, it bloody is!"

And faster...

"Follow! The! Moves!"

Oh, the Devil take it all!

Caroline tossed her sword aside and launched at Thomas' legs, knocking him to the ground. The crowd cheered as his sword went flying. She straddled his waist and pinned down his wrists as strands of her loosened hair trailed around her face. His chest rose and fell rapidly beneath her. Always ambitious, always desperate for success – what kind of lead actor was too ashamed to name his own company? This man would never have her trust.

"You promised you wouldn't get carried away!" Thomas fumed, looking up with blazing brown eyes.

"I lied! As did you!"

Annie rounded off the frantic reel with an uncertain flourish, and the crowd clapped and jeered. Wagon wheels and hooves sounded somewhere nearby.

"Lord Blagdon's Players!" yelled the old woman's voice above the din. The crowd quietened. Her voice wavered. "Again."

Caroline exchanged a wide-eyed look with Thomas.

"Shit," they both said, scrambling to their feet urgently. Caroline brushed some of her unpinned hair away from her eyes. There was the other wagon right in the middle of the road, decorated with Lord Blagdon's flags: a double-headed griffin and three stars. Two women and two men stood there. One of the women was young, with furious eyes and a sword in her hand. The other was plump, with greying hair poking out from beneath her cap, standing as if she were the queen. The younger man would surely be Lord Blagdon's favourite – clean-shaven with fine cheekbones – and there was an elder with a beard who could probably pull wagons for a living. And they all looked rather pissed off.

"They said *they* were Lord Blagdon's Players," someone said to the new troupe as they moved through the swiftly parting crowd.

"Well, we *were*," said Thomas lightly. "Time flies."

Caroline's hands balled into fists. Robert strode towards her, sliding the drum strap from around his neck as he moved. "Get Annie, get everything in the wagon – just leave." He pushed the dying drum into her arms.

"In our defence, we didn't know you were coming as well," Thomas was saying.

Caroline ran to Annie, who stood wide-eyed, clutching her fiddle to her chest. Safe – she needed to get Annie safe. Caroline's fingers closed desperately around Annie's arm, dragging her to the wagon.

"Stay in and stay down," she said as she bundled Annie inside, followed by the drum. She looked anxiously at the others. Thomas stood on the far side of Robert. The two troupes faced each other in uneasy lines as the crowd gathered. Quiet, tense. Caroline grabbed her sword from the ground and marched over to Robert.

"I said, get in!" he said.

"No!" Caroline fixed her eyes on the opposing players. Well, she had wanted a fight...

"Get your arses off our circuit," said the young woman to Robert.

Caroline tightened the grip of her sweating hand on the sword.

"What is the meaning of this?" said a gravelly voice she recognised. The town clerk, a stout, black-haired man, pushed through the crowd.

"They claim to be us," said the bearded man, pointing at Robert. "But *we* are Lord Blagdon's Players. *They* are stealing our livelihood."

"We meant no trouble." Robert moved his arms out towards Thomas and Caroline on either side, palms facing them, as if to either protect them or restrain them. "This was just a mistake."

"Yes, it was," sneered the young man with the cheekbones. "*We* have Lord Blagdon's patronage, not you. Have a care, my friend. The Vagrancy Act does not favour beggars."

"We are not beggars – we are actors!" Thomas shot back heatedly, pushing past Robert's outstretched hand and shoving the man, who staggered back.

Robert grabbed Thomas by the shirt and pulled him back swiftly. "Enough!"

Caroline's throat went dry. She waited, twitchy – tense – ready—

They waited, twitchy – tense – ready—

"Beggars and vagabonds with no licence to perform," said the town clerk, walking closer to Robert until there was an inch between them. Robert did not flinch.

Caroline leaned slightly forwards. Oh, she wanted to fly at this man. Robert's outstretched hand edged closer towards her.

The town clerk looked down his nose at Robert as he growled: "Get out of my town." He turned his back, gave a nod to Lord Blagdon's Players and disappeared through the crowd.

"Get 'im!" yelled some bastard.

Caroline's heart leapt into her mouth as the fine-cheekboned man rushed forwards and punched Thomas in the face, sending him crashing to the ground. At the same time, the elder punched Robert.

"God for Harry, England and Saint George!" roared the young woman's voice, raising her sword as the audience cheered.

Shit!

The woman lunged forwards. Caroline swung wildly; their swords clashed. Anger fuelled every blow, every parry, every riposte. Bloody Hell, this woman was good. There was a stinging thump on her arm – and another – as stones hurled by the plump woman rained around her. The crowd roared, filling her ears – sword flashing blow after blow – stones flying – her eyes working fast – no chance to catch breath—

Somewhere behind her, Thomas' desperate voice pleaded, "Stop! You'll kill him!"

Robert! Her heart lurched. Swords slashed through the air. Blow after blow after—

Something hard slammed into her cheek. The thud resounded in her head.

She gasped, stumbled and doubled over. Her blurry eyes saw another stone fall at her feet. She touched her face. Blood on her fingers. A smack stung her knuckles, and the sword flew from her hand.

Her eyes regained focus. She pressed her stinging hand against her throbbing cheek and glared at the young woman. The woman pointed her sword at Caroline's chest and marched forwards. Caroline retreated until, with a jolting thud, her back hit the market building. Robert? Where was Robert? She looked at the crowd gathered on her left.

Shit. Her stomach knotted.

He was barely standing, his eyes closed and his arm limply draped around Thomas' shoulder. Thomas supported Robert's waist with one arm and dragged his reclaimed sword with the other as he stumbled forwards. Both had blood running down their faces. Caroline swallowed and forced her gaze back to the woman. She needed to stay calm. The crowd applauded and coins landed at the feet of Lord Blagdon's Players as the fine-cheekboned man and the plump woman collected the money with triumphant bows.

"We said, get your arses off our circuit," repeated the young woman. She kicked Caroline's sword, sending it spinning towards her.

Caroline grabbed it and ran to Robert. With a shaking hand she lifted his other limp arm over her shoulders, feeling the warmth of his body. Safe. She had to get him safe. They shuffled towards the wagon. Inside, Annie sat with her knees drawn up and her arms wrapped around her fiddle. Thomas crawled in and helped drag Robert inside before crumpling onto his side.

"The girls..." Robert murmured.

"We're fine," said Caroline. Her voice didn't dare to shake and betray the lie. It never did.

"You're hurt," whispered Annie.

Caroline cupped Annie's tear-stained face in her hands and met her frightened eyes. "We're fine."

Annie nodded frantically as Caroline headed to the driver's seat. She picked up the reins with trembling hands smeared with blood – hers? Robert's? – and with a flick of the reins, Old Bess trotted past the market building. Where to go? Where should she go? The millstream... follow the millstream out of town. They could stop. Wash their wounds.

"We're fine," she whispered and took a deep breath. The thought of a fraying string tormented her – the company she adored was down to a single thread. She wiped her cheek with her bruised hand. She relished the pain. It screamed out her untameable fury. Not just at Lord Blagdon and his players. But at Robert, for getting himself hurt. At Thomas for causing this in the first place.

But most of all at herself, for failing to offer protection.

Failing, as she had done before... on that terrible day when the final thread had snapped.

The image of a body being pulled from the river flashed into her mind once more.

CHAPTER 5: Thomas

"Ow!" Thomas winced as Caroline wiped the cloth more roughly than necessary across the cut on his forehead. Did she have to be so brutal? His head was spinning enough. "Ashamed is such a strong word! I thought they might be a warmer audience if they didn't know our change of circumstances. I was trying to help!"

He sank onto the grass beside the wagon, the darkening clouds reflecting his mood. A heavy sickness sat in his chest. He eyed Caroline nervously as she plunged the cloth back into the bowl of water and wrung it out like she was wringing his neck. Warm blood trickled down his cheek, and Caroline threw him a murderous look as she laid one hand on the side of his face and, with the other, pressed the cloth forcefully against the wound. Was she actually trying to crush his skull?

"Bollocks," she said. "You *were* ashamed! You pretended we were someone else."

"We are *actors*!" he protested. "It's what we're supposed to do. Ouch!" He caught his breath as Caroline wiped his head once more and studied the wound.

"You'll live," she said, giving him the impression that this was rather a bad idea. Hurling the blood-stained cloth into his lap, she went to Robert, her unpinned hair flouncing behind her. Thomas gently touched his forehead. Bloody Hell, it throbbed. He'd only been attempting to win the townsfolk's favour. He just hadn't entirely succeeded.

You are naught but a failure.

He forced himself to look at their manager, hating the wave of guilt that battered him. Robert sat just inside the wagon, his legs dangling over the edge and his eyes still shut. He clutched his ribs, wincing with each breath. Thomas grimaced as his eyes traced the numerous cuts on Robert's body. There would be a good many bruises in the morning. Robert leaned forwards and retched a little, face screwed up with pain. Caroline and Annie began bandaging his ribs with a long strip of linen.

"If it had worked, I would be a hero now, not a villain," Thomas muttered, quietly enough that Caroline wouldn't hear him. Well, she had wanted a tragedy, not a comedy. Two sides of the same spinning coin – and fortune was, yet again, not their friend today.

An eager drop of rain splattered onto Thomas' hand.

"You may have joined when we were Lord Blagdon's Players, Thomas," Caroline ranted as she bandaged, "but we have always been the Ticehurst Players, and there is no bloody shame in that."

He avoided her furious glare by staring down at the grass. It blurred and unblurred before him, and he reached for the ground to steady himself.

"'Course he's 'shamed," slurred Robert. "Look at us. No patron. No stage. No circuit."

"If we're making a list," said Annie as she fastened the bandage, "we also have no skull after what happened with the parson and the goat in Portchester."

Thomas crossed himself, as did Caroline and Annie. They had all vowed to do so whenever someone recalled that dreadful incident.

"Used to love us, Andover..." said Robert. "All my fault... Lost Lord Blagdon—"

"It's not *your* fault, Robert," Caroline said.

Thomas' pa laughed cruelly in his head.

"It's not Thomas' fault neither," said Annie meekly.

He glanced up at her with an appreciative smile, choosing to ignore the look of disbelief Caroline threw her.

"Piero was just better in talent and looks," Annie said with a shrug.

Marvellous. He bit his tongue.

"Annie," cautioned Caroline.

"Though reckon it were his looks that caused all the bother–"

Caroline reached over and put her hand over Annie's mouth, casting an anxious look at Robert.

Several drops of rain tickled Thomas' neck, and a chilly breeze wrapped around him. He sighed. "Listen. We shall find another patron."

"Knocked on ev'ry door... We *are* beggars... This's our future..." Robert winced again. "I'm sorry. It's time."

Thomas tensed at the defeated tone. "Time for what?"

"Final bow."

What? Thomas sat suddenly upright: a rush of dizziness and sickness flooded him. "You would not fold the company!"

Annie pressed her hands to her stomach. "Robert, this company's our family!"

"Listen, Robert," pleaded Thomas as his spinning head caused him to lurch sideways. "This company is destined for great things! We have not failed! We will not fail."

You're naught but a failure.

Robert dragged open his eyes and looked at Thomas. "This feel like success?"

The words hit harder than the punches Thomas had just received. He bit his lip and averted his eyes from his manager's gaze. Everything was falling apart! Thomas took several long, slow breaths and pushed away the temptation to panic. He had not abandoned his home, his inheritance of the inn, and put in two years' hard work for it all to end like this. There must be a way to save the company! A pleading look flew in Caroline's direction, but her face was as grim as a gravestone.

"Oh, Robert!" said Annie. "You're hurt; you're not thinking straight. Have the sleeping draught and rest awhile." Glass clinked as she rummaged through her crate of tonics then raised a bottle to Robert's lips.

"So, we improvise!" Thomas searched desperately in his hazy mind for more words to follow.

"Improvise?" said Caroline coldly. "Like us being Lord Blagdon's Players? Shall we discuss that, Thomas?"

"*Courage and comfort...*" Thomas paused to allow his brother to complete the Shakespearean line, as they had done since boyhood.

Silence.

He frowned. Oh, of course... how foolish. Benedict was miles away in Devonshire. He hadn't spoken half a line of Shakespeare – and waited for his brother's reply – for nigh on a year now. He pressed the damp cloth back to his forehead. His injury must be worse than he thought. "*... All shall yet go well,*" he continued. "We just need time to get back on our feet! For Robert to recover. We just need..." A bloody miracle? "... A new circuit somewhere."

"Oh, and where do you suggest?" snapped Caroline.

"I... don't know." The rush of enthusiasm trickled away and left him empty. His head hurt, his side ached and bile rose in his chest. "Somewhere we have an advantage for once. Where we stand a chance of earning some shillings." He spread his hands. "We need a decent audience; like a home crowd..."

A vague, dark thought began drifting into his mind, like a raincloud on the verge of bursting. "With... free accommodation..." The thought began to sharpen. "Free decent food..." Reaching inside his jacket, his fingers closed around the brass pocket watch from his brother. "And free cider..." His heart sank faster than Titania's bosom. He dropped his voice. "Oh shit."

“All fare better without this company...” Robert gasped in pain as he laid down in the wagon sleepily. “Drop you all where you wish...”

“Devonshire!” The word leapt out. What in Heaven’s name was he saying?! “I wish to go to Devonshire.” Thomas drew in a deep breath, his head spinning worse than ever. “Do you... recall me mentioning that my father has an inn, some miles north of Exeter?”

“No.” Caroline narrowed her eyes at him. “I think you kept that rather quiet.”

“Hmm? Oh. Certain I mentioned it,” he mumbled, waving a hand dismissively. He rocked forwards onto his hands and knees and swayed a little. “Listen, I can arrange everything. We can perform at the inn without charge, raise funds, then we can secure patronage. Drury Lane will be within our reach once more.” Sickness welled inside. “Everything will be fine.” This company was his best chance of success. He had no choice but to save it. One last push... “The show is not over ’til we lower the curtain.”

Annie clasped her hands together. “Will there be real beds? Real pillows with feathers?”

“Feathers,” said Thomas. He tried to summon the energy to stand.

“And decent food?” added Caroline, casting a sidelong glance at Annie.

“My ma’s bread... Best this side of Truro.” Was it working? Hope dared to bloom.

“I’m sorry,” Robert murmured sleepily. “’s over, Thomas.”

“One last try, Robert, I beg you! One!” He staggered to his feet and vomited over the grass. Dragging one foot after the other, he found the wagon and flopped gratefully against it, hearing the gentle patter of raindrops on canvas. “And should we... *not* meet with success... I would not ask you to reconsider.” He summoned his warmest, most tempting voice. “Free cider.”

“All way to Devonshire?” slurred Robert as Annie tucked a blanket over him. “With you three...!”

Thomas strained his ringing ears. Was there... more? Robert's breathing relaxed into an easy rhythm. Thomas looked at Caroline and Annie. "That was almost definitely, probably, a yes. Let's go before he wakes up." With the damp cloth still in hand, he began to crawl into the wagon. Caroline grabbed his arm, exactly where a boot had kicked him. He winced.

"Let me make something clear," she said in a dangerously low voice. "I owe Robert, and I will never forget that. He was devastated when he caught Piero with some woman. Served the bastard right when Robert started thinking with his head instead of his cock." She pointed a finger in Thomas' face. "But thanks to you, now his spirit and his ribs are broken as well as his heart. If you do not make amends, I will personally string you up at a crossroads. And more importantly, this company will be over."

"I know." Flashing lights danced in his vision.

"Robert does not change his mind readily once it is made up, as Piero will testify. We will not get another chance."

"I know..." Everything felt... strangely light.

"So, this had better work."

"Of course it'll work."

"That," she snapped, "is what you said about Titania."

He opened his mouth, but there were no words. A high-pitched note rang in his ears. Breath came short and shallow. Caroline released his arm and marched to the front of the wagon as Thomas half-crawled, half-fell in beside Annie. He glanced at Robert lying unawares as rain suddenly hammered down upon the canvas. Several strongly worded exclamations came from the driver's seat, but the wagon jolted as it set off.

His pocket watch... he needed to look at his... Thomas pulled it from his jacket. His brother had bought it from a pedlar some years ago. The six words engraved on the back were also engraved in his mind.

RICHARD III ACT 1, SCENE 4.

He brought only half of the intended line to mind, for he only ever needed to.

I am his brother...

Who had crept away in the night... abandoned his family... started a new life.

Vision narrowed. The hand and the pocket watch dropped limply to his side.

"Thomas?" Annie's concerned voice was far away. "Are you all right?"

His family were going to kill him.

He toppled into Annie's lap.

Everything went black.

CHAPTER 6: Piero

If it was possible to look like you were strutting as you drove a wagon, Piero was certain he had accomplished it. Shoulders back, head high, chin up – barely acknowledge the people you pass as the wheels and the horses' hooves kick up dust in their pitiful faces.

The two horses led the wagon down the leafy road beneath a darkly clouded sky. He moved his hand to the skirted thigh of the woman beside him. Maria smiled. It served his purpose to keep her happy. Her slender, olive-skinned fingers reached in reply for his own leg. Piero smiled back, knowing with certainty that the remaining person on the seat would not be smiling.

Angelo sat on the other side of Maria, tall and strong, with the same dark eyes and olive skin as his sister. Piero sensed Angelo observing their teasing fingers – a habit of a lifetime, presumably, when you had trained since childhood to watch your sister's every movement, with the sole purpose of keeping her alive.

Piero defiantly slid his white-gloved fingers further up Maria's skirt until they rested at the top of her leg. Then he leaned oh-so-slightly forwards, and his purple-powdered eyes met the waiting, troubled eyes of Angelo. Was there a time Piero might have felt sympathy for him? Perhaps. But kindness was a dangerous affair. It made you vulnerable, and Piero would never make that mistake again.

Angelo looked away and tapped his fingers in agitation on the driver's seat. Piero rested back triumphantly. Angelo must bend, yes, but he must not snap. Angelo loved his sister deeply and if the man snapped, Piero was not quite sure in which direction he might break. It was all a fine balancing act.

One wrong move...

He moved his hand away from Maria and replaced it on the reins. She shuffled closer. Rebellious strands of her dark, wavy hair had escaped her cap and brushed against his face as she murmured in his ear.

"This road feels endless. Must we keep seeking these wretched players?"

"Oh, every performance requires a grand finale, does it not?" Piero said coldly. "It's time to end the show."

Maria's sigh held more than a fraction of irritation, but her fingers slid further and further up his leg until they rested teasingly over his cock. "You had better make this journey worth my while."

"Do I not, my love?" He lowered his voice to a murmur. "Every single time?"

She rested her head upon his shoulder. He felt the warmth of her, but it did not sink any deeper than his skin. It never did.

"The air grows colder. We should stop before it rains," she said. "Why not rest at the next inn and ask to perform? Besides, we might have need of a decent bed."

"We have a game to play, my love. You like games," Piero replied. His pale eyes danced. "And this shall be a fine one."

What would he do without her now? It was hard to believe they had met just a year ago in Portsmouth, when she was entranced by his Hamlet. How she had begged him to join their troupe and use his remarkable talent to captivate their audience, with the dazzling promise of success... Maria could be so persuasive, especially if you were rather drunk on rum and applause, and her hand was working your cock. And Robert...

He pushed Maria to one side, eyes focused on Robert, fingers fumbling with the buttons on his breeches. He threw on a desperate, crowd-winning smile. "Just trying to entertain the audience."

Robert's eyes were full of pain and thunder.

"Robert..." It was barely a whisper.

The fist of the man he adored pulled back and—

His left hand moved to his cheek, his shoulder shifting. Maria hesitantly lifted her head from his shoulder and her hand from his breeches, but he cared not. That moment had passed and no longer held interest for him.

His mood darkened with the clouds, and the anger danced inside him once more as he gripped the reins tighter. He should be grateful – his life was greatly improved without that man, without the company. The thought of a certain sack and its contents, behind him in the wagon, brought him comfort. Oh, there would be no mercy for his prey. The joy of the kill would be worth the toil of the hunt.

A crossroads loomed up ahead. Gallows perched at the foot of a hill on the right-hand side, its frame set against the storm-gathering clouds above it. A young woman knelt in front of it, twisting a single stem of a red flower in her hands. He felt a moment of pity – not for her loss of a loved one, but for her foolishness in having loved at all. Comedy was naught but unfinished tragedy, as the man he hated always said. He looked at the roads ahead. Which direction had the Ticehurst Players gone?

"Good day," Piero called, slowing the wagon to a stop beside her.

The young woman jumped. She rose to her feet and greeted them with a curtsey, wiping tears from her cheeks. She was yet to learn she could live perfectly well without whomever she had lost; yet to learn that she could fill that screaming, aching gap which threatened to consume her from the inside out, and move on with the business of life. Just as he had.

"I seek a company of players who may have passed this way," he said. "A dark-skinned girl, plain and ill-tempered; a flame-haired girl, barefoot and cuddling a fiddle... and a man..." He hesitated as many conflicted and forbidden words sprang to his mind and stole his tongue. "He's just a man."

The young woman nodded, pointing to the road ahead. "I seen 'em pass this way. Few hours ago now, s'pose."

A spark of delight shot through Piero. He disregarded Maria's slump of disappointment and nodded at the girl in front of him. A little flick with his white-gloved fingers sent a coin spinning down towards the wretched creature. "The pain will pass."

He nudged the horses on along the road. Hatred was like a demon that devoured and consumed everything until only itself remained – a demon that could neither rest nor sleep, dancing restlessly in the flames, gorging on memory and clawing impatiently for its chance to play. Now, after much searching, that chance was nearly upon them.

Piero smiled slowly and murmured to the audience beside him. "The game is definitely afoot."

The first raindrops began to fall.

CHAPTER 7: Thomas

Gone were the sage green downlands and the flint walls. The looming hills were now of deep emerald, and the road lined with tall hawthorn hedges. Thomas' stomach gave a little twist.

"We must certainly be in Devonshire now," he said to Annie, who walked beside him, behind the wagon. He had blurted out his home county to Robert as a rash and desperate man. But what choice was there? How he'd longed for the rolling hills and red earth of Devonshire when he had waded through the filth of London, searching desperately for a theatre company. Yet now he would gladly choose the jostling crowds, the endless noise and the shit-covered streets rather than the road ahead.

Inside the wagon, Robert muttered in his sleep. His face bore many colourful shades of bruising, although the cuts were healing well after a week, despite whatever pungent tonic Annie insisted on bathing them with. At least his own injuries had healed well enough without that.

Annie squirmed a little as she walked. "Poor Robert. He weren't pleased about coming so far."

"But he *will* be pleased when we save the company," whispered Thomas. "We will yet change his mind."

Annie squirmed again and wrung her skirts with her hands. "Oh, Thomas..." There was apology and desperation in her hazel eyes.

Thomas sighed. For Heaven's sake! He rubbed his hand over his eyes. "Again? Can you not sing a tune? Relieve your mind of the matter?"

"Oh, Thomas, but 'tisn't my mind needs relieving."

"She is going to kill you. Actually kill you."

Annie bit her lip and Thomas sighed twice as loudly as he needed to.

"Are we nearly there yet?" called Annie.

"I said not to ask again!" floated back Caroline's voice. "And do not tell me you need another piss!"

"I'm really sorry. It's the elderberry tonic! Promise I'll be quick!"

"Right, that's it!" snapped Caroline. "No more long journeys!"

Annie gave Thomas a hopeful smile, but Thomas scowled in reply. This was ridiculous. It was bad enough heading towards your impending doom, let alone dragging it out by stopping every half an hour. After a few more minutes the wagon turned left from the road and bumped over rougher ground down towards a wide stretch of grass beside a stream. Robert opened his eyes, and his hand flew to his ribs.

As the wagon halted, Annie leapt inside, grabbed two empty bottles and disappeared into the bushes faster than Caroline could throw an insult.

"Well, good news – we *are* nearly there," Thomas said to Robert, wishing the weight of his heart could match the forced lightness of his voice. Nearly home. He repressed the shudder. No... It was all going to be absolutely fine...

With the silencing of the wagon wheels, the sound of the babbling stream filled the air. The gentle breeze pushed the clouds on their way and Thomas tilted his face towards the sun, trying to absorb the hopeful warmth of midday. It was a pleasant day in mid-May, enough to normally raise the spirits, but he could find no joy. His stomach jittered as if he were about to walk on stage without knowledge of the play they were performing.

A sturdy chestnut horse grazed on the grass further along the riverbank. Nearby stood a wagon with strings running down its length, adorned with rabbit's feet and colourful ribbons which rippled in the breeze. Beside it was a little campfire and a small table with a candleholder and a couple of stools, but no sign of their owner. He drifted down to observe the stream. On pushed the water with its destined course, tumbling over the pale red and grey stones, refusing to let them impede its progress.

"Thomas," called Caroline, standing beside the wagon. Her fists were balled and her eyes flickered towards the stream. She wore a defiant stare and beckoned him towards her.

Lord, *now* what? He braced himself, his heart growing heavier with every step he took.

"This," she said, "had better be worth it. Ten times we've stopped today, and we've not been travelling two hours! What the Hell did she put in those tonics?"

"Of course it shall be worth it. We'll be at Bampton before you know it, and everything shall be absolutely fine."

Caroline narrowed her eyes. "Do not let her drink any more. I'm hiding the bloody things." She climbed into the wagon and began rummaging around.

Thomas turned to walk down the side of the wagon—

Shit!

Every muscle tensed.

A woman stood there. She wore a long dark red skirt, a matching ribboned bodice over her shirt, and a brown headscarf covering her plaited grey hair. Her face was tanned and wrinkled, and her bright brown eyes looked at him with alarming sharpness, as if they were staring into his very soul. He swallowed.

"Old Dina has a candle. Sees it true, tells it true," she said. A gold-ringed finger jabbed towards him. He startled and leaned back. "You has a question for the candle."

She scurried off towards the other wagon. Who in Heaven's name was this person? And a question for the candle? He had seen such fortune-tellers before but had never paid them any heed. Besides, surely, he was not yet in such a desperate state of misfortune and trouble that he would consult a *fortune-teller* of all people for help?

He sighed.

"Yes, wait! I do have a question!" He rushed after her.

Old Dina stopped suddenly. He forced his legs to halt, almost crashing into her. Slowly, she turned, a smile creeping over her face. "Old Dina knows. She always knows." The brass candleholder on the woman's table now hosted a lit candle and pinned down a piece of paper. The flame flickered in the slight breeze and a small pool of wax began to gather at the candle's top.

The woman sat herself down on one stool and he cautiously sat upon the other, eyeing her with eagerness and curiosity. He cast a glance over his shoulder. No sign of the others.

The woman stared at him. "Old Dina comes from generations of seers. We seek truth, we find truth. Ask the candle–"

He opened his mouth to speak, but the woman leapt up, reaching over the table. What the–? His eyes widened as her hand clasped over his mouth.

"Payment first. Or the candle lies." She removed her palm from his mouth and returned to her stool. Thomas swallowed as his heart rate began to fall. Was this an entirely good idea? Nonetheless, he reached inside the pocket of his tattered jacket for his nearly empty purse, almost dislodging his pocket watch at the same time.

"This is all I have." He dropped a coin into her palm and she studied it for a moment, then looked up at him expectantly. Damn. He reached back inside his purse. "Oh, apart from this one."

She nodded and placed the coins on the table. "Ask the candle."

He leaned closer. "It is my dearest wish to become a successful actor," he said quietly. "I long to perform in the Royal at Drury Lane. I've sacrificed much already – left my home, my family, the inheritance of my father's inn–"

"Old Dina's candle ain't got all day."

"I must know. Will the Ticehurst Players ever have a patron again?"

Old Dina tipped the candleholder, pouring wax over the piece of paper. Thomas stared at it, tilting his head this way and that. He drummed his fingers on his thighs.

"Well? What do you see?" He leaned forwards once more, and for a moment, Old Dina's concentration seemed to waver. Then her bright eyes travelled upwards to meet his.

"Old Dina sees a pocket watch."

Thomas' hand flew to his jacket pocket. "The one from my brother?" It must be a sign!

"Thomas. Bring your arse over here. We're leaving!" Caroline called from the wagon.

"More!" Thomas planted his hands on the table and stared intensely at Old Dina. "There must be more!"

"Good fortune awaits you at Thorverton Fair," she said, returning a look as intense as his own.

"Thorverton Fair?" The place he used to visit with his brother when they were younger! "Good fortune for me or the company? Should I speak of this?"

"THOMAS! If we don't leave now, Annie will need to piss again! What are you doing?"

There was no point now Caroline had seen him. He gave a nod to the fortune-teller and began walking back to the others.

"Find Old Dina at the fair," croaked the woman's voice behind him. It somehow sounded like she was smiling. "She'll be there."

His thoughts tumbled like the stream. The pocket watch. The fortune-teller. Thorverton Fair. He did not readily believe in superstition, unlike Robert who swore by the rabbit's foot and quaked at the peacock's feather. Yet there was something about this old woman. She had seen the pocket watch. Surely it must mean that Benedict would come to his aid and all would be well! If there had been more time, perhaps she could have spoken more of his fate. Of Drury Lane! Perhaps she would have told him that one day he would meet with great success! And finally, Pa's words would haunt him no longer. His heart swelled.

"What *were* you doing?" called Caroline, her voice heavy with suspicion.

"Finding hope!" he said, clasping his hands together. "Surprising where it comes from. But it always turns up."

He ignored her scornful huff as she headed to the driver's seat. He cared not what she thought – a lightness filled him that he hadn't felt since the night before Andover. His step had a decided bounce as he followed the wagon, and his fingers drummed on his thighs. Annie walked beside him, looking greatly relieved in more ways than one. She pointed at the tonic crate holding two bottles filled with dark-yellow liquid, lolling with the wagon's rhythm.

"Did you know it's good for your teeth?" she said brightly.

"To be clear," he said with unwavering firmness, "I have absolutely no problems with my teeth." He gave her a nudge. "Play us a jig!"

Annie needed little encouragement to reach for her fiddle. As the merry tune rang through the air, Thomas' mind returned to the fortune-teller, Drury Lane and the pocket watch.

Before evening rolled in, they pulled onto a clearing by the edge of a dark copse. Caroline's tiredness was clear, and her irritability stabbed at everyone, but that was the least of Thomas' problems. Concern now weighted his earlier buoyancy – what kind of reception would his family offer him tomorrow?

At dusk, the temperature fell, and Thomas was grateful for the comfort of his blanket as he lay beside the crackling campfire. He was also grateful that Caroline sloped off into the shoulder-to-shoulder trees to unleash her mood on whatever the wood had to offer. He glanced over at Robert. The man had barely spoken two words to anyone since he had woken from the sleeping draught, and lay there now in silence, preferring the company of his thoughts to that of his players. Annie pulled the blankets around her as she quietly sang her customary lullaby.

"Lavender's blue, dilly dilly, lavender's green..."

The offering floated through the cold silence of night, for whomever cared to listen. Thomas closed his eyes and bid his body to relax, but his legs were restless, and his mind even more so. He turned and tossed and turned again as Annie's lullaby grew slower and heavier, finally stopping mid-line. Oh, sleep was pointless. Thomas sighed, cast his blanket off and paced around the fire, his fingertips softly tapping his legs. Surely after two years, the rage of his family would have softened! Surely they would have come to appreciate that there had been no choice but for him to abandon the family inn and pursue the stage! And surely Pa's insistence that if Thomas left to become an actor, he would no longer be a son of his, was just an overreaction in the heat of argument! And after all, to Thomas' credit, he had been thoughtful enough to send a letter, several months after his departure, to explain where he'd gone and that he was, in fact, alive.

He slapped his thighs gently with his palms. The company would not fold. It was not allowed to fold! The fortune-teller had seen the pocket watch. He had to stop doubting. There was hope! There *was* hope. He just... needed a plan to nudge it in the right direction.

"Our doubts are traitors..." he reprimanded the campfire.

"Thomas, go to sleep," murmured Robert.

Thomas stared at the fire. Of course, tomorrow the Bard's words would no longer be hanging in the air like an unfulfilled promise. Benedict had probably missed their game sorely. As brothers just shy of two years apart, they had been so close. Thomas smiled.

Indeed, his little brother would surely be overjoyed to see him alive and well – especially since Thomas had sent no word at all for the last eighteen months. Thomas could be dead for all his brother knew! Benedict was always such a slave to his emotion, so it was certain to be a touching reunion. And thanks to Robert's rules, he still had the pocket watch. No, Benedict would be easily managed. Whereas Ma and Pa...

Faster he walked, slapping his thighs again. Thomas needed a plan to deal with his parents: nothing would soften his father's wrath, but if there was some way to persuade Ma...?

"Of course!" He clasped his hands together in delight.

"Will you *please* go to sleep?" grumbled Robert, patting his makeshift pillow of folded blanket.

But sleep wasn't an option. Thomas rushed to the wagon. He had a plan! And there was something he urgently needed to find.

CHAPTER 8: Caroline

A dead, snared rabbit dangled from Caroline's hand as she crept back through the trees, grateful for the abandonment of her cap, and the ease of her breeches. She relished these quiet times, before the night had truly fallen. A moment to gather her thoughts without Annie's chatter, or Thomas' relentless enthusiasm about his latest proposal, or Robert's deafening silence crowding her mind. And it meant there would always be a rabbit or bird sitting by Robert's feet when he woke the next day. Its purpose was twofold – not only to feed the company, but also to remind Robert that she was utterly capable of surviving alone and needed neither his provision nor his protection, lest either she or Robert ever forget.

She could still picture Piero's face the first time it happened. He had complained to Robert about Caroline joining the troupe, clearly liking her as much as a kick in the crotch, which admittedly she would have been willing to deliver on many occasions. Then, in the morning, Robert had seen the bird and told Piero it might be rather handy to have a woman in the company. And how Caroline had enjoyed pointing out that a dead pheasant was of more use to them than a live peacock. Oh, the bastard's expression at that.

As she headed towards the camp, guided by the dimming orange glow of the fire, the amusement soon yielded to hatred. She kicked the twigs and stones beneath her feet as she went. Piero had ruined it all. Things between him and Robert had been strained for a while, and then Portsmouth had happened. Robert had tried to fight the heartbreak, she knew, but now here they were on the brink of collapse, without a patron, without a future, whatever Thomas said. She narrowed her eyes. She was certain he had not mentioned his father's inn before. There was something he wasn't telling them. For a last hope, somehow it didn't seem very hopeful.

Well, even if Robert had no fight in him left, *she* would keep fighting to protect them, especially Annie. She was a sister in all but blood, albeit a frustrating one. And the world wouldn't be kind to Annie – at least she was safe in the company.

She stepped beyond the shadow of the last trees, towards the once-vibrant campfire, resigned to burning itself out. Annie's snoring drifted on the fresh evening breeze as Old Bess grazed contentedly, tethered near the wagon – but there was a flickering light shining through the wagon's thin canvas cover. Caroline frowned. If Annie was snoring and Robert apparently had his head stuffed under a blanket, then...

Now what was Thomas doing?

"Where's it to? Must be here!" she heard the man muttering.

She walked over to the wagon, dropping the rabbit casually by Robert's feet as she went. She peered inside. What the Hell was going on? Thomas was on his hands and knees, rooting around by candlelight, as if he were desperately searching for something. He had turned it all upside down – props were scattered everywhere, and the green curtain lay twisted and tangled amongst them. Robert would be furious. Thankfully the candle was placed at the end of the wagon, far from Thomas' frantic hands. She folded her arms and cleared her throat. He spun around on his knees, looking flustered, surprised and guilty as Hell.

"Thomas, I want some answers."

"No answers needed. Everything is absolutely fine!"

Right. She had no patience to deal with this. She launched herself into the wagon, easily knocked him off-guard and pinned him down with her own weight and the crate of Annie's tonics, which she placed neatly on his arse.

"Oh, for Heaven's sake!" he said. "Move."

“When you tell me what is going on. Suddenly your pa owns an inn, everything is fine, and you are going to save this company. So why are you panicking?”

Thomas sighed as deeply as she supposed was possible when you had a woman and a crate of tonics weighing down on you. “I’m not panicking. Move.”

“Why are you panicking?”

“Move!”

“Why are you panicking?” She raised herself up a little and landed back down on him firmly.

“Oof!”

The tonic bottles rattled.

“Oi!” slurred Robert’s dozy voice from the fireside. “Shut up and go to sleep.”

Thomas let out a frustrated growl. “Fine. I’ll explain. Now get off.”

Caroline stood up, hunched over in the back of the wagon, removed the crate of tonics and shuffled over to sit beside the costume sack. Thomas seemed full of uneasy fire, as if he would have paced up and down the wagon a hundred times if he could. “Speak no word to Robert—”

“What?” came Robert’s irritable voice.

“Nothing,” said Thomas and Caroline at the same time.

“Good!” said Robert. There was the sound of shuffling and wincing. “Then we can all go to sleep.”

“Listen,” Thomas whispered. “Going to Bampton is undoubtedly the wisest move. It is just... complicated.”

“And *how* is it complicated, Thomas?”

Thomas grimaced. “My father is proud, difficult, cannot see beyond his own opinions—”

“Hard to believe you’re his son.”

"I did not leave home on good terms. It's just possible my parents may not entirely welcome me back with open arms." He swallowed. "*Fire*arms, perhaps."

A blaze of fury seared through Caroline. She was actually going to wring his neck. She leapt up. "You're saying this now? Right, I'm sitting on you again!"

"No! Shhh. Listen! Listen!" hissed Thomas. "I have my reasons! Just stop trying to sit on me and do something vaguely helpful!"

His eyes were pleading. She was annoyed at the small pang of sympathy which followed. She knew little about his past, save for the pocket watch he held dear. But like Robert, she knew better than to probe too deeply. When you travelled the roads, drifting from place to place, there was often a reason behind it. The sound of a river and the turned backs of a frightened village floated into her mind...

"And what is vaguely helpful?" she said, more harshly than she meant. She lowered herself back down beside the costume sack.

"My orange neckerchief! I need to wear my orange neckerchief; she is less likely to kill me if I'm wearing it."

"Who?"

"My ma. She made my brother and I matching ones. It's a hideous thing. But I cannot find it anywhere!"

The candlelight flickering revealed the fading bruises on his face and the last few remaining scabs. Yes, Thomas had utterly deserved that beating in Andover. But although he had been hurt quite badly – more than she had realised at the time – he had not abandoned the company. He could have returned to London. But he was still here fighting, trying to make it work. Just like she was.

"You're in luck, I've seen it," she said, ignoring Thomas' melodramatic gasp of joy. She clambered out of the wagon and over to where Annie slept contentedly, and peeled back the blanket. In one arm Annie held her fiddle and in the other the donkey head, with the orange neckerchief tied in a bow around its ear. Caroline slid Horatio gently out of Annie's arms. She shoved it, with more than a little force, into Thomas' stomach, making him grunt.

"Just... sleep," pleaded Robert from beneath his blanket.

Once Thomas had untied the neckerchief, Caroline carefully returned the donkey head to Annie and softly pulled the blanket back over her. Lord, she looked even more vulnerable when she slept. From the day they had met her fiddling near the old castle in Pevensey, Caroline had sworn to protect her. Caroline had seen some bastard steal Annie's little cup of coins and Caroline had made him return it at sword-point before Robert had pulled her away. Of course, Robert had quickly invited Annie to join them, as they all ran for the wagon. Robert's heart was always bigger than he liked people to think. What would have become of Annie without the company? What would any of them do without it?

Frustration snapped inside her. She twisted around and advanced on Thomas. He scurried backwards all the way to the wagon, his hands still clutching the neckerchief, raised in surrender.

"I care not a dog's turd if you left your home on good terms or bad terms, you *will* arrange for us to perform there. The company needs this. Do you understand?"

"Of course I understand!"

"WILL YOU TWO JUST GO THE HELL TO SLEEP?"

Caroline glanced inside the dishevelled wagon and caught a glimpse of Annie's tonic bottles.

"Well, it sounds like you'll need a clear, sharp mind for the morning." She grabbed the tonic bottle filled with yellow liquid and handed it to Thomas. "Annie's sleeping draught. One mouthful only. Get some sleep."

Thomas nodded. "Perhaps that would be wise."

Caroline turned back towards the fire, where a blanket lay waiting for her. She heard the sloshing of tonic as Thomas tipped the bottle; a doubt crossed her mind.

"Wait," she said. "Which bottle did I give you?" There was the sound of tonic being sprayed out violently. Well, it probably served him right. At least his teeth would be sparkling.

The fire spat and crackled its last, desperate breaths before its strength failed. Caroline lay down, pulled her blanket around her and ran through the conversation in her mind. How could this be happening? Not only had Thomas lied yet again, but if he were that concerned about returning home, what hope did the company truly have?

She cast her eyes towards Annie, probably dreaming of straw mattresses and feather pillows. Then she glanced over at Robert: the kind, quiet man who seemed so willing to give love but found it so hard to receive. His theatre company had given her purpose and companionship after her ma, grieving since before Caroline's birth, could finally bear life no longer and had...

Caroline swallowed. Shame and suspicion had overthrown kindness and compassion. She had stood alone in the rain as her ma was unceremoniously buried with a stake through her heart at the crossroads outside of the village. Caroline squeezed her eyes shut. Lord, the weight of it. A silent scream pierced her mind. But with the company and their shows, she had both lost herself and found herself – stepping into other heads and other worlds whilst her own slowly rebuilt. How could it all be ending?

She screwed up her face against the pain and drew deep, shuddering breaths. Fighting for control, fighting for strength. She was hard as stone and had worked extremely hard to become so. She would never love like her ma – giving her heart so completely that when the one she loved was gone, there was nothing of herself left. She would not love anyone in any way. But she would be damned if she failed her new family. She had bound Robert's bleeding arms and saved him once before. She would fucking do so again.

Her breaths came smoother as the silent screaming exhausted itself. Tomorrow, they arrived in Thomas' hometown and discovered the fate of their company. Tears had left her long ago, and she had sworn to cry only when her role demanded it on stage.

But in that moment, as she lay beside the dying embers of the once-vibrant company, she wished with all her heart that she could feel boards beneath her feet.

CHAPTER 9: Piero

Because Piero always walked as if there were boards beneath his feet, people were wont to notice him, and so attention was to be expected. But it was the *way* the old woman stared so relentlessly which intrigued him.

As the last slants of golden sunlight disappeared, Piero drove Young Bess and Iago down to the riverbank, grateful for the two strong horses making good time, and equally grateful for the chance to stop the wagon for the evening. The old woman was dressed in dark red and wore a brown headscarf, with a shawl around her shoulders. She sat on a stool beside a table and a modest fire, not taking her eyes off him for a moment. Her wagon was decorated with rabbit's feet and brightly coloured ribbons hanging on strings tied along its side, and a tethered horse grazed nearby.

"This will suit us tonight," Piero said, jumping down from the seat. The stream would refresh them all, and a wooded area a little way beyond the flat of the bank would provide firewood enough. Maria landed beside him and looked around with a curl of her lip.

"What happened to sleeping in the finest inns? Eating the finest foods?"

"In good time, my love," he said smoothly. "Our act is a success, and the audience adore us. We need only to secure a patron, then the world is ours."

Maria fixed him with an unimpressed look. "And all this will happen once we finish chasing your players?"

There was fire in her soul, and it was one of the things Piero admired about her. He stroked a rebellious curl away from her face and looked into her eyes.

"They are not mine," he said. "*You* are mine."

He closed the distance between them to kiss her, but she drew back slightly. He repressed his irritation.

"I understand why it matters to you so much," she said in a voice edged with frustration. "I do remember what they did to you when you left them. Took your horse and wagon. Robbed you, beat you." She brushed her fingertips against his cheekbone–

He was lying beneath the stars, wearing his beautiful dress and his purple eye-powder, resting in Robert's arms. They were alone amongst the trees in the summer night. What more could he want, apart from to know this man entirely? Robert's breath was warm in his ear... fingertips gently brushed his cheekbone–

Piero grasped her hand and guided her fingers away. The hatred in his heart argued with the warm smile he brought to his face.

"And once their debt is paid, my love, and they come to deeply regret their harsh treatment, we will show everyone how truly unstoppable we are." He guided her close again and was glad that this time he could feel her pushing against his body rather than pulling away. He let his eyes dance for her – like he and Maria always danced around each other in a magnificent but precarious performance. "We are so fortunate to have found one another."

"We need firewood," came Angelo's unnecessarily urgent voice from somewhere nearby.

Piero fought the urge to roll his eyes. Well, the man could wait a little longer. Piero was the one who directed every performance – no one else. He leaned closer and kissed Maria for as long as he bloody wanted – which he always made sure was ever-so-slightly less than she needed.

Always leave them wanting more. They were a fine match, a delicate balance of appreciation, danger and unspoken truth. Two ambitious, fire-filled souls determined to show the world exactly what they were worth. Angelo walked over and gently tugged his sister's arm. Piero was content to let her go, his eyes fixing Angelo with a firm gaze to ensure he remembered which of them was the manager.

"All right, we'll find the firewood," said Maria, her tone impatient as the two of them walked towards the trees.

The smile faded from Piero's face as he watched them go. Two ambitious souls and one frightened one, who threatened to ruin everything. Maria loved him, surely, but she also loved her brother – if her hand was forced, which of the two men did she truly care for more?

And still the strange old woman at the wagon stared at him. "Old Dina has a candle. Sees it true, tells it true."

On the table now was a piece of paper and a candle, its flame flickering slightly. He couldn't repress rolling his eyes this time. Oh, Lord. She was a fortune-teller. He had no time for such superstitious nonsense, unlike...

He huffed the thought away and headed irritably towards the old woman. She might serve some purpose. If nothing else, she had a warm fire. As he walked, she held his gaze with a look of defiance, a look he was willing and perfectly comfortable to return. He stood beside the stool opposite the woman.

"Sees it true, tells it true," she repeated, a little knowing smile appearing on her face.

"I've no need of a fortune-teller's sight, save that of her own eyes."

The old woman's gaze dropped from Piero's eyes to his neck. "You don't believe in the sight, yet you wear the rabbit's foot."

Instinctively, Piero's fingertips reached for the necklace which hung just below his cravat–

Robert's rough fingers brushed Piero's neck, fastened the knot... the day-weary scent of him...

"It will bring you luck."

"You know I do not believe in luck."

Robert's dark, intense eyes met his. "And what do *you believe in?"*

Piero glared at the old woman and channelled his hate into each word. "I believe in revenge."

The old woman jumped up, grabbed his necklace and yanked him across the table, bringing him close to her face.

His heart raced and he stared furiously into this strange woman's knowing eyes. He said nothing, betrayed nothing.

"A troubled past brews a troubled future. Old Dina sees far more than her candle tells her."

Her hand slowly released his necklace. Piero swallowed and gathered his wits. How dare she? Who the Devil did this woman think she was? A hundred sharp words were on his tongue, yet there was something about her which made him hesitate to speak them aloud.

"You seek a patron," she continued, "and Old Dina knows where to find one."

"Then perhaps, good woman," Piero said tightly, "you might be kind enough to share your thoughts without strangling me."

The fortune-teller smiled broadly at that, revealing a few blackened teeth, and held out her palm. Piero did not dare to take his eyes off this unpredictable creature, but he reached into his jacket pocket and pulled out his purse. He dropped a coin into her hand.

Slowly, she moved her eyes from the coin to his face. "Double," she said, and it wasn't a question.

Piero inhaled deeply through his nose and cast his eyes upwards as he dropped a second coin into her palm before exaggeratedly pocketing his purse and folding his arms. With a smirk, the woman picked up the candle and gently tipped the pooling wax onto the paper.

As it began to harden, she bent over the paper, eyeing it curiously. Piero tutted and began to drum his gloved fingers on his arm. She looked up sharply from her studying, thrust out a hand and slapped at his impatient fingers. He glared at her in outrage, then decided it might be wiser to simply move his arms to his sides in a controlled manner. The woman returned her gaze to the paper.

"Old Dina can tell you good fortune awaits you at Thorverton Fair, yes. Yet Old Dina knows you seek more than a patron." She looked up and narrowed her eyes at him.

He narrowed his eyes in return. It was just possible he had misjudged this old woman. She certainly seemed to have her wits about her, and an ally could prove useful. He reached into his jacket and pulled another coin out of his purse. He held it in front of her face, making sure he held his audience's attention, then pressed it firmly into her palm.

"Perchance, good woman, you have heard of the Ticehurst Players."

"Perchance," she said with a sly smile, "Old Dina has."

CHAPTER 10: Thomas

This might be the performance of his life, and he could not allow stage-fright to overcome him. Thomas rehearsed his lines over and over in his head, drumming his fingertips on his legs as he walked behind the wagon. Surely he knew his speech by now. He cast his eyes up to the sky. The sunshine had vanished, replaced by a blanket of grey. The wagon bumped down the tree-lined road towards Bampton. Where was that oak he and Benedict used to climb? Thomas searched the row of trees that sat atop the grassy bank. There it was – the familiar crook of that broad branch. Life had been so simple then. His stomach fluttered and his fingertips drummed once more. He would be home in a matter of minutes.

They had arrived at the south end of town, where the road sloped down into the vale towards the humpback bridge over the River Batherm. Wafts of cider drifted from the nearby Crown Inn which heralded the entrance to the town. But tempting as it was to take his fill for courage, Thomas knew it unwise to turn up at his father's inn rosy-cheeked with cider from another's press. The brown and pink-hued stone of the terraced cottages seamlessly lining the road offered warmth after the cold flint buildings of the downlands. And at the far end of town, the square-towered church rose above the rooftops, with bright green hills rolling behind it. Two years he had been gone – two years of travel and dreams, yet everything here was exactly the same.

Thomas straightened his orange neckerchief and practised his breathing. He had to make this work. They passed the familiar buildings: the long malthouse, its stone walls every shade of brown; beside it the imposing three-storeyed house of Marcus Setherton, the cloth merchant; further along the street was a track which led to old William Jones' carpentry workshop.

The town was busy, and Thomas suspected it must be Tuesday, market day. A gaggle of young women – he knew their faces but not their names – were walking towards the market square, chattering mindlessly, avoiding the horseshit speckling the road by chance rather than observation. Ah! Mr Harper – presumably still the steward to Squire Bickford. Grey-haired and thin-lipped, marching around, holding papers, looking as officious as ever, and—

Shit! Mr Jones!

Heart thumping, Thomas darted alongside the wagon, and out of the man's sight. If Mr Jones' daughter found out he was back...

"Thomas, are you all right?" said Annie.

"Absolutely fine," he breathed. "Caroline, left at the end!"

The wagon swung left as the road leading to the church widened into the busy market square, full of folk selling their wares. And there on the corner was the Star Inn. His stomach knotted and his weight shifted to the balls of his feet as they passed the limewashed stone building with its golden star sign above the oak door. He should be returning home full of pride, as a successful actor; instead, he was returning, just as his father hoped, as a failed one.

Everything darkened ominously as they passed through the carriage arch beneath the neighbouring building to reach the yard, leaving behind the bustling market. Hooves and wheels echoed loudly through the archway until light returned and noise faded. Then everything stopped. What in Heaven's name had he been thinking? They should never have come.

Annie clasped her hands gleefully. "Oh, Thomas, it's wonderful."

"Yes," said Thomas, clearing his dry throat. "It's... marvellous to be home."

Robert walked stiffly over to Old Bess and stroked her face. "Well done, old girl."

"There might be room for her in the stables," Thomas said, pointing to the stone building at the far end. "I'll find you in the market. I should like a few moments with my parents first."

Robert put his hand on Thomas' shoulder and the touch brought him strength. Thomas forced a smile to his face. He would do this – he would succeed, and then Robert would truly be convinced that he had chosen his lead actor well. Annie grabbed a couple of tonic bottles and skipped towards the archway, presumably to inflict them on anyone unfortunate enough to cross her path. Caroline threw Thomas a look which communicated quite clearly that he would likely be disembowelled and roasted on a spit if he failed, then she followed Annie.

In all truth, being roasted on a spit was probably the easier option. He glanced around the barrel-dotted yard. Two years? Lord, it felt a lifetime since he'd left.

Neighbouring buildings of every size and shape pressed around each side. The cider press was in an outbuilding to the left of the stables, and to the right was the gate to their small orchard. They had always been in trouble for scrumping – well, *Benedict* had always been in trouble because Thomas could run faster. Thomas would balance on his brother's shoulders, arms outstretched and hopeful for the prize.

And their bedrooms. Thomas cast his eyes up to the two little attic rooms which overlooked the yard. When they had been beaten as boys for daring to stand on the stage and learn Shakespeare with Lord Pelham's Players, Thomas had leaned longingly out of that window, sore and bruised. He had whispered every word of *Romeo and Juliet* as the players rehearsed, to drown out the unhappiness of his life and the sobs of his brother in the room next door.

His gaze drifted down to the kitchen. It could not be delayed any longer. And the sooner it was all arranged, the sooner they could begin preparations. He straightened his orange neckerchief, crossed himself and opened the back door.

The smell hit him first as he stepped inside: fresh bread mixed with the sweet tang of cider coming from beyond the kitchen door, and the pungent herbs hanging from the ceiling. The kitchen was still the same: a bricked floor with a generous stone fireplace on the left, which had a small bread oven hollowed on one side. A large flour-sprinkled table stood in the middle of the kitchen, bearing a loaf of bread. And standing behind the table, in the middle of slicing the loaf, was his ma.

She was only in her early forties, Thomas forgot exactly whereabouts, but Ma's curly hair seemed greyer than he remembered, poking out from under her cap and framing her plump face. She stared at him with steely eyes. Thomas put on his showman smile and threw wide his arms. And as his clever, carefully rehearsed script vanished instantly from mind to be replaced with stage-fright, he said the only thing he could think of. "Surprise!"

Wordlessly, Ma stabbed the knife into the table, wiped her hands on the apron worn over her brown dress, then marched towards him, her expression darkening with every step she took.

Thomas fixed a smile to his face and braced himself as she reached out a strong arm that was no stranger to rolling barrels and clipped him heartily around the head.

"Ow!"

"Two years gone and only one letter?" She put her hands on her hips.

"I did write it in rhyming couplets!" said Thomas, rubbing his head. "That takes a long–"

"No word for eighteen months! You could ha' been dead! DEAD! No knowin' where 'ee were–"

Thomas raised his hands in protest. "My letter said I was bound for London! Do you know how hard it is to find a rhyme for–"

Ma clipped him around the head again.

"OW! You did notice my neckerchief?"

"Broke your brother's heart leavin' without tellin' 'im!"

"There was no point! He'd shown no interest in coming! Surely this is all in the past!" He edged towards the table. "Is that *fresh* bread?" He reached out hopefully—

A sharp slap stung his hand. "An' as for your pa..." She marched over to the kitchen door and stuck her head into the main room. "JAMES!"

Oh, shit.

He wasn't ready for this. Should he run for the yard? The tall, well-filled form of his pa loomed into the room. Thomas swallowed. Had he always been that broad? He was a child again, head filled with whispering doubts, throat tight with—

Pa lunged, grabbed fistfuls of Thomas' shirt – pushed him back – a painful crash as spine hit table—

His heart galloped as he lay pinned amongst the scattered slices of bread, staring up into raw fury.

"How dare you show your bloody face!"

"James! Mind my loaf!" Ma flapped at her husband. "An' that be no way to greet the boy."

Pa held him there a moment longer, then released him roughly, scowling, and Thomas slid himself off the table, trying to ignore the throbbing pain in his back. He held eye contact, breathing too fast, as he pulled his shirt back into position with a shaking hand. Remember the script. What the Hell was the script? "I have joined a company. We thought to visit... perhaps... perform..." The rehearsed lines danced away at the anger in his pa's eyes.

"You made your choice when you left! Your comp'ny o' rogues aren't welcome here. An' neither be you. An' the state of your face! Been fighting piss-brained with other beggars?"

What could he say? Anything but the humiliating truth about Andover. "I... fell down a horse." Fell *down* a—? He closed his eyes briefly in frustration. What in Heaven's name was the matter with him?

Ma stepped forwards. "The boy has some explainin' to do, but he's travelled all this way."

"Yes, all this way," said Thomas, steadying his voice, "and I beg you to allow us food and lodgings for just three—"

Pa snorted.

"—*two* nights, then we will be on our way."

"You'll need to beg 'arder than that. You can kiss my bloody arse."

Thomas dug his fingernails into his palms. "I realise," he said through gritted teeth, "that I am unworthy to be under the roof of your most precious inn, but being the gracious and forgiving person you are, I beg you – even if we may not perform, please allow us to stay."

Pa's disapproving glare burned into his soul.

"Oh, James!" said Ma, delivering a sharp nudge in her husband's ribs.

"You can sleep where 'ee belong," said Pa.

"My old bedroom?"

"With the horseshit." Pa walked back to the main room, slamming the door behind him. It was only as his chest relaxed that Thomas realised how tight it had been. He breathed deeply to snatch some air.

"You know this inn means everythin' to 'im," Ma said, patting his shoulder awkwardly.

"I know it means more than his sons."

"He worked hard to keep this inn, you know that. His pa's legacy, and his pa's afore, an' meant to be yours. You fair broke his heart chasin' a stage."

Thomas grasped Ma's hands and looked into her eyes. "And it would have broken mine if I had not!" He kissed her on the cheek. "I must tell my company we may stay." Then he grabbed the rest of the unsliced loaf and ran for the back door before her hand met his head.

As he shut the door behind him and entered the yard, air flooded his lungs once more. He rubbed his bruised back, let out a long, frustrated sigh and propped his elbow onto a barrel standing near the back door. Old Bess had moved, and everyone had presumably headed into the market. He stared at the far corner where the stage had stood all those years ago. The players had filled his heart with dreams as they taught him and Benedict to perform Shakespeare and handle swords. He had stepped into other worlds, other minds, and while he stood on those boards, forgetting the dullness of his life and the fights with his pa, he could *be* someone. He had even dared to dream that one day the troupe would invite them both to join the company, that he would stand on the stage with his little brother performing beside him.

Lord, it had all felt so simple then. Two brothers, one stage and a whole world ahead of them. Well, at least they would be reunited now. He couldn't wait to see the overjoyed look on Benedict's face as his long-lost big brother strolled back into his life.

Thomas wandered towards the wagon, its strips of colourful rag flapping in the breeze. He tucked the bread inside the back... and frowned.

Wait.

Both swords had been there, on the right, hadn't they? Now there was only one. Where had the other gone? Footsteps approached behind him. Thomas froze.

"By this good light, had I a sword..." said a voice. It waited expectantly.

"*... I would kill thee.*" Thomas dared not move a muscle. The voice didn't quite sound as overjoyed as he'd hoped.

"Oh, would you look at that?" said his brother coldly. "Such good fortune."

Thomas took a sharp intake of breath as the sword poked at his back.

CHAPTER 11: Benedict

The bastard. Benedict was actually going to kill him. He tried to keep his sword hand and his voice from trembling. "Surely you did not believe that your selfish betrayal would go unavenged?"

The bastard cleared his throat. "We could just forget that bit?" he asked in that ridiculously hopeful voice of his.

"NEVER!" Benedict growled, allowing the sword to poke just a little bit more. He heard another sharp intake of breath. Good. "*Lay on, Macduff...*"

"*And damned be him that first cries, 'Hold, enough!'*"

The traitor lunged forwards into the wagon and swung around to face Benedict, holding the remaining sword. What the Hell had happened to him? Scabs and fading bruises were dotted over his face! Benedict hardened his heart. No doubt a result of betraying someone for his own selfish gain. Bastard.

Benedict flew at him. Their blades crossed in a frantic exchange of parries and ripostes. Benedict delivered blow after merciless blow, thrusting, lunging, gladly unleashing the fury that had built up for two whole bloody years. The traitor was weak – he clearly hadn't been practising hard every day with absolute fury while he had been COMPLETELY ABANDONED AND IGNORED.

"I thought you'd be pleased to see me!" came a desperate gasp as Benedict drove his opponent across the yard.

"Pleased to see you?" Benedict cried in disbelief. He made a sudden turn and angled the fight towards a pile of empty barrels. "How could you just leave? Pa was furious!" The bastard brushed the pile with his elbow and glanced at the barrels nervously. "And you know how cheerful he usually is!" Benedict gave another push, sending his opponent staggering sideways. The barrels toppled, crashed and rolled across the yard.

"Ma was fussing and crying!" Benedict advanced. "Crying and fussing!" The thud jolted through his own body as he pinned the bastard against the limewashed wall, the swords crossed over his chest. "Day and bloody night." Benedict leaned forwards. "Do you have any idea of the agony you have caused me?" Benedict let him push back, purely for the thrill of leading a renewed attack and driving him furiously across the yard again. "There was no word!" His throat tightened. The fear had grown with every day of brotherless silence.

"I wrote home in rhyming couplets!"

"Once! There's been nothing for nigh on two years—"

"Only eighteen months, in my defence."

"I. THOUGHT. YOU. DEAD!" The words burst out and he hated the crack in his voice. Rage and relief charged through him as he lunged again with his blade, as the man scurried backwards, barely defending each blow – stumbling, tripping – into the corner of the yard where the stage had once stood. "And you didn't even..." Benedict hooked his foot around the traitor's leg and pulled, sending him crashing down onto his back, the sword flying from his hand, "... Say goodbye." He pointed his sword down at his opponent's throat, trying to ignore the orange neckerchief.

The man held up his hands in surrender. "Richard the Third, Act one, Scene four."

Every time! Every single bloody time he did this! "That's cheating!" Damn it, his sword hand was shaking. He must not give in. The man never thought of anyone else. He was a self-serving, self-obsessed—

"*I am his brother...*"

That voice... speaking those words. He had come to believe that he would never hear either again. Benedict's chest was rising and falling more rapidly than he wished, but he knew not how to stop it.

"Shakespeare. It's the rules!" said the bastard.

"I hate the rules!"

"You made the rules! It's Shakespeare. Finish the damned line. *I am his brother...*"

A wave of emotions tumbled mercilessly through Benedict as he surrendered to the habit of years. He cast aside his sword, and it clattered noisily upon the ground. "*And I love him well.*"

His brother did not move, but eyed him warily from the ground, as if waiting for an actor to feed him a line. Benedict reached down for his hand and hauled him to his feet. Thomas stood there uncertainly, but with that bloody glimmer of hope in his eyes that he always had. They stared at each other in silence, then Benedict broke, as he always broke. He rushed forwards, flinging himself at his big brother and pinning his arms to his sides. He embraced him for a long time, not daring to let go. Thomas cleared his throat and Benedict pulled back, studying him. He was far thinner. And the fading bruises on his face...

"I suppose you sold the pocket watch."

His brother's eyes widened in what was presumably meant to look like disbelief. "I would sell my soul before—"

"And why have you returned? I wager you're only here because you want something."

Thomas squirmed, as he bloody well should. "W-e-e-e-e-e-l-l..."

"I knew it! That's why you're wearing the neckerchief." Benedict threw his hands in the air and marched towards the back door. Footsteps scurried behind him, and a hand grabbed his arm. Benedict whirled around with a glare.

Thomas looked at him urgently. "I beg you!"

"Good. I'll enjoy that."

"Brother! My company is here! You must persuade Pa to let us perform tomorrow night!"

"Pa? The man who considers all actors to be worthless beggars who need to find a proper occupation?" Benedict huffed at his brother's pleading eyes. How much trouble had he been in over the last twenty-two years because of those bloody pleading eyes?

"I have worked so hard to become lead actor! We need this show! Brother, I am desperate!"

"Oh. You're *desperate*?" Benedict folded his arms. Had this man ever actually considered someone else's feelings in his entire life?

Thomas looked genuinely puzzled. "Well, clearly, I'm desperate! Otherwise, what in Heaven's name would bring me back here?"

"Oh, I don't know! If only you had a brother to visit!" This was hopeless. Benedict headed again to the back door. His brother spun him around and gripped his upper arms.

"Remember Lord Pelham's Players? They told us we belonged on that stage! I had to follow my heart!"

A sigh escaped Benedict, and he looked away. Those had been special times. Maybe he was judging too harshly. He knew how much the stage meant to his brother. And of all people, Benedict knew what it meant to follow your heart, even if it resulted in a complicated mess. His thoughts turned to Sarah, the woman he would spend the rest of his life with – a prospect his brother would never understand.

"BENEDICT!" yelled Pa's voice, from inside the inn.

Benedict rolled his eyes. "I trust he was overjoyed to see you again."

"You could have come with me, you know," his brother said, in a quieter voice. He released his grip on Benedict's arms. "But you said you'd never leave."

Benedict studied his brother. Two years he had been gone. Perhaps life had changed him. Perhaps it was worth a try. "I didn't think you would actually go. Besides, how could I leave," he ventured, "when my heart was here?"

Thomas' mouth dropped open. "A maid? You chose shagging over Shakespeare? For Heaven's sake, Benedict, what is wrong with you?"

Benedict sighed. Perhaps it wasn't worth a try.

"GET YOUR ARSE HERE, BOY!"

Thomas' eyes shone. "Listen, you'll think of something. I have every confidence in you. Remember – tomorrow night! Oh, and Benedict? It truly is good to see you."

Always an afterthought, wasn't he? Benedict sighed yet again. He had forgotten how much he did that whenever this irritating man was around. He turned towards the inn and silently raised a middle finger all the way to the back door, which he shut very firmly behind him.

He placed his hands on the table in the empty kitchen, bowed his head and closed his eyes. He knew not whether to laugh or cry, so he just inhaled a long, deep breath through his nose and breathed out two years of tension and fear.

Tom was alive and well.

And Benedict did not know which annoyed him more: the fact that his brother had strolled back into his life as if nothing had happened, expecting Benedict to stick out his neck and help him; or the fact that Benedict knew without a doubt, of course he bloody would.

CHAPTER 12: Thomas

A maid! Of all reasons not to come with him! Thomas shook his head as he picked up the swords. He would never understand his brother. He would have loved nothing more than if Benedict had accompanied him – all those disastrous fights with Caroline that he could have been spared! But Benedict had insisted his place – their place – was at the inn, and that they should stay, and now Thomas finally knew why. A *maid*!

Thomas placed the swords back in the wagon with a frown, trailing his fingers over one of the hilts. He should have been able to handle his little brother. Benedict would no doubt remind him of this defeat repeatedly. Still, overall things with Benedict had gone well, and while his brother directed efforts to persuade their pa, Thomas could concentrate on gaining permission to perform from the most disagreeable steward in the history of Bampton, and sorting the small matter of the stage, or a lack thereof. He filled his lungs with air, held it for a moment, then huffed it all out. It would all be absolutely fine. He strolled across the yard, under the carriage arch and out into the market.

A small cart rattled past Thomas, heading uphill, towards Exmoor. Stalls of various kinds filled the square... blacksmiths, millers, weavers... but it was the pie-maker which drew Thomas' attention. He licked his lips. What did warm pie and decent cider taste like? It had been so long.

Livestock were taken across the market, their bleating and squawking blending with the merry chatter and bellows of folk selling their wares. And somewhere in here were a depressed manager and the most difficult woman in the world.... Ah! Robert stood beside Caroline, folding his arms and shaking his slightly bowed head. They both looked frustrated. That didn't look promising. For all Robert's commendable features, he was swift to close his mind, and his reluctance to reconsider his options was certainly problematic at times.

And there was Annie a short distance away, the only one looking content as she brandished her death-in-a-bottle tonics confidently and passionately to anyone that moved, undeterred by their lack of interest.

"Removes aches, pains..." Annie called.

"Ten years off your life," Thomas muttered to himself.

He watched as she shoved the bottle in the whiskery face of old Ned Britton, causing the man to startle and the chicken he'd been clutching to escape into the air. As the man and several marketgoers attempted in vain to catch the flapping bird, Thomas pinched the bridge of his nose, then headed to his manager.

"I tell you, one day her life-restoring potions will be the death of someone," he said.

"Leave her be," said Robert.

"Listen, we must make sure our company members are the strongest, most valuable they can be. Yes, I know she's a talented fiddle-player, but—"

"She belongs in this company," said Robert firmly.

"And if there isn't a company?" Caroline challenged, turning to Robert. "Where then does she belong?"

There was an awkward silence as Robert's jaw tightened, and his chest rose and fell in a barely audible sigh. Thomas startled as Caroline twisted sharply around to face him.

"And what news from you, Thomas? Have we your father's permission to perform, with no charge?"

Thomas opened his mouth. Robert's dark eyes were troubled, and Caroline resembled a loaded trap about to spring. It wasn't *really* being dishonest anyway – he was simply providing hopeful predictions of the truth for the benefit of others. So he smiled and clasped his hands together. "Of course we do!"

"Of course we do," echoed Caroline suspiciously.

Thomas observed Robert. A tiny smile from the man, but no sign of joy in his eyes. "Our journey was completely worthwhile!" Thomas added, ducking as the escaped chicken flapped overhead, missing him by an inch. "Ah! And there is Mr Harper, our jovial and esteemed steward." The lean and miserable bastard crossed the square, heading for the market's administrative building at the end of a row of houses. Squire Bickford's steward certainly approved of the jars of cider which Pa slipped him, but the approval had never extended to Thomas himself, something which he suspected earned the steward an extra jar on occasion. He kicked away frustration. "I will enquire about permission for the company to tread the boards."

"When we have boards," said Robert. "The wood in Devonshire must be plated in gold for what it costs."

"You must know someone, Thomas," said Caroline. "Wasn't that the whole point of dragging us here?"

"Y-e-e-e-s," said Thomas. There was indeed a solution to the wood, but it was absolutely a last resort. He frantically scoured his mind for any options – any options at all apart from—

"Thomas Cooper!" sang out a lilting Welsh voice.

Thomas froze. Please Lord, no. "Help me," he hissed urgently to Caroline, but the amused and curious look on her face soon made it clear there would be no assistance whatsoever. Essie Jones flounced in front of him, her skirts swooshing unnecessarily around her.

He was an actor. He could handle this. She hadn't changed at all, her round face bright and beaming as ever. Thomas let out a tiny sigh of impatience as she repositioned the front of her dress a little, for what he assumed she considered to be a more favourable view.

"I heard you was back with some players."

"You always had such an ear for news, Essie," muttered Thomas.

Essie looked Caroline up and down, seemingly unfazed by her defensive expression.

"These are members of my company." Thomas gestured to Caroline and Robert.

"Sorry, whose company?" said Caroline with false politeness, but Thomas was relieved that Essie, as usual, had too much to say to be listening.

"You'll be here for Thorverton Fair, I s'pose?" Essie gabbled. "My cousin Eliza – remember her? Not as fair of face as me, rather ungainly, poor lamb – works as a maid now in Lord Pelham's house and–"

"Lord Pelham?" He tried to readjust to the tested method of only picking out the important words that Essie spoke, which were few and far between. "Does he still maintain a company of players these days?"

"Eliza says he'll be looking for a new act to patronise at the fair and she hopes that..."

Good fortune awaits at Thorverton Fair... Thomas caught his breath. Surely this must be what the fortune-teller meant! She was right about the pocket watch – Benedict had indeed been pleased to see him: well, he hadn't *killed* him. Perhaps everything was finally falling into place!

"... and since you're back," Essie continued as Thomas' ears pricked up, "us could get more properly acquainted." She swayed her hips from side to side – good Lord, was that meant to be endearing?

"Well," said Caroline, "all work and no play makes Thomas a dull boy."

Her elbow shoved into his ribs, and he stumbled towards Essie. He twisted around, throwing Caroline a glare. How dare she? Did she have no idea of the trouble she was causing? The amusement on her face clarified that she had *every* idea of the trouble she was causing. He turned swiftly back to Essie, wondering which of the two women irritated him more.

"That will not be necessary." Thomas sidestepped Essie, only to find she mirrored his movement. For Heaven's sake! He closed his eyes briefly in frustration. As he opened them again, he saw Annie approaching, still brandishing her death potions.

"Ah!" he said, never being more relieved to see her in his life. "Another member of my company. She brews the most remarkable tonics. You should try one."

Annie arrived beside them, smiling at Thomas' words. "This one'll cure all your spots," she said sweetly, offering a bottle. Essie pouted, then flounced away as Annie's shoulders sank in disappointment.

Thomas caught another glimpse of the steward, now at the door of the administrative building. "Mr Harper!" he called, scurrying towards him. Mr Harper turned to face him, looking typically unimpressed. But he *needed* to be impressed. Although it was the squire's permission that was needed, Mr Harper had always dealt with such trivial matters. Without winning him over, there would be no show and no hope. Thomas threw on a smile and enthusiastically reached for the disagreeable man's hand.

"Thomas Cooper, the famous actor, returns," said Mr Harper in a voice as thin as his lips. "If you are indeed famous." He raised a grey eyebrow. "Or indeed an actor."

Thomas bit his tongue and straightened himself up. "I have returned as lead actor with my company! The Ticehurst Players seek permission to perform at the Star Inn tomorrow night."

"The Star? A surprising choice, considering your father's understandable misgivings towards such beggary." Mr Harper craned his neck slightly, and although his eyeline was raised only a fraction of an inch higher than Thomas' own, the steward still somehow managed to look down his nose at Thomas.

Thomas moved slightly onto the balls of his feet. Why did the soles of his shoes have to be so worn and thin? "We shall perform a play by William Shakespeare, a song and a dance. It will be a delight for the whole town to enjoy!"

"With, presumably, the exception of your father." Mr Harper turned his back to Thomas and reached for the door handle.

"Mr Harper!" pleaded Thomas, clutching the arm of the steward's jacket in desperation. Mr Harper stared indignantly at the grasp and Thomas removed his fingers with haste. "I'm certain Squire Bickford would enjoy a fine comedy! And my father has agreed to our performance tomorrow night." The hopeful prediction rolled off his tongue so easily. "I have travelled for days under very trying circumstances to return home to share our successful show. It had a most favourable reception in Winchester!" He reminded himself that he needed to urgently source a new bosom. "You have the squire's ear. I beg you, do not let our travels be in vain."

Mr Harper turned to face Thomas. "Speaking of begging, you are, no doubt, aware of the Vagrancy Act passed last year."

They were not beggars! Hurt roared inside him, but Thomas clamped his mouth shut, lest the words should escape. One ill-favoured decision from this man and everything fell apart. How Pa would adore the sight of Thomas and his company being forced to move on or facing arrest.

You're naught but a failure.

"And tomorrow, you say?" Mr Harper continued, pursing his lips and shaking his head. "To persuade Squire Bickford and handle paperwork at such late notice is most inconvenient."

Thomas repressed a sigh. "What might it require, Mr Harper, to assist you with your 'paperwork'?"

"I am certain you will think of something... generous. Then I'm certain permission will be yours." Mr Harper's empty smile disappeared into his moustache. Then the door of the market building shut promptly in Thomas' face.

Well, it was surely close enough to a yes. Benedict was bound to have savings from his work at the inn – there couldn't have been much he could spend wages on, except for this maid he was apparently courting. Besides, if Thomas made it clear that the company's whole existence and his entire future career rested on this show, *surely* his brother would loan – nay, donate! – some funds to their cause! The fate of the company was in Thomas' hands, and he would not let them down! Thomas held his head high. He would prove to the company he was a worthy successor to the apparently amazing Piero. Even one which surpassed him! The thought swelled in his chest as he spun around on his worn heels.

"Permission will be granted to perform on tomorrow night!" he announced as he approached the others, with his arms spread wide.

"Oh, Thomas!" said Annie, and both of her hands flew to her mouth. Caroline caught the two tonic bottles just in time and thrust them back towards Annie with an admonishing frown.

"The steward will definitely arrange permission?" said Caroline.

Thomas beamed. "Yes!" No.

"And your pa has agreed?"

"Yes!" No. "And with the takings from the show we can invest in props and new costumes and truly catch Lord Pelham's attention! Just as I said, everything will be absolutely fine."

Robert laid a hand on Thomas' shoulder. "You have done well." For the first time in ages, there was a spark of hope in his manager's eyes.

Caroline folded her arms. "We are still in want of a stage."

Thomas sighed. Was this woman never satisfied? And could he really not think of any alternative to the single, terrible option he had in mind? They didn't have money enough, and his brother was unlikely to fund both a stage *and* a bribe. There was only one option, and it pained him more than Shakespeare himself could write. "I do know a carpenter... Well, a carpenter's daughter. I shall make... enquiries."

So be it. But first, he must speak urgently with his brother, before Pa found out, or Mr Harper found out, or the company found out that he was an even better actor than any of them gave him credit for.

CHAPTER 13: Benedict

Benedict stood by the desk at the window, beneath the fragment of angled timber which broke through the suffocating white plaster. Thomas' rag-decorated wagon stood expectantly in the middle of the yard, taking centre stage. Benedict fiddled with his orange neckerchief with one hand, whilst his other ran through his dark, unruly hair. Of all times, Thomas had chosen *now* to return home.

He loved his brother dearly, and he had missed him more than he thought possible. But somehow, Thomas managed to make the whole world spiral chaotically around *himself*. And now, as Benedict was swinging back and forth, trying to make the most important, most difficult decision of his life, Thomas had crashed back into his world and Benedict was sucked into his brother's spiral yet again.

Thumping footsteps pounded up the narrow attic staircase outside his room. There was only one person who had ever moved at that pace around the inn. Benedict rolled his eyes, and the hand holding the orange neckerchief flopped down defeatedly by his side. He turned dutifully from the window to face the bedroom door just as it flew open.

"Everyone else manages to knock," he said as Thomas marched in. His brother still wore the orange neckerchief matching the one in his own hand. Thomas charged over and gripped Benedict's upper arms.

"You know," said Benedict drily, "I've missed you."

“Brother,” said Thomas, his eyes fixed in a merciless stare, “I need to borrow some money.”

Benedict groaned. “*Really* missed you.”

“Listen, you must understand!” Thomas’ grip tightened. “I have naught myself, and without a generous and substantial donation to Mr Harper, the show cannot proceed! And if the show does not proceed, the company will fold! I promise to pay you back after the show tomorrow night! We’ll perform at six o’clock; you shall have your money by ten.”

Those bloody pleading eyes. Was this truly all they had left? What had happened to them as brothers? They stood in the same room, yet they were a thousand miles apart. In childhood and youth, they had been so close. How many times had they climbed that oak tree together on the outskirts of town, their legs dangling in the dappled sunlight, sharing secrets, dreams and lines of Shakespeare? Those times were so precious, despite the one time he had slipped and fallen, hitting his head so badly he’d slept for days. Did Thomas ever think of those days at all? It had become painfully clear, had it not, that Thomas had more room in his heart for a stage than a—

“Brother?” said Thomas. “I promise to return it! Straight after the show! What say you?”

Benedict sighed. “I say you’d bloody better.”

“You have my thanks. I shall not forget it!”

“Like you wouldn’t forget it when you borrowed my shirt six years ago?”

“What shirt?”

“Never mind,” muttered Benedict. He walked over to his messy bed and dropped the orange neckerchief onto the crumpled bedlinen. Then he knelt upon the creaking floorboards and reached beneath the wooden bed-frame. His fingers brushed the coarse material of the sack – the sack he would pack with clothes and belongings, only to unpack it all moments later, with a flush of fear and uncertainty. At present, it laid empty and wanting. He must finally decide: would the sack be full of belongings, promise and new beginnings as it journeyed up to Bristol? Or would it remain neglected and empty, forever imprisoned here beneath the bed?

His fingers reached just beyond the sack for the small wooden box of purses, all filled with carefully saved wages to ease the journey, should it be taken.

"Any news from Pa?" said Thomas eagerly. "Did he mention permission for us to perform?"

Benedict pulled out the box and selected a purse. "He mentioned horseshit. Loudly."

Thomas huffed as Benedict returned the box to its home beneath the bed with a scrape of wood on wood.

"All my life he has told me I am naught! You have heard him!"

Benedict paused and listened carefully. It was not often Thomas let his guard down. For a moment, they could have been boys again, legs swinging in the oak. Yes, Thomas had always borne the brunt of Pa's rage, but that was because he insisted on persevering, on fighting back. He could have saved himself many a beating if he had just kept his head down.

"I will prove him wrong! Prove Mr Harper wrong! Prove everyone wrong!"

But he would never keep his head down, would he? Benedict twisted around and studied the pained expression on his brother's bruised face. Who or what *had* caused those injuries? Presumably, as Thomas wasn't boasting about some conquest, the event had not gone in his favour. Perhaps things had been tougher than he realised.

"Tom," he said, softening his voice as he stood up and returned to his brother's side, "you do not have to prove anything to anyone."

"I beg to disagree," Thomas said bitterly. "With an audience, with success, I am something! Someone! Without it, look at me! What do I have?"

"Well," Benedict said as he dropped what probably amounted to a few days' worth of food on the way to Bristol into Thomas' hand, "apparently you have a brother."

Thomas gave a quick smile. "I shall not surrender my dreams, Ben. Whatever Pa says, I must follow my heart. For if I do not, am I not just a shadow of what I could be?"

Benedict looked at the passion and determination that shone from his brother's eyes, and he longed for the strength that Thomas always seemed to have. His heart stung. If he had been bolder, perhaps he would not be in the situation he now found himself. When they were boys, Benedict would happily settle for the lower branches, but Thomas would always attempt to climb further and further up the tree. And if Benedict was honest, he admired Thomas for his courage and yearned for some of the same. What would Thomas do if he had an empty, waiting sack beneath his bed?

"You'll keep trying?" Thomas said. "You'll find a way?"

Thomas would never let a precious opportunity slip through his fingers.

"Yes," said Benedict, and he meant it. For them both. "I'll find a way."

Thomas slapped his hands on Benedict's shoulders. "When I tread the boards at the Royal, I shall save you a seat at every single show!"

"Every single show," said Benedict flatly. "Can't wait." He studied again the fading bruises and longed for the boy in the tree. "Pa said you fell *down* a horse."

Thomas turned abruptly and waved a dismissive hand as he headed for the bedroom door. "It was a very tall, very wild horse."

Benedict watched him go. Lies, secrets... There was so much hidden now between them. Thomas would surely leave with his company as soon as he had what he came for. Benedict might not see him for years. Perhaps he would never see him again. What if this was the last time they ever talked like boys in a tree? What if this was the last chance to tell Thomas about—

"Sarah," he blurted out, before his mind had opportunity to caution his heart.

"Hmm?" said Thomas. He paused at the threshold and looked back over his shoulder.

Benedict dropped his voice. "I am in love with Sarah." It was the first time he had confessed those words to anyone other than her. It was like a burden lifted from his shoulders, like air finally filling his desperate lungs.

Thomas shrugged. "Yes... I am not best placed to offer advice, nor do I really have the time or inclination. I have urgent matters–"

"Sarah Setherton." Benedict bit his lip. Was this wise?

"*Sarah* Setherton? I know *Marcus* Setherton, the cloth merchant, but I don't recall a sister."

"That is because he does not have a sister." Benedict squeezed out the words. "He has a wife."

Thomas frowned for a moment, then his eyes grew wide. "WHAT? HOW CAN YOU BE IN LOVE WITH HIS–"

Benedict leapt forwards and slammed his hand over Thomas' mouth. "Ssshhhh!" His galloping heart slowed as he removed his hand. "You remember Sarah Westcott? They married only a few months ago."

"Oh, you have surely lost your wits!"

"It was always the family's intention for Sarah to marry well. We kept our courtship a secret, but they forced her hand! Marcus is not where her heart truly lies!"

Thomas shook his head. "Benedict–"

"We ought to have acted sooner. We have tried to move on, but we cannot let each other go! We are destined to be together, Tom! Ma always said I should settle down–"

"Yes, when she said, 'find a wife', she did not mean someone else's!"

Benedict held Thomas' incredulous gaze. His shoulders dropped. Of course, Thomas wouldn't understand. Why had he even bothered? How could Thomas possibly understand what it was like to adore someone so much you physically ached? To burn with shameful guilt at the forbidden love yet also burn with irrepressible passion at the wholeness she alone could bring?

"*Then must you speak of one that loved not wisely...*"

"*But too well.*" Thomas looked at Benedict with a doubtful expression.

"I would die for her, Tom."

"That may serve you well if Marcus should find out!" Thomas' eyes widened with horror, as if a terrible thought had occurred. "Pa... and everyone would despise you if you were discovered. And that may affect custom at the inn and the size of the audience!"

"Audience?" What the–! Frustration growled in his throat as Benedict slapped his forehead with his palm. "Has it ever occurred to you that there might be more to life than a stage?"

"No," said Thomas curtly. He pointed his finger at Benedict. "Listen, stay away from Sarah Setherton. Love will be the death of you!"

"And ambition the death of you!"

Thomas shrugged. "A far more rewarding way to go. Keep trying with Pa. And consider yourself fortunate." He rubbed his hands over his eyes. "After I have made my donation to Mr Harper, *I* must go and get wood for our stage." He grimaced, then walked out of the open bedroom door, not bothering to close it behind him.

The man was impossible! Benedict stomped over to the door and slammed it shut. The orange neckerchief on the crumpled bedlinen caught his eye. He sighed. It was always meant to be one of a pair, but now they were on very separate paths. His heart ached sadly at the truth – they could never be boys in the tree again. He drifted back to the window, scooping up the neckerchief as he went and twisting it with his fingers.

Sarah was with child. It was early still, but before long she would find travel difficult. Marcus was due back from his latest business visit next week and intended to stay home for some time. If they did not leave before he returned, they might never leave at all. They could not continue living two lives. They had tried to forget each other, tried to do the right thing. They were truly in love, and of all things in this cruel world, did not love deserve the best chance it could have?

Thomas might be a stage-obsessed idiot, but if his brother had followed his heart and achieved so much, then why shouldn't *he*? There was more to life than the inn! More than an empty, unfulfilled sack gathering dust beneath a bed! More than secret letters and stolen nights! Thomas was right. He should not be a shadow of what he could be. He should find a way.

Benedict ignored the pleading doubts in his mind. He would head to Sarah, and they would make their plans. By the time Marcus returned, they would be gone, even if leaving town in the heat of scandal meant they could never return. They had to follow their hearts.

And now, with thanks to his brother, he knew the perfect time for them to make their escape.

CHAPTER 14: Thomas

There were ways of getting wood, and there were ways of getting wood, Thomas reflected gloomily as he walked slowly with a sense of impending doom. And this surely had to be the most desperate way of them all.

He paused as a pony and cart rolled by, then continued towards the carpenter's workshop. Yes, others had made sacrifices along the way, he supposed. Robert always made sure everyone else had food and drink before himself and had oft gone to bed with an empty belly. And true, Caroline risked her life poaching at night to try and sustain the company.

But no one had performed a sacrifice as deep and great as this before. The act itself was perilous but the consequences – oh,good Lord – the consequences could be terrifying and far-reaching.

Heart thumping, he crept down the track until he reached the building and, double-checking that no one had spotted him, slid behind it. There was a strip of land maybe six feet wide between the workshop and a stone wall. No one would go there. No one would see. Many planks stood propped against the wall of the workshop, beyond which rested a couple of upright completed coffins. Thomas grimaced. He would rather be buried six feet under in one of those than complete the deed ahead.

But with a heavy heart, he dragged his eyes down to the half-made coffin on the ground, where Essie Jones lay smiling slyly at him, knowing exactly what she was doing. She shuffled her skirts a little higher expectantly.

"The things I do for this bloody company," grumbled Thomas as he unbuttoned his trousers and let them fall to the dusty ground.

CHAPTER 15: Caroline

Old Bess stood with her rope tied to the tethering ring on the stable wall, happily munching hay. Caroline stroked the old girl's mane, the coarse horsehair tickling her palm. If only she could share the horse's contentment. But she didn't. Thomas had been so agitated about returning home that night at the campfire, and yet everything had seemingly gone so smoothly... too smoothly.

There were a few other horses in the stables, but there was still space aplenty. She looked over to where Robert sat resting on a hay bale, one hand on his ribs. He must have felt her staring at him, for he looked up and gave her a little smile. Oh, it was good to see him smile again, even if it didn't quite reach his eyes any more. He was at least beginning to talk about the company's future again. Everything hinged on this performance, but it would not be much of a performance without a stage. With all else apparently in place, all that remained was for Thomas to get...

The stable door opened, and Thomas staggered inside. Pale and wide-eyed, he clung to the door posts. His orange neckerchief was half undone, twisted sideways and looking like it was holding on for dear life.

"Don't tell me you're going to bloody die after all the effort it took to get here," Caroline said. "What the Hell's happened to you?"

Thomas waved a hand, shaking his head slightly. "Wood," he whispered breathlessly. "I did it. Planks. Trestles. Outside. More by the workshop down the road." He inhaled deeply, as if trying to catch his breath. "Great personal cost. But we have a stage."

Robert stood up and his smile widened. He walked over gingerly to Thomas, put his hands on Thomas' shoulders and looked at him in wonder. "I do not know how you did it—"

"Neither do I."

"You look like you need a drink."

Thomas nodded, eyes still unfocused. "Drink."

Caroline folded her arms as Thomas staggered slowly and apparently with some discomfort towards the inn. She looked at Robert – yes, he was stronger, more alive, but as grateful as she was for that, concern still haunted her.

"You put a lot of trust in him." She fixed her eyes on Robert, demanding his attention. They needed this conversation.

"It is the only way the company can work. There needs to be respect and there needs to be trust." Robert poked the hay covering the floor with his shoe. "That's why he had to go."

Caroline repressed the urge to sigh. How did Piero manage to lurk at the edge of every conversation?

"But all his talk of Drury Lane, fame and fortune. The ambition..." She hesitated, hating to think it, hating to say it. "And the *dress*. Just like –"

"He's fine," said Robert abruptly. "He said he would get this company a show, and he did."

It was pointless to push Robert once he had shut down a matter in his mind. Well, Robert could trust Thomas all he liked. She never would. She shook her head as their best hope in the world staggered melodramatically into the inn. The little pile of planks and trestles sat in a handcart propped up against the stable wall. At least that was something. She walked over to the wagon in the yard, and retrieved the hammer and the leather pouch of iron nails from within.

“We ought to build the stage before Annie comes to help and makes it go triangular again,” Caroline called as she dragged over a couple of planks. The two of them formed more trestles, hammering short planks into place, Robert wincing and cursing under his breath as they went. She said nothing. Wiser not to draw attention to his discomfort and pain. His frown deepened until finally he stopped, head bowed, with a hand pressed to his ribs.

“Just let me finish it,” she said, snatching the hammer from his hand.

“What the Hell ’ee doin’?” came the gruff, unfamiliar voice of a man behind them.

Caroline turned to see a tall man twice the width of Robert, large hands forming into fists. His hair and beard were grey, and his face bore the lines of many frowns. He had the same brown eyes as Thomas, but instead of warmth, there was anger. It must be Thomas’ pa.

Still gripping the hammer, she put her hands on her hips. “Making the stage for the show.”

Robert instantly moved beside and slightly in front of her. “Thomas arranged everything,”

“Oh no he bloody didn’t,” said the man.

There was a moment’s silence.

“I’ll kill him,” the three of them said in unison.

Oh, she would give Thomas melodramatic staggering! She stormed towards the back door of the inn, hearing the footsteps of Robert and Thomas’ pa behind. She flung open the door, letting it bang angrily and raged through the kitchen.

“Where is he?” she said.

“Who the Hell are you?” cried a short, plump woman slicing bread at a table. Caroline instinctively swept a slice into her hand as she marched past towards the door on the other side. “Oi!”

Caroline ignored her. There was only one goal in mind. She yanked open the door and was welcomed by the warm tang of cider hanging heavy in the air. She took in the large room with timber pillars, customers dotted around at tables, the bar on the left and... yes! There on the far side, sitting alone by the fireplace, head down on a table and a tankard beside him: the man who seemed to cause thrice as many problems as he solved.

Skirts swishing, she marched towards him, hammer in one hand, bread in the other, fury pulsing through her body. There was a shot of satisfaction as he sat up, wide-eyed and terrified as the three of them marched over. As well he bloody might.

She slammed the hammer down onto the table between his hands. The tankard rocked as Thomas glanced fearfully down at the hammer then up to meet her gaze.

"What the bloody Hell are you playing at?" she said furiously, picking up the hammer again. But Robert reached forwards and whisked it from her hand, at the same time as the woman whisked the bread out of her other one.

Then everyone started yelling at once.

"You lying bastard! We needed this show!" Caroline shouted as Thomas' pa grabbed Thomas by the shirt and hoisted him to his feet.

"How dare 'ee take advantage of my hospitality!" he roared in Thomas' face.

"Get off him!" protested Robert, prising the man's hand away from Thomas' shirt with the hand not holding the hammer. He pulled Thomas around to face him. "How could you lie to me?"

"I wasn't *lying*, just hopefully predicting the–"

"And *you* can give me back that hammer!" Caroline said. She whisked the hammer out of Robert's hand and pointed it at Thomas. "One hundred- and forty-three times Annie had to stop and piss! ONE HUNDRED AND FORTY-THREE!"

"There'll be no more bloody shows at my inn!" Thomas' pa said, grabbing Thomas out of Robert's grasp.

"I said, get off him!" Robert pulled Thomas back.

"He's my bloody son!"

"And he's my bloody lead actor!"

"Oh, leave him be, husband! An' mind that neck'chief!" The plump woman waded in and slapped away the two men's hands.

"And *you* can give me back that bread!" Caroline shouted.

The plump woman looked at Caroline with defiance and stuffed the bread into her own mouth.

"Think of the opportunity," called a young man's loud voice behind them all.

Caroline turned around, as did everyone else. The hammer was whisked back out of her hand, and she tutted at Robert loudly. There, leaning against a timber pillar, was a young man who surely had to be Thomas' brother. He had the same warm brown eyes and dark hair, although it was curlier and more unruly. He wore the same orange neckerchief as he took a small bite from a slice of fresh bread in his hand. The plump woman beside Caroline put her hands on her hips.

"Many people would pay well to see Thomas being a complete arse on the stage, Pa."

Caroline cast a look at Thomas. He looked like he was biting his tongue.

"They'll buy their fill of cider from *you*, laugh at *him*. You'll make a tidy sum, and he'll want to pack up this nonsense forever." The man shrugged, ignoring the burning stare that Thomas was giving him. "I mean, look at the state of him..."

"Yes, thank you, Brother."

"Crawling back home, tail between his legs..."

"Can probably stop now," said Thomas, through gritted teeth.

Thomas' pa glared at him. "A complete failure."

The brother looked uncomfortable and stared down at his bread. "He's not a failure, Pa," he mumbled, taking another bite.

Robert stepped protectively in front of Thomas, his eyes fixed on Thomas' pa. "He is not. His actions may have been foolish and misguided, but I can assure you Thomas is a talented—"

"My arse!" said Thomas' pa, with a rough laugh. "Not a failure? All he ever wanted were Drury bloody Lane." He stepped closer to Robert.

Caroline clenched her hammerless hands. If he laid a finger on Robert...

"If he's such a success," growled the man, leaning into Robert's face, "then why the bloody Hell is he back in my inn?"

Robert's shoulders tensed. He clearly had no argument, but still he stared resolutely at Thomas' pa. She took the moment to exaggeratedly pluck the hammer from his hand, more to prove a point than anything. And Thomas? Was he not going to defend himself? But Thomas stared not at his pa, but down at the floor. Their lead actor, who confidently strutted out Titania and often disappeared up his own arse, reduced to silence in his own home. No wonder he had left.

"The steward has arranged permission to perform tomorrow night," said Robert firmly to Thomas' pa. He paused and glanced at Thomas behind him, as if to check that at least *this* part wasn't a lie. Thomas gave a small nod.

A tense silence filled the room. All the customers were staring at them. Caroline threw a hand in the air and said, "So, are we building our stage or not?"

"There be a lot of wisdom in it," said the plump woman.

"Go on, James!" called a man sitting with a group at a table across the room. "We need some entertainment – unless Rosie Watson be coming tonight!"

"Well, she bloody will if I gets *my* turn!" called out another.

Caroline rolled her eyes at the slapping of backs and raucous laughter that rose from the table.

Thomas' pa pointed at Robert's face, his finger only an inch from Robert's nose. Still Robert did not flinch. "One night only. This had better reap reward." He looked past Robert at Thomas, who reluctantly lifted his eyes to meet him. "And you clean out the piss-pots after."

He crossed the room and disappeared through another doorway on the far side. The plump woman patted Thomas' arm awkwardly then followed her husband, pausing momentarily to clip Thomas' brother around the ear and snatch away the remains of his bread.

Thomas cleared his throat and stepped out from behind Robert. "There," he said in an overly bright voice as he straightened his fist-crumpled shirt and orange neckerchief. "I have arranged everything."

"Yes, you're very welcome," said Thomas' brother drily. He ambled towards the front door and disappeared.

"I shall go and prepare our beds for tonight," said Thomas. "We shall need a good night's sleep if we are to perform at our best."

He began moving swiftly – surely more swiftly than necessary – towards the kitchen door.

Caroline twisted her mouth, letting the hammer swing gently by her side. "Annie will be pleased about the feather pillows." It took every effort to keep her voice under control.

"Hmm," said Thomas, his pace quickening.

"Thomas," Caroline called, making sure the threat was clear in her voice. Thomas approached the kitchen door. "Where exactly are we sleeping tonight?"

"Oh... yes... In the—" said Thomas as the kitchen door shut behind him.

Caroline's jaw clenched and she heard Robert sigh beside her. "You put a lot of trust in him," she said pointedly.

"We need to build the stage," said Robert. And Caroline knew him well enough to hear beyond the steadiness in his voice and hear the hurt.

CHAPTER 16: Benedict

Now he was with her, every doubt in his mind had faded into insignificance. Benedict gazed at the beautiful woman in her cream linen shift, lying beneath him on her bed. He lapped up every detail of her heart-shaped face – the flecks in her blue eyes, the shape of her lips, the curls which cascaded like a golden waterfall about her shoulders.

He pitied his brother for he had never known what it was like to be so deeply in love with a woman. To feel so completely lost in the presence of a person and at the same time so completely found. As if every second of your life was building up to this very moment, and time would surely stand still, for you had finally reached where you were destined to be. Except... today, Sarah seemed strangely distant.

"What is wrong?" He rolled his naked body over onto the other side of the bed, looking at her in concern. "Are you unwell?"

Sarah turned her head away. "Benedict, we cannot steal these moments any longer. I've told you: Marcus returns next week. And now with the child..." Her voice choked a little. "I'm so sorry. This must end."

The world threatened to collapse around him. She couldn't mean it! "No! No, I have been thinking, planning. I have found us a way."

"And *I* have been thinking. I ought to be grateful. I am well provided for." She gestured to the comfortable room, with its rugs, mirrors and wooden furniture. "Marcus is a good man. He treats me kindly. I am told that in time, affection shall grow—"

"But you know it could never be like *this*!" He reached out and grasped her shoulder. "I love you with the strength of a thousand hearts!" Sarah turned back towards him, tiredness in the soft blue eyes he knew so well.

"Please. For both our sakes, come to me no more. Forget what we had."

"No!" He sat upright. Damn it, he would keep the world from collapsing! "We go to Bristol! And I swear, I will always love you, always care for you and the child!"

She reached out a hand and cupped Benedict's face. He clasped his hand over hers. "My heart may belong to you, but my future is here."

She pulled her hand away from his face. He snatched at her delicate fingers and caught them just before they slipped away.

"Tomorrow night at six o'clock my brother performs a show. Then, the eyes of the entire town will be on him. Not us. Meet me by Mr Jones' workshop—"

"I am truly sorry," whispered Sarah as tears gathered in her eyes. "You will love again."

He kissed her hand, and the scent of her skin flooded his mind. His heart ached to the point of bursting. How was it possible to feel this much love? "No. Six o'clock. I promise you; this is possible! And nothing – nothing! – will stand in our way."

A door below them shut. Benedict held his breath. A man's voice called out.

"Sarah?"

"Marcus?" gasped Benedict.

"Benedict!" Sarah shoved him out of the bed, snatching at the fine linen sheets as he tumbled naked onto the floor.

"Shit!" said Benedict as he scrambled on all fours – heart racing – to the chair where his undergarments, breeches, shirt and orange neckerchief were heaped. "Shit-shit-shit!" He pulled his undergarments on – where was his shirt? "Shit-shit-shit-shit-shit!" Breeches on! Damn – they were back-to-front.

Footsteps coming up the stairs...

"Make haste!" hissed Sarah, desperately patting down her hair and arranging the sheets. "Why is he back early?"

Benedict dashed over to the sash window, pushed it open and sat astride it. He turned and blew Sarah a kiss. His heart stung at the sadness that hung on her like a weighted cloak, but he would be strong enough for them both. "Tomorrow, six o'clock! Behind Mr Jones' workshop. I love you."

Then he half-climbed, half-tumbled out of the window. He scrabbled at nothing, unable to breathe. There was a bone-jolting thump onto a bundle of hay propped up against the back wall of the house. Benedict groaned and gathered his senses. No broken bones. He snatched a breath and scrambled away as urgently as back-to-front breeches would allow.

He dashed down the carriage arch between Sarah's house and the malthouse, out of sight of her window. Then, checking he was unseen, he scurried down towards the south end of town until he reached the old humpback bridge over the River Batherm. He stood on the bridge, feeling the rough hunks of moss-speckled stone beneath his palms, breathing slowly and deeply to calm his galloping heart. He watched the shallow river tumble over the stones, travelling on with passion and purpose towards the sea it was destined for. They could no sooner turn their backs on their love than the river could return to the moor.

Tomorrow at six o'clock.

The sack beneath his bed would be filled with a future. He would take courage from Thomas – courage he should have taken long before Sarah's marriage had occurred. He would follow his heart, whatever the consequences. He had one life, one chance to make this work, with the woman he loved more than life itself. She was scared, but she would see sense. And once they were free of this place, Sarah would soon realise they had been right to choose love.

He lifted his head defiantly to the sky and sang.

"There's no man in this wide world... As happy as me..."

CHAPTER 17: Thomas

"Well, that's our new stage built," announced Thomas, throwing out his hands towards the hard-earned planks and trestles in the yard, and trying to ignore the ache of his back and the sweat on his brow.

Silence.

For Heaven's sake. Why was his own company always the hardest crowd to win? Completing the stage ought to be a moment of triumph. The afternoon had swung between bickering and irritated silence. Even Annie had been downcast, mourning the absence of a feather pillow. The only thing worse than Caroline's blunt appraisal of his behaviour had been the quiet disappointment from Robert – the man whose approval meant so much. The man who had been forced to defend him from his own father in his own home.

The day was yielding to dusk and had seemed unreasonably long. Robert stood with a frown, waves of pain flickering across his face. Caroline looked hot and bothered, one hand on her hip. And Annie cast nervous glances towards her as if Caroline were a keg of gunpowder and Thomas a rather dangerous spark. Thomas sighed and tossed the hammer onto the stage. A muffled wave of laughter came from inside the inn. His ears pricked up and he licked his dry lips. The day could yet be saved. He turned to the others. "We have a performance and a stage – great cause for celebration! The evening beckons. Come and taste the best cider in the west."

“And is the best cider in the west still free, Thomas?” said Caroline. “Or was that another hopeful prediction?”

“We have worked hard,” said Robert, before Thomas could answer. “I suggest we go and find out.”

Thomas led them beneath the golden star sign at the street entrance, just in case his pa was waiting with a harsh tongue and a quick fist in the kitchen. Many voices babbled inside, and as Thomas opened the door, the warming waft of ale, cider and woodsmoke wrapped around him like an embrace from an old friend. He breathed it in. When was the last time they had been to an inn, simply to enjoy its pleasures and drink their fill? Candles were dotted on each table, ready to fight the impending gloom, and lanterns hung from the walls, casting light and shadows into the room and up onto the timber-beamed ceiling. The crowd were already merry, several ales and ciders no doubt already warming their bellies whilst Thomas and the others had been building the stage. Thomas spied an empty table in the centre and leaned back a little to peer around one of the wide oak pillars. No sign of Pa... Or Essie. Thank Heaven. Just Ma serving behind the bar. He patted his orange neckerchief gratefully – it should be worth at least two tankards.

“We had better have an audience tomorrow,” said Caroline, as they meandered through the chatting, laughing customers.

Thomas gestured to the inn around them as they arrived at the table. “Do not worry, we shall have one. Observe.” He stepped up onto a wooden stool, then onto the slightly wobbling table and cupped his hands to his mouth. “Oi-oi!” He waited until many heads turned in his direction, then threw out his arms. “The Ticehurst Players will perform A Midsummer Night’s Dream here, six o’clock on the morrow!”

There were a couple of cheers, a raising of tankards. Someone shouted, “Good luck with your pa!” which raised some laughter. Thomas jumped down again and gestured to the folk around them. “A good many of them journey to Thorverton Fair. If we win them over with the play tomorrow, they will no doubt gather around us once more. And a crowd is certain to draw Lord Pelham's attention."

"A Midsummer Night's Dream?" said Robert.

Caroline pointed at Thomas but looked at Robert. "Tell me he is not playing Titania again."

Thomas opened his mouth to protest.

"We are doing A Midsummer Night's Dream again over my dead body," said Robert.

"Oh?" said Annie, looking puzzled. "That's a bold choice."

"Shakespeare yields the best results," said Robert, "but we perform Hamlet. Always draws the crowds. Well... it used to."

Thomas tensed at the heaviness in Robert's voice. "And we will draw marvellous crowds with *every* play when we have our patron." He clambered back up onto the table, holding his balance as it wobbled once more beneath him. "Oi-oi! The Ticehurst Players will perform *Hamlet* here, six o'clock on the morrow!"

"Make up your mind!" someone called across the room as Thomas jumped down again.

"Bloody actors," called someone else.

Annie gasped. "Oh no, wait! We can't do Hamlet!"

"I am *not* standing up there again," said Thomas, with a sting of irritation.

"Oh, but Thomas, we've no skull."

"I'll find one," said Thomas and Caroline at the same time. Thomas' head snapped towards Caroline, defiance written all over her face, and her head slightly lowered like a bull about to charge. Well, she could be as defiant as she liked. Thomas would get the skull: this was the perfect opportunity to win back Robert's favour. "But I truly think we should consider performing more comedy in future."

"Tragedy suits us," said Robert.

"We certainly excel at dying on stage," Caroline said.

"But comedy is popular!"

"Comedy is naught but an unfinished tragedy," said Robert, shaking his head. "Laugh as you will, at the end of the day, happy hearts break, death awaits." His fingers reached for the rabbit's foot necklace. "Then we all play the fool."

One last try. "You speak as a man in need of a comedy."

"I speak as a man who has lived." Robert's voice was soft and final.

Thomas sighed. Three things were certain: one, he would perform comedy at Drury bloody Lane. Two, one of Robert's long dark moods wasn't far away. And three, he desperately needed some of his pa's delicious cider. "Yes... well..." he said. "Tragedy will be lovely. I'll get the drinks."

He headed over to the bar where Ma was serving, twisting his body around the crowded tables and stools, noting every customer who had ever mocked his desire for acting, until he gave up counting. Most of all, he dreamed of the day he could throw a bill in Pa's face – a bill with *his* name, maybe even *his* theatre company, announcing *his* performance at Drury Lane. Oh, he would make this happen, whatever the cost. He had such hopes for this company. They just needed more money and more players, then they could be far more successful! He would not – *could* not – allow anything to come in the way of his dreams—

A woman with olive skin and locks of dark hair escaping her cap pushed in front of him, reaching the bar first.

"Evenin'. You're a new face," said Ma.

"We are a company of three," said the woman in a silky voice, "looking for rooms for the night."

Ma shook her head. "We be full to burstin'." She jabbed her thumb towards the door. "Ask at the Angel, north end of town, jus' past the church."

The olive-skinned woman nodded her thanks as Ma disappeared further down the bar to serve.

"But do come back here tomorrow night if you're still here!" Thomas said to the woman. "My company perform a play here."

"Oh yes." Her brown eyes danced. "I have heard of the Ticehurst Players before."

Thomas raised his eyebrows. "You have? Oh. Good... things?"

"That would be telling. Perhaps I should see for myself if the reports are true."

Their reputation had never gone ahead of them before. What exactly had she heard? "Well, we begin at six of the clock."

"So you said. Twice. There must be a sudden change of heart to move from comedy to tragedy so swiftly."

Thomas brought a smile to his face. Every potential audience member counted. "Ah, but they say at the end of the day, comedy is naught but an unfinished tragedy anyway."

The woman stifled a laugh. "Yes. Yes, they do."

A strange response. It was, in truth, a phrase he had only heard from Robert's lips, so surely she hadn't heard it before? He gave a polite chuckle anyway. "Tomorrow, at six. I can promise you a moving performance."

The woman glided towards Thomas' ear, her movement smooth and seamless, her voice low and husky. "Then I shall look forward to being... moved."

Thomas leaned back. What in Heaven's name was that supposed to mean? He watched in confusion as the woman sauntered towards the front door. She had a confidence about her which reminded him of Caroline, yet not in a don't-argue-with-me-I-have-a-hammer manner, but more of a dangerously playful one. He puffed out his cheeks and gave his head a little shake. Well, it mattered not. Thank Heaven his life did not revolve around women, unlike his unfortunate brother.

Still, that was one more audience member – three, if she brought her two travel companions – and that could only be a good thing. He had promised Robert an eager crowd, but as he listened to the merry folk around him, doubt began to creep in. What if he failed? What if people did not come? What if Pa was right? He passed a hand over his eyes. Lord, he needed a drink. Or three. Possibly more. Ma headed over: he straightened his orange neckerchief and smiled his most winning smile.

The evening passed in a blur of tankards. Thomas was grateful that at least one hopeful prediction had come true. It had been long – too long – since they had drunk their fill of decent cider. And, oh Lord, how good it tasted, sliding down.

And down.

And down.

And then came a little rum. Laughing together.

And down.

Thomas lost sight of his shit-ridden life.

And...

"Here's a health to the company!" he shouted.

People cheering in the blurry room. Oof. Table?

"Cheese!" Annie laughed, leaning on Robert. Holding bloody rabbit foot.

Nice Annie. No hammers with Annie.

His tankard disappeared from his hand.

Caroline drinking it. "Always tastes better when it's free." Tankard back in his hand. "An' when it's yours."

Oh. Tankard down on the table.

"Robert! You are right! No bloody women!"

A hand over his mouth. "Sssssshh." Caroline's voice in his ear. And Caroline's face in front of him. Both of them. "Robert's secret."

Pointing at Caroline. "You. Don't drink my cider." Pointing at... Robert? Well, Robert was there somewhere. "Don't let her drink my cider. I... am going to find a skull."

"No." Caroline pushing him into – Robert's? – Robert's lap. "*I* am going to find a skull."

"I jus' wanna skull." Robert shoving him back on his feet.

Room all spinny.

"Watch Annie." Caroline walking off... sideways?

Floor wobbling. Never used to wobble.

Need to find a skull... Legs so heavy. Wait. Thank Heaven. Empty stool.

Essie coming. Shit. Essie. Shit. Essie. Shit – Essie on his lap. Saying something.

"What? What?" A wave of the hand. "Yes, whatever. Go... go." Essie's lips pushing on his.

What the Hell?

Essie laughing. Essie going.

"Yes, go!"

Legs heavy... head heavy...

Head. Skull. Need to find a Hamlet for a skull.

Oh. Thank Heaven. Empty floor. Just... lying down...

Won't be...

Long...

CHAPTER 18: Piero

Piero climbed the inn's creaking staircase, one hand clamped over his eyes, the other clasping Maria's hand, their fingers entwined. Another of her games. He moved slowly, his foot searching for the next step. He was meant to be trusting the one holding his hand. Of course, he didn't, but he played his part. Trust. The greatest and most foolish mistake a person could make.

"You'll like it, I promise," came her teasing voice.

He bumped into her. He detested this. Why had she stopped? There was movement, her body pressed against his.

"It's more fun when you have your eyes closed," she murmured. Her lips brushed against his, then she pulled away. A tug on his hand, a giggle, and they were moving again. His foot reached for a step – it wasn't there. The landing, then? He bumped into her again.

"Keep them closed," she said.

A key clanked in a lock. A door creaked open.

He was yanked forwards, lost his footing and stumbled – a small jolt of panic, then she tore his hand away from his eyes. Lord, he hated that feeling. Hated being at the mercy of someone else.

But he devoured the sight which met him. In the middle of the lantern-lit room stood a double bed. The creamy bedlinen fresh and tempting, the feather pillows plump and welcoming. Maria wrapped her arms around his neck. All was forgiven.

“I said we would sleep in the finest inns,” Piero murmured as his arms found her waist.

“You also said you would make the journey worthwhile,” she replied, unpinning her cap and hair as dark, thick locks tumbled down. She kissed him again.

The scent of her swept around him.

“And I have other news,” she said in a knowing voice. Her hands dropped from his neck to his jacket, which she began to slide off.

For a moment, the whole world paused. Was this it? Was this what he had spent the last year waiting for, as he built up his act and his success? He held his breath...

“I have found your wretched players.”

Robert! His breath burst out in a gasp before he could stop it.

“And... I know exactly where and when they will perform.”

A dark joy threatened to overwhelm him, but he brought it to heel and smiled at Maria. He began to remove her garments, kissing her as he did so. Oh, this was magnificent. *She* was magnificent. He unlaced her stays, before hastily untying his cravat and casting his shirt and breeches to the floorboards. Only the rabbit’s foot necklace remained, as it always did.

She slid onto the bed, in her shift and stockings, reaching out for him and guiding him down towards her. He closed his eyes as he ran his hands through dark, wavy locks. And as the necklace dangled between their pressing bodies, Piero fought and fought to think of Maria.

Not the man he hated with all his heart.

CHAPTER 19: Caroline

"Fuuuuuuuuuck," groaned Caroline.

She put a hand to her spinning head and opened aching eyes. She was lying on the straw in the stable, legs sprawled over Robert's chest and her head on what she presumed were Thomas'... thighs? A heaviness sat in her chest, and the smell of stale sweat, horseshit and the heady fragrance of hay only made everything worse.

"Don't worry!" came Annie's cheerful voice, followed by Annie's cheerful face in front of her.

Caroline closed her eyes. She couldn't deal with this right now.

"This will help," Annie said brightly, and something smooth and wooden was shoved into Caroline's hand.

She peeked open one eye and glanced at the beaker in dismay. "Fuuuuuuuuuck." She groaned again. She dug her elbow into something soft – probably some sensitive part of Thomas judging by the head-splitting cry he gave – and propped herself up. She opened both eyes, blinked several times and peered into the beaker suspiciously. Her stomach churned. Why was it green? Why the Hell was it always green? At least it wasn't yellow.

"You know it'll help," said Annie. She handed a beaker to Robert and Thomas, who struggled to sit up. "That's the bottle dry, but promise I'll make some more."

"Oh good," grumbled Caroline.

"I'll go and sell some of the tonics." She gave Caroline an excited smile and bounced out of the stable.

Caroline and Thomas gave Robert a pleading look, but he looked back at them with merciless, bloodshot eyes. "We have a show," he said firmly. "On three."

Caroline took a deep breath and grimaced.

"One, two, three," said Robert.

They glugged down the foul liquid. Caroline's hand flew to her burning throat.

"Why do we keep drinking what she gives us?" rasped Thomas.

But a few minutes later, there was a gentle spread of relief as the sickness and headache began to subside.

Thomas sniffed the beaker curiously. "What *does* she put in it?"

"That," said Caroline, getting to her feet with a wobble just small enough to be disguised, "is a question you never ask." She rubbed her dull, aching head and pinned up some of her hair as loosely as possible. "I'll go and drum up more business for tonight."

"And I," Thomas announced, looking at her with such earnest defiance, she could not help but smile, "am going to find a skull."

"As long as somebody gets one," said Robert. He rubbed his temples. "We rehearse in half an hour and we're not using the donkey head like last time. It's a tragedy, not a bloody comedy."

"You'll have your skull," said Caroline, shooting a satisfied look at Thomas. She retrieved her cap from where it dangled on Old Bess' ear and fixed it in place. Then slinging the drum around her neck and picking up the beater, she persuaded her feet to go out towards the market square. Another wave of nausea washed over her and she rested against the cool stone of the carriage arch.

There was Annie, darting like a merry bee through the sunny May morning – which was far too bright for Caroline's liking – brandishing her bottles of tonic hopefully at passing victims. Oh, Annie. She always tried her best. A wave of affection rose, and Caroline forced it down. She would not be like her ma. Not with

Annie. Not with Robert. Not with anyone. Love of any kind could only bring—

A tall man in smart tan breeches and a black cocked hat on his golden-brown hair walked past her down the street. His face was full of sorrow and distraction and his fist clenched around an orange neckerchief, just like the one Thomas and his brother had been wearing. Annie leapt in front of him, almost tripping him over. He looked up sharply, as if he were only just aware of his surroundings.

"Good sir! Seems the burdens of life are weighing you down. I've the perfect remedy." She pushed a bottle in front of his face.

The man gave a polite smile. "No, thank you."

He began to move past her when Annie let out a loud gasp. "Oh, you're not Thomas Cooper's brother, are you?"

Caroline's ears pricked up. The man whirled around to face Annie, wearing a dark frown. Time to rescue Annie again, then. Caroline quickly eased herself away from the wall, ignoring the strange slanting of the ground.

"Thomas... Cooper's brother," repeated the man. He looked like he was trying to solve a rather unpleasant riddle.

"She means no trouble," Caroline called as she headed over, hoping her tone promised that the drum beater in her hand was a considerable threat should he touch one hair on Annie's head.

"Thomas said his brother had a matching one of those," Annie continued as Caroline slipped herself pointedly between her and the man. "I've not met him yet."

The man stood for a moment, staring at the neckerchief, then gave them the briefest nod and marched away.

"Really good for easing the..." Annie called after him, raising the bottle. "BURDENS OF LIFE." Her shoulders drooped.

"Your mouth will see you hanged one day, Annie."

"I'm certain it were just like Thomas' one."

Caroline sighed impatiently. "Oh, it doesn't matter, does it? But since you're in such fine voice today, you can help announce the show. Come on." She banged on the drum heartily, wincing at the noise and hoping the fragile drum would withstand the onslaught. "Ticehurst Players present Shakespeare's Hamlet! Tonight, six o'clock at the Star!"

A couple of women scurried by, paying little heed. They spoke in excited voices and pointed at a piece of paper one of them held.

"Hamlet tomorrow at the Star!" called Annie after them. She raised the bottle. "And a tonic to cure your boils."

The square around them seemed empty. "Where is everyone?" Caroline looked down towards the path leading up to the church where a fine crowd had gathered. "What's going on there?" She grabbed Annie's arm and headed in that direction, banging the drum – still wincing – as she went. "Hamlet, tonight at the Star!"

Another woman's voice called from within the flock of people. "Unmissable!"

Caroline frowned and picked up the pace. The dull headache did nothing for her irritability and patience. Why were the people paying attention down there? *She* was the one with a bloody drum. As they drew closer, she saw the owner of the voice – a dark-haired, olive-skinned woman, clutching a pile of printed bills. Beside her stood a man with short, dark hair and the same olive skin. He was taller than her, slim but with strong muscles, and he silently handed out bills to the crowd.

"Unmissable tightrope act!" called the woman, her smile bright. "Tonight, at the Angel!"

Tonight? A tightrope act? What the Hell? She left Annie behind and pushed through the people. "*We* are performing tonight."

The woman shrugged, but Caroline noticed her eyes dancing. And she didn't like it.

"Death-defying, unmissable—" the woman continued.

Caroline banged the drum louder and yelled as fast as she could. "Shakespeare's-Hamlet-the-one-with-the-skull!"

The woman glared at Caroline, her bright smile vanishing quicker than Annie's potential customers.

"TIGHTROPE!"

"HAMLET!" Caroline banged the drum louder than ever.

The woman moved with speed, grabbed the drum beater out of Caroline's hands and tossed it over her shoulder. There was a gasp from the crowd. Caroline glared at her. How dare—! Her hand shot out and punched the bills out of the woman's grip. Another gasp swept through the crowd as the papers scattered into the air.

The tall man scrabbled at the bills as they drifted down again.

"Leave them, Brother." The woman faced Caroline, meeting her fierce glare unnervingly well. "A temper like a mule with a poker up its arse. You must be Caroline."

What? Caroline blinked, trying to connect thoughts which didn't seem to exist. "How do you know my name?"

The woman gave a dangerous smile, and her eyes danced once more.

Annie shoved the beater back into Caroline's hand. "Come on, please just leave it," she pleaded. There was tugging on Caroline's arm, and she let herself be pulled away from the crowd.

"How the Hell does she know my name?"

"Oh Caroline, you say it'll be my mouth which sees me to the gallows, but it's the fire in your belly what'll see *you* swing." Annie tugged Caroline's arm again. "We ought to head back for rehearsals, or Robert will see us *both* hanged! I wonder if Thomas found a skull."

Caroline looked back at the crowd-stealing woman as the townsfolk snatched bills from the ground with eager fingers. "*She* has a Yorick-sized head."

This was all they needed! Caroline marched back to the inn with Annie fretting beside her all the way. In the yard, Robert and Thomas were placing the swords, props and fiddle at the front of the stage beside the hammer left out from earlier. Her furious eyes met Thomas, and he hastily slid the hammer across the boards to Robert.

"There's a bloody tightrope act!" she burst out, standing next to them with her hands on her hips. "Tonight, at the Angel, wherever that is."

"By the church. A *tightrope* act?" said Thomas. He looked devastated.

But it was the despair on Robert's face which pierced her heart. He shook his head. "Oh, then what is the bloody point?" He sat down on the stage, put the hammer beside him and let his arms flop down by his sides.

"Surely there must be a mistake?" said Thomas.

Annie shook her head and clutched a handful of her skirts. "Heard it with my own ears."

Thomas stepped forwards, eyes full of fire. "We perform anyway! I will knock on every single door in this town! Build an audience! We can do this!"

Caroline nodded. The storm inside her began to ease, but she cast a doubtful look at Robert, still perched on the stage.

"I even found a skull!" Thomas continued.

He reached inside his jacket pocket and placed a small animal skull triumphantly on the stage beside the other props. Caroline moved towards the stage to fetch the small sack she had stashed there overnight. She retrieved a large human skull and set it firmly beside Thomas' offering. Robert glanced over, and a smile flickered across his frowning face but faded before it truly began.

Thomas just stared at the skull, then at her. "Where? How...?"

There was the misty memory of a drunken man pinning her against the wall of the inn, asking where she was from, looking surprised when she answered Shoreditch... Looking even more surprised when she held a hammer to his crotch and told him if he didn't point her in the direction of a local gravedigger, he might end up looking surprised permanently.

"Secrets," she said.

"You did well, I knew you would," said Robert as Thomas' shoulders slumped a little. "But I fear a skull is not enough to save us." His hand covered his eyes. "A tightrope act at the same time."

"We will be fine," said Thomas, passionately.

"Fine?" snapped Robert. Dropping his hand, he jumped up and looked at Thomas with tired, broken eyes. "Forgive me, in what manner will we be 'fine'? We only have permission for one night from the steward *and* your father, we need to purchase props and costumes on Friday, the fair is on Saturday, we need this chance to secure a patron, so we cannot alter the date of our performance, and there is a bloody tightrope act that everyone will want to see, which just happens to be performing at exactly the same time!"

Thomas squirmed a little. "Aside from that, we shall be fine."

"We are not fine, Thomas, we are fucked!" shouted Robert.

Caroline swallowed. Everyone was silent.

He had shouted.

In all the time she had known him, Robert had never shouted at the company. He hardly ever raised his voice at anyone. This was not a good sign.

"We need to rehearse," she said firmly to Annie, ignoring the tears filling Annie's eyes. "Script. Now." Annie darted off into the stables, wiping her face with her sleeve.

Caroline watched Robert for clues. He stood with his hands resting on his hips, staring fiercely down at the ground, as if he was concentrating on locking everything inside him, bolt by bolt, where no one could reach it. Despite his lies, Thomas had done what he had promised, and there had been hope for the company once more. But now all that was unravelling. Robert took a deep breath. A deep breath was good, wasn't it? He was trying, and just about managing, to keep the thread that held him up from snapping.

Annie came towards them, clutching a large handful of papers. "I still can't find the end of Act four, Scene seven."

Caroline hated that scene. The pages had deserved to burn.

Robert took the papers from Annie and laid an apologetic hand on her shoulder. "Thank you," he said gently, looking into her eyes. Then he laid the script on the stage and began rifling through the pages. He handed a pile to Annie and one to a subdued-looking Thomas. "Yes, you're still Hamlet." His hand rested on Thomas' back. "Forgive me."

Caroline held out her hand for her papers and stared at Robert, seeking to make eye contact with him. He briefly met her gaze as the pages were exchanged, then tilted his face away as if he couldn't bear to look at her. Unease edged her shoulders higher.

"We try," said Robert. "We know Hamlet well enough, but we'll go through." He moved onto the centre of the stage as Annie put her papers down and took her position on the far side. Caroline climbed up behind her, followed by Thomas. At least they were up on the boards they now possessed, rehearsing like a company which still had purpose and hope.

Caroline watched as Robert stepped effortlessly into his character – and she longed for that feeling of slipping away from the weight of her own life and losing herself in someone else's. Robert looked out across the yard as Annie approached him.

"*Who's there?*" she called.

"*Nay, answer me,*" said Robert, facing her. "*Stand, and unfold yourself.*"

Annie opened her mouth to reply–

"*Long live the king!*" came a playful voice from the carriage arch. A voice which Caroline knew.

She froze.

Shit. No.

All of them turned around to the owner of the voice. It was like the stage had collapsed beneath her. Not because of the olive-skinned woman and her brother, but because of the man beside them who had spoken. The man holding a bulging sack, with purple powder smeared lavishly on the lids of his gleaming eyes.

CHAPTER 20: Piero

Piero's second-favourite thing in the world was making an entrance. And this would surely go down as one of his most successful ones. He placed the sack on the floor and clapped his gloved hands together loudly and slowly. The bastard Robert, and Caroline and Annie stared at him with open mouths. There was a pathetic-looking man he didn't recognise too, presumably their new lead actor.

"Bravo!" he called, picking up the sack again and strutting towards the stage, aware of Maria and Angelo following like faithful hounds. "The audience will be mesmerised with this tantalising, death-defying performance." He paused, frowned, then feigned embarrassment. "Oh, my mistake. That's us."

Caroline looked like she wanted to kill him. Nothing new. Annie clasped her hands to her mouth. The new actor just looked confused. And Robert...

He swallowed, purely to prepare for his next speech.

Robert was frozen, staring at him in disbelief. Piero narrowed his eyes slightly. What the Devil had happened to Robert's face? There were several fading bruises, and scabs where nasty-looking cuts were healing. An accident? Or had someone discovered his secret and hurt him? It mattered not. The man's wellbeing was no longer his concern. Robert had made that perfectly clear. Piero needed to focus. He was here with a very clear purpose.

And he must be in control.

He jumped up onto the stage, hearing Maria and Angelo climb up behind him. Piero moved himself directly in front of Robert as they formed opposing lines. For a moment, nobody moved, and nobody spoke. Oh, the tension was delicious. A shame that the audience was so small and pitiful for what promised to be such a fine performance.

"You've seen better days," he murmured to Robert. Trying to ignore the thumping of his own heartbeat, he reached out a gloved finger and delicately traced the scab of what must have been a particularly nasty cut above Robert's left eye.

Caroline grabbed the sword from the stage boards and lunged—

It pointed at his chest.

Piero forced his muscles to slacken as he sighed and rolled his eyes.

"You could always just say 'good morning'," he said, "but it appears old habits die hard." He dropped the sack, widened his eyes in mock fear and raised his hands in surrender. "I suppose I should be grateful you are pointing at my *heart*." He glanced sideways at Robert. "What remains of it."

"Oh, Caroline, please!" Annie pleaded, pushing down on Caroline's arm and lowering the sword. She met his eyes. She looked desperate, confused. He quickly turned his gaze to Caroline. Out of the two women, he knew Annie was a far greater threat to him. After all, she possessed a weapon far more deadly than a sword and must be handled with great caution.

"Why the Hell are you here?" Caroline demanded, her sword arm rising again. Once more, Annie forced it down.

"Well, now! I thought you'd like to meet my new, improved companions," Piero said brightly. He turned and cupped Maria's face, giving her an enthusiastic kiss.

"You!" Robert said, in a voice that sounded like he was being choked.

How lovely. He recognised her when Piero did that, did he? Piero broke off the kiss and addressed Robert and the others. "Ah, yes! I forgot. You have met once before." He looked at Robert, ensuring his eyes sparkled with defiance and hate.

Robert looked back with eyes full of pain and thunder.

"Robert..." It was barely a whisper. There was more desperation in that one word than he had ever known in his life. The fist of the man he adored pulled back–

No. He had to focus.

"Maria Violante is a talented tightrope walker," Piero continued loudly, to drown out his own treacherous thoughts as much as anything else. He gestured with a flourish to Maria. "Did you know," he said in a merry tone, "we do not even need a stage? Speaking of which..." He pointed his gloved finger in the air for attention and reached down for the sack. "I found your old one." And he upended the sack and poured – slowly, oh, deliciously – ashes and charred chunks of wood onto the boards. Caroline jumped back quickly. "Oops. Do mind your feet there," he added.

"Piero," Annie begged softly.

NO.

He turned to the young man, with his determined face and blazing brown eyes, and wondered if it was this new actor who had dared to lay a finger on the dress. "Ah," said Piero, sincerely hoping his voice sounded as welcoming as a slow and painful death, "and you must be my replacement!"

"New, improved," the man threw back.

Piero allowed a small smile. The man had fire, at least. Robert had chosen well.

"Yet lacking the livery, I notice?" Piero gestured around them and gasped. "Alas and indeed alack! Do not tell me you lost the patronage?" He made his eyes dance. "After *all* I said to Lord Blagdon about you before I left?"

"You bastard!" said Caroline.

She raised the sword again, lurched forwards.

A bolt of fear—

Annie dashed between them, bright hair flying. She whirled back around, wide-eyed, to face Caroline. Piero regained his composure as the annoying woman skidded to a halt.

"What do you think you're doing?" Caroline yelled at Annie. "Out of the way!"

"Just drop that bloody sword!" Robert said, pointing at Caroline.

"Ah, nothing like a happy family, is there? I trust you are all *very* happy?" said Piero smoothly as Caroline glared at everybody in turn before stabbing the sword into the boards. She pulled Annie roughly back alongside her.

Piero turned his attention to the man he hated more than life itself. Robert was breathing fast, chest moving beneath his white shirt. And there was the rabbit's foot necklace, still tied around his neck.

"What do you want?" Robert said tightly.

Piero tapped his cheek with his finger. "What do I want?" He silenced the screaming inside, and instead leaned forwards to speak in Robert's ear. That familiar scent of him now... Lord, that scent... the scent that used to fill the gaps in his soul. He steadied himself with a quick breath. "I want to watch you beg for mercy. One mistake, when I was pissed, and you took everything from me, everything I cared about. Yet you are nothing without me."

"I do not care about you any more," Robert said.

"A tragedy indeed!" said Piero. "And do you know what's even more tragic? I am going to destroy this company. Slowly. Painfully. I will bring you to your knees." He dropped his voice lower. "You know how I always liked you there."

He leapt from the stage, followed by Maria and Angelo. "Pray, do not let us stop your rehearsals. Undoubtedly you will need all the time you can get. Now... where were you?" He dared to look at Annie who raised her tear-filled eyes to him.

"*Long live the king...*" she whispered.

He risked giving her half a wink, then spun on his heel.

The performance was almost complete, and oh, how beautiful it had been. He reached for Maria's hand and walked on, hearing nothing but heavy silence behind him. How his heart raced with the thrill of it all as he brought the show to its conclusion. He focused on his pace – walking fast enough to hopefully avoid having a sword hurled at his back, but slow enough to make the moment linger. It was all in the timing.

Yes, he loved to make an entrance and capture the audience with his presence. But an exit – creating a lasting impression on the audience as they watched him go, leaving them silently falling in a tangle of thought and feeling – by far wielded the greater power.

Which is why it was his favourite thing in the world.

CHAPTER 21: Caroline

Caroline turned to Robert, fearing the look in his eyes. Dreading the state of his final, delicate thread.

"Robert..." she began urgently.

"Competing against a tightrope act is already impossible. But competing against a tightrope act run by...!" A thousand emotions flew across his face before they were swiftly locked away, and he began to pace the stage, shaking his head. "Why did he have to come back? Why are we always fucking *fucked*?"

"Robert." Caroline reached out and grabbed his arm, but he threw it off.

He put his hands to his temples and stared at the boards. "Just go," he whispered furiously, as if the fight was over and all that was left to do was retreat. "I want all of you to go – now. Pack up your belongings and go! Find someone else who has not failed at everything they touch!"

She cast a desperate look to Thomas, who glanced back at her, concern all over his face.

"Go!" said Robert.

"Robert, we do not want another company!" cried Thomas.

"You have no choice. You are all dismissed, and I am telling you to go!" Robert sat down on the edge of the stage beside the props, rested his elbows on his knees and hid his face in his hands.

"Robert," said Caroline again. "Robert." But he had locked her out. He had locked them all out.

Right. That was it. She clenched her fists. If *he* couldn't fight...

She jumped from the stage, letting the ground feel her anger. She grabbed the hammer from beside the pile of props, faced Robert and hurled it just behind him on the stage. The hammer hit the boards with a resounding smack and bounced away. Robert sat up straight, eyes wide – shocked, overwhelmed, lost – looking right at her. Good. Now she had his attention.

"We have a play to rehearse," she said firmly, toughening her thumping heart which could break at the sight of him, "so I shall make this quick. In case it has escaped your notice, as Thomas says, we do not *want* to go and find another company because, LORD HELP US, we want to work with *you*! We have been together for years, Robert, and we have met dark times before..."

She had bound his bleeding arms a little too roughly.

"Lord knows we have! Yet we have survived. Now we have travelled halfway across the bloody country, and I will not have it all be for naught. Especially not because of a bastard like him! We throw this away now and you are playing right into his hands! We have this chance, Robert, to try and get back on our feet. We do not let him win! Do you understand? We want *you*; we want this company! So, get your arse up on that stage, start acting like a bloody manager and BLOODY MANAGE US!"

Robert still sat motionless, staring at her, wide-eyed.

Oh, she wanted to shout that she knew he was broken, that she knew he was still trying to find a way to survive, to crawl back from the dark abyss stretching hopelessly in front of him, and that he was clinging to that delicate thread, and that her ma had been the same when her pa had died of a fever, that she knew the world had been unfair and unkind to Robert, and she understood that he was shutting them out and pushing them away for that was all he knew how to do, and she wanted to shout that there was yet hope for him, that he had to fight, he needed to stay, he needed to be all right because – for Heaven's sake – she cared so fucking much for him—

These words could not come.

They would never come.

They burned inside her as she snatched at the broken bottles inside his mind and tried to bind his bleeding arms a little too roughly. She stared at him – furious, desperate – hands clenched into fists, breathing much faster than she meant to.

And still Robert stared at her, as if he were listening to her screamed thoughts. Then he stood slowly, moved towards her – what was he doing? His arms closed around her, holding her tight. He had never done this before. Caroline stood motionless for a moment, then wrapped her arms around him in return. She had never done this before, either. As she rested her face against his shirt, his pulsing heartbeat brought a comfort she had almost forgotten.

She wielded swords and hammers inside her mind, fighting the urge to dissolve in a way she hadn't done for years, but then she felt his breath against her neck – he had breath in him yet – as he murmured, "No one could ever manage *you.*"

The tiny smile she gave against his still-beating heart saved the tears for another day.

CHAPTER 22: Thomas

The words bounced in Thomas' mind like the hammer off the stage.

Find someone else who has not failed at everything they touch...

He stood watching as Robert embraced Caroline, without seeming to have any intention of releasing her. Thomas stared down at the boards, his mind twisting and conspiring against itself. *Find someone else.* Another company... it wasn't really a thought he had entertained before. He had *this* company. Robert was exceptionally talented, if rather closed-minded. And despite Annie's somewhat odd behaviour, and the constant frustration which was Caroline, he relished his life with the troupe. But what if Robert was right? What if it was indeed time to reconsider his options?

Where would he go? It was not as if he lacked talent, rather opportunity. When he had arrived in London, he had tried. The managers showed no interest in him: desperate new actors were two a penny and easily shoved aside by desperate experienced actors. It had only been by coincidence that one rainy day last autumn he had stumbled upon the red-haired woman in the street, standing by a wagon decorated with the livery of a lord. She had pressed a soggy bill into his hand, and had chatted to him enthusiastically, saying they were performing *King Lear* because the lead actor had left and their unhappy manager needed to howl a bit, before she tried to sell him what he suspected was a bottle of poison.

And now, the boards of the stage were shifting beneath his feet. That previous lead actor had returned – the one that Annie had claimed was more talented and attractive than himself, although thus far Thomas had seen no evidence to support either count. Uncertainty hovered like a ghost.

"Right," said Robert.

Thomas looked up as Robert took a deep breath and finally stepped back from Caroline.

"Are we rehearsing this bloody play or not?"

Robert's voice sounded determined around the edges, but Thomas could hear the fragility inside.

Caroline pulled out the sword from the stage. The tension so riddled the yard that one poke with the sword's blade in the air and surely everything would just come crashing down around them. Caroline laid it beside the other props as Robert pointed at Thomas.

"Act three, Scene one. You know where to start."

Thomas nodded and closed his eyes to focus.

"Can we not do something else?" Caroline argued. Nervousness tinged her voice. "We have heard this speech enough times."

Thomas tried to banish thoughts of the company, and his future, and the actor who clearly wasn't more attractive or talented than him, and the crushing feeling of worry and desperation which stifled the air. He needed to forget all that and find the Prince of Denmark. Hamlet... Hamlet...

Whether 'tis nobler in the mind to suffer

The slings and arrows of outrageous fortune...

Thomas tried to ignore the barking of dogs and chattering voices and rumbling carts from the market square which now seemed so noticeably loud.

No traveller returns, puzzles the will,

And makes us rather bear those ills we have

Than fly to others that we know not of?

"What about Annie's lines?" suggested Caroline.

"I wish to hear this speech again," said Robert firmly. "And as you pointed out, I am the 'bloody manager', am I not?"

Did everyone have to speak so loudly? Thomas squeezed his closed eyes tighter. Where was his Prince of Denmark?

"Oh," said Annie doubtfully, "but this speech..."

"Is what the audience wants to hear," Robert said. "So, it needs to be good."

Thus conscience does make cowards of us all...

"Thomas?" said Robert expectantly.

Thomas opened his eyes. Was he ready? Regardless, he moved to centre stage. He stood there, legs a little astride, head high, and took a deep breath. He needed to focus. He needed to be marvellous. And although he would speak now to barrels and horseshit, he needed to hope. One day he would take his Prince of Denmark to the grandest stage, and the people – oh, the people in their finery would listen at last.

In his mind, the yard began to transform and colour. Gone was his father's inn, the dark, empty barrels drained of joy, the echo of failure. And in its place was the Theatre Royal at Drury Lane as he imagined it to be, in all its glory. A host of ordinary groundlings filled the area in front of the stage where he stood, yes, but opposite him, at the back of the theatre, were rows and rows of cheering people. And either side of the stage, rows of contained boxes, divided by timber pillars, stretching up ever higher towards the elaborate embossed ceiling, filled with lords and ladies watching him... applauding him... as he spoke:

"To be, or not to be, that is the question:

Whether 'tis nobler in the mind to suffer

The slings and arrows of outrageous fortune,

Or to take arms against a sea of troubles

And by opposing end them—"

A faceless lord in a tall, powdered wig leaned over one of the boxes nearest the stage. Thomas paused as the man called with Robert's voice: *"Find someone else who has not failed at everything they touch."*

But a voice from the groundlings croaked in an old, knowing voice: *"Good fortune awaits you at Thorverton Fair."*

Thomas looked down to see the old woman in a dark red dress and a brown headscarf.

"What do I do?" he whispered to her. "Which path do I take?"

"Thomas!" called the tall-wigged lord.

"Thomas!" said Robert's voice.

The Royal shattered into a thousand pieces like a smashed stained-glass window. Tiny shards of broken dreams. And there once more was the unwelcome reality of barrels and horseshit.

"What are you doing?" asked Robert, casting his hands in the air. "Why did you stop?"

"I..." But he could not make any more words follow.

"Perhaps as well," said Annie, wrinkling her nose. "Weren't your best."

Thomas sighed. Piero had returned... the Prince of Denmark had gone. Why was it all going so wrong?

"Forget this speech," said Caroline. "We should practise the dance at the end. Remember last time? Annie fell off the stage twice."

"I wouldn't have fallen off if the stage were a triangle," Annie said quietly.

"Annie," snapped Caroline, "the stage isn't *meant* to be a triangle!"

Thomas' remaining patience vanished. "And I suppose you know a good reason why we couldn't possibly experiment with a triangular stage?"

"YES. BECAUSE IT DOESN'T WORK!"

"Oh, that's enough," Robert said. He sighed and rubbed his face. "I do not think any of us are in the frame of mind for rehearsing." He pointed at Thomas. "But Annie is right. You perform better tonight, or you're trading places with the skull!" He reached for his necklace and rolled it between his fingers. "Prepare the stage and spread the word: we will give this our best shot." He averted his eyes from their gaze. "The blanket will be down awhile."

Shit. The blanket? They did not have time for this! Robert stepped inside the wagon and hastily untied the blanket which usually remained rolled up and fastened above the open back. It flopped down, coming to rest halfway between the wagon's base and the ground. Caroline visibly tensed, then went to follow Robert. Annie grabbed her arm.

"Oh, but Robert's rules. The company member inside is not to be disturbed!"

"If the blanket's down," Caroline said grimly, "he needs disturbing more than anything." Annie released her grip as Caroline followed Robert, pointedly swept the blanket aside and climbed into the wagon. The blanket dropped silently back into place.

Shit. Shit. SHIT! Thomas pinched the bridge of his nose. They had come so far! He turned to Annie who just stood there, looking lost. "Take the fiddle to the square. We *shall* find our audience." Lord, he wished he believed his own words. "I'll knock on every door and have my brother assist us. We can do this – yes? Yes?"

Annie nodded, picked up her fiddle and headed towards the carriage arch.

Thomas turned his back on the painfully silent wagon and headed for the back door into the kitchen, praying he did not run into his pa. Fortune smiled upon him for the first time that day, as he darted through the inn unhindered. He galloped up the narrow attic stairway two steps a time, setting his sights upon Benedict's door. He pushed down the thumb-latch and burst into the room.

Benedict sat at his little table by the window, directly opposite the doorway, with paper in front of him and a quill rising from the inkpot. He jumped with a strange, almost guilty expression as Thomas strode in. Benedict looked back in dismay at the splattering of ink over the paper.

"It is simple," he said, slamming down his quill and standing up. "You make a fist, and you bang on the door."

Thomas marched towards him. There was no time for nonsense. He grabbed his brother's upper arms, ignoring his brother's sigh.

"Listen, I am in need of your assistance!"

"*How* much longer are you staying?"

"We must attract more people to our play, or I fear the tightrope act will draw them instead—"

"Tightrope act?"

"Keep up, Benedict! It runs tonight! At precisely the same time as our show! Have you not heard?"

"No, because I have had other matters to attend to and my life does not revolve around a stage."

Thomas sighed impatiently. Why was his brother always so unhelpful? "Well, never mind. It's not too late to start helping now."

Benedict wriggled out of Thomas' grip. He had a slightly odd expression on his face that Thomas could not read. "Sorry, Tom. I have urgent business."

Thomas threw his hands into the air. "What? *This* is urgent business! Why do you fail to understand?" He waved towards the paper on the table. "You sit there, writing pointless love poems to a woman who will never be yours!"

"You are wrong," said Benedict quietly, sitting back down at the table. "On both counts."

"Listen! This is my hour of need!"

"Oh, the entire clock is your hour of need!"

Thomas clasped his hands together. "I ask only for you to go and speak word of the play tonight! Is that too much to ask?"

Benedict's shoulders sagged in defeat, as they always did in the end. "Fine. I am writing this letter first and then I will help you."

Thank Heaven! "Make haste, then," Thomas said, striding for the bedroom door.

"And you owe me money!" came Benedict's voice behind him, but it warranted no reply.

Thomas began walking down the narrow attic staircase, hearing Benedict's exasperated sigh and the scrape of his bedroom door shutting. Benedict was proving himself very useful indeed, just as Thomas had hoped. He would miss the help Benedict provided once the company had moved on. He paused for a moment and brought out the watch from his jacket pocket.

RICHARD III ACT 1 SCENE 4...

I am his brother...

It was fortunate indeed that he hadn't sold the pocket watch. Benedict may have been less willing to help if he had. Thomas tucked the watch away and made his way back to the main room, dotted with customers. He collected a couple of three-legged stools for the audience and passed through the kitchen. It was just a few hours before they were due to begin. Usually, he loved the thrill of the show, the eyes of an audience fixed upon him, but today, he wished the applause had already sounded so they could count their money, spend it wisely and head for the fair.

He entered the yard and positioned the stools opposite the stage. He studied the boards, and an unexpected pang caught him off-guard. It had been such a glorious boyhood dream – that he and Benedict would travel together, reciting Shakespeare to anyone who would listen. But his brother had chosen his own path – and a foolish one at that. Still, no doubt it was merely a boyish fancy brought on by boredom, and likely soon to pass, for all his brother's nonsensical talk of lasting love. It was a shame. Benedict would have revelled in the stage. Maybe he might gain a new appreciation for it after watching their show tonight. He drummed his fingers against his legs. Lord, he had better find his Prince of Denmark before six o'clock. His shoulders slumped at Robert's suggestion that if he did not, he should trade places with the skull.

It sat there on the stage with the props. Thomas narrowed his eyes. How the *Hell* had she got her hands on that? He went over to it, picked it up, and stared into its eyeless sockets. Life was tragically short, was it not? Who had belonged it to? Had they once been filled with dreams, and had they ever achieved them? Had they chased their ambition enough, fought enough, sacrificed enough before they shuffled off this mortal coil? He would bloody well make sure that *he* had, before life made Yoricks of them all.

CHAPTER 23: Piero

Piero's pale green eyes stared back at him from the round mirror propped up against the wall. It was time for the finishing touches. He sat at the table in his room. His make-up had been removed for a clean, bold application, and he could see the terrible nakedness in his unpainted face – the vulnerability, the weakness of being revealed as he truly was... and he hated it.

Yet still, he would pause and look on occasion. Sometimes to reassure himself of the benefit of becoming who he was now; sometimes just to see whether that unpainted boy was still in there or if he had been truly lost for ever. That boy who had once dared to trust and love; betrayed by his own sister when she had caught him wearing her clothes, admiring his reflection in the silver-framed mirror in her bedchamber. Something about it had made him feel like he could breathe more easily. Like part of him was staring back with bold truth. He could still remember turning around in panic, frozen in fear, when he saw her reflection behind him, open-mouthed.

Of course, his pleas for secrecy were to no avail, and the consequences... most severe. It was not the last time he was betrayed. Whatever had happened to the poor man he had been caught with in the stables? And it was not the last time others wounded him.

Every hurt, every betrayal weighed him down with hate and shame. It was far safer to hide away his naked, unpainted reflection, and never let a single soul gaze upon it, including himself. And yet, on occasion he would find himself looking... longing... searching. But never for too long.

So, he reached for his little tin of purple powder, dipped his fingertips in and smeared them across his eyelids and just beyond. The terrible feeling of being lost instantly began to fade, and the boards beneath his feet began to reappear. He opened a little box of rouge and swished his little brush into the mix. Then he swept it lightly over his cheekbone—

Robert's breath was warm in his ear... fingertips gently brushed his cheekbone... then his lips.

No.

He closed his eyes for a moment. He performed the same little ritual he used whenever he became... lost. He tilted his head away, as if to remove himself from the thought, then he inhaled and exhaled deeply. He opened his eyes again, and stared defiantly back into the mirror, forcing his eyes to shine darker, harder, more dangerous. Satisfied, he brushed the other cheek. Finally, he painted his lips a brazen scarlet and smiled at the face in the mirror. The boy was nowhere to be seen, and the showman was ready to play. And what a game it would be tonight.

He pulled his black jacket on over his white shirt, giving the pocket inside a little pat. He headed for the staircase, his strut becoming more pronounced, his confidence growing with every stair he descended, so by the time he opened the front door and burst out into the street with a flourish, he was ready and hungry for his audience.

"Come along, ladies and gentlemen, come along!" Piero called into the modest warmth of the evening. He raised his perfectly positioned arms and twirled around on the spot, flashing his painted smile to the people in the market square, particularly the young gentleman in the blue jacket and exceptionally tight breeches. "Come in, one and all, and witness the most incredible, most amazing tightrope act! Purchase your drinks at the bar, friends, then come through to the yard! Fifteen minutes, my good people!"

He gave another little flourish, pleased at the already-bubbling murmur and the stream of people heading for the door. Oh, and there was Squire Bickford and his steward making their way towards the Angel. He smiled. Attendance from the authorities. Their act had taken the town, then. He must remember to mention that little fact to Robert. He would exchange pleasantries with the squire later, but first, he needed to prepare. He headed down the brown and grey stone wall of the inn to the yard at the rear. It paid to ensure everything was in order before he went on his errand.

He stood at the tall wooden gate in the wall and gently twisted the iron ring. Silently, he inched it open and peeped into the yard. The tightrope stretched between two huge x-shaped frames at either end. A ladder rested against the left-hand side of the supporting frames, and it was up this ladder now that Angelo climbed. He reached the top, checked the fastening of the rope and checked it again. Then he climbed down three or four rungs, paused, climbed back up again, checked the rope and checked it again... He rested his head against the ladder, trying to bring his fast breathing under control.

Piero fought against the pang of sympathy which reared, and he won. He always won. If Angelo did not want to work with the act, then he was free to walk away any time. Piero had suggested as much to Maria, believing it would certainly make his own life easier. But she had insisted that they came as a pair. And as much as it clearly agonised Angelo to perform his duties, he showed too much loyalty and care to leave his beloved older sister to go forth alone or place her life in another man's hands. Piero snorted. Loyalty and care... Maria's family was clearly very different from his own.

He watched as Maria walked over to Angelo. Lord, she was beautiful. Her locks were twisted on top of her head, and she wore a black sleeveless outfit adorned with tiny circles of shining mirror glass which sparkled in the evening sun. The outfit was cut low and extended down over her hips and the top of her legs. Black ribbons tied in a bow over each shoulder.

"Angelo," she said impatiently, standing at the foot of the ladder. Her voice softened. "I promise you the tightrope is fine. The tightrope is always fine." Angelo climbed down and took his sister's hands. His look was pleading but she returned a confident smile. "You shall not have to catch me because I shall not fall." She looked around. "Have you seen Piero? The show begins soon."

Piero quickly slipped away. All was ready, all was well. He had time then, for his errand, just as he had planned. He held his head high, strutting down through the market square and merrily directing people up towards the Angel and–

Shit!

Annie skipped through the square, playing a merry jig on her fiddle and calling as she went, "Hamlet! The one with the skull! At the Star Inn, ten minutes!"

It was of utmost importance they did not speak. He ducked away to the side of the square, passing on the far side of customers heading for the Angel, nodding politely as they went, then turning his face away so Annie would not see him. He reached the carriage arch of the Star and slipped into the yard. Barely a dozen people holding tankards – ten of whom were already pissed by the look and smell of it. They sat opposite the stage, which was positioned near the stables, facing the inn. Upon the stage was a thin wooden frame which held the green curtain. He narrowed his eyes. He had bought that with coins from his own purse.

The wagon stood between the stage and the carriage arch, parallel with the stone wall. The back faced the rear-side of the stage behind the curtain, probably acting as a dressing room. Was his dress in there somewhere, perhaps? He slunk along beside the stone wall as the voices of Caroline and the new lead actor came from the wagon.

"Gravedigging is absolutely cheating!" complained the man.

"How can it be cheating if we set no rules?" came Caroline's argumentative voice. "Just because you didn't think of it."

"I did think of it–"

"No, you didn't."

"—and decided it was cheating."

Piero rolled his eyes. Lord above. How in Heaven's name did Robert tolerate them? The agitation in their voices betrayed their nervousness, but he soon lost interest in them. For there was Robert – his slender form standing alone behind the curtained stage, hidden from the noisy audience. One arm was folded across his waist, his other hand raised to his mouth, biting his fingernails. He was also nervous, then. But what exactly was he thinking? Robert's thoughts... locked away and unreachable as they always had been. Piero crept silently, on the boards which lived beneath his feet, until he was so close to Robert that if he had wanted to, Piero could have leaned forwards... stretched out his fingers... nearly touched him...

But the stage was set for a different scene.

Piero casually strolled the last two steps and adopted an innocent expression for the audience who would never see it.

"I came to wish you luck," he announced as Robert startled and faced him. "I presume you still believe in such nonsense."

Robert caught his breath and looked away. "Go and play with your new friends. I shall not speak with you."

Piero pouted his scarlet lips. "Oh, you are no fun any more, Robert. We used to have such fun. And to think I brought you a gift!" He reached inside his pocket for the weapon. Then in a swift movement, he shot forwards, grabbed Robert's hand and slammed the peacock feather into it. "Alas and alack! The evil eye! What was I thinking?" he said in feigned horror as Robert stood paralysed. The rage sang out in his lowered voice. "What. Bad. Luck."

Robert still stared, speechless at the feather in his hand.

"Speaking of which, don't expect the squire and his steward to be in your audience. For some reason it is *our* spectacular show which has taken the town and not yours." He shrugged. "I said I came to wish you luck." He began strutting away, throwing in a little swing of his hips for good measure. "I merely did not specify which kind."

He glanced over his shoulder, and smiled his scarlet smile. "Enjoy your show."

Piero slipped back past the wagon, the bickering voices unaware of the fine performance they had missed.

He strutted on to the Angel Inn.

It was on with the show.

Because it was always on with the fucking show.

CHAPTER 24: Benedict

His brother's show alone was helpful, but having two performances distracting the town was an absolute gift. No one would notice them as they slipped away. Once they had left, once the secret was revealed, there would be no coming back. But they had made their choices. They could not stay here; they could not give up this chance. And it had to be tonight.

Benedict looked around his bedroom, a lump in his throat. The only home he had ever known. He laid his sack onto his crumpled bedsheets. Everything was packed and prepared... everything except for his orange neckerchief. He dropped to his knees and searched one more time beneath his bed. Where was it to? He should have liked to take it as a reminder of home, and it saddened him that he could not find it.

Home had been a strange place, even more so since Thomas had left, but Ma loved him and tried her best. And Pa? Well, the inn meant everything to him, and perhaps in his own way he thought he was doing what was right. He would probably be devastated to discover there were no sons left to inherit. Perhaps the inn would pass onto his Uncle Henry. Benedict shrugged. It mattered not. All he cared about was his future with Sarah, and he had the feeling that once he left, he would suddenly realise what it was like to breathe. He sat back on his heels. Perhaps this was how Thomas had felt two years ago when he had crept away under cover of darkness, without a word.

Thomas. He walked over to the folded letter on the table by the window. He opened it, pointlessly brushing the dried splats of ink caused by his brother's earlier and unnecessarily dramatic entrance. He read once more its simple but heartfelt words.

I must follow my heart.

Richard III Act one, Scene four.

"I am his brother..."

Always.

Farewell.

He swallowed, feeling the weight of the words in his heart, then folded the letter slowly and placed it back on the table. Thomas would find it next time he charged into his room unannounced and uninvited. There was a prickle of irritation – Thomas would probably charge straight back out again, leaving his bedroom door wide open for ever.

In some ways his brother's return was timely – a chance for Benedict to say a final farewell before he disappeared into the world, unlike his brother's sudden departure. Their paths would separate for good as they followed their own hearts. Yet it would be easier if Tom hadn't returned. It wasn't just that being in his presence reminded him of happier times which had long-since gone, but his brother had been there almost all his life. Tom filled a part of his heart reserved only for a brother, and which simply could not be filled by anyone else.

He would miss Tom indeed, despite the man's utter conviction that the world revolved around *him*, his inability to knock although *everyone else managed it*, his insistence that they always did things *his way*, the manner in which he always grabbed Benedict's arms so he couldn't move just because what Thomas had to say was absolutely definitely the *most important thing* in the world.

He gave a little wistful smile. Perhaps he wouldn't miss Thomas as much as he thought. He picked up his sack, slung it over his shoulder and walked to his bedroom door. He opened it slowly, then with a murmured, "Goodbye," closed the door behind him. His new life with the one he loved began right now.

The main room was empty, just as he had hoped. Anyone at the Star tonight was in the yard, and judging by the raucous and provocative noise of a handful of voices, they had drunk a lot before they had stepped outside. Well, at least that would please Pa. As he crossed the floor, the ghosts of his memories danced around him. Running to the kitchen door, nine-year-old Thomas pulling his hand, saying the players were doing *Romeo and Juliet*. Tiptoeing towards the bar as older lads, sneaking drinks by candlelight. Watching powerless as Pa's fist sent Thomas to the floor, his brother's blood speckling the scripts scattered around him... Benedict made it to the front door, and gave one last look over his shoulder. He had never felt so free.

As he slipped outside, the floating song of the fiddle reached his ears, coming from the market square. It was the red-haired woman from Thomas' company – he had seen her in the yard from his window. She played a merry jig, skipping and calling in a slightly desperate voice, "Hamlet! The one with the skull! The Star Inn, five minutes!"

He cast his eyes quickly about the square. It was fairly empty, with the remaining people scurrying towards the north end of town. If he made haste, with his head down, perhaps the woman wouldn't notice him—

"Oooh!" cried a triumphant voice. "Now you *must* be Thomas Cooper's brother!"

Perhaps not. He looked up to find the woman scurrying over with a warm smile.

"Such is my misfortune," said Benedict lightly. "I regret I cannot stop and—"

"I'd recognise you even without the neckerchief."

Benedict smiled politely. Where *had* he put that?

"It's your hair and your eyes, all brown and sparkly." The woman frowned. "Well, the eyes are brown and sparkly. The hair is just brown."

Benedict frowned. "Er... yes."

He glanced up the street, towards the carpenter's workshop. "Forgive me, I cannot–"

"Are you coming to the show? It's nearly on." Her eyes shone. "And we have a real human skull."

"O-h-h-h-h," said Benedict. It was probably better that he didn't know too much about that. "I regret I cannot, I must meet someone urgently."

She nodded and looked a little downcast. Benedict twisted his mouth at the stab of guilt.

"I am truly sorry," said Benedict. "I would have loved to see the show. But I wish you all every success." The words stuck in his throat a little. "Would you tell Thomas I've left him a note in my bedroom? And tell him to forget about the money he owes me. Although he probably already has." Benedict gave her an appreciative nod and managed to walk a couple of yards before a nagging thought defeated him. He turned back to face her. "Please – if he ever goes to sell his pocket watch, would you try and stop him?"

The woman nodded again. "Of course. It's a lovely watch." Then she began fiddling another merry tune, skipping off towards the archway to the Star.

So, this was it.

Excitement, fear, joy flowed through every step he took towards Mr Jones' workshop. He had nearly reached it. Was Sarah there already, waiting for him? He crept down the track, checking over his shoulder as he went. Their story would have the perfect ending. He smiled as he approached, heart thumping, hopes high. There was a glorious lightness in his soul for the first time in his life. He darted around the back of the stone building.

Sarah...?

He forgot how to breathe.

Marcus.

And a broad, thickset man he recognised as Marcus' groom nearby.

His legs could no longer move.

The groom grabbed him by his jacket and slammed him backwards: a thud of skull against stone.

Everything... spinning.

Rough hands releasing him. His back bouncing down stone wall. Another thud. Arse on ground.

Marcus' blurry face... "Mr Cooper, you have made a serious error, and if you so much as glance in my wife's direction again—"

Sarah...

"The consequences will be most unfortunate. I hope we understand each other."

Orange neckerchief dropping into his lap...

"You should look after your belongings, Mr Cooper. I assure you I shall take greater care of what belongs to me." Boots moving. "Deliver the message lightly, Turner. He *is* but a young fool." Footsteps walking away.

Being dragged upwards... feet scrabbling for ground... "Please," he whispered.

The groom's fist pulling back.

Oh—

CHAPTER 25: Thomas

Shit.

The peacock feather in Robert's hand so close to the stage was extremely bad news. They needed to concentrate on their performance, not be distracted by such nonsense. Robert paced up and down behind the stage with Caroline trying to pacify him as she prepared her Ghost costume. Clearly, Piero knew exactly what he was doing.

Thomas smoothed down the black breeches and shirt he wore and grabbed the skull. He needed to focus; needed to think Prince of Denmark thoughts.

"Hamlet-Hamlet-Hamlet-Hamlet," he muttered.

"It is just a feather from a bird," said Caroline.

"It is *not* just a feather from a bird!"

"Hamlet-Hamlet-Hamlet-Hamlet." Thomas glared at the unhelpful skull. It really should be making more effort.

"And it won't count, Robert. You said he wasn't actually on the stage."

"No, but he was bloody looking at it!"

Oh, for Heaven's sake! Clearly, there was no point him trying to think about the Prince of Denmark when all everyone else could think about was their erstwhile lead bloody actor. Thomas slammed the skull down harder than necessary on the portion of stage behind the green curtain. A tooth fell out.

Caroline snatched the feather from Robert and tossed it into the wagon. "Do not dwell on it. That's exactly what he wants. And where the Hell is Annie?" She went over to the curtain nailed to the top of the frame, fingers poised to peep, but Robert pulled her back.

"It's bad luck to look! Do you really think we need any more of that?"

"Do you really think matters can get any worse?"

Thomas pinched the bridge of his nose. The crowd was restless and judging by the smell hanging in the air, Pa had already provided refreshment enough to cause trouble. "Listen, we cannot wait for Annie," he said, turning to Robert. "We need to start now, or we'll lose them."

Robert nodded at Caroline. "Do the introduction."

Caroline brushed down her pale cloak, then stepped from behind the green curtain onto the stage. She was welcomed by a raucous noise, which wasn't exactly a cheer, but at least wasn't a boo.

"Welcome to the Ticehurst Players' performance of Hamlet!" came her voice, fighting against the noise.

"Where's your tightrope?" called someone in the crowd.

Thomas' shoulders sagged.

"Annie!" hissed Robert, looking beyond Thomas. "Come on, quickly."

Thomas gave a sigh of relief as Annie came skipping in and placed her fiddle by the curtain. He fetched the grey cloak laid out in the wagon. "What took you so long?"

"I saw your brother, but he can't come," she said.

Thomas' mouth dropped open as he draped the costume over her shoulders. "What do you mean, 'can't come'? Can't come to his own brother's show in his own back yard? What else could be that important?" He tutted irritably. "If this is to do with that woman—"

“He did say he had to meet someone urgently,” said Annie. She fastened the cloak at her throat.

“I knew it!”

“And he’s left you a note.”

“It had better be an extremely long apology – in rhyming bloody couplets!” Thomas put his hands on his hips. His brother had truly taken leave of his senses.

“Never mind your brother!” said Robert. “Concentrate.” He and Annie both stepped up onto the stage to take their positions.

“*Who’s there?*” said Annie from the stage.

“*Nay,*” said Robert, “*answer me: stand and unfold yourself.*”

A movement to the left past the wagon caught Thomas’ eye. He turned his head to see Marcus – Marcus! – stopping expectantly by the wall. This was going to be awkward.

“Good evening,” said Thomas, feigning a smile as he went over. “You have come to see the show?”

Marcus fixed him with a stern look. “Sarah is my wife, and I will treat her with all the love and respect she deserves.”

Thomas’ heart leapt to his mouth. Marcus knew?

“Please assure him that if he goes near her again, I will not be responsible for my actions.”

Robert pushed back through the green curtain with a dark expression and stepped down. “Trouble?”

“You will find your brother behind Mr Jones’ workshop,” said Marcus.

Thomas swallowed. Benedict... Oh shit.

“I would not leave it too long.” Marcus marched away. And where he had been, eight-year-old Benedict now stood, his face bloody and bruised, just like the day–

A growl of frustration and fear rushed up Thomas' throat. He threw Robert an apologetic look and turned towards the arch – there was a tug on his shirt and Robert pulled him back.

"Don't you bloody dare!"

But the image of his little brother burned too deeply in his mind. Thomas wrestled away from Robert, and ran for the arch, with Robert's furious words hissing after him, "Get your arse back here!"

Anger swiftly began arguing with his fear as Thomas raced towards the workshop. Why the Hell did it have to be *now*? How could his brother be so foolish? Did he truly not think all this would come crashing down around him? Thomas had warned him, and now his brother's idiotic behaviour was jeopardising the show he so desperately needed. By the time he reached the workshop, fear was defeated, and anger was well and truly victorious.

He ran around behind the stone building, past the planks and half-built coffins leaning against the wall. There was Marcus' groom – bigger than Thomas in every direction – and Benedict curled up on the ground – blood streaming from his head, his nose – the groom aiming a kick—

"NO!" Thomas yelled, hurling his weight against the man.

The force, and perhaps the surprise, knocked the groom backwards a step. Thomas readied his fists: oh, he was in the mood for a fight.

The groom glowered at him. "Marcus be a good man, but don' you make him deliver this message twice." He gave Thomas and Benedict a parting glare, then walked away.

His heart racing, Thomas dropped to Benedict's side and grabbed the orange neckerchief beside him.

"Oh, you fucking idiot!" A swelling on his brother's forehead seemed to be bleeding the worst. With shaking hands, he pressed the neckerchief against the wound.

"Tom... Sarah..." whispered Benedict. The look in his eyes made Thomas' insides twist, but he chose to ignore it.

"Shut up!" He lifted the neckerchief to examine the cut. The blood still flowed freely. Thomas sighed and pressed the neckerchief again to his brother's head. Oh, Ma was going to kill Benedict. And as for Pa... It didn't warrant thinking about. And Robert was going to kill Thomas. So was Caroline. Annie would cry. How could he possibly focus on his performance now? Everything was ruined.

Thomas' mind reeled at all the terrible consequences of his brother's poor choices. Benedict was still curled up and breathing fast, but Thomas examined his injuries. Bleeding nose, nasty cut on the bump beneath the neckerchief, a few small grazes on his face, no doubt a sore stomach. Not pleasant but—

"You got off far more lightly than you deserved." Anger still roared through him. "Come on, I'm late! Get up!"

He thrust the scarlet-stained neckerchief into Benedict's hand and hauled him with some effort to his feet. He slung his brother's arm over his shoulders, then they staggered out into the street. A jubilant cheer and tormenting applause floated down from the Angel.

"Oh, hurry up!" snapped Thomas. "And don't you dare drip blood on my Hamlet costume." With every step they took, his mood darkened and the voice in his head grew louder.

You're naught but a failure.

After what seemed forever, they made it through the arch to the yard. Thomas dragged Benedict over to the wagon, grateful that at least the drunken audience hadn't noticed their arrival.

Annie ran over, eyes wide and worried. "What happened?"

"Not now!" Thomas unhooked Benedict's arm from his shoulder, stepping back swiftly as drops of blood narrowly avoided Hamlet's shirt.

"You missed your part, Thomas! We stopped the show and did a song. Robert's ever so cross!"

Why did this have to happen? Thomas roughly propped his brother inside the wagon, beside the costumes laid out in preparation. "Just stay there on your stupid arse!" He snatched the neckerchief from Benedict's limp hand and threw it at Annie. "For Heaven's sake, do not let him bleed all over Ophelia's dress."

He dashed to the stage and brushed the curtain aside with fingers wet and sticky with his brother's blood. Caroline and Robert stood looking furious as Thomas caught his breath and whispered urgently, "Where are we?"

"Just do scene two," said Robert, tight-lipped.

Scene two... Scene two... Thomas opened his mouth—

An egg flew towards him and met its target. Thomas froze as the smelly sogginess splatted over the Prince of Denmark's breeches and slid slowly towards the boards. There was a cheer and a raise of tankards from the audience, followed by Ma's reprimanding voice, "JAMES!"

Thomas' chest heaved. Burning, prickling tears stung at his eyes. Why was it all so unfair? He tried so bloody hard. But the show must go on. He blinked furiously, wiped his blood-smeared hands on his breeches and pushed his feelings to whatever dark corners he could find.

He turned to the pitifully small audience, heart sinking at the rotten vegetables and tankards in their hands.

"*But now,*" Robert said loudly, "*my cousin Hamlet and my son.*"

"*A little more than kin, and less than kind,*" said Thomas, facing Robert. Wait – that was meant to be an aside. What was he doing? His scattered thoughts flew shouting in every direction. Benedict's blood. Rotten eggs. The Prince of Denmark. Pa.

You're naught but a failure.

"*How is it that the clouds still hang on you?*" Robert said with burning eyes and tense shoulders, for all the good actor that he was.

Thomas opened his mouth. Words abandoned him. He searched and searched for his line, but there was naught but deathly blankness. Like the eye-sockets of the skull. He shook his head and whispered, "I... do not know."

"He don't know!" hooted someone. The audience burst into laughter.

"My totter-legged pig could perform better than that!" jeered a man as more eggs launched at the stage.

A horrible hotness spread up Thomas' neck, across his face, and threatened to consume him entirely.

"Where's the skull?" called a woman. "We want to see the skull!"

"Do... the... skull," said Robert as he walked off the stage, followed by Caroline, who refused to even look at him. Oh, his brother had so much to answer for! Caroline marched back over and slammed the skull into his hand. Another tooth fell out. He snatched a breath, then faced the audience. He could do this. He held the skull aloft in his left hand, clutched in his blood-stained fingers.

"Alas, poor Yorick! I knew him, Horatio: a fellow of infinite jest, of most excellent fancy: he hath...borne me on his back a thousand times..."

And he had spoken these words a thousand times, yet all he could conjure in his mind was the image of a broken, bloodied Benedict ... not the lines he needed to speak.

"Let the skull do it!" someone yelled.

A potato hurtled towards his hand. There was a thump – the skull went flying out of his hand.

Thomas gasped as the audience whooped and applauded, despite another scolding cry of, "JAMES!" He frantically chased the rolling skull across the stage, reaching for it with shaking, scarlet, clawing fingers and wishing he could throw it back at his father. Heart pounding, he stood his ground, raised the skull again and tried desperately – Lord, so desperately – to save something of this moment. But there was nothing, just nothing left to save.

"Where be your gibes now? Your... your gambols? Your songs?" he shouted pointlessly over the booing audience.

His voice dropped in defeat.

"Your flashes of merriment..."

Benedict was broken. He himself was broken. What the Hell had happened to them both? Was this really the answer to their dreams? He let the arm holding the skull flop to his side, and knowing no one could hear him anyway, he whispered,

"That were wont to set the table on a roar?"

There was no Theatre Royal before his eyes. Just the humble yard of a pestilent inn where an audience was so uninterested that even the rotten cabbages had ceased to fly. A few people staggered out, and he heard the words, "tightrope" and "refund". Yet there was one person looking directly at the stage, meeting Thomas' tear-filled eyes with his gaze, smiling darkly, and more than satisfied with the performance which had been delivered.

Robert and Caroline stormed over, with Annie scurrying behind.

"JUST... DIE!" Robert instructed Thomas and Annie, eyes sparking with sadness and rage.

Annie laid down on the boards and Thomas joined her, lying with his back to the audience. He felt the warm boards beneath his cheek, saw the blood on his fingers curled around the skull, heard the drunken laughter of the people behind him, thought of his brother in the wagon...

"*Take up the bodies,*" said Robert's defeated voice. "*Such a sight as this becomes the field, but here shows much amiss. Go, bid the soldiers shoot.*"

Then Robert's shoes marched past his face.

"I think they've finished," said a voice.

Someone cheered. "To the tightrope act!"

Stools scraped on the ground. One person clapped politely. He guessed his ma. Then a second person clapped slowly... loudly... deliberately... presumably to ensure every meeting of his disapproving hands resounded for ever in Thomas' ears. And as he listened to that terrible, echoing sound, Thomas would gladly have traded places with the skull.

CHAPTER 26: Thomas

Knowing what awaited him behind the curtain, lying dead on the stage was without question the wiser choice, but slowly and reluctantly, Thomas dragged his body up from the boards. His heart sank: Ma was heading over. He quickly hid his blood-smeared fingers behind his back. Far better she knew nothing about the condition of her younger son. He attempted a smile.

"Did you enjoy the show?"

"Yes, that were..." began Ma, then frowned. "What *were* that?"

"Oh... We – we like to experiment."

"Yes." And there was a weight of doubt in the word. "Well, at some point, you'll have your fill of experimentin', an' when that time comes, don't fret – your pa'll always find barrels for 'ee to roll." It sounded like a death sentence.

"Thanks, Ma," said Thomas. They needed a trap door for the stage so it could just swallow him whole.

Ma's face brightened. "Can't be stoppin'. Your pa's already gone to the tightrope act. Never seen a tightrope walker afore! Proper exciting it be. And folk are sayin' their showman could charm the very birds from them trees!" She patted Thomas on the shoulder and scurried off through the archway.

"Thanks, Ma," he said flatly to the empty yard. His pa had led the vegetable assault, his ma was more interested in the rival act, and his brother... Oh, Lord... His head dropped to his chest for a moment, then he made his way with heavy feet behind the stage to the wagon to deal with the next problem on his increasingly long list.

Robert stood leaning against the stone wall of the yard, face in hands. Caroline stood beside him, holding the pottery takings box and looking like she would prefer it to be a hammer. Annie sat on the edge of the wagon and looked up sadly at Thomas. He placed the skull carefully on the boards behind the curtain in an attempt to preserve its few remaining teeth, then headed over.

"He's sleeping," Annie said. "Tended him best I could."

Thomas gave a little nod. He peered inside the wagon. There was the idiot, eyes closed, motionless, with the blue bow on Ophelia's dress beside him splattered with his blood. For Heaven's sake! Even unconscious, his brother had managed to worsen matters!

Caroline held the takings box aloft. "Well," she said, her voice dripping with fury, "shall we?"

"Is there any point?" said Robert. He dropped his hands from his face, and they fell to his sides.

"Maybe things are not as bad as they seem," said Thomas, out of habit rather than conviction.

Caroline hurled the box to the ground, harder than necessary. A deafening smash echoed in the abandoned yard and shattered the remaining hope that Thomas so desperately clung to. A handful of coins and a button sat amongst the shards. Thomas' eyes began to swim as he stared down.

"And there's three people waiting in the street for their money back," said Annie.

"How will we even pay the performers' fee at the fair with this?" raged Caroline. "And we were a laughingstock, Thomas! The only reason they will gather around us at the fair will be to rid themselves of unwanted vegetables!" She put her hands on her hips. "Shall we draw Lord Pelham's attention to that?"

"You do not understand what happened!" Thomas said. "I had to go to him. He is family!"

"This company is a family!" snapped Caroline. "Or it was! But don't worry, because at this rate, you will have plenty of time to spend at home with yours."

"Enough," said Robert quietly.

Caroline walked over to Thomas until her face was just inches away. He held her gaze, absorbing her fury, as he deserved. "I detest Piero with all my heart. But you are not half the lead actor that he was."

Robert cast her a stern look. "I said enough!"

"And *I* said you put too much trust in him!"

Thomas pressed his trembling lips together. The words pierced deeper than a blade, and it hurt even more that Robert spoke no word in reply.

"Come on, Annie," Caroline said sharply as Annie scrabbled to pick out the coins and the button from the ground. "Show me who you said could have their money back." She glared at Thomas, then shepherded Annie away.

The man Thomas had wanted so desperately to impress stood there still, looking at him with a mixture of devastation and disappointment. "Robert..." Thomas began, unsure what would follow.

Robert shook his head. "We shall speak later." Then he walked off alone towards the stables.

Was it possible to feel any worse than this? Thomas looked at Benedict with increasingly blurring eyes. He needed to wake his brother and drag him up two flights of stairs before Ma came back. But all he could do was slump onto the stage behind the curtain, close his eyes in despair and let his mind turn over and over the disastrous events of the night.

"Problem?" said a playful voice which barely contained its delight.

Thomas startled and looked up.

Piero stood opposite him, leaning casually against the yard wall, arms folded. "Robert's not the easiest person to get on with, is he? Never listens when you try to explain. Refuses to change his mind. Pushes you away when you try to draw close." He unfolded his arms and raised them in despair. "And Lord, the moods!" He folded his arms back across his chest. "To be fair, he does make up for it in other areas." Piero looked at him intently, watching, waiting.

Thomas could not summon the strength for a fight. "What do you want?"

Piero kicked away from the wall and strutted towards him. "Merely to congratulate you on your show. I love what you did with the..." He peered past the green curtain and glanced doubtfully at the stage. "... Cabbages."

Thomas sighed.

As Piero rotated, his eyes widened at something he saw in the wagon, and he moved swiftly towards it. Thomas leapt to his feet, body tense. What was he doing? Piero lifted Benedict's leg up in the air with one hand and slid out the blood-flecked costume with the other. With a dramatic flourish, he let Benedict's leg fall with a careless thump onto the wagon, causing Benedict to moan and stir slightly. Thomas tracked the man's every moment, his heart beginning to pound.

Piero folded the costume delicately over his arm. "No one," he said in a low and menacing voice, "*no one* touches my dress. Nor do they carelessly spill blood upon it." The gaze from his pale eyes was dangerous and piercing.

Was he going to punish Benedict? Thomas edged closer to his brother and stood between him and Piero's wrath. Of all the times for his brother to be unhelpfully unconscious.

"You're new," said Piero, "and I suspect you have a great deal to learn. So, just this once, I shall accept a heartfelt apology."

Thomas gritted his teeth. "Then... my apologies."

Piero tutted. "Heavens above, surely you can do better than that. You are the lead actor, are you not? I said *heartfelt*."

“My... apologies.” His feigned sincerity brimmed with frustration. No wonder Caroline hated this man.

“There!” Piero’s countenance brightened in a startling change of demeanour. “Practice makes perfect, does it not? You clearly have a wonderful career ahead of you. And since we are friends once more, I have some good news to impart. We shall see you at Thorverton Fair.”

The fair? He was going to the...? Why was their path bedevilled with such persistent ill fortune? He wanted to shout, wanted to rant at this man. But he did not have any words left, so he said nothing.

“I hear Lord Pelham seeks an act to patronise. Robert must be devastated after losing his patron.” Piero shook his head sadly. “Truly, a shame. But...” He pointed a finger in the air. “... it need not mean the end for you all. Admittedly my act will likely acquire Lord Pelham’s patronage, and gain security, finances, opportunities and fame. But fear not, *you’ll* still have...” His voice faded away. He frowned and tapped his finger thoughtfully against his cheek, then gave a slight shrug. He spun on his heel and strutted towards the arch, the costume still draped over his arm. Piero paused, and he placed a hand on the blood-stained bow. Then without turning around, he murmured, “Send my love to Robert.”

Thomas clenched his fists as Piero sauntered through the archway and into the square. He roared through his tightened jaw and kicked the wagon wheel. Pain shot through his foot, but he cared not. What the Hell would the others say when he told them he had just let Piero walk away with their best costume? Benedict stirred again. Thomas glared at him. To think he had once dreamed of travelling the country in the company of this man! Judging by his brother’s poor decisions and reckless actions, Thomas had probably been spared a miserable fate! He launched himself into the back of the wagon and shook his brother’s shoulder furiously.

“Wake the Hell up!”

And he hardly waited for Benedict to open his eyes before dragging him away. It took longer than he hoped to get Benedict up all the stairs, but Thomas refused to feel gratitude towards the tightrope walker distracting his parents. In Benedict's bedroom, Thomas hurled his brother onto the messy bed. It was by luck rather than judgement that Benedict's head met his pillow.

"Do you understand what you have done? We needed that show, Benedict!" he said. He yanked his brother's shoes off and flung them, one and then the other, across the room, caring not for any damage they might cause. The first shoe landed on the chair and the second hit the table. Something fluttered down onto the floorboards and caught Thomas' eye: a piece of folded paper with a single word written upon its folded side.

Thomas.

Thomas paused in his wrath. What was that? He went over, picked it up with blood-stained fingers and unfolded it.

I must follow my heart.

Richard III Act one, Scene four.

"I am his brother..."

Always.

Farewell.

Without warning, Thomas' legs lacked the strength they needed, as if all the devastation from the evening bore down upon them at last. He let himself flop onto the floor, sitting with his head in his hand. He stared at the letter and read the words over and over. Once upon a simpler time they had been two brothers on a stage, two boys up a tree, enjoying each other's company. Where had it all gone wrong? He glanced back at Benedict. His brother's face was screwed up with discomfort and pain. Thomas sighed deeply, exhaling all the frustration in the world. He lifted his eyes to the heavens, although chances were, he was beyond help from there now. Perhaps they both were.

He tucked the letter into the pocket of his breeches and went to a low chest of drawers in the far corner. A pitcher of water stood atop the chest, beside a bowl and washcloth. Thomas poured some water into the bowl and brought it over to the bed. He perched on the edge, immersed the cloth in water and gently tended the grazes and bruises. Then he folded the cloth and laid it over the lump on Benedict's forehead.

It was just like the day–

Guilt clawed at him as he steered his thoughts away.

"We love each other, Tom," Benedict whispered. "She expects a child. It must be mine."

Thomas stared into the bowl of scarlet-tinged water, a far more comfortable sight than the brokenness in his brother's eyes. "I don't think it is any more, Ben." He made a point of keeping the harshness from his voice, but Benedict's face still crumpled with pain. "Rest. You'll feel better in the morning."

Thomas set the bowl on the floor and headed to the door. He must have left it open. He looked back at the bed and for a moment, he saw his unconscious eight-year-old little brother, lying there with a cold, damp cloth to ease the swelling on his bloodied head...

Benedict had sat in their favourite oak that day, swinging his legs as they played their Shakespeare game, but Thomas had insisted they climbed higher and higher to get a better view of the river. The thin branch he had trodden on had snapped, and for a moment, he had lost his balance and swung wildly, knocking into Benedict and sending him tumbling down to the ground. Thomas had lied and told him that he'd slipped, and Benedict, having no memory of the event, believed him. That was one of Benedict's many faults – he trusted too easily and paid the price for that, as did others around him. Now Benedict lay there, heartbroken and injured, and Thomas' show and reputation had been ruined.

Thomas sighed, and with a last, heavy-hearted look at his little brother, walked out of the bedroom, pausing to shut the door quietly behind him.

CHAPTER 27: Piero

In the main room of the inn, the darkness was winning, and the air began to chill. Piero sat in a chair beside the expiring fire. In another chair beside it, his dress was laid out carefully. *His* dress, although it did not – and could never – belong to him alone. It was late and the Angel was deserted now, although he thought he still heard the glorious echoes of applause. The fire burned low, and before too long, it would splutter its last desperate, futile gasps, and he had nothing to feed it... except...

He reached inside his jacket for the folded flyer, and his white-gloved fingers carefully smoothed it out on his knee. He read the note again, each word burning his eyes with hate.

THE TICEHURST PLAYERS PRESENT

A MIDSUMMER NIGHT'S DREAM

BY SHAKESPEARE

FOLLOWED BY A SONG AND A DANCE

THE RED LION

"And now?" came Maria's voice from the doorway, breaking through his thoughts.

He did not look up but stared on into the flames. "We win a patron, and they do not."

Silence.

"It's late," she said. "Come to bed."

Silence.

Her sigh was followed by the sound of her retreating footsteps. He pulled out the rabbit's foot necklace beneath his cravat and rolled it between his thumb and middle finger – the necklace which hung like a millstone around his neck and would do so until the story met its inevitable finale.

"*Good fortune awaits you at Thorverton Fair,*" reminded the old woman's voice in his mind.

"Every show requires a grand finale," he whispered. "It's all in the timing." A tear ran down his smiling face as he softly sang: *"I'll always remember your kindness to me..."* He tucked the necklace away and cast the bill into the fire. The edges caught alight and curled, and the desperate flames devoured their final prey.

"Here's a health to the company," he announced to the empty room.

The dying flames flickered on.

CHAPTER 28: Thomas

In the main room of the inn, the darkness was winning, and the air began to chill. Thomas sat on a stool beside the expiring fire. It was late and the Star was deserted now, although he thought he still heard the sickening echoes of jeers. The fire burned low, and before too long, it would splutter its last desperate, futile gasps, and he had nothing to feed it... except...

He reached in his breeches pocket for the note from his brother, his fingers brushing the watch that he had placed there for safekeeping. He read the note again, each word burning his eyes with discomfort.

I must follow my heart.

Richard III Act One, Scene four.

"I am his brother..."

Always.

Farewell.

There could be a way... No, it was unthinkable, surely. He discarded the note onto the table beside him.

"So, *that* was what you walked out on your family for?" came Pa's slurred voice from the doorway, with an unsteady shuffling of feet on bricked floor.

Thomas startled. He did not dare meet his father's eyes, so he stared at the hearth.

"You apologise for abandonin' your family an' our livelihood for your own selfish ambition, an' I'll forgive 'ee. You can come home."

And that was all he had to do. Would it not be easier to end this exhausting fight? Allow his dream to linger as a dream forever, and just come home? It might be easier, but was it right?

"No," Thomas whispered to the fire. Then he took a deep breath. He stood up, his legs shaking beneath him, and faced his pa. "The stage is my home."

Pa marched over swiftly for someone on the wrong side of a great many drinks. Thomas couldn't move, betrayed by his own muscles – the man grabbed him by the Prince of Denmark's shirt and shook him. There was a sickening rip. "You stop this nonsense, you shit-breech fool! You are no actor! You are naught but a failure. An' all you've done is prove it to the whole town!" He released Thomas roughly.

Thomas staggered backwards, arms flailing – knocking over his stool with a crash. There was a stinging thump as his shoulders and the back of his head met the stone of the chimney breast. He regained his balance swiftly, stepped forwards once more and glared back at his pa. He would stand his damned ground.

"Understand, Thomas. You belong here!"

"I will prove to you that I do not!" His hands formed fists. He blinked his filling eyes, and the blurriness cleared.

"All you will prove," slurred Pa, "is that you be twice the bull head I took 'ee for. I'll knock sense into 'ee."

Pa staggered a few steps closer. Thomas readied himself, lifting his fists higher. His heart galloped like a wild horse. He had never hit his pa before. He swallowed as the man threw out a fist.

Thomas blocked the blow – a hefty punch landed on his forearm. Pain bloomed but he did not falter. His fists clenched tighter, daring his pa to come again. And if he did, Thomas would get there first.

His pa wobbled a little and scowled.

Thomas leaned forwards. He would stand his damned ground!

Pa eyed him darkly. “You know there be no future for ’ee beyond these walls.” He shoved a nearby chair with unnecessary force, sending it crashing onto the floor. Thomas flinched. Even after all these years, he still flinched. His jaw clenched as Pa staggered across the main room.

As soon as the bastard disappeared through the doorway, Thomas’ arms and shoulders dropped, but his chest still rose and fell quickly. He touched the back of his head then examined his shaking fingers. No blood. His hand closed over his bruised arm, and he looked down at his ripped costume. The rage and sadness building in him all night – or was it all these years? – finally broke. He always tried so hard! So bloody hard! The tears rushed into his eyes, then streamed down his cheeks. He picked up his fallen stool with trembling hands. A roar emerged from the depths of his soul and burst from his throat as he hurled the stool across the inn. A crack echoed through the room as it landed.

His hands flew to his head. He stood there, breathing fast, as every timber beam in the ceiling bore down upon his skull. He pulled out the watch from the pocket in his breeches, the treacherous thought gaining traction.

“Good fortune awaits you at Thorverton Fair,” reminded the old woman’s voice in his mind. She had seen a pocket watch.

“The show is not over ’til we lower the curtain,” he whispered. Then he tucked the pocket watch away, safely out of sight. But the note on the table still stared at him, with a heartfelt and brotherly plea.

He wiped his wet cheeks with the ball of his hand as he softly sang: *“For we may or might never all meet here again...”* He picked up the note with trembling fingers, paused for a moment, then cast it into the fire. He could hardly bear to watch as the edges caught alight and curled, and the desperate flames devoured their final prey.

“Here’s a health to the company,” he announced to the empty room.

The dying flames flickered on.

***

I have set my life upon a cast

And I will stand the hazard of the die.

William Shakespeare

Richard III, Act five, Scene four

***

CHAPTER 29: Thomas

The morning had not started well. Robert was in pain after all the activity, and Caroline had enjoyed reminding everyone whose fault his condition was before storming away. She had no need to. The many bruises on Robert's body might have faded to a sickly yellow, but the guilt in Thomas' mind had not faded so swiftly. He was glad to leave as Annie held a tonic-soaked cloth to Robert's aching ribs. Besides, he had a deed to perform, and regrettably it would not perform itself. He stood outside the kitchen door, beneath the blue sky and gentle morning sun, sickness weighing in his chest, pocket watch weighing in his jacket. He took a deep breath and stepped inside. It would all be absolutely fine.

Ma was scrubbing the flour-sprinkled kitchen table, and Pa was fixing the leg of the broken stool, both oblivious to the dreadful news he was about to deliver. Pa's heavy eyes and furrowed brow suggested he might benefit from the morning-after tonic that Annie had given them after their night of indulgence. A blurry image of a smiling Essie popped into his mind. What? That was strange. He shook the image away. He must concentrate. Everything rested on this.

"I have grave news of great consequence," Thomas said, moving his hands behind his back, so his parents couldn't see his fingernails digging into his palms. "Benedict has made a grievous mistake which could ruin his entire life and jeopardise this inn. And we all know how much you care about," he paused and looked at his pa, "your inn." Was there truly no other way? No, it would all be absolutely... "He has unwisely engaged in a relationship with Sarah Setherton, Marcus Setherton's—"

"He done what?" exclaimed Ma, hands flying to her cheeks.

"I'll kill 'im!" Pa slammed the stool into the ground, breaking its leg again. He headed for the door into the main room.

Shit! Thomas dashed ahead and blocked the doorway, heart thumping.

"An' I'll kill *'er!*" ranted his ma. "The boy has a good heart. I'll wager 'tis that strumpet leading him astray."

"This is a serious situation indeed," said Thomas, watching every twitching muscle of the angry man in front of him. He was likely the only thing standing in between Benedict and certain death right now, for which his brother had better be bloody grateful. "Marcus is a popular man, and folk will not take kindly to the scandal." Pa tried to move past him. Thomas tensed and stood his ground. He had done it last night – he could do it today. "Your business will likely suffer, but I have a proposal which may, in fact, save... your... arse."

Pa narrowed his eyes and tightened his fists. "An' just what might that be?"

Thomas swallowed, then raced out his plan. "We leave imminently for Thorverton Fair and Benedict joins the company. The affair cannot continue. Nobody finds out and your beloved inn, thank Heaven, remains unaffected." He held his breath. Pa looked like he wanted to smash everything, including Thomas.

"And what you be wantin' in return? Don't you be tellin' me that you're doin' this for Benedict's benefit."

Thomas dropped his mouth open and feigned disbelief. "I'm his brother!" Guilt burned his tongue at the memory of the cremated note.

"Don't you give me that shit." Pa leaned closer, and Thomas stepped backwards, until his back bumped the door. "You're a selfish bastard! Always have been, so tell me: what is in this for you?"

"If you insist on something in return, then speak no word of this arrangement to Benedict. You may thank the company for solving your problem by donating a sum of money—"

Pa gave a snort of laughter and folded his arms.

"Just enough to pay the performers' fee for the fair and invest in more planks for the stage." Was it working? "Everybody wins."

Pa leaned closer still, resting one hand on the door behind Thomas. The smell of his breath assaulted Thomas' nostrils.

Thomas did not dare to move. But he met Pa's hate-filled stare with defiant eyes. He had done it last night – damn it, he *could* do it today.

Pa sneered. "I'd sooner set fire to my own arse."

Ma pushed forwards, and Thomas could breathe again. "Husband! It'll be the worse should he stay. Folk'll talk a'right. 'Tis better he go, if only 'til the dust settles and the boy's come to his senses." She shook her head. "He must be bewitched!"

"He must be a bloody fool! Bringin' shame on the family."

"There is no time to waste," said Thomas.

"Then you'd better move your arse, hadn't you?" said Pa.

Thomas swiftly stepped aside and tried to persuade his body to relax as Pa stormed off into the main room.

"Never liked that Sarah," said Ma. "Her ears be too close together."

Thomas stared at his ma quizzically. "What?"

"Never trust no one with their ears set too close together."

Thomas shook his head in bewilderment.

"He'll be nursin' a broken heart, I s'pose," Ma continued. "No doubt it'll pass, but you make sure you mind him."

"Of course." Doubts tickled his mind – exactly how taxing would a heartbroken Benedict be? Well, for all his pained expressions now, his brother would surely recover swiftly once Sarah was removed from his sight. And, besides, once they had finished at the fair and Benedict had served his purpose, Thomas could always send his brother home if it all became too arduous. Pa might not be best pleased to see Benedict returning quite so soon, but then, Thomas hadn't specified any timings, had he?

"An' you'd better be sendin' more'n one letter a year," chastised Ma.

"I'm already working on a rhyme for 'Pelham'," said Thomas. Ma smiled and a huge rush of affection for her surged through Thomas. He moved forwards and wrapped his arms around her.

The kitchen door behind them flew open. Thomas startled and broke away from the embrace.

"That'll see you through the gate alone." Pa slammed a little purse of money into Thomas' hand. "I won't be payin' for no stage. An' you keep your part of the bargain. Henry's workin' at Thorverton Fair again this year."

Thomas' heart sank. Uncle Henry. The man who disapproved of him most in this world, after Pa.

"I'll send word to him. An' if your brother don't turn up with 'ee, your poxy beggars can kiss the fair goodbye."

Thomas didn't even try to keep the bitterness from his voice. "I expect no less." He gave his ma a quick nod, then bounded for the main staircase. A dizzy lightness spread through him. He had done it! He had secured funds for the fair! Lord Pelham was once more in their sights! Robert would be delighted. And yes, fair enough, Benedict might possibly be slightly unconvinced at Thomas' intervention in the short term, but surely he would come to see the wisdom of it all with hindsight.

Thomas dashed up the stairs two at a time, tucking the purse into his jacket pocket. All that remained was to simply persuade his brother to join the company – he sped along the hallway – persuade Robert to *let* his brother join the company – he ran up the attic staircase – and then everything would be absolutely—

A faint singing in an unsteady voice made him skid to a halt and listen.

"Here's a health to my dear lass... that I... love so well..."

For Heaven's sake! All this over a woman? Clearly, the sooner his brother left, the better. He marched into Benedict's room, knocking on the door as an afterthought as he entered.

"Good news, Brother!" he said brightly. "There's someone I need you to... meet..." The words died a tragic death as he took in the sight before him. Benedict lay draped on the bed, one leg drooping down to the floorboards. A black eye was beginning to develop, his grazes were ringed with redness and the bump on his head was still bloody and prominent. He looked worse than last night. But even more discouraging was the bottle dangling in his hand, which dropped down with a forlorn clink to join the ridiculous number of empty bottles laying spent around his bed.

Thomas' hope faded into annoyance. "How can you be pissed already? It's nine o'clock in the morning!"

"Time for 'nother drink, then." Benedict sat himself up, swayed and fell face down on the other side of the bed. He gave a grunt of pain.

Thomas rubbed his hands over his face. For the love of Shakespeare! Benedict couldn't possibly meet Robert in this condition. Surely there was *something* that could be done? *Something* that would help?

He snapped his fingers.

Annie!

"Time for another drink indeed," he said, hastily retrieving Benedict's shoes from where he had hurled them the night before. "And I know the perfect one."

Getting his brother to stand up was testing enough, let alone persuading him to walk down two flights of stairs. Fortunately, Benedict fell down the first staircase, which sped up the process considerably. But the main staircase was closer to the kitchen.

“Just don’t say anything or do anything,” Thomas hissed as anxiety twisted inside him. Everything rested on a fine balance. He needed to reach Annie before they bumped into Robert or his parents. If Ma saw the state of Benedict, it would only serve to delay matters as she fussed over him. And if Pa saw him, the furniture would probably start flying around again. He glanced nervously at the kitchen on their left as they stumbled through the main room of the inn. Thank Heaven it was early enough in the day to be empty of customers. His parents’ voices came from the kitchen, and Thomas clapped his hand over Benedict’s mouth as they inched towards the front door.

Thomas let out a sigh of relief as they stepped out into the street, cursing that they had to take the long way around to the yard. Why was nothing ever simple? He dragged Benedict through the arch to the yard, where Annie was lifting a plank from the stage. At last, some good fortune!

“Annie!” he hissed as loud as he dared. He cast a look to the stables. Robert was probably still resting inside.

Her eyes widened, and her hand flew to her mouth, dropping the plank with a clatter. She studied Benedict and tilted her head with a warm, sympathetic expression. But Thomas had no time for that.

“Annie! You must have a tonic that sobers up a body without actually killing them! It must be quick before Rob—”

Robert emerged from the stables, one hand pressed to his ribs.

“—ert!” finished Thomas, throwing a wide smile on his face. It would all be absolutely— “Good news! Pa recognises our talent and has donated the performers’ fee for the fair!”

Robert’s face softened, although the darkness in his expression hadn’t truly left. “Well, that is some consolation after last night’s disaster.”

Thomas’ scrabbling fingers tried to reach inside his jacket for the purse, but his yet again incredibly unhelpful brother leaning against him made it impossible. He unhooked Benedict’s arm from his shoulder to retrieve the purse.

"And why's he here?" said Robert, nodding at the swaying Benedict as Thomas handed the purse over.

"Let us start anew," said Thomas in what he hoped was a warm and winning voice. "This is my brother, Benedict—"

Benedict collapsed in a heap on the ground. Thomas tightened his mouth, then hauled his brother to his feet, hurling silent curses at him the whole time.

"No," said Robert, firmly.

"Listen," said Thomas from Benedict's armpit as he hooked his brother's arm back over his shoulder. "He's a talented actor—"

"No."

"—a fine swordsman! Although not as good as me."

"Doesn't sound right," slurred Benedict.

"Imagine the sword-fights, Robert! Imagine the crowds we could draw at Thorverton Fair! Imagine what he could do for the company!"

"Do for the company?" said Benedict and Robert at the same time, one sounding confused, the other incredulous.

"Like make the lead actors miss their scenes and ruin the show?" Robert passed his hands over his tired eyes. "It's work enough keeping you all out of trouble without tending to a bloody drunkard as well! No."

"But I did mention before Winchester that we should expand our company. We'd be able to achieve so much more. And he's well versed in Shakespeare. *Out, out, brief candle...*" He looked expectedly at Benedict, who stared at the ground as if he were trying to work out exactly where it was. Thomas gave him a little shake.

"Hmm?"

"Rules."

"Yes... rules," said Benedict. "*I* made the damned rules. *Life is but a walking shadow... a poor player who...*" He took a breath. "*... fruts an' strets his hour upon the stage... and then...*"

Benedict lurched forwards, grabbed Robert's arm and vomited. Annie gasped. Thomas pinched the bridge of his nose as Robert's face turned to thunder.

"Is fine," said Benedict, patting Robert's arm. "I missed the shoes." He looked down and frowned. "I did not miss the shoes."

"Oh, that was beautiful," said Annie awkwardly. "I'm just not sure about the ending."

"Look at the state of him," said Robert. "He is trouble. If he were the last player in Hell, he would not join this company. And I will not change my mind." One hand clutching the purse, the other pressed against his ribs, he walked gingerly back to the stables.

"He's right, that man," said Benedict. "I'd not leave. Not while my heart is here and..." He groaned. "I really need to piss."

With a rush of frustration, Thomas unhooked Benedict's arm, caring not if he stood or fell. "Well, you can go and bloody do that by yourself. I want *my* shoes to stay clean."

Benedict staggered forwards, bouncing off the stone wall of the yard, and using it to steady himself as he headed – more or less – for the archway. Thomas sighed in frustration. He could tell Robert that Pa had paid to have Benedict removed, but that wouldn't exactly dispel Robert's fears that Benedict was trouble. No, the truth, as usual, would have to be an absolute last resort. As Benedict, by some miracle, safely reached the end of the archway, Thomas turned and grabbed Annie's upper arms. "The tonic! To sober him up?"

Annie shook her head sadly. "I used it all for our sore heads yesterday morning, remember?"

Damn. Why had he drunk so much on Tuesday night? Essie's face flashed into Thomas' mind once more. Why did it keep doing that? He pushed it away as he released Annie's arms. There must be another solution.

"I know he's your brother, but maybe it's for the best he don't come? Robert's right. We do have trouble enough, and we really need to impress Lord Pelham."

Thomas was painfully aware of all the above but—"No," he said resolutely. "I'll find a way. There's always a way. I just need to work out what it is."

Annie nodded. "Have you seen Caroline?"

"Fortunately not," said Thomas, recalling the unnecessarily harsh words she had spoken earlier.

"Oh, Thomas, I do worry when she goes off all upset and angry."

Thomas shrugged. "She'll be fine." He drummed his fingertips on his thighs and began sifting through his mind for a plan. At the present, surely, Caroline's whereabouts was the very least of their worries.

CHAPTER 30: Caroline

The square-towered church cast nearby shadows in the morning sun as Caroline stood by the wide oak doorway of the Angel Inn. She glanced over her shoulder. The last thing she wanted to do was bump into Piero, not unless she had a sword in her hand, anyway. She tightened her grip on the wooden beaker. She might not have a sword, but she did have something potentially more dangerous.

She twisted the door-ring and stepped inside. A few customers were still breaking their fast at the tables, and the smell of smoked bacon and fresh bread made her mouth water. Caroline narrowed her eyes. So much for Thomas' promise of free food, comfortable beds and a hearty welcome. It had, like everything else, been naught but lies. Her eyes scoured the inn for the person she sought. And she found her.

Maria seemed unaware of Caroline's presence, sitting alone at the table on the far side, looking lost in her own thoughts, eating her fresh bread, having slept in her soft bed with her venomous lover, the pair of them determined to ruin everything that Caroline now lived for. But she would not let a cocky tightrope walker and a bastard of a peacock ruin that, not while there was breath in her body. She edged around tables and customers until she reached the oblivious woman. Caroline slammed the beaker upside down on the table in front of Maria, pleased to see that she jumped considerably.

"What do you want now?" said Maria in a bored tone, defiantly meeting Caroline's gaze.

“I want to play.” Caroline pulled out the stool opposite Maria and sat down hard, keeping her hand on the beaker.

“Please,” said Maria, pointedly. “Do have a seat.”

Caroline lifted the beaker to reveal the bone dice. “We play Highest Points. One game.” Many was the time these two dice had rolled at the campfire evenings. Annie was always willing to play, caring not if she won or lost. Thomas was a terrible loser, suggesting the dice were weighted or broken and demanding another chance. Robert sometimes played to humour her if she pestered him enough. Maria looked at the dice now as she had probably looked this morning, empty-bellied, at her bread and bacon.

“What if I do not wish to play?”

“Oh,” said Caroline, hoping her judgement was correct, “I know you want to play.” Everything rested on this. Maria was a mistress of risk. She gambled every time she walked the tightrope, did she not?

Maria slowly tilted her face to meet Caroline’s stare, the hint of a smile curling at her lips. “And the stakes?”

Caroline reached under her skirts and untied the little purse around her leg, not breaking her gaze with Maria. She grumbled inwardly at the pathetic weight of the leather pouch, despite the addition of a few small stones along the way to bulk it out. She placed it on the table. “Our takings, and your takings from last night. Winner takes all.”

Maria picked up the little purse, clearly judging its weight. She gave a little laugh and dropped it back onto the table with a telling grind of stone against coin. “Why would I be interested in your pitiful pennies? We earned a handsome sum.”

“Because it’s not about the money, is it? It’s about the risk.” The glint in the tightrope walker’s calculating eyes did not escape Caroline’s keen poacher ones. “You risk losing some coins, which you could easily replace. Yet I am risking everything. Our company hangs by a single thread.” The words almost stuck in her throat.

"This is all we have, and without it, we will fold. I am sure you'll agree that increases the value."

Maria pushed her plate aside, clearly now with an appetite for more than bread. "My brother has our purse. The contents are yours should you win. After you."

Caroline snatched up the beaker as her heart began to speed. If her gamble did not pay off... She dropped in the two dice and shook the beaker with a wish and a prayer. Then she hurled the dice onto the table, watching as they rolled, danced, holding her breath—

Four and a three.

A fair score. She released her breath, hoping Maria didn't notice. "A word of advice," she said as Maria collected the dice and placed them in the beaker. "One slip, one fall – that's all it takes. Don't assume he will catch you."

"My brother would always catch me, but I never fall."

"I wasn't referring to your brother." Caroline stared intently as Maria shook the beaker.

"He loves me."

"He loves the audience you bring."

Caroline's eyes bore into the cubes as they tumbled.

Five and a two.

"At least I bring him an audience," said Maria, lightly. "We play again."

Caroline picked up the dice, berating her trembling fingers, and shook them in the beaker once more. "He will drop you as soon as he lands—" The dice bounced across the table, her heart in her mouth—

Six and a three.

Caroline smiled. "—a higher score." Robert would be so proud of her, coming back with Piero's takings.

Maria's smile faded. The cubes of bone rattled furiously inside the beaker once more, then out they cartwheeled to determine the company's fate. Caroline held her breath – please, PLEASE–

Five.

And a five.

Five... and a five...

Caroline stared at the treacherous dice, her mind and body frozen, as if staring at them could change the black spots they displayed.

Shit.

Shit, what had she done?

"One slip, one fall," teased Maria as she scooped up the purse with delicate fingers. "That's all it takes."

Caroline didn't notice Maria leave. All she noticed was how fast she was breathing as she clutched the edge of the table. Their takings weren't much, but they needed them so desperately. Robert would be devastated, and he was fragile enough. *What had she done?* She tried to relax her tightening throat. Fear and anger forged seamlessly together until she could no longer tell them apart. Then she slammed her hands decisively on the table. Survival wasn't about sitting and sobbing. Survival was about finding a way. And she would bloody well find one.

She marched to the front door of the Angel, and out into the street. This was all Piero's fault. How dare he come to this town, seeking to destroy them when *he* was the one who had broken their trust? She had always known the bastard had cared more for an audience than another living soul, and one day, oh, she hoped Maria discovered that, too. And how dare that woman take her purse when she *knew* how much it meant to the company? The town passed as a blur, for somehow she was already at the carriage arch leading to the yard of the Star Inn. Annie was loading planks into the wagon.

"Oh, good. You're back!"

Caroline jumped into the back of the wagon, rummaging through the props. How dare they both?

"Caroline?"

How dare life be so cruel? She had failed to save her ma and now she was failing to save the company. And how could she be foolish enough to care when she had sworn to herself that she would *never* love anyone? A blade of silver poked beneath the green curtain.

"Caroline?"

She grasped the sword and was out of the wagon, half-running for the carriage arch before Annie could stop her.

"Where are you going with that?" came Annie's anxious voice behind her. "Robert!" Footsteps hurried towards the stables.

Despite the fury blinding her, Caroline had sight enough to avoid colliding with Thomas' pizzle-headed brother and the key-jangling constable who dragged him, declaring, "You'll think twice afore pissin' on my cabbages again!" And she had mind enough to tuck the sword behind her back as they passed.

Through the market, towards the church, into the Angel yard she went – where Maria's brother had his back towards her, bent over, dismantling the wooden tightrope frames. His fingers must have slipped, for wood clattered noisily to the ground. Which is why, she supposed, he didn't hear her coming, and why she was able to lean over from behind, hold the sword just below his throat and hiss in his ear:

"Where is my purse?"

The man stiffened and began to breathe rapidly. "My sister – she said—"

"I care not a turd what she said! I've changed my mind. Hand over the money!"

With fumbling fingers, Maria's brother reached inside a pouch tied to his waist and wordlessly passed a purse behind him, but Caroline shook her head, frustration and embarrassment mixing with impatience and fear.

“No, not that one. The smaller one is ours.” She needed to make haste. “I just want ours back. Quickly, before—”

Caroline froze as a dagger appeared across her own throat.

“Old habits really do die hard,” murmured Piero’s voice in her ear. “Oh, just so we’re clear: this is the part where you drop your sword.”

Cursing the man behind her with all her being, Caroline allowed the sword to slip from her sweating hand and fall defeated to the ground with an angry, resounding clang.

“Angelo,” said Piero, and she could hear the delight sparkling in the bastard’s voice, “fetch the constable.”

CHAPTER 31: Benedict

Cold on the lock-up floor. Cold.

Arms flopped by side.

How had it come to this?

Cabbages. That was how it had come to this.

Not the cabbages' fault he needed a piss...

Life. Life's fault. Life pisses on your head... like you're a cabbage.

Sarah loves cabbages.

CHAPTER 32: Caroline

Caroline tried to wriggle free of the bushy-bearded constable's grip on her arm, but it was unshakeable. His thick fingers bruised her arm, and his large iron keys jangled ominously on the ring attached to his breeches. There was a flurry of interest around them as they headed through the square, and Caroline feared they were heading for a round lock-up on the far side. It was built of brick and its wooden door had an iron-barred hole for a window at the top.

"I heard they were naught but beggars," said a woman somewhere.

Caroline writhed again in the constable's grasp. "You cannot trust anything that Piero Grimaldi says! He's a liar!"

"That's funny," said the constable. "Same's he said about 'ee."

He bundled Caroline along with such haste that she stumbled to keep up. As she went, she caught a glimpse of a confused-looking Maria.

"I didn't want their money! I wanted mine!"

"Witnesses saw you enter the yard with a sword," the constable said matter-of-factly as they approached the lock-up. "Not looking good for you, is it?"

"To get my purse back! The other man handed over his by mistake! If the magistrate thinks I was stealing theirs, he will see me hanged!" Caroline protested as they arrived at the little building.

The constable swung her around. "But you *was* stealin' theirs. You lose it in a wager, maid, then 'tisn't your purse no more." The constable's grip tightened as he wrestled the keys from his breeches. He put one in the lock, turned it with a noisy clank and threw open the door.

"You be in luck, Cooper," he called inside the lock-up. "Out."

"Jus' got comfortable," slurred a man's voice.

"OUT."

Caroline watched as Thomas' brother stumbled out, his face a shocking mess of bruises and cuts.

"An' don't you be pissin' on my cabbages again!"

Thomas' brother swayed to a halt in front of the constable. He jabbed his finger against the constable's chest. "Don' care wha' you say, Mr Richards... wha' Tom says... anyone says." A look of hurt appeared on his bruised face and he spoke with a fragile defiance. "She loves me more'n cabbages."

Caroline frowned. What the Hell? The constable's grip tightened. There was a whirl of brick around her as she was hurled inside. She quickly regained her balance and threw herself back towards the door as it slammed shut in her face.

"Oi!" she said as the key turned in the lock. "I need to send word to Thomas Cooper!"

"That's not askin' very nicely, is it, maid?" the constable said, appearing at the bars.

"Please!"

The constable gave her a stern look and walked away, the sound of jangling keys swallowed up by the intrigued voices of the spectating townsfolk around them.

Caroline flopped onto the cold floor. Even on a bright May morning, the gloomy building was chilling and damp. She shivered and drew her knees up to her ever-tightening chest, rubbing her bruised arm. Time forgot to pass. The world was unravelling in a nightmare.

“Shit!” she shouted and slammed her clenched fists onto the ground beside her, relishing the dull pain of the impact. She could swing for this; she really could swing. There came the sound of hurried footsteps approaching the lock-up. What of Annie? Who would protect her? And who would watch—

Robert’s face appeared at the bars, brown eyes wide and fearful. She leapt up to the door as he poked his fingers through the bars. Clasping them with her own, she forced the fear from her face, as always.

“Are you all right?” he demanded. “Have they hurt you?”

“I’m fine, and I didn’t want his bloody purse! I just wanted ours back!”

“Why the Hell did he have our purse? What have you done?”

“Oh, what do you think? I was gambling with the tightrope walker.”

“Gambling? Have you lost your wits?” The despair and disbelief in Robert’s eyes stung her heart. Lord, she wished he would just shout at her and give her an excuse to shout back. “How many times have I told you to think before you act?”

“Well, I don’t listen to you, do I?”

“Perhaps you should bloody try it sometimes!” He sighed. “Shit.” With the hand not holding hers, he ran fingers through his hair. Caroline hated the fear on his face and in his voice.

There came the sound of running footsteps and Annie appeared, her fingers desperately reaching for Caroline’s other hand. Caroline poked her fingers through and held Annie’s as reassuringly as she could.

“Oh, Caroline, what if you swing? Tell me you won’t swing!”

“No,” said Robert, looking at Caroline fiercely. He put his free arm around Annie. “I will never let that happen. Thomas is speaking with the constable and the town clerk. Caroline, I will not let them hurt you.”

“I will speak with them myself!” said Caroline. She was hard as stone, she reminded herself. She had to be. “Just bring them here because apparently I am stuck inside an ice house!” The cold of the lock-up bit her again and as Robert gripped her fingers even more tightly, she wished that his jacket – warm and safe and smelling of him – was slipped around her shoulders.

There were more footsteps and Robert and Annie turned their heads.

“Yes,” came Thomas’ voice.

“Yes, we’re fine?” asked Annie, pleading in her voice.

“Yes, we’re fucked. Again. The town clerk wouldn’t even discuss it with me!” He sighed. “Apparently, he really enjoyed the tightrope show last night.”

Caroline gave a little shake of her head. Oh, Piero would be loving this! He had always hated her. He would be making the most of this opportunity. He would probably be in the audience, watching and applauding as she stood on her final stage, a rope around her neck. What had she done? What had she *done*? She couldn’t get air into her lungs... ringing in her ears...

“Breathe,” instructed Robert’s firm but distant voice. His hand gripped hers more tightly. “Caroline, breathe.”

Caroline took a deep breath and rested her head against the iron bars, willing the lock-up to stop spinning.

“Listen to me. Sit down,” said Robert, squeezing her fingers. But Annie slowly slipped her hand away from Caroline’s grasp. Caroline looked up at the movement – her vision tilted. Her heart ached at the desperate panic in Annie’s eyes.

“Annie...” began Caroline, fear and apology bleeding together as one.

But Annie shook her head, then turned and ran, her tangled fiery hair flying behind her.

“ANNIE!” Caroline yelled, pulling her fingers away from Robert’s grip so she could shake the bars. But Annie was gone. A devastating sick feeling hit Caroline's stomach. For the first time since the day they had met at the castle, Caroline was utterly powerless to protect her.

CHAPTER 33: Piero

"Caroline is in the lock-up," came Maria's voice.

Lord, surely that wasn't a trace of concern he heard? Piero fastened the harness on Young Bess, the leather straps warm and tough in his ungloved hands. How beautifully sweet it had been to hold that dagger to Caroline's throat. She had always hated him. From the moment Robert had brought her back to their camp and announced he had found another member for their troupe, she had been naught but antagonistic. Piero had tried to persuade him it was a mistake, but once Robert had made up his mind, it rarely shifted. As he knew all too well.

"She made a serious error of judgement. I believe the lock-up will serve her well," he said simply. He turned around. Maria stood there in the stable doorway, framed by the warm morning sunlight – a harsh contrast to the stormy expression on her face. He sighed inwardly. Robert's moods had always been quiet and withdrawn; he became an unlockable mystery. Maria's moods were decidedly more vocal and tiresome.

"We were only playing a game!"

"And she lost and you won." He led Young Bess through the Angel's stables, her hooves muffled on the straw-covered floor. Maria stepped aside, hands on her hips, as Piero brought the horse out into the yard. Angelo was hitching Iago to their wagon, his hands swift and nervous. Piero left Young Bess standing and sauntered over to Maria. Why did she have to be so difficult? He cupped her face in his hands and stared into her eyes. "Look, isn't that what you wanted, my love? To play the game, and to win?"

"I did not know it would lead to this! What will become of her?"

Piero shrugged. "This was her mistake, not yours. I told you, they are thieves and liars. Do not forget that they stole my horse, my wagon and left me beaten on the ground. I will press my charges, and she will pay the price. They deserve their comeuppance; we deserve success." He softened his expression and smiled warmly at Maria. "And we shall have it." He leaned forwards and kissed her lightly. "Won't we, Angelo?"

The man's eyes were burning him, and Piero looked over his shoulder to where Angelo stood, staring at them. Angelo nodded, and turned away, fiddling unnecessarily with Iago's harness.

"I shall speak with the constable and make known our plans to leave for the fair," said Piero. "We want an excellent position and time to prepare." He smiled again at Maria. Was it reaching his eyes? Judging by her icy look, he doubted it. "The patronage will be ours, my love, and soon everyone will know the wonder that is Maria Violante." He kissed her deeply, with a flicker of irritation that she barely responded after all his effort. Maria and the tightrope act were all that he had left in the world, but they needed him, and they followed him. He broke away before she did. "I suggest you both find food for the journey. We would be wise to leave this place as soon as we can."

"We would have been wiser not to have come at all," said Maria coldly.

If that was her mood, there was little point in attempting to win her. Piero busied himself with the harness on Young Bess until he heard his two companions' exiting footsteps and a slam of the gate in the wall. He paused his fingers, listening. They had definitely gone?

Silence.

He released the sigh which had been aching to escape and rubbed his eyes with his hand. This was merely a minor upset. Once they were in the throes of a bustling fair, Maria would forget about Caroline and the Ticehurst Players, exactly as *he* had learned to do.

He studied Young Bess. What was it about horses? The way they looked at you with those deep, knowing, faithful eyes. A horse would never break your trust or break your heart. Piero stroked the face of Young Bess, running his palm over the soft coat on her cheek down to her jawline. He gazed into her brown eyes, thinking as he often did of another dear horse. He had hoped to sneak into the Star Inn stables and see her one last time before their paths parted for ever.

Dear Old Bess. On those days when the tension between him and Robert had run high, those days when everything felt... stretched, how that faithful horse had brought comfort. The only one who cared apart from—

Running footsteps sounded across the yard. Piero snapped from his thoughts. He dropped the necklace he was absent-mindedly holding and whirled around. Annie stood there, pale, wild-haired and teary-eyed. Her fists were clenched by her side, and she shuffled on the spot with nervous restlessness.

"How – how could you?"

Oh, Lord. He knew at some point this moment would have to come, and it was crucial that he

did

not

break.

He swiftly summoned up every hateful feeling and furious thought he could conjure, before the unpainted boy in the mirror could cry out to her. In his mind, he smeared more purple powder above his eyes, painted his lips and arranged his face into a look of boredom.

"And it is charming to see you, too," he said with an uninterested tone, returning his attention to Young Bess.

"She – she is a sister in all but blood!"

"She is a pain in the arse," said Piero. He stroked Young Bess, willing this dangerous moment to be over. He caught a glimpse of the sword Caroline had used, resting against the wall of the yard. Aware of the tear-filled eyes burning into his back, he retrieved the weapon then, laying the blade across his hand, he presented the hilt to Annie. "At least *I* am no thief."

Annie took the sword, letting its tip touch the ground with a tinny clang. He wanted to rush back to the safety of Young Bess, but he ensured his step was measured, controlled. He could hear Annie's breathing slowing down, but that was hardly reassuring. She needed neither rage nor sword to destroy him. He concentrated on the feeling of Young Bess' smooth coat beneath his fingertips and stared desperately into the horse's deep, knowing eyes.

"She could swing."

"Oh yes!" said Piero brightly as if the idea hadn't occurred to him. "I suppose she could."

"Piero, please!"

It was a heartfelt whisper, and it reached him deeper than he was entirely comfortable with. That was what she truly thought of him, then? That he would stand by and actually let Caroline hang? Once upon a time, she would never have believed such a thing. But once upon a time, matters were very different – in the merry days and nights when he and Annie would dance together, laugh together, perform together. And in his darker moments, when her sweet nature would soothe his troubled soul, and he could almost believe that not everyone in the world would hurt him.

He had not yet confessed to Maria, but as much as he disliked Caroline and was keen to teach the wretched woman a lesson, of course he did not want her death on his hands. He was all too aware of the ever-present threat of the noose for men like him, and he didn't much fancy putting more employment opportunities the hangman's way. Besides... with Annie's arrival, a far more satisfying plan was beginning to assume form in his mind. He looked into Young Bess' eyes and smiled.

He sighed dramatically. "You know, it's so very touching, the way you all bleat around her, though I truly fail to see the appeal, myself." It was a gamble, yes, but oh, this could all work out so beautifully. He looked over his shoulder at Annie. "Do you know what I wonder?" It was all so perfect, and he made his eyes gleam dangerously as the final pieces slotted into place. "I wonder how far you would go to save her very precious neck."

CHAPTER 34: Caroline

A great many feelings coursed through Caroline as she sat in the lock-up, and the more these feelings tumbled inside of her, the more they came back to one person who was responsible for the situation they were all in – and it wasn't Piero, and it wasn't Maria.

Thomas.

The infuriating man was outside now, pacing restlessly back and forth in front of the lock-up, drumming his hands against his thighs. Once she had finally convinced Robert that she was quite well and not about to drop unconscious onto the cold, hard ground, he had gone to try and seek out the constable and the town clerk, leaving Thomas to 'keep an eye on her'. Where the Hell did Robert think she was going to go? Thomas paced by again. For Heaven's sake! Didn't that man ever stand still?

Caroline huffed loudly, removed her shoe and threw it at the bars, the closest she could get to Thomas' head. There was a loud clonk as shoe hit metal. Thomas stopped pacing and peered inside, looking nervous and agitated. Caroline scowled at him. It was not as if it was *his* neck on the bloody line.

"Any sign of Annie?"

"No. As when you asked me five minutes ago."

"Well, where's Robert?"

"Still searching for the constable, I presume." He turned his back to the door. "As when you asked me five minutes ago!"

"What is taking everybody so long?" Caroline wriggled her foot back into the shoe. Worry and frustration trampled mercilessly on her patience. She needed a bloody good argument with somebody and Thomas, at least, served some purpose there. She stood up, smoothed down her skirts and jabbed her finger through the bars.

"This is all your fault," she said, "bringing us to this town."

Thomas gave a sharp, indignant laugh. "Me? *I* was not the one gambling the company's takings—"

"Which I had no choice to do since *your* pizzle-head brother ruined our show!"

Thomas pointed his finger back at Caroline through the bars. "And what of *your* erstwhile lead actor? If you hadn't aggravated him so much, we might have had an audience!"

"Not for long! Your performance was hardly remarkable. You even dropped the skull!"

"Drop the—? I did not 'drop' the skull. I simply *used* a prop in an unusual and surprising manner."

Caroline opened her mouth to retort, but Thomas glanced away, up the road.

"Robert and Constable Richards," he said urgently.

Caroline swallowed hard, and she and Thomas exchanged a nervous glance. This would be either good news or bad news. She could hear Robert's angry voice getting closer, which didn't sound like good news. She gripped the bars with both hands, feeling the cool of the metal against her palms as she tried to peer out.

"And I demand a full trial—" Robert ranted, stopping outside the lock-up and pointing at the constable.

The constable sighed and threw his hands up in despair. "An' if you let me speak a word, I's tryin' to tell 'ee the charges are dropped. The maid be free to go."

Thomas looked at Caroline, a look of relief on his face.

"Free to go?" Caroline's chest suddenly lightened. She wanted to cover her face with her hands and drop to her knees. But instead, she put her hands on her hips and said, "I should bloody well hope so."

The constable reached for his ring of iron keys and noisily jiggled one inside the keyhole. Thank Heaven her time in this place had been over quickly...

Caroline folded her arms as suspicions began to knit together.

Too quickly.

There was a clank as the lock released. The constable pulled open the door and gestured to Caroline to come out, but she narrowed her eyes. Something wasn't right.

"Why exactly am I free to go? I am not leaving until I have answers."

The constable, Thomas and Robert gawped at Caroline in disbelief.

"The tightrope master came to me a short while ago," said the constable. "Explained it were all a mistake."

"Mistake?" She shook her head. "No. He would never admit a mistake!"

Robert moved urgently forwards, his hand reaching for her. "She knows not what she says."

"Yes, she bloody does," Caroline protested. She stepped back pointedly from Robert, ignoring his exasperated look.

The constable shrugged and patted a pocket, creating a jangle of coins. "'E says it were a simple mistake. And 'e compensated han'some like for any inconvenience caused to me."

"Caused to *you*?" said Caroline, putting her hands back on her hips.

The constable sighed impatiently. "Look, you leavin' or not?"

"Yes, she is," said Robert, giving Caroline a firm and frustrated look. He reached inside the lock-up and grabbed Caroline's hand.

Caroline huffed loudly, shook off Robert's hand and walked out by herself. A few bystanders were watching in the street, pointing and whispering. Well, let them stare!

"An', Cooper?" the constable grumbled as he secured the lock-up once more. "Tell your piss-head brother to stay away from my cabbages!" The constable muttered as he trundled away.

Robert faced Caroline, put his hands on her shoulders and studied her. "Are you all right?"

"Oh, he's up to something." Caroline stared furiously back at Robert. "He has got to be. This is all part of his game."

"But are you all right?"

She hated being unsure of what was happening. Hated that vulnerability. Hated Piero. "And you know what we're doing? We're playing right into his sneaky little hands!"

"ARE YOU ALL RIGHT?" Robert said loudly.

"Oh, of course I am!" Caroline lied, with more irritation than she intended. She wriggled her shoulders away from his hands.

"Good," said Robert. His look of concern dissolved into a brooding frown. "Then if you have finished almost being killed, perhaps we may go to the fair?"

"Speaking of which, I have matters to attend to," said Thomas, and strode off purposefully.

Caroline forced her thoughts to clear. "Where's Annie?"

"I found her. She's at the stables with Old Bess," Robert said as he and Caroline headed towards the Star Inn. "She is fine, just a little shaken."

Well, that was something at least. She walked on with Robert towards the Star, with Piero dominating her thoughts. This wasn't a mistake. This wasn't just a change of heart. Oh, he was playing at something, without a doubt. And surely it would only be a matter of time until they found out the exact nature of the game.

CHAPTER 35: Thomas

With Caroline released, Thomas turned his attention to his next problem: Benedict. The man had only gone to piss. Where in Heaven's name was he? And how was he going to persuade both Robert and Benedict that it would be a wise move for his brother to join the company? Surely, they could see it made sense! They must reach the fair! He wove through the market square and his heart groaned as he remembered: Piero would be waiting for them in Thorverton. And as much as he hated to admit it, Caroline was right. Piero didn't seem the kind of person to show mercy out of the goodness of his heart, or admit mistakes, so why did—?

Essie skipped into his path and Thomas stopped abruptly. Her cheeks were flushed, and her smile wide. His whole body slumped. "Not now."

"Oh, Thomas," she said, "I've the most wonderful news!"

"Lovely. Excuse me," said Thomas, trying to move around her. She mirrored his actions and blocked his path yet again. He cast his eyes to the heavens and inhaled deeply.

"Pa has given his blessing for the marriage!"

Thomas' ears pricked up and his gaze snapped down to Essie. "Marriage? Thank Heaven for that. And who is the—" poor, unsuspecting, "—lucky man?"

Essie looked confused before giving a trill of laughter. "Oh! You be practisin' your comedy again."

"Practising my…? I do not need to practise my comedy," Thomas said indignantly, "whatever Benedict may say."

"Took me ages to persuade Pa," Essie prattled on. She pulled a grumpy face, put her hands on her hips, and spoke gruffly: "'Not havin' a girl o' mine settlin' for a vagrant.'"

"Vagrant?" Something stirred at the back of Thomas' mind.

"Oh, don't you be worryin'. I explained there wouldn't be no more vagrantin' once we be married. We'll be here for ever!" She gestured around her.

"Here? Forever? We?" The words dropped with such weight that they could have smashed on the ground. Something dozing in Thomas' mind was desperately trying to wake up, trying to break through into consciousness as if it were a matter of life and death.

Essie smiled and grabbed his face, pulling it towards her. What the Hell? His eyes opened wide, and he froze as she kissed him.

Floor wobbling. Never used to wobble.

Need to find a skull… legs so heavy. Wait. Thank Heaven. Empty stool.

Essie coming. Shit. Essie. Shit. Essie. Shit – Essie on his lap.

"No, you can't sit on my lap, 'cos I know your pa. He sees you on m'lap, that's it! We have to marry."

Saying something. Can't hear. "What? What?"

"We do have to marry! I'll tell Pa!"

A wave of the hand. "Yes, whatever. Go… go."

Essie's lips pushing on his. What the Hell?

Thomas was still frozen in the market square as Essie kissed him.

WHAT.

THE.

HELL.

A storm of panic whirled through his very soul. Essie pulled away, releasing her grip on his cheeks, and smiled sweetly. Then she flounced away, pausing to look over her shoulder. And he saw in her narrowed eyes then – as clear as day – the deadliest, most satisfied look which a stable cat might give a mouse fatally trapped in its claws. Shit-shit-shit-shit-SHIT! Thomas' legs all but buckled beneath him. His stomach churned, he struggled to breathe, and as he stared at her disappearing figure in wide-eyed terror, all he could manage was a rather choked whisper: "We need to leave."

It was fear rather than muscle that carried his shaking legs at great pace back towards the Star. With every step he took, the terror grew, but he could not let his fear present itself to the others. He must steady his nerves and be of sound mind. By the time he reached the stables, he had a plan – an uncomfortable but desperate plan. Yet again, he had no choice. Life had forced his hand.

The others had finished dismantling the stage. Several planks were propped up against the yard wall and the wagon stood beside it. Caroline and Robert seemed to be in the middle of a lively debate about the hammer, but Thomas paid no heed to their words, nor to Annie's downcast face. Instead, he marched towards them like a man pursued by the very hounds of Hell.

"Well," he said brightly, "it's been good to come home. We have secured the entrance payment for the fair..." He picked up a short plank from the stage and dropped it into Robert's arms. "Caroline's not going to die..." He picked up another piece of wood and chucked it at Caroline. "All in all, a great success. We can leave absolutely immediately with no delay."

He hurled another plank into the wagon, then turned to face his companions with the winning smile of a showman. They all returned a slightly confused frown.

"The sooner we leave this town, the better," said Robert.

"Couldn't agree more," said Thomas, and he darted past them towards the stables.

He stepped inside, casting a quick look at Old Bess as she snorted and swished her tail, watching him disapprovingly with her big, innocent eyes.

"Don't look at me like that. It's all for the best," Thomas muttered to the horse, yet the guilt still gnawed at him as he reached for the wooden crate of Annie's tonics. With a furtive glance over his shoulder, he began frantically pulling out each bottle in turn.

"Why does she make so many?" The rush of relief as he found the sleeping draught was immediately followed by another sting of guilt. Thomas hastily dismissed it. There was no time for indecision. His future was at stake: not only did they need to reach the fair, but they now needed to leave with utmost urgency. He held the bottle down low by his side, poked his head out of the stable door like a terrified mouse, then scurried to the back door of the inn.

"Oi," said Caroline. "Are you helping us with these planks?"

"One moment," Thomas called as he dashed into the kitchen.

Ma was in the corner, wringing out some wet cloths. She looked up as he entered and for a moment, Thomas startled at her narrowed eyes.

"An' what you up to now?" she asked, suspiciously.

"Nothing, Ma! When am I ever up to anything?" he lied, hurrying past her. Then he paused, went back to her and kissed her forehead. "More than one letter a year." He gave her a little, sad smile before heading to the main room of the inn.

"Well, don' you let your pa catch 'ee bein' up to nothin'," rang her sharp voice behind him.

The customers in the main room were engrossed in their own conversations, and paid Thomas no heed as he ducked behind the bar and retrieved a bottle of rum. He gulped a mouthful or two for himself – Lord knew he needed it – feeling the comforting warmth hit his throat, then poured a generous measure into Annie's tonic, his heart thumping and his eyes ever watchful. Then he gulped another mouthful of rum for good luck – Lord knew he needed that too – and went to the front door. He paused and cast a glance around the inn... this place that had made him... or broken him... He allowed the conflicted thoughts and feelings to wrestle inside him for just a moment, then he slipped out into the street, closing the Star Inn door behind him for the very last time.

The square was busy with folk milling around. He searched with restless urgency, taking a step left, looking – a step right, looking – Benedict-Benedict-Benedict-Benedict. Where was he to? "For Heaven's sake," he muttered, "why is there never a brother around when you need one?"

Shit! There was Essie on the far side of the street talking with another young maid. Mrs Richards, the constable's jolly wife, walked by, leading a donkey by a rope. Thomas ducked down and scurried along beside the donkey – wondering how exactly his life had come to this – until he hoped to have passed out of Essie's vision. He poked his head up and gave a little sigh of relief as he saw Essie moving on in the opposite direction. He straightened up and looked again for—

Oh, for Heaven's sake! There he was, a little further down the road, slumped in the stocks. His legs drooped hopelessly out of their wooden prison, and his arms dangled at his sides. A pitiful sight indeed, but Thomas marched over with purpose and resolution. Benedict lifted his bruised face up to look at him.

"I'm stuck, Tom. Only stopped for a rest."

"We do not have time for this," Thomas said briskly as he put down the bottle, lifted the top of the stocks with one arm and grabbed Benedict with the other.

"What does time matter if there is no Sarah? What does anything matter?"

"Ssshhhh! Have a care," hissed Thomas as he arranged Benedict into something resembling an upright position. Then he reached down and picked up the bottle, pulling out the cork with his teeth, and spitting it away. "Just drink."

"Good idea," said Benedict, taking the bottle.

“Of course it’s a good idea – it’s mine.”

Benedict took a hearty mouthful, then wrinkled his nose and stuck out his tongue. “Tastes strange...” He sniffed it. “Smells strange.” But he raised the bottle to his lips again.

“Quicker,” said Thomas impatiently. He tilted up the bottom of the bottle, causing Benedict to take several urgent gulps. Benedict spluttered. “How do you feel?”

“As if my heart has been ripped into a thousand pieces.”

“Hmm,” said Thomas, nervously observing the market square. “Well, it’s a bit of an experiment. I’m not sure how long it will take to—”

There was a loud smash as the tonic bottle hit the ground, and a loud thud as Benedict followed. With a rush of relief, Thomas bent down, reached under his brother’s armpits and heaved him upwards with some difficulty. It was at an agonisingly slow pace that Thomas dragged Benedict back to the Star, his brother’s decidedly unhelpful heels scraping along the stones and dust as they went. Dragging a bruised and unconscious body through the streets in broad daylight raised its questions, but Thomas declined the occasional bemused offers of help, hoping it would lessen the unwanted attention, and explained lightly that his brother was just somewhat the worse for drink, which was, to be fair, more or less true.

By the time he arrived, aching and breathless, in the yard, Thomas could feel his shirt sticking to his back, his brow tickling with sweat and his patience beyond dangerously thin. Old Bess was already hitched up to the wagon, facing the archway, and Robert stood beside her, stroking her mane. He turned to look at Thomas and his face darkened.

“Not if he was the last player in Hell,” Robert said firmly.

Thomas huffed. Fine. He was too hot and too tired. The truth it had to be.

“Listen,” he panted. “Forgot to say... a little awkward... our admission to Thorverton Fair entirely depends on him coming with us.”

Robert just stared at Thomas in disbelief as Caroline appeared, walking down the side of the wagon, looking as if she might explode.

“What?” she snapped.

“Please say yes quickly,” pleaded Thomas. “He’s heavier than he looks.”

Robert clapped his hand over his eyes, then dropped it and pointed at Thomas. “After we have finished with that fair, he is coming straight back here! And you and me are sitting down for a little talk!” He jabbed his thumb crossly at the wagon. “In.” Then he turned to Caroline, a look of utter exasperation on his face. “Why the Hell do I put up with you two?”

Thomas didn’t listen to Caroline’s sharp-tongued answer. He concentrated on his screaming muscles as he dragged Benedict to the back of the wagon, where a concerned Annie rearranged the planks of wood and the donkey head to accommodate him. Thomas had done it! He had secured their entrance to the fair. They could perform in front of the patron, exactly as he had planned. Exactly as he had wanted. Then... why was there not an ounce of joy in his heart?

As Annie and Caroline walked alongside the wagon, Thomas followed behind, trying to avoid staring at his unconscious brother and persuading his own sinking heart that everything was – of course – going to work out absolutely fine.

But as the wagon lumbered its way out of town, he heard shouting. He twisted around to see Essie hoisting up her skirts, running through the street towards them. His eyes widened. And he was off, as if someone had ignited gunpowder up his arse – speeding past Annie, Caroline, Robert, Old Bess and down the road, with Essie’s furious voice yelling, “Come back here, Thomas Cooper, you bastard!”, followed by a stream of explosive Welsh language, and finishing with a mercifully distant, "I'll ruin you at Thorverton Fair!"

The journey was awkward and silent. They stopped at some open land near a coaching inn to rest for the night, but despite a thriving campfire on a warm May evening, the atmosphere was remarkably frosty. Whilst Caroline, Robert and Annie silently encircled the fire, Thomas remained in the wagon with Benedict, torn between watching him obsessively and not bearing to look. How long would it take for him to wake? As the temperature began to drop, he glanced at the others, all sitting hunched and disgruntled, staring at the flames. Annie was his best chance of help. He edged over and crouched down beside her.

"Would you help me with my brother? He will become cold so far from the fire."

Annie nodded, and as she followed him to the wagon, Caroline's pointed remark carried through the air: "Now do you realise that hiring Thomas was a mistake?"

Thomas' heart stung at the deafening silence.

"He's not very happy, is he?" said Annie softly, peering at Benedict. "He must have drunk a fair barrel full." She grabbed his legs, and Thomas held his brother's limp body beneath his arms. Benedict's head lolled lifelessly to the side as they shuffled towards the others.

"Y-e-e-e-e-e-s..." said Thomas in a low voice, pushing his tongue into his cheek. "Annie... what would happen to a man who had accidentally drunk your sleeping draught mixed with a rather generous splash of rum?"

"I don't know. But I spent ages perfecting the amount of laudanum, so you only need a mouthful."

Thomas grimaced as they neared the fire. "Y-e-e-e-e-s, but what if they mixed it with rum and had somewhat more than a mouthful?"

Annie frowned, then a look of horror swept over her face. "Oh, Thomas! What have you done?"

"What I had to!" Thomas whispered, with a heavy heart. "I had no choice if we want to save this company!" He was expecting more fussing but instead Annie looked strangely sad and nodded. "But he'll be all right?"

"I don't know, Thomas." Her worried gaze dropped down to Benedict.

They laid him down on blankets by the warmth of the fire. He looked so peaceful, and content, asleep in a place where his bruises and broken heart could not reach him. The bump on his brother's head still looked very tender. Thomas dampened a cloth and pressed it gently over the injury. Yes, his brother had acted rashly and unwisely, and the wounds were a consequence of his actions. But as Thomas knelt beside the brother who had trusted him, and whom he had betrayed, drugged and abducted in the space of a few hours, he began to wonder if they were more similar than he had realised.

As the stars appeared and dark swallowed up the evening, the company lay with their backs towards each other and the fire. Annie hadn't sung her lullaby and the night air felt strangely empty without it.

Thomas faced his brother, hating himself more with every slow minute that passed. His fingers closed around his pocket watch as he recalled the merry soul who had given it to him out of love. Then he reached yet again for the reassuring pulse in Benedict's neck, and the warmth of his slow, rhythmic breath on Thomas' hand. Thomas rubbed his heavy eyes but doubted sleep would come until his little brother was safely awake.

"Please understand, my whole future rests on this fair," Thomas whispered to Benedict. "Good fortune awaits, I have been told. And it is as well you are free of that place. Everything... everything will be fine."

His head filled with images of a furious Caroline, a disappointed Robert, a horrified Annie, a vengeful Essie, a dangerous Piero and a bruised, unconscious brother who was yet unaware of his treacherous abduction. Perhaps it might be wise to reconsider the definition of 'fine'.

Despite his restless thoughts, he began to lose the battle with his eyelids. He had surely rested his weary eyes for only a few minutes before he opened them again. There was movement over by Old Bess. He raised his head from his blanket as someone tiptoed away.

CHAPTER 36: Piero

The deal was a gamble, but then life *was* a gamble, was it not? Piero rested his head back against the cool stone wall of the coaching inn and closed his purple-powdered eyes for a moment to clear his mind. The lanterns outside the front door of the inn creaked noisily in the late evening breeze, and merry singing came from within, where Maria and Angelo waited.

It was most unlike him to feel stage-fright, and he deeply resented the fluttering in his chest. Maria never seemed to feel concern, although her brother felt enough for them both. No, Maria was fearless as she played her way through life. She had gambled when they had first met, approaching him after *Hamlet* with a dazzling proposition. She had tended his bruised cheekbone and his bleeding heart and kissed them both better. They had built up their dreams as he had built up his hate. Maria had followed him as he had danced his merry dance, hunting the company and seeking his revenge. And she had enjoyed the thrill of the chase and the fun of the game... but now? Now, with their task nearly accomplished, she was growing restless, desiring to secure a patron and travel further afield, gathering fame and fortune. Everything he had always dreamed of.

Robert had indeed been humiliated, and the company teetered precariously on the brink of collapse. It was written like a perfect script, was it not? There was just one more gamble before he broke the Ticehurst Players and left them in his wake for ever. But as he stood there waiting, the risk of this gamble unnerved him, and the stage-fright crept in. The dice were rolling. He needed to make sure he won.

He heard the slow, rhythmic clip-clopping of hooves. His purple-powdered eyes flew open, and he took a quick, deep breath. He grounded himself on those imagined boards beneath his feet. Which position to adopt? Careless and unbothered, arms folded and leaning against the wall? Commanding and defiant, head high, chest out? Angry and unbreakable, steely glare and legs slightly apart? For Heaven's sake! Which was the perfect one?

The clip-clopping hooves came closer and, by the swaying light of the lantern, he saw his beautiful horse, plodding faithfully towards him. Lord, it hurt; hungrily, he searched for every detail of the third founding member of the company.

Piero began to discern the outline of a figure, and he resisted the urge to claw at the ruins of the old world which had crumbled around him. He must not break. Instead, he crossed his ankles, folded his arms, and examined his white-gloved fingers. Careless and unbothered, then.

The figure moved into the light of the lantern and stood there uncertainly, but Piero focused on the horse. He pushed himself forwards from the wall and with a delightful air of indifference walked over to the horse he had always held so dear. His painted eyes met Old Bess' trusting brown ones, and – damn it – he could not help but falter as he turned his back on the figure and reached out for Old Bess' head.

"We meet again, old friend," he whispered, and in that moment, he was surely the loneliest boy in the world.

"You don't have to do this," came Annie's soft voice.

Piero swallowed. He refused to look at her. The horse had cracked him more than he had predicted, and Annie could break him utterly now with little effort; the unpainted boy would appear to her, and—

"And Robert didn't have to throw me out," he said sharply, "but such is life. And I quote: 'comedy is naught but an unfinished tragedy.' I am just rounding the story up."

"But we're all so fond of Old Bess, and if you take her, we cannot get to the fair!" She grabbed handfuls of her skirts. "And if we don't win the patron, he'll fold the company!"

"And there's the tragic ending," he said. "Aren't stories wonderful things?" He stroked Old Bess' soft face. He must stand firm on his boards. The gamble was paying off.

"I know things weren't easy," said Annie gently. "I know he hurt you."

Lord, did she ever stop? He focused on the coarse strands of Old Bess' mane beneath his white-gloved hands. His chest tightened, and his patience began drumming its fingers.

"I tried to talk to him," Annie gabbled. "I'm certain he regrets it, but you know when he's sad, he just pushes people away—"

"I do not know what I ever saw in him," Piero said carelessly.

He must not break—

"The same as he saw in you!"

—the tension inside pushing him, willing him, to break, to burst—

"Well, thank Heaven we're both past that now. It's been marvellous reminiscing. Were you leaving now?"

"But you hurt him, too. What you did with that tightrope girl, Piero!"

There was the sound of a crack in his mind. He whirled around to face her, his eyes dancing a little too defiantly beneath their painted lids. "Shall we remind ourselves of the situation? I was pissed and she approached *me*. Robert wouldn't listen, hit me, stole my possessions, then you all left." He must not break. He pulled a puzzled face. "And yet, somehow, *I* am the villain." He glared at her, daring her to utter a single word.

"I miss you."

He caught his breath at the tremor in her voice. Heaven above! Why did she have to come so close to ruining everything all the damned time? Tempting him to fail, to fall, to implode, and he hated, hated, how much he desperately longed to...

"Then rather unfortunately, you shall have to continue to miss me, for there is no place for a person like *you* in my life." His words cut through the air like a poisonous blade, leaving naught but silence.

Annie recoiled as if she had been slapped. One hand flew to her stomach, the other to her mouth. He fixed her with a cold stare. Old Bess' rope fell to the ground. Annie cast one last tearful look at the horse, then ran, taking her choked sobs with her into the darkness.

His heart stung and he screwed up his eyes. The unpainted boy opened his mouth to scream his apologies – to beg for her to return, but Piero tightened his jaw. He would not break. And in order to do that, sometimes other people had to be broken instead.

He buried his face in Old Bess' neck. He snatched a desperate breath and fought his burning eyes as he filled himself with her warmth and her smell. He had not fallen.

"You cannot take that horse," came a vaguely familiar male voice.

Piero startled, then spun around, quickly choosing a face of arrogance and calm as he did so. There was Robert's precious lead actor – whoever he was – his brown eyes flashing and fierce. The poor, dear boy. Although how marvellous that he had made an appearance – it would make the moment sweeter and the exit far more satisfying. After the near disaster with Annie, he needed some light relief.

"Oh, this horse?" he quipped, feigning innocent confusion. "The one I've just taken?"

The lead actor leapt for Old Bess' rope. As he did so, Piero jumped forwards, and grabbed the man by his shirt, catching him off-balance. Piero pulled him close until their faces were almost touching.

"Ah, now you see," Piero began in a low and threatening voice, with just the perfect touch of playfulness, "if Old Bess does not come with me, I shall have to return to your charming hometown and tell your charming constable that I dropped charges under duress." Uncertainty flickered across the face of the new actor. Not a mistake Piero would have made. Amateur. "They'll come for Caroline and then it all gets rather... messy."

There was despair in the other man's eyes. Already? Disappointing. He was expecting more of a fight, but the new actor's initial fire was fading fast, and he looked tired and defeated.

Piero gave a loud, pitying sigh. "Look, this is nothing personal." Unless... "Wait, are you shagging him?"

"No!"

"This is nothing personal," Piero continued calmly. "And it's been marvellous fun, but all good things must come to an end. The patron is ours. And as for the company's fate..." Lord, surely those weren't tears in the man's eyes? "I am sorry for your loss. Doesn't feel good to lose something you care about, does it?"

His white gloves released the man with a dramatic flourish. He left the new actor standing alone in the dark and the cold as he strutted away with his prize, congratulating himself on a rather lovely exit.

It had been a gamble as he'd rolled the dice, and it had been closer than he cared for.

But he had won.

CHAPTER 37: Thomas

They had lost.

Thomas was the most hopeful person he knew, but as he crept back to the dying campfire, he knew there was nothing left. Everything he'd hoped for, everything he'd worked for... it had all drifted away like fading smoke between his fingers. He spoke no word to Annie, who was curled up and sobbing quietly with her head under a blanket. He suspected she hadn't even noticed he had followed her. Besides, he was in no mood for conversation.

He checked his brother's pulse and his breathing, then laid beside him on his back, just staring up at the star-speckled blackness, completely devoid of hope and answers, and dreading the sunrise. The company would discover the horse gone and Annie's betrayal, and everything was going to turn rather spectacularly to shit.

And he was right.

"How could you?" Robert said to Annie, in a pain-laden voice which was far worse than shouting. She stood there, with her head bowed and her hands clutching her skirts. "Old Bess – to *him*! Old Bess, Annie!"

"Listen, she made the right choice," said Thomas. "Our hands were tied."

Caroline pulled out one of the swords from the wagon. "We go after him. The coaching inn, you say?"

Thomas grabbed her arm. “He will be long gone.”

“Thanks to you!” Caroline hurled back at him, stabbing the sword point-down into the ground. Thomas swiftly released her arm and stepped backwards, just in case. “Why didn’t you stop him?”

“I had no choice!” Thomas pointed at Caroline. “I had to let him go to save *your* bloody neck!”

Robert turned to Caroline, hurt etched on his face. “Why did *you* have to gamble our takings?”

“To save the company!” Caroline said angrily, throwing her arms in the air.

“Which is going to fold anyway!” Robert said. “Because thanks to the three of you, we have just lost our horse!” He flopped down on the ground, drew his knees up and ran his fingers through his hair.

The silence was awkward as Hell. Annie’s eyes filled with tears and Caroline put her hands on her hips and stared so furiously at a nearby oak tree, Thomas was surprised it didn’t wither and die. Surely, after everything, it wasn’t going to end like this.

“I’m so sorry, Robert,” said Annie. She glanced around for unwelcome listeners. “I wish none of this had to happen. I know sometimes he was a bit difficult—”

“A bit difficult?” Caroline said, looking up with an incredulous expression.

“—and he broke your heart...”

Robert rested his head in his hands. “He meant everything to me.”

“He... he made a mistake,” continued Annie loudly, her hands scrunching and releasing her skirts. “Well, maybe more than one, but everyone makes mistakes. And...”

Thomas slightly tilted his head and looked at Annie curiously.

“... and I reckon losing Piero was yours!” Annie finished, a brief, triumphant smile flickering on her face, before her wide-eyed, anxious look returned.

Robert did not speak and did not move. Caroline stepped over towards Annie and pulled her aside with a frown. "Hold your tongue. You have spoken enough."

Annie stared down at the ground. Thomas looked at the company in front of him, and the brother lying on the grass behind him. Everyone – everything – was broken. The company had fallen apart, along with his dreams. Were there any options left? Out of habit rather than inspiration, he wracked his brain. "We could walk to Thorverton?"

"We couldn't carry everything: the stage, the props, the costumes," Caroline said, and nudged Benedict with her foot. "An almost-dead body."

Benedict's head lolled over to the other side with a small moan. Thomas caught his breath.

Thank Heaven... Benedict was stirring! Oh shit... Benedict was stirring!

Annie gasped and her face lit up. "I've an idea."

"Your last idea cost us a horse," Caroline pointed out.

"And saved your life!" Annie replied. Caroline was unusually silent. "It is a really good idea. Say you'll come with me!"

"What choice do I have?" snapped Caroline as Annie pulled her over to the wagon. "Because Lord knows what you will do next without someone to mind you!"

Annie loaded bottles of the tonic into Caroline's arms and took some herself, heading for the road.

"Where are you..." began Thomas.

But Benedict sat up slowly and groggily, with a hand to his bruised head. Thomas' attention snapped to him. It was a strange list of feelings that hurtled through him: relief, happiness, nervousness, guilt... and it ended in downright dread.

"What's all the shouting?" Benedict mumbled, looking around him dozily. "What's going on?"

"Ah, Brother," said Thomas, eyeing the sword Caroline had left blade-down in the ground. Fortunately, it was within grabbing distance. "How are you feeling?"

"This isn't home," said Benedict, sitting straighter and looking around with more alertness.

"Depends on your definition." Thomas risked a nervous smile.

Benedict pointed at Thomas. "You. I'm looking at you, and I'm very cross with you, and I can't remember why. What have you done?"

"Me? I haven't done anything."

"Oh, you've always done something," said Benedict, and Thomas flinched at the growing frustration in his brother's voice. It was possible this wasn't going to go very well.

Robert moved his hands away from his head, flopped them over his drawn-up knees and began to watch with interest. Thomas cast another quick glance at the sword as Benedict's eyes widened.

"You gave me a drink!"

"I don't think I gave you a drink."

"You gave me a drink! It didn't taste right..."

"Use your head," said Robert. "It was a sleeping draught."

What? Thomas threw Robert an exasperated look. It was definitely not going to go very well.

"A sleeping draught?" Benedict stared at Thomas, clearly going through a list of feelings himself, which appeared to be rapidly ending in downright fury.

Time for the sword. Thomas leapt forwards, and grabbed it, holding it in front of himself defensively. "Listen, Brother, I can explain–"

"Sleeping draught? You drugged me!" Benedict staggered to his feet and stumbled towards the wagon.

“A small price to pay for sparing you from further heartbreak! And almost certain death! Marcus *will* kill you, Ben!”

Benedict reached the wagon and rested with his hand against its side, looking like he was going to vomit. He turned back to look at Thomas, who gripped the sword tighter and raised his other hand in surrender. Perhaps he could still save this.

“So, all this is for my benefit?” said Benedict.

“I am concerned for your wellbeing!”

“You ought to be concerned for your own.” Benedict reached inside the wagon and drew out the other sword. “There’s more to this, isn’t there? What’s the real reason?”

Benedict flopped against the wagon for a moment, catching his breath, then began advancing towards Thomas, his steps growing stronger and steadier. Oh shit. Thomas tightened his grip.

“Listen, I had no choice,” he gabbled. “It was all arranged with Pa!”

“You *told* him!”

“I was supposed to bring you away, preserve the family’s reputation—”

“And what do you get out of it?” said Benedict, chest heaving as he pointed the sword at Thomas. “My wellbeing?”

He lunged. Thomas gasped and brought up his sword to meet his brother’s. The blows fell relentlessly as Thomas desperately parried each attack, walking backwards all the time.

Benedict growled with each clash of the blades.

“What...

...do...

...you...

...get?”

A dull thud at Thomas’ back: the trunk of the oak. His brother’s sword pointed at his chest. Thomas tried to think of a way out and swiftly concluded there simply wasn't one. He tossed his sword to the grass and refused to meet his brother's eyes.

"Pa paid our way to the fair," he said quietly.

"What?" breathed Benedict.

Thomas stared down at the twig-strewn ground. Anywhere but at his brother. It was too painful. "Without you, we are denied entry."

Silence had never been so agonisingly silent.

"Everything – EVERYTHING! – you've ever done is because you love your fucking stage above all else! Don't you?"

Thomas said nothing as the sword pushed closer and dented the shirt beneath his open jacket.

Robert stood up. "That's enough," he said gently.

"Just give me one reason why I should come with you and save your arse!" raged Benedict. "And don't you dare quote bloody Shakespeare at me! One reason!"

The guilt weighed his head down but slowly, painfully, Thomas dragged his eyes up to meet Benedict's. He had betrayed his little brother's trust. And Benedict was perfectly entitled to go home and leave Thomas without hope, without a future, exactly as he deserved.

"Then we are no longer brothers," Benedict spat, with all the hurt in the world in his breaking voice.

His sword landed with a grass-softened thump near Thomas' feet, then he turned away. Thomas rested his head back against the oak, heart close to bursting. There was but one thing he could say. "Because I'm sorry."

Benedict twisted around to face Thomas. "You have never apologised for a single thing in your whole fucking life!" His voice cracked with what Thomas uncomfortably supposed was many years of frustration.

And all he could say quietly was, "I know."

Thomas looked into Benedict's tear-filled eyes and saw the anger melting into sadness then flashing back into anger once more. His little brother stumbled sideways, closed his eyes and inhaled deeply. He doubled over, resting his hands on his knees. Was he... all right?

"I have walked away from my brother once before," said Thomas as Robert moved towards Benedict, "and I do not wish to do it again."

"Because I serve your interests!"

"Because," Thomas said, swallowing down the tightness in his throat, "my brother matters more than he knows, and I want him here."

Benedict dragged himself upright. "You are despicable." He glared at Thomas, then staggered backwards.

Robert caught him before he fell. "Come on, sit down," he said, steering Benedict further away from Thomas. Benedict half-sat, half-collapsed onto the ground, tentatively touching the bump on his head, then burying his face in his hands.

Thomas slid down the oak to the ground, leaned his head back against the uneven bark and closed his burning eyes. They had lost their takings, their horse, the chance of attending the fair, the hope of securing a patron – and now it seemed he had lost his brother as well. His dreams, his plans, his hopes... It had all been for naught, in the end. And Pa was proved right. Thomas could not be more of a failure, for there was simply nothing left to lose.

Robert's footsteps walked towards him. "He handles a sword even better than you."

Thomas waved a defeated hand. "We just use different tactics."

"And mine work," said Benedict sharply.

"Robert!" came Annie's cheerful voice.

Thomas opened his eyes and looked around. Annie approached with Caroline, a dark-haired man... and two horses.

"What are they?" said Thomas, scrambling to his feet and pointing at the horses.

"They're horses," Annie said brightly. "From the coaching inn. They have spare ones, see."

The dark-haired man looked at Thomas. "I can take 'ee as far as Thorverton, no further, mind, then I's bringin' 'em home." He walked the horses towards the wagon and began to harness them.

"How have you done this?" said Robert, heading for Annie.

"I made it right." Annie squeezed Robert's arm. "Said I would."

"But how?" said Robert.

"Annie gave him all her tonics," said Caroline.

"And Caroline gave–"

Caroline threw her a warning glance as Annie clasped her hand over her mouth. Robert reached forwards and grabbed Caroline's ringless hand.

"No," he said, pointing at her. "Ask for it back. I will not have my players parting with their–"

"Robert," Caroline said firmly as she snatched her fingers away, "your players will do what they bloody well like. Because this company is their family. And for some reason – Heaven help them – they insist on fighting for what they love."

Robert just stood there, looking at Caroline and Annie, saying nothing. His mouth tightened and distorted for a few moments, and a little shadow appeared on his jaw. Then he seemed to regain control and gave a sharp nod.

A strange lostness struck Thomas. Did Robert ever look at him like that? Thomas was the replacing and replaceable lead actor, the one that had brought nothing but disappointment and trouble. The one that did not truly have a place. Thomas thought again of the Theatre Royal at Drury Lane. Where indeed *was* his place? He risked a glance at Benedict, who caught his eye and promptly looked away.

Robert picked up the sword by Thomas' feet and passed it to him. Thomas nodded gratefully as he took it. Robert picked up the sword's brother and offered it wordlessly to Benedict. Thomas hardly dared to breathe. What would his brother do? There was a moment's pause, then Benedict reached for the hilt. Thomas' throat tightened and he knew not whether to smile or cry, so he simply stood there. Robert looked at them both in turn, as if he were exasperated that there were two of them. Then with a loud sigh he turned to Benedict, jabbed his thumb at the wagon and said, "In."

Benedict clambered into the back and flopped onto his side, hands covering his face. Robert headed to the driver's seat to sit beside the man from the inn, and moments later, the wagon began to roll towards Thorverton. As Thomas walked alongside Annie and Caroline, a thought occurred to him.

"Annie... you gave him *all* the tonics." He paused and lowered his voice. "Surely not the piss one?"

She nodded. "His teeth will be sparkling."

"Oh Lord," Thomas groaned.

Annie plucked her fiddle from the wagon and soon a merry jig sang out into the morning. She smiled at Thomas as she played, and he found himself smiling back. It was often surprising where hope came from. But it always turned up.

CHAPTER 38: Piero

Every inch of the oak-dotted field was flooded with colour and noise as performers prepared for the fair tomorrow. Such a ripe opportunity, surrounded by a ready audience, but Piero was not in the mood. Even so, he willed the boards to appear beneath his feet, held his head high and nodded to fellow performers. A young man in a group of jugglers cast him a curious look, but Piero was in no mood for flirting. Comedy was but an unfinished tragedy, and now the show had all but ended for the broken company. There was just one last matter to take care of.

He searched for the anger locked inside his heart. It wouldn't take long to find, but he was going to need it. He sauntered on with Old Bess beside him, weaving through people, stalls and wagons in the heat of the day. The smell of heady ale and sharp cider mixed seamlessly with sweat and horseshit as people pushed and shoved in their haste to claim spots and build stages.

He did not look at Old Bess. He did not dare. They walked together, her rope in his white-gloved hand, as they had done before.

The hooves of the horse clip-clopped along the flint-speckled track. Piero walked closely beside her, the rope in his hand. The element of surprise would have been preferable, as making an entrance was his second-favourite thing in the world. But it was impossible to arrive quietly.

"Close your eyes!" he called into the empty field they had found for the night.

Piero hadn't stopped smiling since he had bought the horse from the farmer. Their dream was becoming real – they would set up their own little theatre company – just them and a stage, against the world. With the horse, he and Robert could move more easily from town to town, never in one place for too long – where judging eyes might pry, troublemaking voices might whisper, and a hangman's hands might begin to twitch. On the road they were free. They were who they were meant to be.

Robert sat, his slender frame leaning against the wide oak deeper into the field, his long legs stretched in front of him. One hand was placed trustingly over his eyes. His jaw-length wavy hair and his pale shirt rippled teasingly in the breeze. Piero longed to truly know this secret of a man: the quiet, protective man who always thought more than he spoke. The man who had brought meaning back into his life.

"Keep them closed," Piero said. They were just a few feet away. Oh, this was going to be wonderful. The hand not holding the rope reached to pat the horse in appreciation...

The hand not holding the rope formed a fist as they walked on. It was anger, not sorrow which would help him now. A tall, curly-haired fire-juggler threw four flaming batons into the air, nearly knocking over his bottle of oil in his effort to catch them. Their fierce colours split the cloudless blue sky above them as they flew. There was something so beautiful, so terrifying and so final about fire. And right now, Piero's heart burned.

They passed a troupe of easily forgettable dancers, swishing brightly-coloured ribbons as they rehearsed. A group of men sang rousing sea shanties and raised tankards of ale – and had presumably done so for several hours beforehand judging by the fact that one of the members had just fallen off the stage in a giggling heap. The clear, strong harmonies rang through the air. But their bearded faces – apparently a requirement for such songs - were not who he was looking for.

There were another troupe of players, three men and two women, standing on a prop-littered stage with a green curtain at its rear. A clean-shaven man with a willowy figure was hammering a sign into the ground: 'The Ashton Players'. He stopped, admiring his work. Another man in his company passed him, clapping a hand on his back. Piero fought to keep the scowl from his face. How lovely. A happy company. Well, one day it would all fall apart and *then* where would they be? As the willowy man returned to the stage, he noticed Piero standing there and gave him a passing smile. Lord, his eyelashes were long. Piero gave a little nod in return. They were not who he was looking for.

He walked on, trying to fill his ears with the noises of the fair. But the mournful silence grew louder with every step as he wove through the carts and wagons. Did this really need to happen? Annie's voice in his head. *You don't have to do this.* Doubt threatened to betray him. He needed to feed his anger and hatred – feed the demon that devoured and consumed everything as it danced restlessly in the flames. He must not break. His muscles tensed and he began to feel stronger.

Gorging on memory.

Clawing impatiently—

His feet faltered. There was that wagon, decorated with rabbit's feet and colourful ribbons. And there was the old woman in the same dark red dress, sitting beside the small table, her back towards him. She whirled around with unnecessary and alarming speed and looked straight at him.

Piero startled. He held the old woman's gaze coldly, shaking his head at the ridiculous knowing smile which spread across her face now. Knowing? Did she truly know his rage? Did she truly know his pain? He narrowed his eyes.

She knew nothing. NOTHING!

Yet her gaze burned relentlessly into the rabbit's foot necklace beneath his cravat. He cared not! Not for the old woman and her foolish words! Not for the necklace! Not for Robert! He breathed deeply to steady himself and glared at the tiresome old crone. Then he tossed his head before strutting on, pulling dear, faithful Old Bess beside him. He walked faster, letting the rage drive his legs.

He had come so close – so close! – to falling once before. And what had all that pain, all that fear, all that hope amounted to? Naught!

He had been a fool to trust Robert! A fool to think that it might have been love! It had always, always been a lie! But lies cannot last forever. This was the ending of it all. Every show must end, and oh, it would end with such raw, deserved fury. Piero lifted his head. He could scream flames in his pain and burn himself and the whole world around him, leaving naught but ashes and devastation behind! He made his pale eyes dance beneath their purple armour. He led Old Bess on with renewed determination – in defiance of Robert, in defiance of love, in defiance of the whole fucking world.

And he found who he was looking for.

He stood before the stage where the five acrobats stretched, twisted and bent into unthinkable forms. He ignored the rapid beat of what remained of his heart, slowed his breathing and painted his face with a pleasant smile. He raised the arm not holding the horse's rope—

—in a perfectly poised flourish. "Ta-daaaaa! Our show is on the road! Open your eyes!"

Robert's hands dropped from his eyes, and his mouth opened. He scrambled to his feet and walked over to the horse. His dark eyes sparkled. Lord, he was beautiful when he smiled like that.

"She's perfect!"

"Not the youngest, but she's sturdy and strong. I propose we name her Old Bess."

Robert turned his adoring gaze from the horse to Piero. Despite the impending dusk, Piero felt like the sun had just risen and bathed him in new warmth and light. Surely all he needed to do was to fall, to melt into this gorgeous man: abandon himself and give himself entirely... except... he never would. Piero had sworn he would never be the boy in the mirror again. He had built his stage, and he must walk on it for ever.

Robert reached forwards, cupped Piero's face and kissed him. The day-weary scent of him... Piero wanted nothing more than to fall...

"And I have a gift for you!"

A gift? Robert reached behind the oak trunk. He looked over his shoulder at Piero. Then he pulled out a simple but beautiful dress with an embroidered top, ribbons on the shoulders, and a blue bow. Piero caught his breath. The unpainted boy pressed his fingertips against the glass. This was surely the beginning of something so special.

"For Titania," said Robert, with a smile. "Or... whatever you wish."

For perhaps the first time in his life, Piero could not speak.

His tightened throat almost stole his voice. He clung to rage at this final test and refused to feel the years of love and loyalty which stood silently beside him – the devastating reminder of how it all could have been. He refused to look at the last true friend he had in the world. He would not break.

Instead, he looked at the acrobats and forced the words out. "Good afternoon," he said calmly. "I hear you are in want of a horse. Perhaps I may be of assistance."

And the loud, screaming, rageful fire inside him drowned out the crack of a breaking heart.

CHAPTER 39: Thomas

The gate at Thorverton Fair had struck terror into Thomas for as long as he could remember, because his Uncle Henry minded it. Now, in the late afternoon, as he followed the wagon down the track hemmed in by blackthorn hedges, there was the same feeling of tension he had known since boyhood.

Thomas knew there was bitterness between the brothers, which exploded on the rare occasions they met. Pa, as the elder, had been left the precious inn by their father, and now the inn was supposed to pass to Thomas. It had been the source of many an argument and Uncle Henry had made his concerns perfectly clear: the inn would suffer if it was left to a good-for-nothing dreamer like Thomas, or a happy-go-lucky layabout like Benedict, and it should be sold to Henry and his son instead. Thomas had never known his grandfather, but he did occasionally wonder what kind of person had raised two such disagreeable men. Unlike Pa and Uncle Henry, he and Benedict had been united in their disinterest in the Star instead of being torn apart by their desire for it.

As he walked beside Annie and Caroline, Thomas cast a look at his brother. He was dozing somehow as the wagon rocked unnervingly in and out of the many horrendous ruts caused by the wagons which had travelled before it. A violent jolt caused Benedict's eyes to fly open.

The wagon rumbled to a halt. A tightness spread through Thomas. Had word from Pa reached Thorverton? Was that Uncle Henry's gruff voice muttering somewhere?

“Thomas!” Robert beckoned from the front.

Quickly smartening his jacket and crossing himself, Thomas positioned a smile on his face as he rounded the wagon. “Uncle Henry!”

The man stood there, blocking the gate, arms folded. He was shorter than Pa, and beardless, but wore the same permanently angry expression. Who in Heaven’s name had given him the task of welcoming folk to the fair, and how many bottles of rum had they consumed before arriving at that odd decision?

“Jus’ Henry to you,” said Uncle Henry. “Your pa sent out a rider. An’ ’e don’ pay for nothin’ readily. Seems very keen to send your brother out of town.”

Thomas held up his hands in protest. “I assure you, Uncle, all is well. Benedict is in the back of the wagon, and we can absolutely enter the fair with no argument or delay at all.” He led his uncle around to the back of the wagon.

“Good for nothin’, the pair of you, I’s always said.”

“Yes, you have,” said Thomas tightly.

“Performin’ like beggars when the inn needs mindin’—”

“Yes, I know,” Thomas said through gritted teeth. “But as you can tell, we are late arriving and must begin preparations. So...” He gestured towards Benedict. “You can see, my brother is present, well and delighted to be accompanying us.”

“Thrilled,” said Benedict flatly, folding his arms.

Uncle Henry peered in. “What the Devil ’appened to your face, boy?”

“Fell down a horse,” Benedict said. He threw Thomas a challenging look.

Thomas cleared his throat. “Anyway,” he said quickly to his confused-looking uncle, putting his arm around him and drawing him away, “I realise we are late to arrange a pitch...” He pulled out the purse of money from his jacket, which his uncle promptly snatched from his hand. "I trust you have somewhere we may perform?"

Thomas studied his uncle with nervous, eager eyes. He wouldn't put it past his uncle to take the money for the inconvenience of merely speaking with him and then bid the company leave. His uncle frowned at him as Thomas held his breath.

"You can 'ave yonder barn," Uncle Henry said, pointing to a small wooden structure on the top, far side of the upward-sloping field. "Only inside it, mind, not the space around it. I'm sure you'll find it... perfectly suitable." He gave Thomas a look of deep disapproval and walked back to the gate.

"A thousand thanks, Uncle Henry!"

"Jus' Henry," came the gruff reply. "An' don' you be causin' no trouble or I'll send word to your pa."

"Wouldn't dream of it," called Thomas. The wagon rocked forwards once more and Thomas smiled at Annie and Caroline as they followed it. "Well, that went better than expected."

"We'll see," said Caroline.

As they headed up and across the field towards the wooden building, Thomas looked around anxiously. Was the tightrope act here? Who else was performing? The field was bustling. Stages and pitches were set up already, and the tang of cider, ale, meat and pastry drifted welcomingly on the breeze. Carts and wagons were dotted all over the grass and—

There was the one belonging to the old fortune-teller, with its string of rabbit's feet and bright ribbons along the side! Thomas slowed his pace slightly as Caroline and Annie passed him by. Where was the old woman? Was she there? He must seek a word with her before the fair was over; gain more insight about his future. She had said good fortune awaited him here and oh, how his heart begged that to be true. He ran a little to catch up with the others.

Aside from the fortune-teller's wagon, there was a huge tent further along on the right, troupes of dancers on stages far larger than their own, a few other theatre companies judging by the green curtains, several jugglers, a man on stilts, puppeteers, a dog performing tricks and – oh Lord, was that a fire-juggler? They would have a fight on their hands, but they had not come this far to fail now! And it was a large, busy fair. With a bit of luck, they might not even run into—

"Shit," said Caroline as Annie gasped.

Thomas followed their gaze. The large tent on their right had its sides rolled up. Thomas' heart sank. The olive-skinned man who worked with Piero was inside, setting up the tightrope frames. The tightrope walker stood outside the tent, amongst a group of curious performers and stallholders. "Stay away from those thieving players!" she announced, pointing at their wagon. "They're naught but trouble."

Caroline's fists clenched and she turned towards Maria.

"No!" Thomas hissed. He grabbed her upper arms from behind. "Shall we not give them reason to believe her?"

The tension in Caroline's arms slackened slightly and he released his hold.

"Why is it that everywhere we turn that bastard is there?" said Caroline as she once more followed the path of the wagon.

Thomas eyed her as he walked alongside. They could not afford to ruin this opportunity, for it was likely to be their last. He would need to watch Caroline like a hawk.

The small wooden barn was some distance from the main throb of the fair, next to a hedge that ran the length of the field. Thomas wrinkled his nose as they approached. What in Heaven's name was that smell on the breeze? The grassy scent of horseshit, yes, but there was something else. Something sweet, sickly and rancid.

As the wagon drew near, Thomas' heart sank lower. If Pa could see what Uncle Henry had done, surely all would be forgiven between them. *This* was the building that his uncle considered to be perfectly suitable: little more than a long, tumbledown hut, constructed of badly joined planks. It was clearly in the process of falling apart and looked like it needed very little encouragement to finish the task. The doorway faced the rest of the field, and whatever was causing the smell inside seemed to be attracting a great many flies. It was clearly unloved, unwanted and neglected, barely surviving at the edge of the field. It looked in desperate need of a patron.

"Well," said Thomas brightly. "Here we are!"

He turned to Caroline, Annie and Robert, who stood staring in dismay.

"This?" said Robert. "This is where we are to perform?"

Thomas searched desperately for a cheering thought. "We will have a fine view of the fair!"

"Not if it collapses on top of us, we won't," said Caroline.

"Oh, I'm sure it'll be a lovely theatre," said Annie, her voice weighed with doubt. She poked her head inside and swiftly retreated, holding her nose. "Once we clean it out," she added in a pinched, nasal voice. "We're going to need a shovel."

Robert sighed. "I will make enquiries." He turned to the man from the inn. "We thank you for your help."

The man nodded and cast a dubious look at the barn. "Good luck."

"We shall have no need of luck," said Thomas, as he swatted at a particularly persistent fly.

The man cast an even more dubious look at Thomas, then led the two horses away.

Robert moved closer to Caroline. "Did you see?" he said quietly.

"Well, at least when we shovel out the horseshit, we know in whose direction to chuck it," she replied.

For a moment, Robert neither spoke nor moved, then he turned and walked slowly towards the heart of the fair.

Thomas screwed up his face as the breeze carried a fresh wave of the stench from the barn.

"I'm *so* thankful you abducted me. I had no idea the life of a strolling player was so enchanting," came Benedict's flat voice at his shoulder. "For the love of Shakespeare, tell me you have drink."

"We have no need to commiserate with drink," said Thomas. He tried to summon hope from wherever it had fled. "We are at the fair! We have a pitch! We have a stage—"

"I'm so excited I may piss myself."

"Everything will be absolutely fine!"

Annie poked her head inside the barn again and began to violently retch.

"Oh good," said Benedict sourly, and his footsteps stomped away.

Thomas let him go. It was probably better to have some distance between them for the moment. Besides, the barn clearly needed preparations for their patron-winning performance tomorrow. Caroline peered inside more closely.

"There's a half a dead sheep in there," she said, folding her arms and looking at Thomas with what he feared was a clear indication of who would be moving it.

Annie retched again. Thomas looked to the heavens and clung with desperate, determined fingertips to the words of the fortune-teller...

CHAPTER 40: Old Dina

Good fortune awaits you at Thorverton Fair.

Oh, Old Dina loved this life. With quick, clever eyes, she looked around at the bustling fairground, making a swift headcount of those lost, tormented souls she had spoken to on her journey here, making a note of those she was yet to meet, and making an estimate of the coins she would raise with such encounters. They came to her with questions, doubts, fears and purses. One was coming towards her now: the tall, slender man with the dark hair and the brooding face. She never forgot a face, even if it was bruised and bloodied in the back of a wagon. She noticed everything, for a keen eye and a sharp memory served her well in this line of business.

She picked up a stick and went over to the little campfire she kept. She dipped the stick into the flame, humming as she waited for the fire to catch. She even remembered the name of the company – the Ticehurst Players. She lit the candle in front of her on the table, beside the paper. She sensed mystery about this man. There was something she had not quite worked out, and that bothered her. She wriggled her spotlessly clean fingers, determined to make the catch this time.

She watched the man walk. She always studied how they walked. You could tell a great deal from that. He moved tensely, with no easy swing in his limbs. When there was tension, it was all locked inside – inside the body, inside the mind. Frustration in this one, yes, but also such burden, such heaviness about him. And he was drawn to her, like a moth to flame – the way he tried to walk on past her but kept giving little sidewards glances. He believed in the power of fortune-telling, then. He was tempted. He would need little encouragement, rather disappointingly. It was more satisfying when it required a little effort. Still, the game was there for the playing, and it was always good to win.

"Old Dina sees it true, tells it true," she called.

A turn of his head; a slight pause in his movement.

"You has a question for the candle. It consumes you. Come, ask."

And over he came. Pfft. Too easy. The man was at the point of desperation, then. The point of breaking. He did not fight it, and he did not attempt to conceal it – very telling. She gestured to the little stool opposite her, and down he sat. Wordless, brooding, a sad storm in his eyes and his face and his soul. She enjoyed the silent ones who liked to think. They were more of a challenge, harder to crack. But she would indeed crack him, like a nut, until he sat there bare and exposed, his shell destroyed. But first, she needed more clues. There were always clues.

She held out her hand for a coin, her mind racing as she observed him. He reached into a purse – flat, weightless – it did not jingle. He rummaged to pull out a coin... his final coin, then? Oh well, it would have to do, and she would not push for more. He dropped it into her palm.

His face still bore bruises although they had faded considerably – it was attack rather than accident, she'd wager, judging by the number and position of the blows. But his cuts had healed well, so he was probably well cared for – held in high regard by his company. Yet his face had a remarkable closedness about it. A reluctance to share and express. A wall. He had been hurt before, then. Or he had spent so many years hiding a deep secret, his face had forgotten how to reveal anything, lest his secret should escape? Perhaps both.

There was a string around the quiet man's neck, and a little bulge beneath the top of his pale shirt. She recognised the shape, and seeing how willing he was to come to the candle, she'd wager her entire takings at the fair tomorrow that it was a rabbit's foot necklace which hung there. Curiously, he tilted forwards slightly as he sat, not eager and engaged, like the other actor in his company, the one who was so desperate for success. This one sat refusing to speak or meet her gaze, leaning towards her as if the thing which hung around his neck weighed like a millstone.

And still the man was silent, avoiding eye contact and staring instead at the candle flame. Unwilling, or unable to ask for help. Needing her guidance yet refusing her access. At the point of desperation and yet unable to voice it. Very, very interesting. She pocketed his coin and just about resisted the urge to rub her hands together in absolute delight.

She had one more piece of information, which twisted into a question: what was his connection with the one who had sought the quiet man's troupe? The attention-seeking, strutting man who loved the sound of his own voice and believed his own lies; who wore the rabbit's foot yet believed not in the sight but in revenge; the man with the purple-powdered eyelids who clearly hid behind a mask; who seemed so lost but knew not how to be found; whose pale green eyes looked like they burned with fury and hate until you noticed how clearly they burned with tears and—

Oh.

Oh...

Of course. She should have been quicker than this – she was distracted perhaps by the sheer volume of people she had met as folk travelled to the fair. It was all so obvious once all the game pieces were set in place. She smiled smugly. She sat back a little on her stool and folded her arms as the impatient candle dribbled wax down its side. She would pour it soon enough on the paper and impart her wisdom. Oh, this – this was going to be fun.

"You believe in the sight," she croaked. They liked her to croak. "Old Dina already knows your question but only you can ask the candle."

She would force him to speak. She wanted to hear it for herself. She put her fingers around the candle, ready to pour the wax onto the paper. Oh, she loved this life. And she smiled in sweet victory as the shell began to crack, and the brooding, desperate man broke his dark, wounded silence to speak the words she had predicted:

"Could I ever have a future with the person I love?"

CHAPTER 41: Piero

Piero watched Maria from the doorway of the tent as she begged her brother to come down from the ladder, and in his heart, he knew he watched her because he did not trust her. She was growing increasingly restless and resistant, and everything between them felt as stretched as the tightrope between the frames. He could do worse than Maria, yet he did not love her. He never had and he never would. But then, that was the wisest way to be, was it not?

With Maria, he had a path to success. A path to an adoring audience. He could not – would not – truly give his heart. The audience was his lover on the stage, and Maria was just his lover between the sheets. He would keep both for as long as he could, fill his ears with their cheers and applause and moans of pleasure. Without them to drown out the empty silence which threatened to destroy him, what would he become?

She called once more to Angelo to come down from the ladder, but her brother's anxious fingers were locked in their ritual of touching the rope and tapping the frame. Finally, he came down and stood with his face in his hands.

"I beg you..." Angelo began, but Maria shook her head, peeled his hands from his face and held them.

"It breaks my heart to see you like this," she said, "but I cannot give up this life. You cannot ask me to leave it behind."

"If we could have but two more catchers?" Angelo said. "Even one!"

"Piero is right: the more catchers we have, the less spectacular the show."

"I do not like that man!"

"Well, I love him, and he loves me."

The words stung Piero and brought instant discomfort. She had never confessed this to him, and he had never uttered those words aloud to another person in his life, not even –

They danced beside the campfire to Annie's fiddle. Robert lifted Piero's hand high, and Piero twirled underneath, dress flowing. Their eyes locked; the words burning his tongue—

He would never say those words. The shape, the sound of them repulsed him – if you spoke these words to another person as truth, you were as good as curled up, naked and helpless on the floor, at the mercy of the listener. Not a position he particularly favoured, and Maria was most unwise to make such a confession. Still, it was useful information to know.

Maria sighed. "His showmanship is unrivalled, and he is of great benefit to us. And once all this unfortunate business with these players is done, matters will improve, I promise."

Angelo's eyes flickered back towards the tightrope.

"Angelo, the tightrope is in good order and needs no further attention! However, *I* would like your attention! 'Tis the eve before the fair – come on, let us drink and be merry!"

Piero quickly ducked out of the tent doorway and hid beside the wagon. He glanced at Young Bess and Iago nearby, tethered to their posts and munching the grass. Maria dragged her reluctant brother out of the tent, on towards the stalls, where the drinks flowed, and the meat pies, sweet tarts and delicacies tempted the stallholders as they made their final preparations. But it wasn't the food and drink that held his interest. Piero's fingers closed around the matted fur of the rabbit's foot.

He had seen *their* wagon roll in a few hours ago, and head for the pathetic little barn in the far corner of the field. Must they insist on prolonging this grand finale? The show was begging to end. But tomorrow he would win the patronage, the company would be defeated, and they need never darken his stage again. But since they had somehow managed to make it to the fair, it would be impolite not to give Robert a little gift to celebrate his arrival.

Piero climbed into his wagon, heading for the wooden chest. He rummaged inside and retrieved his little tin box. He carefully removed his glove and dipped his fingertip into the purple powder, then smeared another layer across his eyelids. A fresh application of armour would be beneficial.

He took a deep breath and headed for the tumbledown barn. Why were there so many flies? And what was that stomach-churning smell on the breeze? Well, it served them right. As he approached, he heard voices and a fiddle inside the barn. A merry jig tumbled out, rather incongruous with the somewhat amusing bickering between Caroline and the new actor over the condition of the barn. Caroline's choice of words had their usual feminine charm, and Annie's joyful music seemed incapable of appeasing her. Another torrent of unladylike words hit the air, followed by a shovelful of dung.

"Oi!" yelled the irritated voice of the new actor.

"Well, move faster next time," came Caroline's voice.

Piero couldn't resist a smile. Yes, he disliked her for her antagonism and the way she stole Robert's attention, but she was a fighter, like himself, although their tactics were vastly different. Fighters deserved more than a noose. Perhaps he and Caroline might even have been friends if they had somehow learned to battle side-by-side instead of face-to-face.

He headed on towards the wagon where a pair of tight, dark breeches and... that arse... poked outside. Piero cast a cautious look over his shoulder. Surely the other performers down at the fairground wouldn't see him behind the wagon here. He had a precious moment of freedom to act as he bloody well wanted. He tiptoed over and acquired the perfect position, leaning against the wagon, arms folded, one leg crossed over the other, the toe of his boot pointing down at the ground. He was ready for his second-favourite thing. He took a little breath, feeling the reassuring firmness of the boards beneath his feet.

"Oh dear," he said, lightly. There was a sudden clatter of dropped things from inside the wagon. A delicious thrill rippled through Piero. Robert emerged swiftly and clumsily. "Don't tell me you have lost your horse as well as your stage?" He turned his head oh-so-lazily to look at Robert.

Robert's dark eyes were intense beneath his frown, his expression closed. Always so closed.

"What have you done with my horse?" said Robert calmly.

Piero held his position. "*My* horse is sold. Rest assured, she is in good hands. I would not place her in any other."

The frown on Robert's face softened slightly, and Piero would have given every guinea he had ever held to be privy to his thoughts. But this was all so very curious. There was no argument? No anger? Piero had just sold the darling horse they had founded the company with all that time ago. Why wasn't Robert grabbing handfuls of Piero's shirt and pushing him furiously against the wall of the barn? Their bodies just inches apart... Robert's breath on his skin...

Robert took a step closer towards him, looking at Piero with those deep, brown eyes and a wary expression. Piero responded by stepping away from the wagon and facing him, narrowing his eyes and tilting his head in challenge, hoping his increasing uncertainty remained disguised. Whatever this was, it was not in the script.

"That day at Portsmouth, when I said you should leave the company..." Robert began.

"And Caroline threatened to remove parts of my anatomy if I returned."

"Perhaps..." Robert continued, "perhaps we both acted in haste."

"You mean, after you refused to listen to anything I had to say and rode off with the horse and wagon I paid for, leaving me beaten and bleeding on the ground?" Piero shot back as he searched Robert's face for clues. What game was Robert playing? He needed to find out the rules, bend them, break them, throw them back in the man's face.

Robert took another wary step closer, as if he were approaching a cornered animal. "We had something beautiful, once. I am not sure where it went."

Piero swallowed.

"You deserved a second chance," Robert said gently. "*We* deserved a second chance."

No. This was more lies. Robert believed in second chances as much as Piero believed in luck.

Robert took another step closer, his eyes fixed on Piero... those eyes that the unpainted boy had so nearly lost himself in as the fire crackled and smoke pirouetted up into the indigo sky. "We could put the past where it belongs."

He tensed. Was this Robert admitting his defeat? Or was this Robert admitting—? He hated that he noticed his own breathing. He was here to aggravate matters further, not to listen to lies disguised as forgiveness or apology or whatever the Hell this was.

"Oh, it's a little late for that now, is it not?" he said, in a perfectly pitched tone, both light and dark at the same time. "Besides, I now have everything you could not give me. A successful company... an adoring audience... an attractive lover..." He flicked his white-gloved hand carelessly towards Robert. "And I believe we are about to win a wealthy patron."

He edged forwards, defiance in every step, until their faces were just inches apart. He tensed his chest, his throat. His breathing must be under the strictest control. Let the anger swirl inside him. He would never be the unpainted boy again. "Remind me," he said in barely more than a growl, "why would I come back?"

Robert shuffled an inch closer, his gaze flickering down to Piero's lips then back up to meet his furious stare. Robert was breathing faster – his chest rising, falling. Piero reminded himself to breathe at all.

"Because," Robert said softly, "we were enough."

That was it.

Piero killed the distance between them, cupped Robert's face and kissed him... Lord, the feel of him... the scent, the taste... It physically hurt and he wanted to fall here for ever. He pulled away first, still holding Robert's face, delighted by the spark of desperate hope in his dark eyes. It made his line all the sweeter.

"It was never enough," Piero said, venom overflowing in his voice.

He paused for just long enough to savour the utter devastation on Robert's face, then he dropped his hands from Robert's cheeks with a dramatic flourish, spun on his heel, and walked away.

"See you anon," he called over his shoulder. He walked on, gasping desperate, silent breaths and swallowing desperate, silent screams. His face contorted with unbearable pain and regret; his tight chest ached so much, he thought he might simply drop to the ground and live no more.

Making an exit was his favourite thing in the world... but as he strutted away on dissolving boards, he did not even know in which direction his legs were taking him.

CHAPTER 42: Maria

Maria watched Piero from behind the wooden barn as he walked away from the manager of the Ticehurst Players, and in her heart, she knew she watched him because she did not trust him. Yes, she liked him. She liked his playful style, the way he made her feel. She had easily singled him out when she had seen him on the stage with these players. He had held the audience in the palm of his hand like no other performer she had ever seen before. And yes, she had wanted him.

It was hard to succeed in this world as a tightrope walker, and it was even harder when you happened to be a woman. She needed a loud, confident voice to draw the attention to her, so she could continue to do what she loved, and Angelo did not have the demeanour for such business. Piero was perfect.

She was both the actor and the audience, promising an ambitious, attention-seeking man fame and fortune as they travelled the world. He had been drunk in Portsmouth, and easily tempted, and she had sealed the dream with a kiss and a quick hand. Was she dishonest and unkind? Perhaps, but so was the world. She needed to survive. She had promised Papa as he lay dying that she would look after her little brother by whatever means necessary. And in her defence, she had not known about Piero's involvement with the players' manager. Would she still have acted the way she did if she'd known? Probably.

He made his way down the hill now. From time to time he would change course, stumble uncertainly – as if his mind and his legs were not in harmony. He was lost. So very lost. A stab of pity struck her, followed by a prickle of guilt. She had witnessed this lostness before.

When the players' wagon had rolled away and left him behind, she had bathed his face, bathed his soul and offered him the new life he needed. The new love he needed. For so many days he had drunk and drunk and barely spoken. But in time, he warmed to her, took to her arms, then took to the rest of her body, although she had never been sure whose face he imagined when he closed his eyes and kissed her. Now she was certain. The love of the past had never left him. And neither had the anger. Maria had hoped that the administration of what he perceived as justice would enable him to move on, so she could finally have the undivided attention of his mind and perchance his heart.

Yet here she stood. Losing his attention. Watching him kiss another. And it wasn't just the kiss. It was the way he had looked at the manager: how they had stood barely inches apart... the tension, the desire sparking between them... That was how he ought to be looking at *her*. The endless months of hunting had not been just the petty revenge of a showman. She finally understood the severity of the threat. Piero was tied to this damned company like that damned rabbit's foot was tied to his neck.

It was clear, then. The players would have to go. You played the game to win – that's what Piero always said. Well, if he could not separate himself from them, she would do it for him and lead him out from the prison of his past and into their promising future. She would steal Piero away for a second time and prove to him that they belonged together. She had not come this far just to lose him and the security he brought for her and Angelo. She would do whatever it took to keep him.

Piero strutted on towards the heart of the fair as the man he had kissed gasped, as if Piero had been his very air, and now it had been snatched from him. Then the manager marched inside the barn.

She must be swift.

She glanced over her shoulder, ignoring the racing of her heart and the pricking of her conscience, and darted towards the players' wagon.

CHAPTER 43: Caroline

Robert stormed like a whirlwind into the barn. Annie's merry fiddle instantly silenced. Caroline tensed. What the Hell had happened? His breathing was distressingly fast, his fists clenched. The image of a smirking bastard with purple eyelids sauntered into her mind.

"What has he done?" said Caroline, rushing towards him.

Robert let out a roar which sounded like his soul had been torn in half as he kicked the wooden wall. A plank slipped down. Caroline froze halfway towards him. He pulled back his right hand and punched the wall twice, let out a growl of pain, then booted an unshovelled pile of dung across the barn, missing Thomas by half an inch.

This was not good. She swallowed as Robert marched over to the corner and sat down, drawing his knees to his chest and burying his face in his hands. Blood trickled from his knuckles. A shiver of panic ran through her mind. They could not – must not – begin to slip down that slope again. The single thread... She had fought so hard to keep this company together since the bastard had left, but with either his presence or his absence, Piero seemed utterly determined to destroy them and utterly capable of fulfilling his desire. She took a deep breath. Calm. She needed to keep calm and keep her head, not let her fear tip – as it so easily did – into anger.

Annie crept towards Robert and sat beside him uncertainly. "We gave away the nettle tonic," she whispered to Caroline.

Caroline stared again at the bleeding hand hiding his face.

She snatched broken bottles away, bound his bleeding arms a little too roughly.

"Robert," she said, edging closer. "Look at me."

Her stomach tightened as she knelt beside the kindest man she had ever known, willing him – please – not to just push her away and lock her out as he always did. Why could he not understand he didn't have to always lower the blanket door and suffer alone?

"Look at me."

And he dropped his hands from his face and met her gaze. His face spoke of a devastating brokenness that Caroline swore she would never know for herself. Not like Robert. Not like her ma. For the first time since she had known him, Caroline saw the tears spill from his eyes. There were no words for this.

Something inside her burst. She threw her arms around him, and he let her. She held him tight, so very tight, as silent, choking sobs made his body pulse. She swallowed and blinked more often than she should have needed to, and hoped the strength of her arms spoke the words that she swore she would never say.

After a short while, the pulsing sobs subsided. Was it safe to let him go? Did she want to ever let him go? Her fingers slackened their hold, retreating slowly, as if to reassure him they were never far away. She dropped her arms and sat back on her heels. She needed to clear her mind. She needed to be strong. "Right, I don't care what that bastard has done or what he has said. Robert, you need *us*, not him. And *we* perform for the patron tomorrow and *we* need to be ready."

Too many broken heartbeats passed, and Robert remained silent and motionless. Caroline glanced up at Thomas. Would he help? He stood in the middle of the barn, staring at her.

"Robert, she is right," said Thomas, taking a couple of tentative steps towards them. "We have so little time, yet we are here despite all that has conspired against us! Please – we deserve this second chance!"

"I know." Robert's voice was barely there but speaking was an improvement.

Caroline looked at Thomas with approval. He had his faults – she could in fact form quite a long list – and the idiot's breeches were splattered in dung in two separate places, for Heaven's sake, but his passion could not be doubted. And maybe, for the moment, that was enough.

"I just always hoped that we could find a way," said Robert.

Yes, he had a gift for seeing the potential in lost souls, but why couldn't he accept that some people were simply too much trouble? "Robert, listen to me. He is a selfish bastard and he's never going to change. You deserve better than him."

Robert said nothing.

"Oh... but..." said Annie.

Caroline shot her a furious look. How dare she come to Piero's defence! "Annie, clean his hand," she said firmly. "Thomas, we build the stage. Come on."

Her legs betrayed her with their shakiness as she stood. She and Thomas walked outside, away from the lingering smell and warmth of the barn. There was a rush of air, as if all the feelings inside her had been stealing away her breath without her realising. The world tilted. She put her hands to her head for a moment and took a deep breath.

"You are... all right?" said Thomas awkwardly, moving opposite her, facing down the hill.

Caroline dropped her hands as her head cleared and treated his words like a statement, rather than a question. "Robert would have fared a good sight better if he had never met that man." She thought of her ma, and how she spoke once – only once, when she was wet with tears and drink – of the irreplaceable love she had shared with her beloved Samuel when they both worked in service, how he had died of a fever before their wedding, leaving her lost, heartbroken and with child, and how she would never love again. She looked at her finger. Gone was the ring her pa had gifted her ma as a promise of his love. The ring her ma had gifted Caroline before she went to the river. The ring she had parted with to save the company she loved. The bitterness of life forced its way to her tongue. "Love brings naught but heartbreak."

"And is a woeful distraction from greater purpose," agreed Thomas. "My brother is a testimony to that. So much talent wasted – for a *woman*." He gestured with a dismissive hand towards Caroline.

She narrowed her eyes slightly. "And Robert. So much talent wasted – for a *man*." She returned the gesture to Thomas.

"At least two of us in this company have clarity of sight. We may yet make it to Drury Lane."

Caroline sighed. "Let us see if we can first make it to the end of this bloody fair."

"We shall be fine," Thomas said. "Everything will be absolutely..." His gaze drifted over her shoulder down the hill, then he slumped. "Oh, Lord."

Caroline put her hands on her hips as Benedict came up the sloping field towards them, carrying two large wooden beakers, drinking heartily from each in turn as he headed towards the barn.

"Benedict!" sighed Thomas, melodramatically raising his hands in frustration. "Why must you insist on being so unhelpful?"

"Why?" Benedict's voice was bitter. "You would never understand, Tom. Don't concern yourself. I'd hate to distract you from your precious stage." He staggered inside the barn.

Caroline and Thomas both watched as Benedict went to Robert in the corner.

"You look as I feel," Benedict said, handing Robert a beaker which he took in the hand not being bandaged by Annie. Benedict sat beside him as Annie fastened the bandage and sat on the other side of Robert. The three of them there in a row, lost and forlorn.

Caroline and Thomas both sighed together.

"Stage?" said Caroline. She was very much in the mood to hit things hard with a hammer.

"Stage," said Thomas and clambered into the wagon.

Caroline peered once more inside the barn. Robert and Benedict were both drinking. That was the last thing they needed—

"No!" cried Thomas.

Caroline's head snapped in his direction. That was panic in his voice. She rushed towards him. "What? What now?"

Thomas was on his knees in the wagon, his back facing her. He turned around with a look of utter dismay and held up the Puck costume in one hand. Slashed. Ruined. Strips of green material flopped and flapped hopelessly. Her stomach tightened. No! Then Thomas held up his other hand. The donkey head – impaled and split by the sword.

"Horatio," breathed Caroline, and her hands flew to cover her mouth before she could disguise the shock. Devastation turned to rage. A scream of frustration tore its way through her gritted teeth. "I'll kill him. This is him! Or her! It must be them!" She leapt into the wagon, pushing Thomas aside and began rummaging breathlessly. The drum was destroyed – the final thread slashed; its fragile skin pierced by the other sword. The costume sack! They only had a few precious costumes left, damn him! She tipped the sack upside down. Yes, everything had been damaged, except—

"Where's the dress?" she said. "They've stolen the dress!"

Thomas cleared his throat. "Yes, well. I didn't mention that."

"Didn't mention what?" Patience was no longer an option.

"It wasn't my fault! It was after the show, and apparently, he wanted it back."

"He 'wanted it back'? And you just let him take it?" Any vaguely positive thought of Thomas made a hasty exit.

"He can be rather persuasive at times or perhaps you've not noticed!" Thomas sighed. "At least the skull has survived."

"IT'S ALREADY DEAD!" cried Caroline. "There's only so much more damage they could do! Speaking of damage..." She shoved a plank aside, reached for a wooden box beneath it and opened the lid. There, at least, was the leather sheath, with thin straps for tying it to her leg. And inside was nestled the wooden-handled knife, its blade sharp and ready to serve. But instead of cutting a poached rabbit, she had another purpose in mind. "I have had enough."

Rage propelled her out of the wagon at a neck-breaking speed, and she heard Thomas' footsteps hurrying after her.

"What are you doing?" he said, striding alongside. "Have you lost your wits?"

"I would rather lose my wits than this company, although at this rate I SHALL LOSE THEM BOTH!" She marched with purpose down the field. "We are going to the tightrope tent."

"You *have* lost your wits!" Thomas said, grabbing Caroline's arm and pulling her around.

"Don't you touch me!" Caroline wrenched her arm free. Thomas took a step back and raised his hands in surrender.

"Have you so soon forgotten the call of the gallows?"

"We send them a little message so they understand if they trouble us again, they will have a fight on their hands."

Thomas looked at the knife. "The tightrope."

"The tightrope."

Thomas twisted his mouth. "We are merely repaying in kind, after all."

"They will come for us again if they think they can. You have seen Robert's state of mind." Caroline pointed the sheath back towards the barn. The single thread... "We do not sit back and take this from them."

Thomas looked grim and nodded. "We must make haste."

For once, he wasn't wrong. She did not want to leave Robert drinking with Thomas' brother for too long and besides, the day was in its golden finale and they had a stage to build before darkness fell. But this was as vital to their success as a stage. Caroline bent over, reached beneath her skirts and tied the thin leather straps around her leg. She stood up and her defiant eyes met his concerned ones, then they made their way swiftly down the field.

The largest tent had a straight top that slanted down at the ends and sides which were now rolled to the ground. Caroline tucked her fingers around the flap and peered inside. The tightrope was stretched high up in the tent between two frames, with a ladder propped against the left-hand side. There was no sign of anyone.

"Watch the door," she said to Thomas as they both stepped inside. "Any moment they could come back. If we're caught, we'll likely be thrown out of the fair."

"*More* than likely if my uncle has anything to do with it."

Caroline headed for the ladder and began to climb, her skirts swishing unhelpfully. Piero was welcome to the bloody things.

"Let me do it. You are going to break your neck in that!"

"I will if you keep distracting me!"

The wooden rungs were smooth beneath her sweating palms. She dared not look down, but she refused to feel respect for the woman who climbed up here and performed Heaven knew what on this rope. Caroline reached the top. Shit, it was a long way...

"This is unwise! I beg you, come down!"

"Just watch the door! I'm trying to concentrate," she said. She steadied herself on the topmost rung of the ladder. Her heart thumped and a wave of panic swept over her. Had she ever been this far from the ground in her life? There was a small ledge at the top, less than a foot wide. Caroline eyed it suspiciously. She leaned forwards onto the ledge, hardly daring to breathe...

One slip, one fall...

She rarely wore stays, and the absence of them now under her clothes allowed her to feel the little wooden platform digging just below her ribcage.

"How can I catch you if I'm watching the door?"

"I don't need you to catch me!" she growled breathlessly. "I need you to watch THE BLOODY DOOR!"

She took the frustrated sigh beneath her as an indication that Thomas was finally doing what he was told. She reached out a trembling hand as far as she could and grasped the rope. Desperate fingers reached beneath her skirts for the knife. She cursed the dress again – unhelpfully trapped between her and the ladder. Her breath stuck in her throat as she rolled herself slightly to the left, to release enough material to reach for her knife. Her sweating hand found the smooth wooden handle...

The ladder rocked slightly – panic swept over her – she gasped.

"Shit!"

"Are you all right?" Thomas' urgent voice called, his footsteps running towards her.

"DOOR!" She regained her balance. Her breath came in bursts. Her heart thumped in her ears. As Thomas' footsteps retreated, she took a deep breath to calm herself. Bloody skirts. Bloody ladder. Bloody tightrope. But she had her knife, and she had control. She needed to be swift.

She fought for balance with every movement of the treacherous knife as it glided back and forth. The rope began to fray and weaken. Maria would, of course, realise as soon as she reached the top and probably long before the show. There would never be any real danger of her treading on it. They were merely causing a stir, playing their game, shaking the dice onto the table and hoping for a higher score.

"Make haste!" said Thomas somewhere beneath her.

"I am!" She studied her handiwork. The rope was still attached but unsafe. Almost hanging by a single... thread... Oh, that served them well.

No time to sheath the knife. She tucked it carefully between her teeth. With every rung she went down, her body relaxed a little more, until she jumped proudly from the last couple of rungs. She let out a triumphant breath. Tucking away the knife, she smiled at Thomas, ashen-faced at the door, and sailed past him with shaking legs, feeling very smug, very sick and very grateful for the ground beneath her feet.

CHAPTER 44: Piero

The ground had vanished beneath his feet. The boards were gone. The audience had gone. There was nothing but flashes of Robert's devastated face in front of his eyes. The noise and excitement of folk enjoying a merry evening before the fair whirled vaguely around him. But he couldn't hear it, he couldn't feel it. There was only the lost, sad-eyed stare of the unpainted boy in the mirror who knocked desperately on the glass. But that person was dead, killed many years ago by a world which did not attempt to understand him and so feared him instead, and what remained in the mirror was merely a voiceless ghost, forever trapped. And it was safer and better that he stayed there.

Piero's legs took him in the direction of a certain wagon. He took deeper, calming breaths as he approached. The world and its audience began to appear around him again, their voices and movements becoming clearer as he walked. He held his head higher and gave his hair a half-hearted toss.

The timing... It was all in the timing... and his timing had always been perfect, so he couldn't possibly have arrived at the old woman's table a little prematurely. He ignored the tears running down an unpainted face, trapped in a mirror far away. Instead, he sat on the stool opposite the old woman, hastily hardened his expression and said with an icy voice, "It appears I have need of your services once more."

That infuriating smirk appeared on the old woman's face, and she held out her hand for a coin. There was something so intriguing yet unnerving about this woman, and he did not dare break eye contact with her as his white glove reached for the purse inside his jacket. Her eyes sparkled with knowledge that she couldn't possibly have as he leaned forwards and dropped the coin into her open, waiting palm.

Her other hand shot out.

What the—?

She grabbed his rabbit's foot necklace, pulled him close, lifting him off his seat. How the Hell did she keep catching him off-guard? Piero rolled his eyes and sighed in frustration. "Will you just stop doing that?"

"Old Dina sees more than her candle tells her." Her breath was warm on his face. "You wear the rabbit's foot, yet you don't believe in the sight, you believe in revenge." Piero huffed with annoyance yet found himself listening desperately. She looked up at him with those knowing eyes.

"Old Dina sees that once you believed in love. And one day, you will again."

And he felt as if he had been punched in the stomach, lying curled up, helpless, naked on the ground, trying so hard – so fucking hard – to find a way to breathe. Somewhere, a silent fist pounded desperately inside a mirror, but Piero would not acknowledge it. He dared not. He fought and caught his breath. He narrowed his eyes and tilted his head oh-so-slightly.

"How lovely," he said with mock politeness. "Now may I have my necklace back?"

Her fingers slowly released their grip. The old woman smiled at him, but Piero threw her an annoyed look as he returned to his stool, tucking the necklace pointedly back beneath his cravat.

"That's better," he said frostily. "Now, *dear woman*, you said good fortune awaited me at this fair. Perhaps we should help it along a little. The lead actor of the Ticehurst Players finds himself in need of wisdom."

"Does he now?" The fortune-teller folded her arms. "And just what might the candle show Old Dina?"

The unpainted boy sadly lowered his fist and faded from the mirror. In his place appeared a man with his head bowed down. He lifted his face slowly upwards until he stared back with defiance: the face of a showman with purple-powdered eyelids.

Piero smiled.

CHAPTER 45: Maria

Voices flowed loud and free in the drinks tent. Maria devoured the heady scents of ale and cider that wrapped around each other in the early evening air, overpowered from time to time by the smell of roasting meat and woodsmoke on the breeze. Performers mingled easily, despite the competition. Folk sang, drank and spoke of their hopes for the fair. Some boasted that their act would attract the patron, some only wanted a decent income to fill their depleted coffers. Others simply hoped that the good weather would last or the bold and hungry rats that scoured the field wouldn't get their stock of pies.

Maria nodded her thanks at the man behind the table, who took her coins and handed her two wooden beakers. She passed one to Angelo, then knocked her beaker against his. While Angelo sipped his drink unenthusiastically, Maria guzzled in celebration. She cursed those wretched players, and her own foolishness for agreeing to hunt them down. But now, at last, it was ended.

Caroline had made it quite clear in the Angel that the company was about to fall, and Maria had given it a thoughtful little nudge over the edge when she had visited their wagon. With no company, there was nothing for Piero to pursue. She let the sweet, tangy liquid slide down her throat, then sighed as she watched her little brother take another half-hearted sip.

She did not have the heart to tease him or provoke him into merriment. She gave an inward sigh. Every night before a show was the same: he was preoccupied with thoughts and rituals that seemed odd to her but made sense to him. If she hadn't dragged him out tonight, he would be there, tapping both frames which held the tightrope, always four times on each side. Yes, it greatly troubled her that he struggled so, but who else in this world would she rather depend on than him? If she should fall – not that she ever would – who was better placed to catch her than the brother who adored her, and had worked with her since childhood? It had been the two of them against the world for so long since their parents had died. The two of them living together, working together, as was the family tradition, as it was always meant to be. She would do her utmost to provide for him and protect him from harm and knew he would do the same for her.

Would Piero? The way he had kissed that manager haunted her... but with the players' imminent fall, his attention would surely return to where it belonged. They needed each other, and she could not imagine a future without him now. An idea brewed in her mind.

"Hold this," Maria said, handing Angelo her drink and ignoring the questions in his eyes. She pushed through the crowd of merry folk. A large man stumbled drunkenly into her, clutching at the sleeve of her shirt, and Maria threw him a sour look and elbowed him away. She peered outside the tent for Piero. Dusk was not far away, and the warmth of day had already surrendered to the freshness of evening. Where was he? She searched through the crowd, trying to...

There he was, coming towards the open-fronted tent where she stood, although his course seemed set for the tightrope tent further along to the right. His head was high, and there was a confident strut in his step once more, as if he expected all eyes to be upon him, lapping up his every move. And here she was: being the audience he so desperately needed. He did not look in the mood for drinking and merriment, but looked straight ahead with a dark and distracted expression. Perhaps she had exactly what he needed to hear.

She pulled out a couple of hair pins beneath her cap and let a lock or two tumble down, then she swayed out of the tent. A seductive smile spread on her face as she intercepted his path. He stopped abruptly, and she snatched the opportunity to wrap her arms around his waist, staring up into his pale eyes and trying to ignore their lack of interest. She tilted her head and kissed him enthusiastically, noting with frustration that there was little response.

"I had an interesting thought," she murmured, wrapping her arms more tightly around him.

"So it appears," said Piero. Was that a hint of irritation in his voice? "Although I regret to inform you, I am in no such mood tonight."

"Actually, it is a different interesting thought." Maria smiled. "You flatter yourself too readily."

"One of my vices, so I'm told." He sounded so far away.

"My interesting thought..." she said, hoping to draw him back. "I was thinking how we must give Lord Pelham a show he cannot forget. Steal the attention."

Piero looked towards the little wooden barn at the top of the field. "And prove to those players that we have everything they do not..."

If nothing else, Piero had taught her the value of capturing an audience. "Everything," she murmured. Maria put a hand on the side of his face and steered his gaze back towards her. Damn it, she would make him look at *her* the way he looked at *him*.

"What exactly were you thinking?"

"I already intend to perform the acrobatics upon the rope, as you know. But what if..." She paused. It was all in the timing, that is what he always said. "I am blindfolded."

She could almost feel the thrill ripple through him as a smile spread across his face. A genuine one... how rare they were.

"Oh, you are marvellous, my love."

And for a moment – one special moment – she looked into his dancing eyes and could almost believe she was the keeper of his heart. Had she ever been? Perhaps, at first, when he was drunk and dizzy and wanted the crowd to beg for more. But really it was all about *them*, wasn't it? For if *she* could be marvellous, the players would seem less so, and his pain would lessen. And so, they performed this elaborate dance – never meaning what they said, never saying what they meant, until it was difficult to tell the truth and lies apart.

She tried to shake the thoughts from her head so she could focus. The game was still in play and she needed to set the pieces in place.

"We must only tell Angelo at the last moment. We keep him away from the tent until I am about to perform." Just as Angelo protected her, she would protect him from harm as she had promised, whatever risks were necessary. Securing the patronage would mean they could afford one more catcher, then he would not be alone in his duty. Her brother's desperate pleas echoed in her mind. It would surely be worth Angelo's momentary suffering to secure such a thing.

"We will do one performance only in the morning," said Piero. "Let us build to that moment and Lord Pelham and the people will come. We can perform in the afternoon without the blindfold. Once will be enough." Piero's head turned towards the barn once more. "How could anyone compete with that?"

She would not be defeated that easily. Maria shifted closer, making certain he felt her breath on his neck. She whispered into his ear: "Join me in our tent."

He leaned slightly closer. They were still strangely bound to each other: there was yet hope. She would keep on playing, as he did. One last game as the dice danced across the table and the stakes rose again.

She smiled back coyly and pulled away from him first, slowly, letting her fingertips trail down his chest, down his body, lingering at his breeches.

"Give me a few minutes to prepare something... special." She swayed off towards the tent, desperately hoping his gaze was following her, and not daring to look back in case it was not.

CHAPTER 46: Angelo

Angelo disliked the way Piero watched his sister, as he did now. Watching Maria was Angelo's job; it should not be Piero's. Angelo stood at the edge of the drinks tent as fingers of anxiety tightened around his throat. He placed the beakers down on a nearby table. Clearly his sister had no want of hers, and he was in no mood for drink. All he wanted was to protect his sister.

She had always been the confident one, the bold one. The one who showed the talent on the tightrope and trapeze as Papa tossed her easily in the air, this way and that, and taught her to master her mind as she balanced far from the safety of the ground. She was naturally fearless, thriving on risk. And Angelo, cautious and nervous, trained from a young age to watch – always watch – every movement, every muscle. For one day his watchfulness could be the very thing which would save his sister's life. Why could she not understand that was what he was trying to do?

He watched Maria now as she sauntered towards the tent. And he watched the untrustworthy, ambitious man who also watched her. His own hands were tied so fast, as if the tightrope itself bound them. They needed another catcher and neither his sister nor this man would listen. It was a disaster waiting to happen. A disaster he needed to prevent.

His chest began to tighten. Panic began to build.

He tried to steady his breathing. If he didn't, he would soon be kneeling on the ground, clutching handfuls of grass, gasping and suffocating. The arrogant man barely tolerated *him*, let alone listened to his requests. How did his sister enjoy his company so much? He needed to plead with Maria again, beg her to persuade Piero. He would speak with her now. He left the merriment of the tent and turned to follow.

"Angelo," came the man's voice, and Angelo stopped and closed his eyes briefly in dismay. How could a name be spoken with such contempt? Angelo turned around to face him as Piero headed over with a meaningful strut and a fixed gaze.

"Look," Piero said in a low voice. "*I* wish to show those players the measure of my success and win the patronage. *You* clearly wish my relationship with your sister to end. I propose an arrangement."

Angelo hesitated. This was not what he was expecting. What was Piero up to?

"For the first show only, when I am certain Lord Pelham will visit, there is to be no catcher."

Angelo held his breath. No catcher? The words ran with blind panic around his head. No catcher... no catcher...

"In fact, I propose you are not present at all. With this spectacular and exceptional performance, we will surely win the patronage. And with that patronage I will employ a second catcher, perchance even a third, to protect your sister."

No catcher...

"And for my part, I promise that I will end our relationship." Piero stared at him intently. "She will no longer share my bed, yet we will continue to work together successfully. And you must speak no word to Maria of any of this." He shrugged. "Is this not the perfect solution to our problems?"

Angelo just stared, his mind racing, chest tightening, fingers clawing at his throat. He needed to breathe.

Piero rolled his eyes. "I do not have all day."

But if it went wrong? He could not voice the words.

Piero tutted impatiently. "Look, nothing will go wrong," he said, as if reading Angelo's mind. "It will be the same performance, the same routine. Just one show. What say you?"

Was there a choice? What would Maria do in his place? She would take the risk. She always took the risk. Could *he*?

"Oh," Piero added lightly, raising his forefinger, "and if you do not find this agreeable, then perhaps it may be better if we parted ways. By that I mean your sister and I go one way, and you another. I can offer her success and fortune. If you sabotage her career and her chance of securing a patron, she will not thank you for it. I can always find a different catcher."

But Angelo watched her; always watched her! He needed to breathe.

A dark expression flitted across Piero's face. "As it turns out, company members are easily replaceable."

Air couldn't reach his lungs. Maria would take the risk. He found himself nodding.

Piero smiled, and there was more delight in his eyes than Angelo cared for. "You have made a wise choice. I suggest you make yourself scarce in the morning so as not to disrupt our arrangement. I will conjure up an explanation for your absence." He turned to go, then rocked back on his heels as his eyes danced. "Oh, and you may wish to sleep beside the horses tonight." He gave Angelo a little wink, then strutted off towards their tent, in the manner of a man who knew what he wanted and would risk everything to have it.

One performance. Just one, then she would no longer be partnered with this unpleasant man.

Just one performance where he must be absent from the tent, unable to watch her.

No catcher...

He needed... to breathe...

Angelo darted behind the drinks tent, clutched the trunk of a tree and was violently sick.

CHAPTER 47: Thomas

The morning of the fair did not start smoothly. Much to Thomas' frustration, Benedict was suffering from the after-effects of sneaking out of the barn once everyone had fallen asleep and drinking whatever he could find, which apparently was quite a lot. Thomas and Caroline had finally told Robert and Annie about the ruined props, which had resulted in Robert swearing for four and a half minutes straight according to Thomas' pocket watch, followed by – on Annie's tearful insistence – a solemn burial for Horatio behind the barn.

The mood was far from great, and when Thomas had dared to suggest that possibly everything might turn out absolutely fine, Caroline had hurled the skull at him. Only Annie's fiddle-quick fingers had prevented Thomas from adding a broken nose to their list of problems.

At least they had eaten. Caroline and Annie had gone down the field earlier on and had returned with their skirts laden with food. Although, judging by the *pace* in which they had returned and Annie's flushed cheeks and twitchy eyes, Thomas was dubious as to the exact way the food had been acquired.

Thomas looked out of the barn doorway eagerly. Visitors were arriving and performers were already displaying their acts. Above the heads of what appeared to be an admiring crowd, he could see the fire-juggler's flaming batons flying against the blue sky. Over by the gate where Uncle Henry stood, more carts entered, laden with people.

Excited voices burbled away, with drums, fiddles, whistles and songs competing with the many callouts from entertainers for attention. Thomas scowled enviously at the fire-juggler's crowd and looked back into the barn at their own audience.

One old woman – motionless, presumed asleep – sat slumped on the hay bale which Benedict had drunkenly stolen last night because the scent apparently reminded him of Sarah's house, or some such nonsense. The green curtain hung from its wooden frame at the back of the stage, and Caroline stood upon the boards, looking extremely fed up and speaking in her best Lady Macbeth voice.

"The raven himself is hoarse

That croaks the fatal entrance of Duncan

Under my battlements."

To be fair, her performance was impressive, although Thomas fancied if he had to face one of the two women in a deadly mood, he would choose Lady Macbeth over Caroline in a heartbeat. Robert stood in the corner, leaning against the barn wall, his left arm folded across his chest and his bandaged hand covering his eyes. Next to him, Benedict sat on the ground, mournfully examining an empty beaker.

Thomas tutted, marched over and nudged him with his foot. "Stop it! Heaven knows you've already had enough!"

"Oi," said Caroline, putting her hands on her hips. "Is anyone actually listening?"

"I am," said Annie. "It's very good."

Caroline just sighed as Annie turned to look doubtfully at the old woman.

"I think she's dead," Annie whispered to Thomas, with a grimace. She walked hesitantly over to the woman, whose white-haired head was dropped down upon her chest, her mouth slightly open. Annie peered closely... then, with a pointing finger, gave the woman a prod on her arm. The woman gave a wail of surprise as she jolted awake, which was met with a wail of surprise from Annie, remarkably in perfect harmony.

"And that," said Caroline, throwing her hands in the air, "is the best response we shall have from an audience today."

The old woman stood up and dusted herself down. "How long till you start walkin' the tightrope?"

Thomas pinched the bridge of his nose. Caroline folded her arms and glared. And Annie helpfully pointed downfield towards the tightrope tent. The woman swore under her breath and shuffled disgruntledly out of the barn.

"This is hopeless," said Robert flatly, removing his bandaged hand from over his eyes and letting it flop by his side. "Annie, play some jigs. The music may attract custom." He pointed at Thomas and Benedict. "You two, go and drum up some interest before Lord Pelham arrives so we do not look like we are complete failures. Go."

Benedict sighed and let the hand holding the beaker drop to his side, but Thomas nudged him with his foot once again, somewhat more forcefully. "Come on, get up." Thomas didn't bother waiting for Benedict to move, knowing full well he would not. Instead, he reached down and dragged him to his feet.

As they made their way down towards the throb of the fair, with the sun on their backs, Thomas eyed his brother nervously. They had hardly spoken since their arrival, and not just because Benedict apparently preferred drinking to talking. It was all very difficult. Even if – when – they won the patron, Robert did not want Benedict in the company and intended to send him home – a fact that Benedict was unaware of but would probably approve of. Returning him was an obvious solution that would please everyone, aside from Pa and Marcus, yet... was it the wisest course of action?

Despite their empty barn, the fair was full of people, atmosphere and enthusiasm. Thomas frowned. It was all rather strange. They had worked hard to remove the dead sheep, clean out the horseshit *and* be rid of the flies, so there was little reason for their lack of custom, apart from the rather remote location. They passed a troupe of Morris dancers performing to the beat of a small drum.

"Thank Heaven you no longer have a drum," muttered Benedict. "My head aches enough."

"But why are they not coming to us?" said Thomas. Was there something else? A familiar voice cut through the noise. Thomas listened carefully. It was a Welsh voice – a Welsh voice that was extremely pissed off.

"I warn you, stay away from there," Essie was saying at full volume, standing in front of a barrel on an upturned wooden crate and pointing to their barn, addressing everyone she could. "Those Ticehurst Players are bad folk." As she turned, she connected eyes with Thomas and smiled smugly. "Lying bastards, they are!" The man with the little trick-performing dog stopped in front of Essie, watching her with interest. "Heartbroken, I was!"

Thomas grabbed Benedict by the elbow and pulled him away. "Well, no wonder our custom has been so poor!"

"Why does she speak so ill of the company?"

Thomas sighed and rested his hands on his hips. "It was all a simple misunderstanding through no fault of my own!"

"What misunderstanding?"

"If anything, it is I, not her, who experienced the greater trauma!"

"What trauma?"

Thomas watched as Essie jumped down from the wooden crate, linked her arm through that of the man with the dog and headed towards the pies. Thomas dropped his voice. "We were nearly wed."

"WED?" Despite his fragile state, Benedict exploded with laughter, one arm grabbing Thomas' arm, the other grabbing his aching head. Thomas tutted and frowned at him but then his expression softened. Was this not how they used to be? How things were of old, before Thomas had left for London? It seemed a lifetime ago. Then Benedict's laugh died, and his face was full of sorrow. "I should have wed Sarah."

"Brother, there is more to life than women and–"

Lord Pelham! There, parading past them in the opposite direction, went Lord Pelham! He was as tall as Thomas, round-bellied and perhaps the same age as Pa. He wore an exquisite silvery-blue knee-length jacket with a matching waistcoat, and a fine, powdered wig which was so tall, it surely threatened to topple over at any moment. He walked around like he owned the place, which he probably did.

Thomas remembered that when Lord Pelham's players had visited the inn, they had spoken about his interest in art and music. To think that now Thomas and his own company had a chance to pursue him as their patron! Lord Pelham had a merry demeanour and a twinkling eye and was clearly enthralled in the fair as he observed its artists. Behind him walked a young, male servant with dark skin, bearing a large piece of paper which he appeared to be consulting.

"Lord Pelham!" hissed Thomas to Benedict, slapping the back of his hand across his brother's chest. "He's visiting all the acts. Come on, quick! We must draw a crowd!" He dashed back towards the barrel where Essie had stood. He used the wooden crate to clamber atop the barrel, took a deep breath and threw out his arms.

"Oi-oi! Come and see the Ticehurst Players! Sword-fighting! Shakespeare! Both at the same time!" he yelled. He looked around. It had caused barely a ripple. He cupped his hands around his mouth. "WE HAVE A HUMAN SKULL."

Quite a few of the people nearby stopped what they were doing and turned to look at him, some with a look of shock or disgust on their face. Thomas shrugged, slightly disconcerted. "Well... it was already dead when we found it."

The folk returned to ignoring him and continued with their own business. Thomas ran his fingers through his hair and sighed. If only they still had a bloody drum. Lord Pelham was heading for the tightrope tent. Two women chattered excitedly as they walked in the same direction. "That's what I heard, over in the tent," said one to the other as they were swallowed up by the crowd.

As Thomas watched them from his vantage point, his eye fell upon the bright ribbons and dangling rabbit's feet of a familiar wagon nearby. Perhaps it was time for a word about this supposed good fortune, for he hadn't seen a great deal of it thus far. He jumped down from the barrel. Benedict stared forlornly at nothing, but Thomas steered him onto the crate.

"Listen, just get up there and perform something."

"What?"

"Shakespeare! Anything! And direct people up to the barn! I won't be a moment."

Benedict climbed up onto the barrel. "*Shall I compare thee to a summer's day?*"

His brother's heart-wrenching voice faded from Thomas' ears. His attention was fixed on the ribbon-strewn wagon. The fortune-teller was already watching him expectantly from her table, her arms folded and her candle burning as he approached.

"You told me to find you at Thorverton Fair," Thomas said, sitting on the stool opposite her.

"Old Dina did."

"You told me good fortune awaited me here."

"Old Dina did. She sees you could have a successful future, find great wealth and prove your true worth."

"I knew it! The Ticehurst Players shall find a patron?" Finally! The good news that Thomas had longed for. All this suffering would be worthwhile. Except... "I have no coin for the candle." He patted his jacket in dismay.

The fortune-teller scowled. "Old Dina will gift you this one."

"I thank you wholeheartedly! I shall make sure to send custom your way!" Thomas said, watching as the old woman picked up the brass candleholder and poured the molten wax on to the paper.

Thomas tipped his head this way and that as the wax slunk into its new form. "What kind of fame and fortune do you see? Lord

Pelham's coat of arms?" He snapped his fingers excitedly as a thought occurred. "His wig!"

Old Dina hunched over the puddle of wax, then slowly looked up at him. "Old Dina sees a tightrope."

"What?" he breathed and glanced over at the large tent. "A tightrope? But..." He saw Lord Pelham approaching it now. "What does that mean? How is that concerned with my future?"

He frowned at the wax-splattered paper, reaching for it; there was a sharp sting across his knuckles as the old woman swiftly slapped his hand away.

"Take it or leave it. Old Dina's candle won't speak no more."

The tightrope act...?

The fortune-teller leaned forwards. "That means you leave Old Dina now."

"Oh. Of course." Thomas nodded his thanks and stood up, walking back towards Benedict, who stood on the barrel.

"*So long lives this, and this gives life to thee,*" his brother implored, presumably not to the crowd but to the woman miles away who could no longer hear him and no longer help him. Then he stood silent and abandoned as the crowd flocked past him to the tightrope tent. Thomas sighed. They ought to return to the barn and prepare for Lord Pelham.

Good fortune awaited him at the fair. The candle had revealed that fame, wealth and a successful future could indeed be his.

But not in the way he had thought.

CHAPTER 48: Piero

Piero stood in front of the tightrope, staring at the wonderful crowd. The tent was full. Even other acts had come to watch. Singers... dancers... the fire-juggler... The thrill coursed through his veins as he gazed upon the excited, chattering faces of the delighted audience who had come to see him and his spectacular act. It had paid well to drop those young boys a penny to spread the word, for the fairgoers had clearly heard that for this one show only, not only was the tightrope walker to be blindfolded, but she would also perform with no catcher. But Maria, who had been preparing herself in the wagon, had not. Another risk, another gamble, as the dice rolled.

Maria stood beside him now, confident and excited. She was dressed in her fine black costume, the bows delicately tied at her shoulder, hair fashioned on top of her head and the black blindfold in her hand. Doubts flitted treacherously across Piero's mind. He pushed them away. She was capable. She was talented. She had done this routine a thousand times. Even with a blindfold, she would be perfectly safe.

Lord Pelham, wearing an oversized powdered wig and with a servant beside him, sat upon the only chair. Piero noted his approving expression, mirrored the smile and performed a flourish which moved smoothly into a sweeping bow. Then slowly he rose, his very soul crackling with delight. All eyes were on him, waiting... watching... longing... Everyone held their breath for the showman as he commanded his audience. Lord, it felt good. This was what it was all about.

"Where is Angelo?" whispered Maria beside him. "You said he had matters to attend to. Why is he not yet here?"

Piero raised a hand to calm her. It had been far more pleasant without Angelo nervously checking the tightrope before the performance. "I have arranged for him to wait and enter once you are blindfolded. It is all in the timing, is it not?"

She nodded, and they both smiled at the audience. She held his gloved hand with a confident grip; he lifted their joined hands triumphantly. This moment was his. This moment was theirs. And it would surely be the turning point of their fortunes.

"Ladies and gentlemen!" he called. "My name is Piero Grimaldi, and I bid you welcome to the greatest show you will witness this day – dare I say this year! Feast your eyes upon the magnificent Signorina Maria Violante! For she will risk all as she performs a most daring and perilous act upon the tightrope..." It was all in the timing – "... Blindfolded!"

He closed his purple eyelids and inhaled the gasps, cheers and applause of the audience as if it were the air he needed. He dropped hands with Maria and took the blindfold from her. He held it aloft, waiting for the murmur from the crowd to die down, before placing it over Maria's eyes. He tied the black ribbons at the back of her head with shaking fingers.

"Take the greatest of care, my love," he murmured in her ear, and he meant it.

"I have nothing to fear," she whispered back, and he believed her.

He took her hand and led her gently, slowly, towards the tightrope frame on the left, where the ladder rested. She was the mistress of risk. He was certain she would have approved had she known the full truth of the circumstances. Perhaps he should have told her. After all, she had wanted to give Lord Pelham a show to remember, had she not? Every held breath in the room bore testimony to the fact that they were doing just that. Even so, he tensed as Maria's searching hands gripped the rungs of the ladder. Was this a mistake? Had he taken a step too far? But all the performers wanted the patronage. They had to be outstanding.

She put a foot on the first rung.

They had to play the game.

Piero's heart began to beat uncomfortably faster. Maria was completely unaware that for the first time in her entire life, her brother would not be standing beneath the tightrope with his faithful hands. For the first time, Maria's life was in *his* hands.

The dice tumbled across the table as steadily, confidently, Maria began to climb...

CHAPTER 49: Angelo

Grass blades gripped in fingers–

need to breathe – need to breathe–

sorry, Papa–

can't breathe – no air–

going to die–

no watching–

no catcher–

no–

no–

NO–

CHAPTER 50: Thomas

A tightrope.

The fortune-teller's words were all Thomas could think of as he guided a downcast Benedict back up the sloping field to the barn. She had seen a tightrope. Behind him, Thomas could hear snatches of Piero's voice introducing his act, which was followed by an eruption of cheers and applause. Ahead of him, the mournful ballad of a fiddle drifted down on the breeze, accompanied by a very faint but stubborn smell of dead sheep.

"Robert, for Heaven's sake, stop staring at that bloody skull!" came Caroline's voice. "And as for *you*..."

The fiddle's doleful tune cut off abruptly. Caroline came marching out of the barn and all but threw the skull together with Annie's fiddle and bow into the wagon.

"Just for five minutes!" Caroline ranted as she went back inside. "Before we *all* start staring at the bloody thing!"

Oh Lord. That didn't sound promising. Thomas ushered Benedict inside the barn. Robert was lying motionless on the stage, staring up at one of the many holes in the roof.

"I'm certain people will arrive soon," Thomas said as Benedict flopped down once more in the corner.

Caroline shook her head and snatched up one of the swords. "*I'll* find us a bloody audience."

"Help!" gasped a man's voice.

Thomas turned and saw the tightrope catcher, gripping the doorway of the barn and looking like he might faint. Robert sat upright as Thomas looked anxiously at Caroline. The sabotaged tightrope?

But it sounded like Piero's show had already started. "Why are you not in the tent?" he asked, unsure if he wished to hear the answer.

Caroline cast down the sword and spoke urgently. "What is wrong?"

The tightrope catcher took some desperate breaths. "Piero Grimaldi. You – you know him."

"Has something happened to him?" said Robert, jumping down from the stage.

"I do not trust him! My sister – she may be unsafe. I cannot go! I swore – not to catch."

"Swore not to catch? But is she not blindfolded?" said Benedict.

"What?" the man and Thomas said at the same time. Thomas whirled around to Benedict, his mind leaping to a multitude of possible scenarios, which all ended in tragic and premature death. That was not the plan! That was never the—

"I heard people speak of it while you were gone," Benedict said to Thomas. "Why should that concern you?"

Thomas gripped the catcher's shoulders. "Surely you noticed the damaged rope?"

The catcher's blank look said it all.

"Oh shit," breathed Thomas, hearing Caroline gasp beside him. He ran from the barn, his feet pounding the grass, aware of desperate footsteps following behind. Why was the tent so far away? He knew it had been a mistake! He heard no screaming, unless it was drowned out by the rapid heartbeat in his ears. On he ran down the hill, across the field. There was the tent! The door flap was open; Thomas charged in, a desperate, silent prayer on his lips, aware of Caroline and the catcher rushing behind him.

Maria was right at the top, blindfolded, one foot upon the platform, the other poised in the air, about to tread upon the—

CHAPTER 51: Maria

"STOP!" yelled the panicked voice of a man below.

Maria startled. The certainty of her next step was stolen by the sudden cry. She wobbled – swayed – desperate for her balance to return as the terrified gasp of the audience flew up to reach her. Papa's voice in her head – she must not panic – must not panic. She forced clarity into her mind. She regained her balance, placed the poised foot back on the platform and hastily untied the blindfold with trembling fingers.

She stared at the rope in front of her. What the Hell had happened to it? Frayed – as if someone had attacked it repeatedly and ferociously with a blade. She had not noticed it from below. For the tightrope had always been fine... and Angelo took care of everything. She looked down. Caroline and the lead actor ran across the ring, stopping beside Piero. What was going on? Why were those wretched players always there? And where was—

Angelo appeared beneath the rope, his shaking arms outstretched and ready; his troubled eyes meeting hers. Watching her, as always. She stepped backwards from the platform, lowering her foot and grateful for the first time in her life to feel the rung securely beneath her.

One slip, one fall...

"I understood, Mr Grimaldi," called Lord Pelham, "that the blindfold was to be present, and the catcher was not! It appears, dear fellow, you have it the wrong way around!"

No catcher? The crowd burst into laughter and there was a loud ripple of jeers as Maria continued down the ladder. What was Lord Pelham talking about?

"Forgive me, my lord," came Piero's charming voice.

Maria's feet touched the ground, and she went straight to Angelo's waiting arms. He embraced her desperately, gasping for breath. His hand cradled the back of her head. His whole body was shaking, and she held him tighter.

"Angelo, what is happening?"

"I will rectify the situation, my lord," Piero said. "There appears to be some kind of mistake." His voice was colder now, laced with a fear and fury that Maria hadn't heard before.

"Apparently so," said Lord Pelham. "Your tightrope walker is now on the ground instead of up in the air! Perhaps we shall watch *you* walk the tightrope, Mr Grimaldi?"

The crowd around him laughed again as Maria pulled free from her brother's embrace. "The tightrope has been damaged," she said to Piero. He glanced up at the rope. Anger burned in his eyes and Maria fought the urge to step further away.

"My lord, I beg for your patience whilst I sort this misunderstanding," said Piero, giving the players a deathly stare. "I am uncertain why these players have run into the tent and ruined my act."

Maria looked at Caroline, thoughts beginning to connect. Had they...?

"My *heartfelt* apologies," said the lead actor. His eyes lingered on Piero, who looked on the verge of exploding. The actor took Caroline's arm and tried to move in the direction of the tent door. "We bid you good day."

Piero dashed in front of them and Maria moved to his side. She narrowed her eyes. They were not leaving without giving some answers.

"And I must bid you good day as well," said Lord Pelham. "Mr Grimaldi, as entertaining as this has been, I am a busy man. A shame indeed. Although if you ever need a new act, perhaps you could turn your hand to comedy." He made a motioning gesture to his servant, who jumped to his feet. They headed for the tent door, swallowed by the swarming crowd which followed, murmuring in disappointment.

"No, wait! My lord!" Piero objected, fighting to follow Lord Pelham.

"Doesn't feel good to lose something you care about, does it?" called the lead actor with an air of smugness about him. Piero turned to face him, rage in his eyes.

"We played your game, Piero," said Caroline. "You lost."

"Oh, do not suppose the dice have stopped rolling," said Piero darkly, then he pushed past whoever he could and fought his way out of the emptying tent.

Maria turned to Caroline. "And do not suppose I have finished with you! Tell me why you burst into our tent." This woman was fast becoming the bane of her life. "What know you of our damaged rope?"

"And what know *you* of our damaged props?" Caroline retorted.

Any doubts disappeared with one look at her face. These bloody players! "How dare you touch my rope?" Maria waved a furious hand. "I shall report you to the fair manager! You have cost us the patronage!"

"And you may have cost us everything! Although I should be grateful to you."

"Grateful?" Maria frowned.

"You have taken Piero off our hands. You are welcome to that man, if he will still have you after this."

If he would still have her? The thought had never occurred to her.

"I am not sure he will have *me*," Angelo said. His hands moved to her shoulders and there was deep concern in the eyes which perfectly matched her own. "He threatened that if I didn't allow this, we would part ways. He would find a different catcher!"

"A different catcher?" Maria shook her head in disbelief. How could Angelo think that she would even entertain such a thing? She lifted his hands from her shoulders and gripped them. "I promised Papa I would take good care of you."

"And I you! I only left because..." Angelo took a breath. "He offered to end your relationship if I was absent this once. I do not think his love is as sincere as you believe. Forgive me."

The words stung and Maria looked away from her brother's concerned face. Piero was willing to end the relationship if it secured him a patron. Just like that. Caroline was right – he would likely abandon her when a better proposition appeared. The bastard. Yes, they had danced around each other since the day they had met, yet now it was painfully clear: they might meet each other's wants, but never each other's needs. She could fulfil his desires with an audience and her bed. Neither would ever really fill his aching emptiness.

Perhaps they had both wanted to believe the lie of their love. But it could never be truth. Truth was that kiss at the barn. It mattered not if he loved men, or women, or both, or none. All that mattered was that he did not love *her.* Perhaps she had never truly loved him either. For so long they had both played Highest Points, and now the dice had finished tumbling, it seemed they had both lost.

"I warned you: he thinks only of himself." Caroline pointed to the doorway. "You have seen what he is capable of, and Lord knows what will come next."

Maria frowned again. His eyes had burned with such anger. And the path he walked seemed to be growing darker every day.

"You do not have to follow him," continued Caroline. "The show is not *his* – it is yours."

"I would not ask you to give up your tightrope," Angelo said, squeezing her hands. "It is in your blood; it is our life. But please, I beg you: could we find another way?"

Maria looked at her little brother. The one who had risked everything to save her. The one who always stood by her, whose strong arms she would rely on until the day they stopped performing and the day she stopped breathing. They had each other for ever. Who did Piero have? When he had kissed her, and lain in her arms, they had never truly been together. When he performed before a devoted crowd, applause would still die and leave him abandoned on an empty stage. She had her brother. Piero? He was utterly alone.

A cry sounded somewhere outside the tent. "FIRE! THERE'S A FIRE!" It was echoed by other voices yelling in panic.

A fire? Maria exchanged a quick nervous glance with Caroline. He hadn't...? As they all burst through the door flap, the smell of smoke and burning wood – and what exactly had come next – rushed to meet them. But as they entered the field, Maria stopped and grabbed Angelo's arm.

"No," she said simply and sadly. She watched as Caroline and the lead actor ran up the field to where their barn was ablaze.

CHAPTER 52: Piero

The flames screamed on Piero's behalf. As exits went, this was surely the pinnacle of his success. He spectated from behind the broad tree, a safe distance away. A tower of dark smoke commandeered the blue sky above the barn, and the smell of destruction drifted across the field. So, now who had won?

Chaos tumbled around him as the panicking audience threw buckets of water at the barn and wagon. The wind and the oil hastened the fire – surely the crowd could see only defeat awaited them? The furious flames roared and crashed and consumed their prey swiftly and without mercy. Yet now the force of his rage had been unleashed, it had passed its peak. Such ferocity could not be sustained and alongside the hatred and anger and pain, something else began screaming inside him – the silenced voice of an unpainted boy.

He hadn't seen Robert and Annie come out. Fingers pressed against the mirror and the face which stared out watched in horror. Where were they?

Sickening cracks sounded over desperate shouts as several defeated planks plunged down to a fiery grave.

He swallowed. Where were they? They must have got out.

Annie. He would never – never – mean Annie any harm. She was the sweetest person he had ever known. He hadn't thought – he didn't mean—

And Robert...

A rush of dizziness swept over him. There was no air.

WHERE WAS ROBERT? Was he safe? Damn him! He hated this man! Hated the way Robert had a hold on his life! Hated the way he made Piero care! WHERE THE HELL WAS HE?

His breath came fast. He leaned against the tree, wrapping an arm around the rough bark, looking anxiously from place to place. Fuck. What had he done? Why hadn't the old fortune-teller stopped him lighting a torch from her fire? Stopped him from taking the fire-juggler's oil and dousing the barn? She must have known! Didn't she know every bloody thing?

The field span. Robert? Annie? WHERE THE HELL WAS ROBERT? He didn't want – he didn't mean—

Red hair! Red hair: yes, there! His legs buckled a little, he clung tighter to the tree. There was Annie in the audience, coughing, hands flying to her face. Safe. Lord, she was safe. And if Annie was all right, then...

Robert pushed people aside to reach her.

Time stopped. The silent screaming inside stopped.

Piero drew desperate, gasping breaths into his tight chest, his head bowed. His shaking fingers dug into the rutted bark of the tree.

They were safe.

His breath began returning and he looked up. Robert embraced Annie in his strong, gentle arms then studied her face intently as he always did to ensure a person was safe. Once, a lifetime ago, Robert had looked at *him* like that... before the world fell irreversibly apart.

The disintegrating barn held no interest now. The audience became irrelevant, merely muffled noise and bucket-throwing blurs. On the fringe of the crowd, some movement did catch his attention: the new actor and Caroline running towards the burning remains. No doubt their precious lead actor would take matters from here.

Piero turned around, his back to the trunk, and slowly lowered himself down to the ground. He closed his eyes and leaned against the bark, unable to move, unable to think. He just needed to keep breathing in the overly-warm air. What remained of his heart pounded too loudly in his ears. Above the sound of its rapid rhythm and the deafening crash as the roof finally caved in, the voice of the precious new actor shouted the same word over and over again...

CHAPTER 53: Thomas

"BENEDICT!"

Everything blurring – a rush of people – smoke – and overwhelming noise – shouting – collapsing wood – consuming fire – crashing into – arms flying at faceless bodies slowing him – get out of the fucking way!

"BENEDICT!"

No sign. Robert! Annie! Running towards them. Caroline there first, throwing her arms around Annie, grasping Robert's hand.

"My fiddle was in the wagon!"

Grabbing Robert's shoulders. "Where's Benedict? Where is my brother?"

"I do not know!" Robert's eyes wide. "Isn't he here?"

Chest tight, looking wildly – so many people – smoke spreading –

"He did come out, didn't he?" Annie's voice.

A crash. More burning wood falling. Oh Lord. What if – what if Ben was still...

Shit! Releasing Robert's shoulders – throwing off jacket – starting for the barn. Strong arms gripping him – pulling him back. Thomas thrashing – thrashing—

"NO!" Robert shouting in his ear. "NO!" Arms wrapping around his chest.

"Get off!"

"I cannot let you go in there!"

"I am his brother!" Thrashing. "I AM HIS BROTHER!"

"*And I love him w–*" Coughing.

Robert's grasp slackening. Ben? Whirling around. Searching. Over there! Ben! Pushing through people, shaking legs somehow running.

"Ben!" Reaching him, grasping his upper arms as if life depended on it. Benedict: so pale, stumbling, coughing. "Are you all right? Can you breathe?"

Benedict nodded. That was all he needed. He threw his arms around his little brother, holding him as close – as tight – as he could, pinning his arms to his sides. The chaos around him faded. It was just them, as it always used to be.

"Well *now* I can't breathe," wheezed Benedict, wriggling slightly. He coughed again.

"Thomas," came Robert's gentle voice from somewhere. There was a hand on his back.

Thomas stepped back from the embrace, keeping his trembling hands on his brother's shoulders and snatching a desperate breath himself. The noise around him flooded back into his ears. Benedict staggered again, and Thomas steered him away from the blaze and eased him down into a sitting position. Thomas dropped down onto his knees beside his brother and ensured their eyes met. "Take some deep breaths. Stay here. You'll be safe." Then he marched back towards the burning barn.

Buckets of water were thrown here and there as new spits of flame broke out on the grass. But there seemed to be the gradual realisation that there was nothing anyone could do but let the raging fire burn and burn, until exhausted and spent, it defeated itself.

Thomas' eyes were drawn to the remains of the wagon as he passed. The canvas was already gone, leaving only tiny pieces of burning material drifting mournfully in the air. The fragile wooden frame was alight, and inside he could just make out the burning circle of the ruined drum and the empty sockets of a skull staring at him through the hungry, licking flames. A funeral pyre. That's what it was.

Somebody shoved an empty bucket into his hand, and Uncle Henry's gruff voice said in his ear, "Horse trough, boy. Down the field. Go."

His arms and legs did as they were bid, as he filled his bucket and flung water at the dying wagon. But his mind was elsewhere, filled with half-thoughts, all chaotic, dancing and uncontrollable as the flames. After each bucket he hurled, he glanced down the field at his little brother, sitting with his head and arms resting on his drawn-up knees. Safe.

The man from the drinks tent brought his table up and began serving while customers, confident that the immediate risk had passed, admired the show as if it were a celebratory bonfire. Lord Pelham sat on a chair, with his servant seated beside him, captivated by the display. Within the hour, the spectacle was over, and the wagon was naught but a charred and broken carcass. Much like the company. Thomas swallowed. Perhaps there came a point when you had to accept that you tried so hard – so bloody hard – to save something, but it was impossible, however much hope you had.

A great many people still stood around, talking and watching. A short distance away, Robert sat on the ground with an arm around Annie. She rested her head on his shoulder as Caroline walked over and sat on the other side of Robert. Thomas' jacket was folded up beside Robert expectantly, but Thomas could not bear to be with them – could not bear the inevitable conversation about the ending of it all. So he stared at the wrecked skeleton of the wagon and kept his distance. Without needing to look, Thomas sensed the comforting presence of his brother alongside him.

Thomas turned to study him: Benedict was still pale. He reached for his brother's shoulder. "You are all right?"

“I am fine.” But his voice lacked its usual strength. “Your wagon...”

“It’s all gone.” There was a twisted feeling in his guts. “Everything we worked for. All my hopes.”

“What will you do now?”

Thomas stared at the devastated frame. In his mind’s eye, Pa came walking out from behind it, smiling in satisfaction.

“If we did not acquire the patronage, it was decided the company should fold.” Thomas ran a hand through his hair. “I crawl back to that inn. I suppose we both do. How can I face him and admit that I’ve failed? That I have lost everything.” And with those words spoken out loud, his eyes burned. He covered them with his hand and tried to blink the tears away.

A hand squeezed his shoulder. “Tom, I do not care about a famous actor with a famous company. I care about my brother.”

Benedict pressed something smooth into Thomas’ hand. Thomas looked down. His pocket watch. It must have fallen out of his jacket when he had thrown it to the ground.

“My brother matters more than he knows,” said Benedict. “You have not lost quite everything.”

Thomas’ throat tightened. He gave a little nod. When was the last time he had been so grateful for his brother’s presence?

“Shouldn’t you be with your company?” Benedict said and slowly walked towards them.

Thomas followed with a heavy heart. The company was ending, but at least he still had his brother. And when the two of them returned empty-hearted to the inn, they would once more have the companionship of each other as they somehow tried to rebuild their drained and dreamless lives.

Benedict flopped down beside Annie. He stared blankly at the two piles of ash with small lumps of charred wood in front of her. Taking great care to avoid eye contact with anyone, Thomas positioned himself opposite Robert.

"You did your best," said Robert.

Thomas forced a tiny smile at the kindness in his voice.

"I am truly sorry it ends this way," said Robert. "It is not as I hoped."

"It is exactly as Piero hoped," Caroline said. "There's no doubt this is his handiwork after what happened to the tightrope."

Thomas shot her a sidelong glance, then looked anxiously at Robert, who wore a puzzled expression.

"Tightrope? What happened to the tightrope?"

Caroline opened her mouth to speak, but Thomas jumped in. "To be clear, sabotage was *her* idea. I just didn't disagree."

"Sabotage?" said Robert, his mouth hanging open. "You sabotaged the tightrope? She could have died!"

"Well, so could we," said Caroline, pointing at the remains of the barn.

Annie looked up at Thomas. Poor Annie, how pale and tired she looked. "I think this is my fiddle." She picked up a handful of the ash and let it trickle through her fingers to the ground. She wiped her eyes with the back of her hand. "We've lost everything."

Thomas looked up to see Lord Pelham still seated, watching a man on stilts attempt to dance. "Not quite everything," he murmured. He pushed himself up again from the grass and got to his feet, threw on his jacket and tucked his watch into the inside pocket. Passion and purpose began to fight once more through the gloom. "Listen, Piero has kindly brought us an audience. Why waste the opportunity? One last performance together. One last farewell. The show is not over 'til we lower the curtain."

"I think this is our curtain," sniffed Annie, picking up the second pile of ash and pouring it to the ground. Then she frowned and looked at both piles in turn. "Or is that one my fiddle?"

"Well," said Thomas, waving an impatient hand. "The show is not over 'til we bloody well take our last bow, whether or not we have a curtain. Brother?" He reached out his hand for Benedict, who smiled and took it. Thomas pulled him to his feet.

"Reckon it'll be a fitting goodbye," said Annie, brushing dust and ash from her skirts as she stood up.

Thomas turned to offer a hand to Caroline, but she was already standing. Only Robert stayed on the ground, staring at the piles of possibly curtain and possibly fiddle with his dark, brooding eyes.

"Robert?" said Thomas. Would he agree?

With a hand on his ribs, Robert eased himself up and looked at everyone in turn. Then a sad smile spread on his face and he said: "*Is all our company here?*"

A rush of emotion travelled up Thomas' throat and he swallowed it back down. Now was not the time. "We need to gain some attention," he said, keeping his voice steady. "And, regretfully, this is the second time our stage has been reduced to ash."

"Shoulders?" said Benedict.

They could be back in the orchard, preparing to scrump. An unstoppable smile burst across his face. "Shoulders."

Benedict leaned over as Thomas climbed on his brother's back, his legs either side of Benedict's neck, wobbling a little as his brother slowly stood up. But up they went, until Thomas was above the heads of the crowd. He threw on the winning smile of a showman, thrust out his arms, then yelled at the top of his voice: "Oi-oi!"

CHAPTER 54: Caroline

For that moment, as they stood there amongst the charred remains of their lives, it was like coming home. There was a sudden and dangerous rush of affection for them all, even Thomas. She had been desperate to protect Robert from another disastrous lead actor, unable to bear the consequences should Robert be hurt once more. Thankfully, Thomas had not been able to replace Piero in every respect, yet the strength of his ambition, and even his passion, had made it clear he ought not to be trusted. But hearing him call out for an audience now, her heart warmed a little.

Thomas could have just walked away – he could have kissed a tightrope walker and left them for a greater show. Yet had the company continued, Thomas might have been exactly what they had needed. Of course, she would never admit that Robert was right, and she was possibly *less* right on this occasion, but perhaps Robert had been wise to place trust in Thomas. Perhaps he had seen something that she had not. After all, Robert did seem to have a particular talent for finding whatever was lost and broken and bringing out the best in them.

Their last show, then... amongst the ashes of what might have been. She pushed away the regret of the past and the fear of the future and focused on the present. They would make it special. People were looking at Thomas now, up on his brother's shoulders. He looked a complete idiot, wobbling around up there, but she suspected he didn't give a toss. Annie skipped around the two in a circle with her hands outstretched towards them to draw attention.

Caroline cast a look at Robert, half-expecting to see him clapping his hands over his eyes and shaking his head slowly in despair, but he had a smile both on his face and in his eyes as he watched them. When was the last time she had seen that? Oh, he was so beautiful when he smiled like that.

Thomas called out:

"The actors are at hand, and by their show,

You shall know all that you are like to know!"

Annie skipped over to Caroline and kept skipping on the spot as she spoke. "But that's from... I thought it was A Midsummer Night's Dream over Robert's dead body?"

"Could be an interesting show, then. Besides..." Despite everything, Caroline could not help but smile. "Perhaps comedy suits us."

"Short pieces so we keep them with us," instructed Robert in a low voice, coming over to them. "Annie, long sticks for swords."

Annie nodded and skipped off as Thomas half-climbed, half-fell off his brother's shoulders and launched into a possibly not entirely planned somersault, followed instantly by a monologue, to the amusement of the crowd.

"*I do much wonder that one man, seeing how much another man is a fool when he dedicates his behaviours to love, will, after he hath laughed at such shallow follies in others, become the argument of his own scorn by falling in love: and such a man is Claudio,*" announced Thomas to the crowd, with a wag of his finger. She watched as Thomas paraded up and down in front of the people, continuing his speech.

"You put a lot of trust in him," Caroline murmured to Robert.

"And now you see why?" He gave her a smile.

If only things could be different – was there any way, any way at all, that they could change Robert's mind? As Thomas began to round off his monologue, he threw an enquiring look towards Caroline. She moved forwards as Thomas bowed dramatically, her mind searching rapidly for what to perform. *Much Ado About*

Nothing? A Midsummer Night's Dream? Yet as she took Thomas' place, her thoughts went to but one speech. *Henry VI.* She prepared each line in her mind with such passion, such fury, as if these were the last words her soul would utter. It was the audience she faced... but the words were spoken to the man who had healed something lost and broken and yet needed to heal himself:

"Great lords, wise men ne'er sit and wail their loss,
But cheerly seek how to redress their harms.
What though the mast be now blown overboard,
The cable broke, the holding-anchor lost,
And half our sailors swallow'd in the flood?
Yet lives our pilot still..."

Caroline paused as Annie skipped across the stage in front of her, carrying two long sticks and looking extremely pleased with herself as she handed them to Thomas and Benedict. Refusing to be distracted, Caroline worked through her speech:

"... the ship splits on the rock,

Which industry and courage might have saved..."

but as she finished, she wondered whether she spoke more to herself than Robert:

"Why, courage then! what cannot be avoided

'Twere childish weakness to lament or fear."

She gave a small and defiant nod to Robert but he would not meet her eyes. She swept into a slow curtsey as people clapped, then joined Thomas, Annie and Benedict as Robert took centre stage. What would he choose to perform? He took a breath and began:

"To be, or not to be, that is the question..."

Thomas huffed indignantly beside her. "He said only I would play Hamlet."

"... The slings and arrows of outrageous fortune..."

"Never mind that," hissed Caroline to Thomas, "we need something lighter now. You and you—" She pointed to Thomas and Benedict. "Get ready to fight."

"But we cannot interrupt Robert in the middle of a—"

"Yes, we bloody can. Go."

"And by opposing end them—"

She gave Thomas a shove forwards and he danced in front of Robert, brandishing the stick-sword to the crowd, who gave a little cheer. Benedict gave her a sidelong glance, then swerved out of her reach before she had chance to shove him, too. Robert bowed, then came over to Caroline, giving her a suspicious look.

"What?" she shrugged. "You said short pieces."

They watched side-by-side as Thomas and his brother displayed an impressive fight, considering they were each wielding a piece of dead wood – a fight which Thomas clearly lost, despite announcing himself as the victor to the audience before bowing.

Annie made her entrance as the brothers exited, dancing and singing a merry song about a maid who had run away with the fair folk. As Annie began the final chorus, Caroline looked at the audience. They were beginning to grow restless, and Caroline knew they could not keep performing like this for ever. Oh, how she wished they could. But it was time – as much as she hated it, as much as it hurt like Hell – for the final act. Annie sang the closing few lines about the fairies, then glanced over to Robert and Caroline, looking unsure at what was to happen next.

Fairies... Should she...? Caroline looked over at their lead actor, standing shoulder to shoulder with Robert. Well, this was the last time they would ever perform together. Why the Hell not? Besides, she was beginning to put a lot of trust in him.

Annie dipped into a low curtsey, and: *"Ill met by moonlight, proud Titania,"* Caroline called to Thomas, as she hurriedly took her place on the invisible stage.

Thomas looked towards her, his eyes momentarily wide in surprise, and Caroline couldn't resist a little smirk at catching him so off-guard. But then he parried as he walked over slowly to join her, "*What, jealous Oberon? Fairies, skip hence. I have forsworn his bed and company.*"

"*Tarry, rash wanton,*" replied Caroline, strutting a little closer towards him. "*Am not I thy lord?*"

"*Then I,*" said Thomas, moving closer in turn, holding her gaze with his warm, brown eyes, "*must be thy lady.*"

They worked through the scene seamlessly, and with every line they spoke, Caroline hated that they stepped word by word, syllable by syllable, inevitably closer to the end of it all, until:

"*Give me that boy and I will go with thee,*" she said.

"*Not for thy fairy kingdom,*" he replied. "*Fairies, away. We shall chide downright if I longer stay.*"

They turned to the audience. Caroline reached for Thomas' hand and held it aloft as they took their final bows. And she hoped the approving smile she gave him suggested that he was perhaps not an entirely terrible Titania.

And what now? Could they do more? Could they squeeze out one more desperate performance and change Robert's mind? Breath stuck a little in her throat. Caroline was not ready to exit this stage, to exit this life, but Robert stepped forwards, his arms open as if to embrace the audience one last time. And Caroline had no choice but to slip her fingers away from Thomas' hand and the two of them moved to the wings once more. Caroline watched, hardly daring to breathe, as Robert stood for a moment in silence. Although he would push her away during his moments of pain, Caroline had watched him well enough to know when he was close to breaking. A little shadow would appear as his jaw tightened. His voice was just that little bit breathier, and he would pause more often as he spoke:

“Ladies and gentlemen. We have been the Ticehurst Players. *And whether we shall meet again, I know not. Therefore our everlasting farewell take... For ever... and for ever... farewell.”*

He dipped down into his final bow, and Caroline swallowed hard. Her eyes prickled treacherously, but by her own rules, there would be no tears. And if the tiniest amount of water escaped her eyes before it was swiftly brushed away, it was because the stinging smoke still hung heavy in the air.

CHAPTER 55: Piero

As Piero's mind calmed, he began to regain control, reprimanding himself for his carelessness and his weakness. Applause rang out and he got to his feet, peering around the tree to look towards the wrecked barn. He shook his head in disapproval as the troupe embraced, congratulating each other on managing to hold the audience's attention for five minutes. It was embarrassing to watch. He could captivate hundreds with a tightrope act, and he might even entertain royalty one day. Thank Heaven such pitiful moments were behind him. He didn't miss it at all.

Besides, once he had smoothed matters over with Maria and Angelo they could plan their next move. But first, a little plan of his own. He waited patiently. It was all in the timing... and... There! The new actor, whoever he was, realised Piero was looking directly at him. Piero's finger flew to his lips, then he curled his white-gloved finger in a beckoning movement, resisting the urge to smile as the man marched towards him furiously.

Piero took his position centre stage in front of the tree, leaning easily and confidently against the trunk, arms folded, one leg crossed across the other, and the toe of his boot pointing down at the ground. Casual and unbothered, then...

"How dare you?" ranted the new actor. "We could have been killed! I will be reporting you!"

Piero dropped his jaw, widened his eyes and splayed his white-gloved fingers on his chest. "Your accusation is cutting indeed. Yet... where is your evidence?"

"Oh, someone will have seen you! They must have."

"Perhaps," said Piero with a light shrug. "And what of my tightrope walker? It transpires that she could also have been killed because somebody tampered with the tightrope." The new actor frowned, doubt flickering all over his face. The man truly needed to work on concealing his feelings. All Piero had to do was to stay calm. He was in control. He was winning. He raised his forefinger up in the air. "I have the perfect suggestion. Neither of us draw attention to our terrible acts of life-threatening sabotage, and we all walk away from this fair in one piece, with an even score, going our separate ways..." Wait for it, wait for it: it was all in the timing. "Unless..." The word landed.

"Unless what?"

Piero looked over the man's shoulder and rolled his eyes. Robert, Annie, Caroline and the fool who had bled all over his beautiful dress were on their way over. He must execute the plan with haste.

"Look, what did he promise you?" he said urgently as his dancing eyes sought to captivate the new actor. "Fame? Fortune? The security of a patron? Surely you see all Robert can offer is failure. I saw how you held the audience. You are magnificent." He threw on the winning smile of a showman. "You and me. Two successful actors with a tremendous tightrope act—"

"The fortune-teller saw a tightrope," the man murmured thoughtfully.

It was working. "You can grasp the success you crave!"

The man gave Piero a strange look which made Piero tilt his head to one side. What the Hell was that look? It couldn't be pity?

"Has it ever occurred to you," the new actor said, "that there might be more to life than a stage?"

Piero sighed and shook his head in disappointment. Fine, it would be the new actor's loss. It clearly wasn't worth the fight. "One day you'll learn," he said, giving the man a strange look in return. And what the Hell was that look? Ah yes. PITY. "When those you trust betray you, at least an audience will love you."

And Lord, here were the rest of them now, lined up and facing him – how lovely, and so on and so forth. He folded his arms. The new actor stretched his arm out towards Caroline, as if to suggest she exercised restraint. Well, good luck with that. Annie looked as if she felt a million different things. The fool who had dared to bleed over his dress hung back, clearly unsure of his place in any of this. And Robert... his dark eyes fixed on Piero...

He swallowed.

And Robert...

"So tragic!" announced Piero, dramatically slapping his hand over his heart, or what remained of it. "So tragic for the company to lose everything."

"We didn't," said the new actor, whoever he was. "Not quite everything."

Piero snorted a cold laugh in his direction. He ran his eyes along the soot-stained, bedraggled company, standing there side-by-side, together. Something odd caught in his throat. Most likely, it was pity for the wretched creatures. Because he didn't miss this... at all.

A handbell rang down by the burned barn, and the distant voice of Lord Pelham's servant called. "All ears! Gather around for Lord Pelham's announcement!"

Caroline threw him a look which could have felled the tree behind him. "One day, it will all fall apart for you. I am only sorry I won't get to see it. Don't bother with him, Thomas."

Ah, so that was his name.

Caroline walked away. Thomas gave Piero one final look of quiet anger then followed her, with the one who had bled over his dress trotting uncertainly behind them. Heaven above. Surely she didn't approve of this new actor? Well, good luck to him with that, too.

Annie and Robert remained. Robert stared at him, and what the Hell was that supposed to be in his beautiful, deep eyes? Regret? Sadness?

No. Lies. It had only ever been lies. Piero lifted his chin a little and made sure his eyes shone with coldness and defiance and hate.

Because he did not... miss Robert... at all.

Robert's gaze dropped momentarily to Piero's neck. Piero glanced down. Damn it. The rabbit's foot necklace was visible beneath his untidy cravat.

The bell rung once more. Piero met Robert's eyes.

"I hope the tightrope act brings you all the success you desire," Robert said. His voice was slightly breathy, and a little shadow appeared on his jaw. "Good luck, Piero." He blinked a couple of times, then leaving Annie standing there, Robert turned his back on Piero and walked away.

Piero fought to summon his voice. "I do not believe in luck," he called after Robert.

Robert paused, his back still facing Piero, his swinging arms coming to a stop. "And what *do* you believe in?" came his voice, quiet but strong.

Piero opened his mouth to speak, and the unpainted boy shouted and pleaded inaudible, unspeakable words...

He said nothing.

Robert's head dipped towards his chest for a moment. Then he lifted it up and walked away.

Piero swallowed. He stood there and blinked a few times... just to... just to clear his eyes... the smoke was... He took a breath to calm himself.

He was a showman. An actor. A performer. Even if the very theatre collapsed around you, it was on with the show. It was always on with the...

He turned to Annie, glad of an excuse to tear his gaze from Robert's back. Her capless red hair was half-unpinned, her soot-smudged face was pale and her eyes were weighed with sorrow. They used to be so merry.

"Well," he said brightly, over the sound of silent screaming, "now that's all done, I have a gift for you." He reached behind the tree for Annie's fiddle and bow and placed them in her hands. She gasped then looked up at him with joy. "Surely you know I would never let that burn."

Annie gave a cry and flung her arms around his neck, embracing him tightly, despite – or perhaps because of – the fiddle and bow in her hands. He tensed and did not return the embrace. This was dangerous. She had the power to destroy him. He should pull her arms from his neck and step back. His hand twitched, ready to pull her away. Except he couldn't.

Robert was gone.

Walked out of his life for ever.

He closed his eyes. He gasped for breath, as if the air around him had ceased to exist, and he threw his arms around Annie in return. The warmth of her sunk deep into his heart, deep into his bones. Lord, it all hurt. Why did it all hurt so bloody much? He rested his head against hers. He had known the risk; he had known the danger he faced if he spent too much time in her company. Now here he was, standing in the middle of a tightrope, losing his balance. Tears filled his eyes far too readily; his throat closed and made a choking sound. His body threatened to shake. There and then, while Annie held him, he could so easily fall. And oh, how he wanted to fall and then cry for a thousand years. The unpainted boy pressed his face against the mirror, his eyes wide with hope.

"Will I ever see you again?" Annie said into his chest.

He just had to fall. But would Annie catch him? And even if she did, what then? He would not ask her to leave Robert and Caroline, she would not bear it – and besides, he could not imagine her place in a spectacular tightrope act. Maria and Angelo were waiting for him. The many adoring audiences in his future could give him all the love he would need.

He opened his eyes. "My act will find another patron in time," he said, controlling the waver in his voice. "We will travel the country and the continent. Fame and fortune beckon us, so I do not think our paths will cross again."

Gently, kindly, he moved Annie's arms from his neck and retreated from her as he crossed the tightrope and made it safely to the other side. The unpainted boy sadly lowered his gaze. "But no one – *no one* – will ever love him like..." The words died, like the boy in the mirror. He begged his choking throat to relax. "Look after him."

Annie wiped away her tears and nodded. He planted a kiss on her forehead. "You are marvellous," he said, trying to be as distant as he could. "And do not let anyone ever tell you otherwise."

Annie nodded again, and with a loud sniff, she began to walk away, leaving him standing alone beside the tree.

"I would have caught Maria," he called after her, "if she had fallen."

Annie looked over her shoulder. "I know." She gave him a small smile then headed back towards the company, swinging her fiddle as she went. He did not continue to watch her: it was wiser that he did not. Instead, he fixed his sights on the tightrope tent where he belonged. The Ticehurst Players were, finally, no longer a part of his life. He was free of his bonds. And he had a new future which he could now dedicate himself to.

He breathed in deeply, breathed it all out, then headed across the field. He had not seen Maria and Angelo during the chaos of the fire. Knowing the patronage was lost, they were probably busy packing up. He could see the horses and wagon had already moved, presumably hitched up behind the tent. He imagined dipping his fingertips into the tin and smearing the purple powder on his eyelids as the showman prepared to win the hearts of his audience of two. He would reignite their excitement for the act after the disappointment of failing to acquire a patron. There was the small matter of blackmailing Angelo, but the lad always did as he was bid, and Piero could easily smooth things over.

Making an entrance was his second-favourite thing. So as he reached the tent, he held his head high and perfected his posture. He would be confident, in control. All the world was his bloody stage, so he pushed aside the door flap, and walked upon the ground as if he were treading the—

He froze.

His feet had forgotten how to move. His heart had forgotten how to beat. But his eyes could still see. And everything had gone, except for the useless, worthless tightrope, tied to a roof pole above and dangling down in the form of a noose.

No.

He choked on nothing.

No.

With an increasing sense of despair, he ran behind the tent where he would surely see Young Bess, Iago and the wagon with all his belongings, waiting for him.

NO!

All he saw was a small tin box on the ground, crushed and misshapen, as if it had been run over. With shaking legs, he walked over to it and examined it with fingers he could barely control. Inside was empty, except for a few smudges of purple desperately clinging to the metal tin. And in the mud his purple eye-powder was spilled and spoiled, mixed with dirt. He released a roar of hurt and anger and hurled the useless tin as far as he could. His breathing became frantic. Rage flew through him once more, and there was yet one person who deserved the full measure of it!

He ran out into the field, where empty stalls and tents stood, their owners and customers all gathered by the burned wood and ash to hear Lord Pelham announce his chosen ones. But there was one person who would not be there! One person who had never cared about any of that! And his feet pounded towards that wagon, a furious scream in his throat. He caught her just in time.

Old Dina climbed up into the driver's seat with a definite jangle in her pockets and a definite grin on her face.

"YOU!" Piero cried as his feet slammed to a halt beside her wagon. He thrust an accusing finger towards the old woman, caring not if he looked calm or in control. He was well past either. She turned to look at him, seeming unbothered. His breath burst out in desperate, broken gasps. "You told me that good fortune awaited me at Thorverton Fair!"

The woman shrugged and tightened her headscarf. "Old Dina didn't think you believed in the sight. You believed in revenge."

Once you believed in love. And one day, you will again.

She cast a look over her shoulder at the wrecked barn. "Old Dina reckons you has what you wanted." She patted her jangling pockets and gave him a grin. "And so has Old Dina."

Piero's chest heaved, and the world blurred with tears. He was lost. He was utterly, utterly lost. "Then what am I to do?" he found himself saying. The break in his voice mirrored that in his heart.

The old woman gave him a knowing look. "Old Dina told you good fortune awaited you at Thorverton Fair."

"It did not!" Piero spat. "You lied!"

Old Dina shrugged again. "We'll see." She gave him a little wink. "Won't we?" Then she chuckled and flicked the reins. The wagon began rolling away over the field. Something small came flying towards him from the driver's seat, heading straight for his face. His shaking hand shot up and caught it, out of instinct rather than anything else. He opened his hand. A rabbit's foot necklace.

“What the Hell am I meant to do with this?” he called. The old woman’s irritatingly knowing smile burned in his mind. “You know I do not believe in luck!”

He shoved the pointless thing into his jacket pocket, then reached up to the rabbit’s foot still hanging around his neck. His trembling fist clenched around the foot. One pull! One pull and he would be free of the damned thing forever; cast it away like an unwanted relic from a bygone age! He began to tug the necklace down... Just one pull! His chest wanted to explode, and the world blurred again. One! His grip weakened...

“DAMN IT ALL!”

His arm dropped to his side. Every muscle in his face tried to fight the tears. Why did it all hurt so much? Everything he had cared about was gone. Maria, his eye-powder, Old Bess, the dress that Robert... Robert... And at last, he broke. The tears escaped their prison, but he did not sob; he did not wail. He never did. His crying, as from childhood, was silent and numb, so no one would hear, and no one would know. On and on he walked as the tears quietly fell, stumbling amongst the deserted stalls, staring at the ground, not knowing or caring where he went. He had been here before and somehow, he would find a way to survive.

Then his feet stopped, and he looked up. As so often seemed to happen, they had stopped in front of a stage. There was the sign, hammered into the ground by the long-lashed, willowy man: ‘The Ashton Players’. He wiped the tears from his face and glanced around. No one had seen. No one knew. The troupe would surely benefit from a commanding lead actor who could hold audiences in the palm of his hand.

Well, then.

It was on with the show.

Because it was always on with the fucking show.

The unpainted boy in the mirror pushed his fingertips to the glass and whispered a beautiful, voiceless promise before he disappeared to wait in the wings, and Piero clambered up onto the stage. There was a loud round of applause which came from the crowd by the burned building. Piero inhaled it all like air, held his head high and walked to the centre, feeling the boards once more beneath his feet.

He positioned himself perfectly, lying down on his side, elbow resting on the boards, hand propping up his head. By the time the troupe returned, his eyes would have cleared and only he would know his tears had been there at all. He would push away the pain which threatened to tear him into a thousand pieces, and he would forget the rabbit's foot necklace which he could never discard. He would wait there, patiently poised upon their stage. It would be worth the wait to see the look on the company's faces.

After all, his second-favourite thing in the world was making an entrance.

CHAPTER 56: Thomas

So, this was it – time to say farewell.

It had not been a surprise that they had not won the patronage. Instead, Lord Pelham had offered it to a troupe of acrobats, who had been so excited they formed an enormous human tower, jumping on top of each other's shoulders, and stood there looking a little uncertain as to how they would all get down.

Folk were milling around, buying drinks for the road as they prepared for the journey ahead. With the disaster of the fire, Uncle Henry had rung the bell and announced that the fair was closing early, although Thomas' pocket watch told him it was barely afternoon. Bands of dark grey smoke and an uncomfortable warmth still hung in the blue sky. Murmurs of excitement and satisfaction at the spectacle still rippled through the field as voices chattered and carts began to rumble.

Thomas stood with Caroline, Robert and Annie in a strange, awkward group by the charred remains of the barn. As they watched the departures around them, they were all undoubtedly thinking the same thing – the thing that no one wanted to voice. Thomas glanced over at his brother. Benedict sat a couple of yards away, his knees drawn up and his head dropped down, and the long stick that had served as his sword by his feet. The swords... Thomas looked over his brother's shoulder to the charred remains of their wagon. Would they have survived the fire? He grabbed the piece of wood in front of Benedict and headed over. Poking the stick around, he sifted through the burned remains of his former life, trying not to list the losses. He just wanted to find the swords. And there they were, buried and filthy – but a glint of silvery hope amongst the dark ashes. He retrieved them, brushed off the worst, and took them back to Robert.

"Some signs of damage," he said, "but they would still have value."

"Perhaps." Robert shrugged. "I have no use for them. You and your brother may keep them."

Thomas nodded, waiting for some sharp comment from Caroline about him needing the practice. But she said nothing. More importantly than practice, the swords would be a welcome distraction. Thomas sighed. How in Heaven's name was it going to work when they went back to the inn? How would Benedict cope with seeing Sarah and Marcus around the town, especially once the baby had arrived? He imagined, with a foreboding sense of gloom, that it would involve many drunken visits to the stocks and the lock-up. He had never seen his brother as broken as this. It was going to be horrendous, and he was thankful that at least he himself would never be at the mercy of a maid.

"We cannot stand here 'til nightfall," said Caroline. "Where will you go, Robert? Back to the farm you worked on?"

"I'm not certain. There's nothing for me there." The pain in Robert's eyes was almost tangible.

"You don't need him, Robert," said Caroline, quietly. "You'll find someone else."

Robert nodded. "I hope one day he finds the happiness he seeks."

"I hope one day he gets a good kick up the arse," muttered Caroline.

Annie trailed her fingertips over the instrument. "Well, he saved my fiddle. I can still play in the towns, like before."

Thomas looked at her thoughtfully. Clearly, to perform such an action, Piero held her in the highest regard. Thomas had always considered Annie to be the weakest member of the troupe. But perhaps she simply showed her strength in different ways. He would miss her. Not her cooking, perhaps, but her care. Her willingness. Her friendship. And Caroline? She was terrifying and unpredictable and should never be allowed near a hammer, but he was so used to her blunt manner, the way she kept him on his toes, that life would feel strangely quiet without her. And Robert? He had given Thomas something to believe in. Damn it. He would miss them all.

Uncle Henry's handbell rang again, presumably to encourage any dawdling performers to get the Hell out of the field. Thomas swallowed and found himself shaking his head. He didn't want life to return to how it was before. Yes, they had no stage, no wagon, no horse, no props, no costumes, no skull, no money... But they did have a fiddle and two damaged swords. And damn it, they could have a company! They were enough! The thought, the passion, the love grew stronger until—

"Robert," he said, spinning around to face Robert, who looked away. "I know that it was agreed if we did not attract a patron, the company would fold..."

"Thomas," said Robert, with a sigh.

"I promise you I tried my best to fill the role, and I know that I was never as good as—"

Robert put his hand on Thomas' shoulder. "I was right to put my trust in you."

He was? Despite all the trouble that Thomas had caused? Thomas swallowed. His throat tightened for a moment. The words spurred him on. "Then trust me now, Robert! Look at us. We are all still here! You are still here!"

Robert folded his arms and held his gaze.

"Do you not see? None of us can actually leave!"

"Thomas..."

"Who cares about a patron?" Thomas said, gesturing wildly and noticing the smile on Caroline's face as he did so. "Yes, it makes life much easier, but we have a fiddle! We have swords, more or less. We start again!" He stared at the most superstitious – but surely the most appreciated – manager in the entire land. "And the show is not over 'til we lower the curtain."

Please!

Robert moved his hands to his hips and looked at Thomas with eyes full of doubt, indecision and longing. But Thomas returned the gaze with the defiant passion he felt for this bedraggled and beautiful company. Robert looked to the heavens and flicked his hands upwards in exasperation. "When we have a curtain?"

Thomas' voice was defeated by a rush of feelings. He sprang forwards and embraced the man, smiling as Robert's hand warmly patted his back.

The handbell sounded with a definite ring of irritation.

"Shall we get our arses moving, then?" said Robert as Thomas stepped away. "Somewhere out there, though Lord knows how, we have a bloody show."

Robert was right: Thomas had no idea how this was going to work. They had even less now than they had started with, although he could hear Benedict's voice in his head, disagreeing. His brother still sat on the ground, his bruised head resting in his hands. Thomas reached into his jacket, and let his fingertips brush the pocket watch. Robert had said in Bampton that Benedict couldn't accompany them beyond the fair. And true, he would be another mouth to feed, and judging by his mood, another problem to deal with on top of everything else. But Thomas couldn't bear the thought of sending him back to Pa and that town. Could he be sure his brother would be safe from harm, caused either by another's hand or Benedict's own?

"Listen," said Thomas, pushing his palms together, then pointing them at Robert. "He's a talented actor, Robert, a fine swordsman! He almost won that stick-fight—"

"I did win that stick-fight," muttered Benedict.

"He almost won that stick-fight, Robert! Imagine how we could show the swords! I will keep him out of trouble, I promise." He walked over to Benedict. "If you want to come."

"I don't want anything, Tom. There's nothing for me ahead," Benedict said, still looking at the ground. "I've lost the woman I love, my child, my future... I have nothing left."

"Well," said Thomas as he knelt beside Benedict and rested a hand on his shoulder, "apparently you have a brother."

Benedict lifted his head. Thomas looked into his brother's heartbroken eyes, and sincerely hoped the love shone from his own.

Benedict gave a small smile. "*And I love him well.*"

"You look as I feel," Robert said to him. He untied the rabbit's foot necklace and held it in his hand for a moment before hurling it into the charred remains of the barn. He stared at its landing place, and a strange little shadow appeared on his jaw. Then he went over to Benedict. "We all need a new beginning sometimes," he said in a voice that sounded stronger than before. "The road is a good place to find one."

Robert placed one hand on his ribs and stretched out the other. Benedict paused, then he held out his own and allowed Robert to pull him back on his feet.

"Well, then," said Caroline. "*Once more unto the breach, dear friends?*"

Robert nodded. "*Once more.*"

And as they travelled on from the fair together, down the deep-rutted track, Annie lifted her soft voice and began to sing.

"Kind friends and companions, come join me in rhyme.

Come lift up your voices in chorus with mine.

Come lift up your voices all grief to refrain,

For we may or might never all meet here again.

Here's a health to the company, and one to my lass..."

"*Let us drink and be merry,*" joined Caroline, raising an invisible bottle to Annie, "*all out of one glass.*"

"*Let us drink and be merry, all grief to refrain,*" Robert sang.

"*For we may or might never all meet here again,*" belted out Thomas with such enthusiasm that Caroline put her hands over her ears.

They continued in song as they went onwards down the lane, to wherever their feet and their future would take them. Only Benedict remained songless. Thomas slipped a hand over his shoulders, and hoped with all his heart that in time, his little brother would be merry with song once more.

Two brothers, one company and a whole world ahead of them. Good fortune did indeed find him at Thorverton Fair. Thomas didn't know how it would all work out, but he knew that it would. It always did in the end. He smiled.

Everything was going to be absolutely fine.

***

***

All the world's a stage,

And all the men and women merely players;

They have their exits and their entrances,

And one man in his life plays many parts...

William Shakespeare

As You Like It, Act two, Scene seven

***

Here's A Health To The Company

Kind friends and companions, come join me in rhyme
Come lift up your voices in chorus with mine
Come lift up your voices, all grief to refrain
For we may or might never all meet here again

Here's a health to the Company and one to my lass
Let us drink and be merry all out of one glass
Let us drink and be merry, all grief to refrain
For we may or might never all meet here again

Here's a health to the dear lass that I love so well
Her style and her beauty sure none can excel
There's a smile on her countenance as she sits on my knee
There's no man in the wide world as happy as me

Here's a health to the Company and one to my lass
Let us drink and be merry all out of one glass
Let us drink and be merry, all grief to refrain
For we may or might never all meet here again

Our ship lies in harbour and ready to dock
I wish her safe landing without any shock
And if I ever I should meet you by land or by sea
I will always remember your kindness to me

Here's a health to the Company and one to my lass
Let us drink and be merry all out of one glass
Let us drink and be merry, all grief to refrain
For we may or might never all meet here again

(Traditional)

Author's Note

This book is a work of fiction set in the past about broken people finding hope and finding themselves. Some facts have been read, absorbed and cast merrily to the breeze in pursuit of storytelling. There was no bridge as described in Bampton in 1715, although there is one now. The road into Andover might be a little on the wonky side with an unexpected bridge, and a slightly altered market building from Dunster has somehow landed in the middle of town. Language has an anachronistic twang to it in places, although if I wrote fully in eighteenth century West Country dialect, we would all give up. And there will always be unintentional errors in books: if you find some, I humbly ask for your forgiveness and raise you a pint of the best cider in the West to toast your astuteness.

The language is interesting. As part of my research, I devoured *How to Swear Like an Elizabethan in Devon* by Todd Gray (The Mint Press, 2016). These people did not hold back. In fact, I'm not entirely sure how they breathed during the lengthy sentences they hurled at each other. But although some phrases may seem dated today (such as "bally rag", or "'giglet"), it is reassuring to discover some – such as "kiss my arse", uttered by a woman in Totnes to a Reverend, no less – have graciously stood the test of time.

Finding comedy in the past is always wonderful, as sometimes history is portrayed in such a serious manner. People knew how to laugh then, and needed to, as we do now. I wanted to bring this flavour to my work. This was one of the reasons I was so enchanted by Samuel Ryley's *The Itinerant*. Printed in the early nineteenth century, it's a semi-autobiographical piece about life as a strolling player. Reading his work is like spending time with a friend. The informality, the humour, the enthusiastic exclamation marks: it was all a delight, and I wish I could have sat by a fireplace beside this man and talked with him.

Some of my favourite quotes include: "Oh Heavens! What a motley group – their complexion and habiliments reminded me of Macbeth's witches..."; "*The play's the thing, in which I'll catch the...*

[affections of Miss K.]..."; "He wore a garment which once bore the name of shirt and still gave that idea..." But perhaps what I loved most of all was the merriment he described in the players' nature. He speaks of meeting the manager of a company, who tells him, "We players are a set of merry, undone dogs, and though we often want the means of life, we are seldom without the means of mirth. We are philosophers, sir, and laugh at misfortune; even the ridiculous situations we are sometimes placed in are more generally the cause of mirth than misery."

They loved what they did. I understand this love and merriment. Plays and performing have always been part of my life. As a primary-school child, I loved creating and performing plays with a small company of long-suffering friends. I persuaded the teachers to let us show the plays during assembly and at one point we were performing a new one every Friday. I also performed mummers' plays in town centres and fairs with a children's folk dancing troupe I had helped set up. I had no idea how to dance at a disco, but I could strip-the-willow, form a star with swords and enthusiastically whack the sticks of fellow dancers like there was no tomorrow. Raised in a folk-loving family, I spent my childhood trailing around rural inns and folk festivals, watching dance troupes perform to the accordion and fiddle, enjoying the merry banter as the warm smell of ale drifted on the breeze. It was like stepping back in time and I loved it far more than the modern day. Writing this book felt like coming home.

My dad was from a working-class family and he often wished he had become an actor. It wasn't really an option for him but he still performed and entertained others at every opportunity, taught me folk songs and took me to the theatre when he could. He is the reason I set up the David Banks Performers Fund (**https://www.dbpf.org.uk**) to help support financially disadvantaged final-year students at drama school and help performing arts be accessible and possible for people from all backgrounds; we need diverse voices because that is and always has been the reality of the world.

I'm very interested in ordinary or forgotten voices: those voices which perhaps couldn't shout as loudly as others through the passing of time. Voices of working-class people, neurodiverse individuals, people with disabilities, people who identified in different ways and many more. All these communities existed in the past as they do today. But their voices are often quiet. So, although there were companies of strolling players who were well known and documented, I longed to explore those who lived more hand-to-mouth, and about whom few records were made.

There were so many companies like this, and we will never know who they all were. But they were here. They existed and they mattered. They lived, loved and performed, existing simultaneously in both the heart and the edges of society, scraping in the pennies wherever and however they could.

Research unearthed some wonderful treasures, such as a description of a company of known players competing with other acts in the same town in different inns, including a tightrope act. Now, that gave me an idea...

Looking into tightrope performers of the past led me to Signora Violante (1682-1741), an absolutely incredible woman who deserves her own story one day. Although the character of Maria isn't based on this real person, she shares the same surname and profession as a nod of respect. Although any woman who can reportedly walk the tightrope whilst balancing a child on her shoulders, with swords strapped to her legs and a child dangling from each ankle, deserves way more than a nod of respect.

Another strong woman in my story is Old Dina. In the 1700s there were plenty of fortune-tellers around who travelled the roads and frequented the fairs, some considered genuine, some less so. And what of Old Dina? Does she truly possess the sight? Does she simply observe and apply her knowledge of humanity? Or is it a little of both? At this point, I do not know, and I'll tell you why. I enjoy knowing my characters inside out: we go for walks, and chat outside of the story, starting as acquaintances, becoming friends, and ending with me being someone they trust to tell their story. Perfectly normal, honest. However, I find it often takes longer to truly reach the heart of three types of characters: very broken ones, very shy ones or very secretive ones. They all have their reasons for keeping themselves to themselves. And the first and last in this list will often provide information which isn't entirely truthful.

Old Dina falls into the last category. Usually, I gently probe until my character cracks like a nut (and as I write this that I realise how much Old Dina and I have in common!) and we can move forwards with the story together. Old Dina is the first character I've allowed to keep a big truth from me. Partly because I suspect that if I probed too deeply, she would simply persuade me to part with my own money and secrets, then disappear before I'd got any information out of her. But also, because she's keeping her secret for a reason, and I reckon that if *anyone* knows exactly what they're doing in this story, it's Old Dina. So, I'll respect that and be guided by her. In the meantime, decide for yourself what you think of her gift.

Caroline was another very secretive character. When she finally revealed her truth to me, I could totally understand why she was so reluctant to share. We live now in an age where people are actively trying to break down and destroy the stigma surrounding mental health and suicide. People are talking more about it and my hope is that conversations continue to happen and lives continue to be saved.

Back in 1715, this was far from the case. The lack of understanding, combined with fear and strong religious condemnation resulted in a harsh view of suicide, which was considered a crime against oneself. People who had died by suicide were usually buried by the wayside – most often at crossroads during the night – and sometimes with a stake through their heart. Although personal attitudes and regional practices varied, it wasn't until the Burial Of Suicides Act in 1823 that things dramatically changed. The suspicion and fear surrounding suicide also extended to loved ones, and relatives could find themselves shunned by their communities. Although there is still a long way to go, I hope Caroline would look at the world today and see the progress. Let's keep talking, keep listening and keep reaching out.

Setting a story in a time where attitudes were quite different from today is always challenging. You want to balance being faithful to predominant attitudes of the time with speaking your truth as an author and communicating with a modern readership. Sexuality is another area where this is the case. Obviously, queer people have always existed, so it made sense that there were queer characters in the storyworld, and a company of strolling players seemed a wonderful place to find them.

The Buggery Act of 1533 meant male sexual intercourse was punishable by death, or if there was a lack of evidence or the accusation was reduced to "attempted buggery", men were sentenced to imprisonment, fines or potentially violent assault in the pillories. Blackmail and reporting to the authorities was common.

As seen at the fair, Robert and Piero needed to keep their eyes open and make sure their behaviour did not arouse suspicion. Even so, it's important to note that some people in the community were sympathetic and didn't agree with the lawmakers. People have always existed who defied society and challenged expectations. And it certainly wouldn't be a surprise to find some of those people travelling on the road, performing Shakespeare.

I was fifteen when I first discovered the Bard in *A Midsummer Night's Dream* at school. I fell in love with the language, rhythm and energy of the words. I studied Shakespeare at A-Level and degree level. When I started researching eighteenth-century players, I was delighted to find that despite the wealth of available plays, Shakespeare remained very popular, especially *Hamlet* and *Macbeth* which could reliably pull a crowd.

I was delighted to weave the words which inspired me as a young person into this novel and hopefully encourage others to delve into his plays. What did surprise me was that the curse of Macbeth wasn't really a "thing" until the 1920s. It seems that only with hindsight have people built the superstition into the robust legend it has become today. I had to break this news to a somewhat disappointed Piero, who had hoped to play this to his advantage, but hey, you can't have everything.

I hope this provides some insight into how and why I wrote this book and some of the interesting research I uncovered. Thank you for reading.

Acknowledgments

There are always many people to thank at the end of a long project, and this one is no exception. First and foremost, my thanks must go to my husband Alyn and our six children, for putting up with me disappearing back into 1715 on a regular basis, and for their enthusiasm for the project. A special thanks to Alyn for managing the layout and formatting of this book and doing such a great job with the marketing images and videos.

Thanks also to my parents, David and Kate Banks, for instilling in me a love of books, theatre and folk music between them, which came in rather handy.

All books are a culmination of work from a wide-ranging group of people. Various people have kindly given some thoughts and feedback into the story along the way, so a big thank you to Julia Churchill, Kate Walker, Lydia Brown, Dave Cohen, Adam Lavis, Sarah Lidstone, Mellie Buse, Claire Barker, Liz Monument, Joanna Tilley, Lizzy Goodchild, Su Bowler, Michelle Halsey, Rachel Stevens and Natalie Westacott. I really appreciate your help. Thanks also to The Niche Reader beta readers who shared their thoughts, and to Drew Hubbard at PrideReads for the sensitivity reading.

Grateful thanks to Catriona Camacho for the line and copy editing, and to Ally Wilkes for proofreading. The book is stronger because of your valuable help. Thanks also to Sarah Christie for creating such a brilliant cover.

Of course, I am indebted to William Shakespeare for the inspiration and the quotes. As a player himself, I hope he would approve of this book.

And thank *you* for reading this book (even this bit!), and joining me as I stroll along with these players. Here's a health to the company.

About The Author

The Players Act 1 is New York Times bestselling Amy Sparkes' debut novel for adults and the first part of a trilogy. Amy is the author of more than 25 children's books translated into over 15 languages, including BBC's The Repair Shop Stories and The House At The Edge of Magic series.

Alongside being an author, Amy works as a writing coach, manages the David Banks Performers Fund supporting drama school students in financial difficulties, and runs Sword & Fiddle Productions with her husband.

She lives in Devon, England and is married with six children and a pet skull called Minchin who lives on the mantelpiece and dresses up for Christmas.

www.amysparkes.co.uk

Printed in Dunstable, United Kingdom

65556810R00190